THE CROSSROADS

A NOVEL

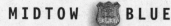

MIDTOW  BLUE
SERIES

F. P. LIONE

Revell
Grand Rapids, Michigan

© 2005 by F. P. Lione

Published by Fleming H. Revell
a division of Baker Publishing Group
P.O. Box 6287, Grand Rapids, MI 49516-6287

Printed in the United States of America

Library of Congress Cataloging-in-Publication Data
Lione, F. P., 1962-
    The crossroads : a novel / F. P. Lione.
        p.   cm. — (Midtown blue series)
    ISBN 0-8007-5961-3 (pbk.)
    1. Police—New York (State)—New York—Fiction. 2. Christian converts—Fiction. 3. New York (N.Y.)—Fiction. I. Title. II. Series.
PS3612.I58C76 2005
813′.6—dc22   2005012378

Scripture is taken from the New King James Version. Copyright © 1982 by Thomas Nelson, Inc. Used by permission. All rights reserved.

Times Square and the other New York City landmarks described in this book exist, as do the recognizable public figures. But this is a work of fiction. The imaginary events and characters are the product of the author's imagination, and any resemblance to any actual events or people, dead or living, is entirely coincidental.

This book is dedicated to Jesus, love personified. We who once walked in darkness have seen a great light. It's your love for us and in us, and it never fails.

And to Frankie, our strong, bright child of promise. We love you more every day.

1

On December 31, the Crossroads of the World become the Center of the Universe as the eyes of the planet look to Times Square when the old year ends and the new year begins. Over the years millions of people have come from all over the globe to witness the brilliant spectacle that only happens in New York City. A billion others watch by television as an illuminated ball is dropped from the top of One Times Square, at the most famous intersection on earth, as the deafening cheers of the wild crowds below greet the new year.

New Year's Eve in Times Square is controlled chaos. Roughly eight thousand cops keep between five hundred thousand and a million people under control because we corral them like livestock behind police barricades.

The New Year's event is a culmination of input from the mayor's office all the way down to the garbage pickup. Dick Clark, the celebrities, and the performers make the whole thing look effortless, but it's not. What goes on behind the scenes is very different from what you see on your television. There's a lot that goes into the annual celebration, and before the last piece of confetti is swept up by Sanitation on New Year's Day, it's already on the planning tables for the following year.

My name is Tony Cavalucci, and this is my tenth year as a New York City cop. It is my eleventh year working New Year's Eve in Times Square. I went into the Academy in June and was assigned my first New Year's Eve in Times Square six months into my career. The first time I worked it, I was a rookie just starting my FTU or Field Training Unit. FTU is where you go when you first get out of the Academy and before you're assigned to a precinct. I had graduated in December, worked Times Square on New Year's Eve, and then spent my first six months at the FTU in Coney Island. I got assigned to the precinct in Midtown Manhattan right before my second New Year's Eve.

At my first New Year's Eve, I was posted at a barrier on 40th Street and 7th Avenue with instructions not to let anyone into Times Square. Since I was green and had no idea what to expect, I spent most of the night at Bellevue getting stitched up after I was hit in the head with a bottle. Had I been assigned inside Times Square, whoever tossed it would have already been searched and the bottle would have been confiscated.

Last year I was fortunate to be on the job at a time when I could count off a year, a decade, a century, and a millennium all in one night, and be part of the history that started nearly a century ago.

On December 31, 1904, Adolph Ochs, the new publisher of the *New York Times*, hung the first ball on top of One Times Square. A rooftop fireworks display at midnight celebrated the completion of the Times building and the renaming of Longacre Square to Times Square. The first illuminated ball was dropped from One Times Square in 1907. Except for two years during World War II, when the people gathered in the dark to listen by loudspeaker, it has been celebrated that way ever since. Long ago, when it was a "gentlemen only" celebration, men came here on New Year's Eve in their finest evening clothes and rang in the New Year with merrymaking and order.

By this time next week I'd be crawling on my hands and knees looking for bombs under parked cars in some parking garage in Times Square, because nowadays some people like their merrymaking with explosives and large crowds.

But now it was the night before Christmas Eve, and I was standing in the muster room, the thirty-by-thirty-foot room where roll call takes place. I was taking the last hit off my cigarette and waiting for my partner, Joe Fiore, to come up from the locker room.

Garcia, a cop from my squad, was standing in front of the shoe-polishing machine that said "Club Members Only." He was lighting the can of shoe polish on fire to soften up the wax. He put the top back on the can to put the flame out. He waited a minute, then opened it back up and smeared some on his shoes. I heard the revolving brushes of the shoe-polishing machine thumping as he shined his shoes.

I picked up a copy of the *New York Post*, thankful that the headline didn't have anything to do with the recent presidential election. After six weeks of the New York papers having a field day with the state of Florida and the Supreme Court's duking it out over the voting numbers, it was time to move on to something else. The papers were relentless, and every day headlines like "Florida Fiasco," "Gore Loser," and "Sissy Al's Going Down Kicking and Screaming" were plastered across the front page. They seemed to be having the most fun with Al Gore, and we were all sick of hearing about it. The headline "No End in Sight" said what we were all thinking—enough already.

I was almost glad to see the paper picking on the cops again, and I scanned an article about low morale among the NYPD.

The police commissioner says the low morale is overstated, but morale is on the rise. Yeah, right. The veteran cops say that morale began to nose-dive back in 1995 when a two-year wage freeze slapped us in the face, followed by two of the worst scandals the department has ever seen.

I leaned my back against the doorway and stepped away, wondering if I had dirt on my back now. I put the paper back in the radio room, trying to brush off my back as I walked. It's not that the precinct is dirty. In fact, I could still detect the faint smell of pine from the floor recently being mopped, but I doubt they ever wash the walls.

It looked like someone had tried to spruce the place up a little by putting a Charlie Brown Christmas tree at the entrance of the muster room. The tree was leaning precariously toward the radio room, and only every other light was lit. Someone was having a little fun with the decorations, and I leaned in to get a closer look.

There was toilet paper garland—someone had taken a roll and wound it around the tree. A bitten donut was pushed on the top of it in place of a star. It looked like a chocolate-covered Entenmann's to me. A 28, the form we fill out to ask for time off, was pushed through one of the branches. It was a request for Christmas Day off from one of the day tour cops, and "Denied" was written across it in red magic marker. About four condoms in their wrappers were taped to the bottom branches with white adhesive tape. I laughed out loud at a Polaroid of Mike Rooney glued onto a green piece of construction paper cut into a wreath. The picture was of Mike Rooney asleep on one of the benches down in the lounge. Someone had written "Insert here," with an arrow pointing to Rooney's mouth.

"Where do they get this stuff?" I heard Fiore's voice beside me.

I turned and shook his hand, and he pulled me in for a hug

like he always does, slapping my back in affection. "Sneaking up on me?" I smiled.

I've worked with Joe since last June when my old partner, John Conte, was injured and needed knee surgery. When Fiore became my partner six months ago, I had been on a downward spiral from too much drinking and too much time alone. He stood by me through a dark time and brought me into his life and his church. I've learned a lot from him in the last few months about God, and we've become as close as brothers.

"Finish your shopping?" Joe asked.

"Just about. I have to pick up Michele's earrings in the morning," I said, then added, "You didn't tell Donna what I got Michele, did you?"

"What are we, in high school?" He shook his head. "Donna's not gonna tell her what she got for Christmas."

Donna is Joe's wife, and Michele is a friend of Donna's. Last summer I met Michele at Joe's house, not impressed with anything but her legs. She didn't seem my type, no makeup, no long nails, no big hair. I met her again at Joe's church and took a second look. She leaned more to a classic type, refined I guess you'd call her. I didn't realize I liked that kind of woman. Looking back, I think I just didn't have much exposure to women outside of happy hour and turtle races. Michele has a little boy, Stevie, who is four and a half, but she's never been married. She's thirty-three, a school teacher, and pretty much everything I've been looking for in a woman.

"How 'bout you? You get everything you need?" Joe had been shopping a lot at the Toys R Us in Times Square. He's got three kids, two boys and a baby girl, so he did a lot of the shopping to give Donna a break.

"I'm done," he said with feeling. "Now all we have to do is wrap it."

Sergeant Hanrahan gave the fall in order from the podium in the muster room.

"The color of the day is green," he said, indicating the city-wide color that plainclothes officers would use to identify themselves if stopped by uniformed officers. Knowing the color of the day would keep them from getting shot when they went to reach for their badge.

Our precinct is made up of different sectors. Port Authority, Penn Station, Times Square, the garment district, Madison Square Garden, the Empire State Building, Grand Central, 34th Street, part of the theater district, and 42nd between 7th and 8th ("the Deuce"). Each sector handles a piece of this.

He gave out the sectors without looking up.

"Garcia."

"Here."

"Davis."

"Here."

"Adam-Boy, 1883, four o'clock meal." That designated their sector, the number of the RMP they'd be driving, and their meal hour.

He went through Charlie-Frank, which is McGovern and O'Brien, and David-George, which is me and Fiore, without incident. When he got to Eddie-Henry, Connelly answered "here," but Rooney bellowed "Yo," causing the boss to raise an eyebrow. The boss moved on to the foot posts, robbery posts, and the substation, and ended the sectors by speaking to Noreen Casey, his driver.

"Casey, 2455, four o'clock meal. Nor, make sure you grab me a radio," he said.

John Quinn from the four-to-twelve was bringing in a collar, a drunk and disorderly we could hear yelling before he even got in the door.

"Who do you think you are?" his collar bellowed. "Do you know who I am?"

"I don't care who you are," Quinn answered in a bored, tired voice.

"Lou, this guy's hammered," Quinn said as he stopped at the desk. "Do you mind if I just take him in the back?" He was pulling the guy in backward by his cuffs.

"I pay your salary!" the drunk said, inviting a whole slew of comments from the roll call.

"I want a raise."

"So you're the guy holding back our pay increase!"

"This job sucks!"

Quinn ignored this, taking the drunk back toward the metal gated door. The lou buzzed him in, and he went back toward the cells.

The boss ignored the heckling from the ranks as he went into "It's been brought to my attention that there's been some congregating on the front steps before the day tour finishes roll call."

"Oh, here we go," someone groaned from the back of the room.

Hanrahan held up his hand. "Apparently the CO came in early and saw ten to fifteen guys gathered on the front steps of the station house."

"Oh, gimme a break," Rooney yelled.

"I know." The boss nodded in understanding. "Just do us all a favor and stay around the block until the day tour is done with roll call. We don't want to bring attention to ourselves, especially if the CO comes in early."

Hanrahan finished up with "Be careful, there's probably gonna be some late-night Christmas parties, and there'll be drunks spilling into the streets. It's gonna be busy out there, all the stores are open late for the last-minute shoppers."

I walked over to the radio room, surprised to see Vince Puletti working. He had enough time on not to be working Christmas week.

"Hey, Vince, whatcha doing here?" I asked as we shook hands. He had big beefy hands and a big pot belly. His bald head was mottled with age spots, and over the last few months he'd been out sick a lot.

"Ah, tonight's my last night. I'll be here for Christmas, then I'll be in Florida for ten days." He could use the sun, he was looking kind of pasty. He had been having some problems with his stomach and some chest pain. At first they thought he was having a heart attack, then they said it was some kind of hernia.

"Feeling okay?" I asked, concerned.

"Yeah, don't worry about me, Tony. I'm too mean to die," he said, not looking mean at all.

"Just don't work too hard," I said as I pointed the antenna of my radio at him.

"You can count on it."

"Hey, Tony," he called as I turned.

"Yeah?" I looked back at him.

He gave me a "come here" signal with his hand.

"What's up?" I asked.

"You still on the wagon?" he whispered.

"Yup," I nodded.

"How long has it been?"

"About five months," I said. He looked like he was thinking.

"Is there a bet going?" I asked dryly.

He held up his hands, "Mike Rooney only gave you two weeks. Me, I said you could do six months."

"Thanks for the vote of confidence, Vince." I shook my head as I walked away.

I stopped by the front desk, where Fiore was talking to the sarge.

"Hey, Joe, Tony, Boss," Nick Romano said as he came out of the muster room. Romano's a rookie that Fiore and I look out for. We drive him to post and have coffee with him, and teach him all the little things that nobody taught us. We only do it because his father was killed in the line of duty, otherwise we would antagonize him like we do the rest of the rookies.

"Can you give me a ride to post?" he asked. His hair, which had been spiked and bleached white at the tips over the summer, was now dark again, cut short, with just a little spike in it.

"Romano," Rice and Beans from the four-to-twelve called. They came in as we were leaving. "Can you do me a favor?" Beans asked. "Central gave us a job about thirty seconds ago for a dispute at 705 8th Avenue, a couple of guys are arguing over there." The dispute was at an Irish pub across from the Milford Plaza. Central stands for Central Communications, those phantom voices that transmit our jobs from the 911 operators. Central's operators each work one division made up of three commands. When 911 gets a call, they dispatch it to Central, who transmits it to us.

"Sure, no problem, that's my post. I'll check it out when I get up there," Romano said, writing it down in his book.

"We'll drop you off up there and back you up," Fiore told Romano.

We walked out to the RMP, which stands for Radio Motor Patrol, or sector car. It was cold out, in the low thirties and expected to dip down into the twenties overnight. It was sunny this morning, but clouds had started to come in and we were expecting some snow showers in the morning.

We drove up 8th Avenue, holding off getting coffee until we answered the dispute.

"How long were you on the job before you got Christmas off?" Romano asked from the backseat.

"Don't expect it anytime soon," I said, lighting a cigarette.

I pulled up in front of the bar. It was an older bar, smoked glass front window, white brick face. I've been here before; they get a big lunch crowd that comes in for the five-buck buffet. It's an all-you-can-eat deal, and they put out a spread of corned beef and cabbage, roast beef, turkey with stuffing, mashed potatoes, and vegetables. They also have shepherd's pie and a pretty good potato soup.

The food draws the crowds, mostly construction workers, but the place makes its money on booze. It's quick and easy to get your food, leaving the rest of your lunch hour to drink. I've seen guys scoff down a plate of food and drink six shots of whiskey to wash it down.

The tinted window with the big shamrock on the front kept us from seeing inside. I took a last drag off my cigarette, tossing it into the street. We opened the front door into a small hallway with wood paneling. We walked into the bar through an inside wooden door with a glass cutout.

A small Christmas tree was perched on a table in the corner in front of us. Three small tables were in front of the window, and a twenty-foot bar ran along the wall. Christmas lights were strung along the bar and around the window. To the left was an open area with a stainless steel buffet counter, now long since cleaned up from lunch.

Leftover food smells, cigarette smoke, and booze hung in the air. Past the buffet counter and up to the kitchen door were wooden tables with wooden chairs pushed in and out at odd angles. A couple of chairs were overturned, and the floor was wet.

Toward the end of the bar we saw two men. One was in a Grinch costume, the other in a Santa Claus suit. They were pummeling each other on the floor of the bar. Beside one of the barstools, the head to the Grinch costume was lying on its side on the floor. Even in the dark bar, the face on the Grinch mask looked strange—small droopy eyes and thick black eyebrows sewn on, giving it a maniacal look.

Santa's hat and beard were on the bar next to a glass of beer and an empty shot glass. A pack of Kools was next to the red hat, and one was smoking in the ashtray.

The bartender in his white apron was standing with his hands on his hips, watching them scuffle. Three or four people sat at the bar, giving little interest to the drama around them.

"Good!" the bartender yelled in his Irish brogue. "Now the cops are here to take your sorry hides to the slammer."

Romano went toward them, and I grabbed him by the jacket. "Whoa, let's let them tire themselves out a little before you separate them." It's been my experience that it's smart to let them run out of steam a little so if they throw you a punch, there's not much force in it.

"These guys stand up on 42nd Street and take pictures with the tourists," Romano remarked.

When we got within about five feet of them, we could smell the sweat mixed with beer. Santa looked like a harmless old man, somewhere in his sixties. His black patent leather belt was broken, hanging open around his waist. The white trim on his Santa suit was now black from the dirt on the floor, and when he rolled over he had a foot print on his back. His face was blotchy where he took some punches, his left eye was swollen, and his lip was split and bleeding.

The Grinch had gotten the best of Santa; aside from a couple of choke marks on his neck and a knot over his eye, he looked okay. He was younger than Santa, heavyset with dark brown hair that was sweaty and disheveled. The Grinch's suit was torn at the collar, revealing a white thermal shirt underneath. His hand was cut, probably from the broken glass on the floor.

15

"Alright, guys, it's over now," I said as I grabbed the Grinch. Fiore came up next to me in case the Grinch started to swing again.

"Nick, grab Santa," I said to Romano.

"I'm not gonna lock up Santa," Romano said, looking horrified.

"We can't leave him here," I pointed out.

"I want them both out of here!" the bartender shouted. "They've been fighting all night."

I still had my gloves on, and when I grabbed the Grinch to cuff him, my hold was slippery on his wet fur. He smelled like a wet dog that'd been rolling in beer.

"When was the last time you washed this thing?" I asked the Grinch, wrinkling my face in distaste.

"I don't know," he said with a shrug.

Nick was standing next to Santa, making no move to cuff him. "Nick, cuff Santa," I said. "We'll sort this out at the precinct."

"Great, I locked up Santa," Romano said miserably.

"And the Grinch," Joe added, holding the more docile Santa's arm in back of him while Romano put the cuffs on him.

At this point the Grinch was breathing heavy, looking at Santa menacingly. He pulled away from me and screamed, "I'll kill you!" as he threw himself at Santa.

"You're a mean one, Mr. Grinch," I said dryly. "Now leave Santa alone." He hocked some spit at Santa, catching him on the front of his furry red jacket. I whipped him around. "If you spit at him again, I'm gonna put your mask back on you and you can spit on yourself." He looked at me defiantly and spit on Santa again. I sighed and walked over to the Grinch head, pulling it a little roughly onto his head.

"He took my money!" he said. It sounded muffled under the mask, but I could hear what he was saying.

"Shut up!" I said, "Look at me." I pulled on his cuffs to pull his stare away from Santa. I couldn't see where his eyes were through the mask and looked in the general direction of his face. "Did you see him take your money?"

"No, but I had a twenty on the bar."

"So anybody could have taken it. You probably drank your-self through it and don't remember," I said. The mask was giving him a deranged look. The eyes on the mask were nothing more than two slits and left him looking like he just shot heroin or something.

Joe got the information from the bartender: name, address, phone number, and a brief summary of what happened. Then he picked up Santa's beard, holding it up to let the beer drip off it. He got Santa his red hat and cigarettes, and we marched them out to the RMP.

We put Romano in the backseat, crushing him between Santa and the Grinch.

"Ah come on, these two stink!" Romano said with disgust. "Why do drunks always wet their pants?" Joe and I laughed at him but rolled down the windows in the back. "You're gonna clean that backseat, Nick," I yelled toward the back. "I'm not smelling that all night."

"Nick, what post you got?" Fiore asked him, calling Central.

"Robbery Post 4," Romano said.

Fiore gave Central Romano's post and told them he had two under, meaning two arrests. He asked them to have a bus (ambulance) meet us at the station house. Better to have these guys looked at—the last thing we needed was to have Santa Claus die while in custody.

Vince Puletti started laughing as soon as we walked through the front doors of the precinct. "I guess the Grinch made the naughty list!" he cackled, cracking himself up.

Terri Marks, an old-timer, was working the desk tonight. She's got about eighteen years on and is probably somewhere in her midforties. Because she was inside, she had no vest on. She had a winter tan. She goes to a tanning salon regularly, sunning herself into a piece of leather. She has these piercing blue eyes, almost silver really, and her hair is dyed a dull red. I hear eighteen years ago she was gorgeous, but she looks like a hair bag now.

She kept her face impassive as we walked over to the desk. We caught Lieutenant Coughlin by surprise. He peered over the top of his glasses, then put his head down and snorted. He looked up again, straight-faced.

"Whaddaya got, Romano?"

"I got assault three on both Santa and the Grinch," Romano said nervously. When he saw the lou looking at Santa, he added, "We got a bus coming to the house."

"Sure," the lou looked at Joe and me. "We don't want Santa sick for Christmas."

"He stole my money!" the Grinch insisted, mumbling the words.

"Uh," Romano stammered, "the Grinch said Santa stole his money off the bar."

I saw the look of distaste on the lou's face as he caught a whiff of these two.

"What's with the mask on the Grinch?" he asked, eyeing the mask suspiciously.

"He's a spitter," I said.

"Take them in the back and keep them separated. Then come back out and do the pedigree sheet." He sighed, then added, "Search them good and see if Santa has any of those magic corn kernels that make the reindeers fly. My wife's got a cat I want to get rid of."

"Nick?" Terri Marks said seriously as Romano started toward the cells. "For the pedigree sheet, what do we got, the North Pole and Who-ville?"

"Come on, Nick, I'll help you get them to the back," Fiore said.

While Joe went back to the cells with Nick, I took some alcohol pads and wiped down the backseat of our car. Fiore came out, and we stopped on the corner of 35th and 9th to get some coffee.

While I was paying for our coffee, I heard Central give us a job on 35th Street between Broadway and 7th. It had come over as a 10-22, past larceny from an auto.

We drove out, heading east to the back of Macy's where their loading dock is located. Three empty trailers were backed up into the loading dock bays behind the store.

There was a woman talking on her cell phone, waving us down. She flipped her phone shut and walked toward our car. I pulled up behind the car she was standing next to, a black Porshe that was parked on the south side of 35th Street. Joe radioed Central, telling them we were 84, on the scene.

She was wearing a fur coat that came to about her ankles. I could see black high heels and stockings sticking out under the fur coat. She was a cool blonde, probably midforties with that well-kept look rich women have.

"Somebody broke into my car. He broke the window and took my presents," she said, indicating the driver's side window that was missing.

I took out my flashlight as I walked over to the car. I shone the light inside the car. In the passenger seat I saw the porcelain part of a spark plug used to break the window.

The woman was looking at us like we could do something about her stolen packages.

The weeks between Thanksgiving and Christmas in Midtown are packed with people. As Christmas gets closer, shoppers and perps compete to buy or steal those last-minute gifts. Perps make the most of the season by doing some shopping as they watch unsuspecting consumers relieve themselves of their heavy packages, put them in their cars, and go back to shop some more. Then the perps usually use the spark plug to gain access to the gifts—the porcelain part is heavy enough to break any window, and you just can't find rocks on the streets of Manhattan. The perps stand a couple of feet away from the car and throw the spark plug as hard as they can at the window, shattering it in one easy move. Then they help themselves to all the gifts and bags people are stupid enough to leave in the backseat of their car. After that, the perps use the latch inside the car to pop the trunk and make off with all the really good stuff the complainant didn't want anyone to walk by and see in the car.

"How long has the car been here?" I asked.

"I came out about forty-five minutes ago and put the packages in the car. I forgot the table linens I needed, so I ran back into Macy's about a quarter to twelve." She held up a brown shopping bag. "I have the linens, but all my presents are gone," she said with a disgusted sigh. "I was so glad to get back in the store before they closed. I would have had the table linens and the presents finished." She shook her head, "They were already wrapped."

I looked at my watch, it was now 12:30. "How long ago did you call?"

"About fifteen minutes ago."

"Whoever it was, they're long gone." I said, looking into the car.

The glove compartment was open and a gum wrapper was on the seat, along with small pieces of glass from the shattered window.

"Not much glass in here," I looked back at her.

"I brushed most of it out of the car already," she said. I looked down to see glass on the street in between the curb and the car. I was wearing gloves so I wouldn't cut my hands. I brushed the rest of it out, picking up a couple of pieces in the console. I picked up the gum wrapper and she said, "And he helped himself to my gum too."

"Does your insurance company cover the contents of the car?" Fiore asked.

"I don't know." She rubbed her forehead. "Now I have to shop all over again. I had it all wrapped already, and now I have to do it again," she repeated. "I'm having thirty guests for Christmas Eve dinner tomorrow, and I don't have time for this." She turned to Joe. "He took the book to my Porshe, the one you keep in the glove compartment. What is he going to do with that?"

"Maybe a souvenir," Joe said with a shrug. "I don't know what to tell you."

"What are you doing out so late? Couldn't you finish this in the morning?" I asked her. I know she had to shop, but this was a dark and desolate street; you'd think she'd know better.

"I wanted to finish all my shopping so I could concentrate on dinner tomorrow." She rubbed her forehead again and asked, "Are you going to dust for fingerprints?"

I'm glad I didn't laugh and say, "Not for this, lady." They weren't coming out for a smash and grab.

Joe said diplomatically, "We'd have to see if someone from the evidence collection unit who is latent print qualified is working."

"How soon can they be here?" she asked.

"It would take a while. Unless you're willing to wait here for a few hours and have powder all over your car, maybe you should check with your insurance company to see if you're covered. How much was in there?" Joe asked. "If it's only a couple of hundred dollars in gifts that you're probably not gonna get back anyway, it's not worth having your car dusted for prints."

She shook her head. "I can't believe I have to do this again."

"Thank God it's stuff you can replace," Joe said. "Do you have your receipts?"

"Some of them—the rest were in the bags."

"We'll do a report," I told her. "Then when you get a list for the rest of the items from your credit card bills, you can come down to the precinct and add them on. Did you use a credit card to buy the gifts?"

She nodded, "Yes."

We took her info, she gave us an Upper East Side address and a list of the receipts she had on her.

"Thank you for your help, officers," she said, smiling. "Merry Christmas."

"No problem," I said. "Merry Christmas to you too."

We got back in the car, and a job came over from South Adam for a robbery in progress.

"South Adam to Central," South Adam radioed.

"Go ahead, South Adam," Central responded.

"I have a pickup of a 30, West 38th and 6th, happened two to three minutes in the past. We're looking for a dark-skinned male Hispanic in a camouflage army jacket with a hood. Suspect armed with a machete, last seen 6th Avenue and 38th."

A 30 is a robbery in progress, and 38th Street was three blocks from where we were. I smiled and raised my eyebrows at Fiore as I turned the car around. I pulled into one of the empty bays of the loading dock, threw my lights on, and drove the wrong way on 35th Street, toward Broadway.

2

*H*erald Square is between Broadway and 6th, so I figured I'd zip over to Broadway or 6th from 35th Street and maybe catch the suspect running down our way.

"You looking tonight?" Joe asked, meaning did I want to make an arrest.

"No way, tomorrow's Christmas Eve. You?" I countered.

"Can't, lots of company coming."

As I got to Broadway, Joe and I took a fast look up and down the block. When I proceeded to 6th Avenue, Joe said, "Wait up, Tony."

"Whaddaya got?" I looked around, trying to see what was up.

"Look." He pointed to Herald Square. "Someone is ducking behind the statue."

He was talking about the statue in Herald Square of Minerva, the goddess of wisdom, holding her shield over her two bell ringers. It's a memorial to James Gordon Bennett Sr., the founder of the *New York Herald*.

We were on the north side of the statue, behind it. The statue faces south. Herald Square is enclosed with a wrought iron fence, so people can enjoy the park without having cars jump the sidewalk and plow into them. The park is triangular with three exits, and he could wind up on 34th Street or on either side of 35th Street, depending on which side of the statue he ran from.

"He's been running, I can see he's breathing hard," Joe said quietly.

I leaned forward to take a look. I couldn't see the perp, just the plumes of smoke as his breath hit the cold air.

Joe got on the radio, "South David to Central."

"Go ahead, South David."

"We got a possible at three-five and six."

"10-4."

We both got out of the car. I cut the engine and took my keys. Joe and I loosened our guns from our holsters, keeping our right hands on our guns and our radios in our left hands.

We were at the opening at 35th and 6th. As we reached the sidewalk, he bolted. We could hear him running and hear the rustling of a plastic bag. We stopped and hunched down to see which way he went. We spotted him running westbound on 35th Street, where we just answered the smash-and-grab job.

Good, I thought as he ran down 35th. *We can trap him on this street—if he had run down Broadway, he would have had an open street with subway access. He must have panicked and couldn't orient himself, or he never would have run this way.*

Joe and I started to run after him. As I passed the RMP, I realized I'd have time to get in the car and chase him down 35th Street. Joe kept after him on foot. I jumped in the car, turned the ignition, and spun the tires.

I heard Joe radioing Central, "I'm in pursuit on 35th Street going westbound toward 7th Avenue." The other units joined in.

"South Adam responding."

"South Eddie going."

"South Sergeant responding."

I threw my lights on as I turned down 35th Street. I saw the perp running in the street about thirty feet in front of Joe, not even halfway to 7th Avenue. I was contemplating opening my door to whack him from behind when he cut in between two parked cars, slowing down on the sidewalk but still running.

As I passed him I didn't turn to look at him, but I could see him carrying a long, black plastic bag in his right hand.

While the streets in Herald Square were shorter, this length of 35th Street was unusually long, about a block and a half, the whole length of Macy's.

I kept him in my sights with quick glances in my sideview mirror. When I got about fifty feet ahead of him, I screeched to a halt, threw the car in park, and shut off the ignition. I grabbed my keys in case he threw me a head fake to get past me and drove off with the RMP, leaving me and Fiore swinging in the breeze.

I jumped out of the car, leaving the door open. I pulled my gun out and tried to set my eyes on where he was so I could move in his direction. He was still on the sidewalk, with Joe running about thirty feet behind him.

He was about forty feet away from me. I raised my gun up now so I'd have my sights on his chest. In the distance I heard the screeching of tires, but I paid no attention to them.

Up until this point my only thought was getting in front of him to trap him. Now he was bearing down on me. The bag in his right hand was pumping up and down in time with his moving legs. I could hear his labored breathing, his face still a shadow in a camouflage jacket. I had about eight to ten seconds till he'd be on me.

This is the moment the department can never get you ready

for no matter how much tactical training you have—that split-second decision you have to make on your reaction to his action.

I wanted to let this guy know I'm not here to play games with him. I decided if he tried to run around me, I'd holster my gun and tackle him down. The seconds are short and the options are few. For him, he'd be in one of two places tonight, dead or in jail. For me, if I hesitate, he stabs me or I shoot him. Not looking good for either one of us at this point.

I decided right there that I'd be the one going home at the end of the night. If he raised his hand with the bag, I was gonna shoot him, more than once. Perps have been known to keep coming with a knife even with a couple of bullets in them.

"Drop the bag!" I yelled, my gun aimed at his chest as I looked straight at him.

When he saw the gun in my hand, he stumbled down to a walk. He had a hood on. I didn't see that before. It was one of those nylon ones that roll into the collar of the jacket. It was pulled tight around his face, circling his features.

Our eyes locked, his wide and dark, almost black. I didn't see fear in his eyes, more like uncertainty. Not good.

My right arm was extended, straight out with my left hand cupped under my right hand holding my gun. I had both my eyes open, with my gun sights on his chest.

"Drop the bag now!" I yelled again, taking slow steps toward him.

He was tired now; he'd been running since 38th Street and 6th Avenue, pausing only for a couple of seconds at the statue in Herald Square, then running down here.

Steam was coming from his nose and mouth. I didn't know if he was thinking of dropping the bag or coming at me. The only thing I was thinking is, *He has a machete in that bag.*

I was about ten feet away from him now. I could see the sweat on his face and the whites of his eyes as he stared at me. I looked down at his hand for half a second and saw him tighten his grip on the bag.

I heard the screech of tires again, and in my peripheral vision I saw a sector car turn the corner off Broadway with the turret lights on.

I gave him my last command: "I'm not going to tell you again, drop the bag *now!*" I closed my left eye to pinpoint my sights. I saw his eyes widen, and I was vaguely aware of someone talking. He stopped and began to turn to the right, then he flew forward, facedown onto the sidewalk.

I had forgotten about Fiore. He came up from behind the perp and tackled him to the ground. As soon as Joe had him down, I closed in the last couple of feet. I stepped on the perp's hand holding the bag, careful not to step on Joe's hand holding his right elbow. I used the arch of my foot on his wrist so he couldn't move his hand.

I heard the acceleration of the sector car approaching from Broadway. South Adam was on the scene first, with Rooney coming next from 7th Avenue, and the sergeant behind him.

I holstered my gun and reached down to grab the bag. I threw it to the side, a couple of feet away. Joe took the wrist from under my foot and cuffed him. I moved to kneel on his neck to keep him pinned, pushing down on his upper back so he couldn't move.

"Give me your other arm," Joe said, breathing heavy but still giving a clear and precise command. As Joe cuffed his other wrist, I came off his neck.

"Everyone okay?" Sergeant Hanrahan asked.

"We're fine," Joe said as he grabbed one of the perp's elbows and I grabbed the other.

"Come on, get up," Joe said as we got him to his feet. He got up, keeping his head down, still breathing heavy.

I lit a cigarette. I noticed that my hands were shaking. I took a deep drag and blew out the smoke in relief that Joe and I would be going home tonight.

Joe called Central to "slow it down" so no one else would be rushing to the scene.

Garcia got out of his RMP, stuck his head in the rear window, and said something in Spanish to an older woman sitting in the backseat. She peered out and pointed at the perp, nodding furiously as she rattled off in Spanish.

We're allowed to bring the complainants to the place where we stop the perp so they can make a positive ID. Technically he wouldn't be under arrest until she made a positive ID. We're not allowed to bring a suspect we have in custody back to the complainant's location, because the courts feel we'd be swaying the complainant. It's been argued that since victims are upset, if we bring a suspect to them and say, "Is this the guy?" they're more likely to say, "Yeah, that's him" about anyone we produce. The only exception to the rule would be if a victim is seriously hurt and likely to die and can't be brought to the location to identify the perp.

Garcia walked back to Joe and me and confirmed, "This is the guy."

I picked up the bag and pulled out a machete. It was about two feet long with a black handle and metal blade.

"Was she cut? This looks like blood." I showed the stained blade to Joe and Garcia.

"It does look like blood," Garcia agreed. "No, she wasn't cut."

"I wonder whose blood this is," I commented.

The sarge saw us looking at the knife and walked over. "Whaddaya got?"

"Looks like blood," I said, showing him the blade.

"Hers?" He indicated his head toward the car where the complainant sat.

"No," I said.

"We'll let the lab figure it out. Don't put it back in the plastic bag," Hanrahan said.

"Are you guys looking to collar?" Garcia asked.

"No, are you looking?" Joe asked.

"It's a good collar." He sounded excited.

"Robbery two, Merry Christmas," I handed him the bag and the machete.

Usually with something like this, it's an unwritten rule that whoever catches the perp gets the collar. Since neither Joe nor I wanted overtime tonight, we could give the collar to Garcia. The ADAs (Assistant District Attorneys) don't come in until 9:00 a.m. anyway, and Christmas Eve would slow the arrest process down, so he could drag it out to a full tour of overtime. Sometimes in a situation like this there would be a fight about it. South Adam got this as a pickup and it was a good collar, but Joe and I caught the perp. If I had shot the perp, nobody would have wanted it 'cause it would lead to a whole slew of investigations.

Joe, Garcia, and Davis searched the perp, finding money in the inside pocket of his jacket. Joe counted out three hundred in new, crisp twenties.

"She said he took three hundred off her," Garcia said, taking the money as evidence. "Boss," Garcia called to Sergeant Hanrahan.

"Did she ID him?" Hanrahan asked.

"Yeah, besides the machete, he had the three hundred bucks she said he took."

The sarge looked at me, "Who's taking the collar?"

"Garcia wants to take it."

He nodded, "Noreen and I will take the complainant. Put the perp in Garcia's car."

When Garcia and Hanrahan left, Joe and I hung out with Rooney and Connelly for a few minutes, going through what happened with them.

We went to the all-night deli at the corner of 35th and 7th for coffee. We sat in the car outside the deli, drinking our coffee and talking about the machete perp.

I looked over at Joe and said, "When you ran up and tackled him, I heard you talking, but you were talking too low for me to hear what you were saying."

He shrugged, "Yeah."

"Who were you talking to? You weren't talking loud enough for the perp to understand you." I lit another cigarette, my third in the last twenty minutes.

"I was praying." He said it like it was nothing.

I thought about that for a minute. I wasn't praying. I wasn't thinking about anyone—not God, not Fiore, not Michele, not Stevie—just if I was gonna have to shoot that guy. I wondered why I didn't pray.

"Didn't that distract you?" I asked. I wondered if stopping to talk to God would blow my focus.

"Not at all," he said and paused. "If anything, it helps me concentrate. When I was running down after him, I was praying, asking God if he was carrying a knife. I asked God to help me, and when the perp ran under a streetlight, the light caught his right arm and I saw the outline of the machete."

"I couldn't tell from where I was if he had a knife, I just took it that he did," I said.

"Then once I saw the knife, I knew he was coming down at you, and I didn't want him to stab you. So I asked God to help me take him down before you got hurt or had to shoot him. He was so intent on you with the gun, he forgot I was behind him. He slowed down some, but I was still running and hit him full force. Hurt my shoulder a little too," Joe said as he rubbed his right shoulder.

"You alright?"

"Yeah, but I'll be sore tomorrow."

"I didn't even think to pray. Why is that?" I never seem to be as good at this as Joe is.

"It's not something that happens overnight—you develop in it."

I nodded, not sure I wanted God in my head while I'm trying to work. "Hey, what'd you think about that stuff they were saying last Sunday at church?" I'd been wanting to ask him about that.

"What stuff?"

"The stuff about the star the wise men saw in the East. Pastor was saying it appeared in 6 BC. How would he know that?"

"Tony, I'm sure it's a historical fact. The star was never seen before that," he said.

"I always thought it appeared the night Jesus was born," I said. "Oh," I added, remembering something else about it, "he said that the wise men didn't go to the stable and see Baby Jesus. He said they went to the house when he was older."

"That's in Matthew, chapter two," he said with a nod.

"I know where it is, I read it with Pastor last week. I just always thought that on Christmas Eve, the wise men went to the stable because they saw the star over where the manger was," I said, still surprised at the information.

"And?" he asked.

"I never heard it that way before, and I'm having a hard time being convinced."

He looked at me like I was nuts. "Let me get this straight: You're having a hard time believing what you read in the Bible over some Sunday school story somebody *told* you?"

"I never heard it before," I said defensively. "No one in my family ever heard it that way either."

"I never heard it any other way," he said, "so I don't have a problem with it. I can understand it throwing you a little, but I believe what the Bible tells me. Most people think there were three wise men too, but the Bible doesn't say how many there were, just that wise men visited Jesus."

"It's not throwing me, but are you sure it's true?" I know it seemed like a little thing, but it made me wonder what else I was wrong about.

"It's true. Ask Pastor to show you where he got his information. He'll tell you."

It was about 2:45 now. The street was quiet, the stores on 34th Street were all closed. Even though it was a Sunday, they'd all be open bright and early for Christmas Eve. I picked up the newspaper, reading an article about mad cow disease in Germany.

"Did you know Germany has over fifteen hundred kinds of sausage?" I asked Joe.

"What are you reading?" He laughed.

"About mad cow disease in Germany. It says that there's fifteen hundred kinds of sausage, most made with pork and beef, and that the average German consumes . . ." I scanned the article for my place, ". . . fifty-five pounds of sausage a year. That's more than the Italians."

"Yeah, but I bet we eat more than fifty-five pounds of macaroni a year," he said.

That was probably true. "It says they use cow brains for sausage—we don't do that?" I asked, horrified at the thought.

"Not that I know of. Let me see that." He took the paper from me and read through the article.

"I'm glad I'm eating fish for Christmas Eve," I shuddered.

"Me too."

We sat in the car, talking and reading the paper, until 3:15 when we got a job.

"South David," Central called.

"South David," Fiore answered.

"We have a 54 unconscious at three-nine and eight."

"10-4."

We took 35th Street to 8th Avenue, driving north up to 39th Street. A male white was laying facedown over the subway grating on the southwest corner of 39th Street.

He appeared lifeless when we walked up to him. His head was facing 8th Avenue, resting on top of his folded arms.

I'd seen him around; he's usually across the street near the liquor store on the southeast corner of 39th Street. He was wearing dark pants and a stained, green plaid thermal jacket. One leg was pulled up close to his body, the other was stretched out with the shoe half off. He was wearing old sneakers, one with no lace in it, the other was knotted in a couple of places to hold it together.

He was lying on the subway grating so he'd catch a blast of heat whenever a train went by underneath him. There was a rumpled paper bag next to him with a pint of Thunderbird sticking out of it.

I put my gloves on while Joe tossed the bottle into the garbage can.

I nudged him with my foot. "Hey, buddy, you alive there?"

He moaned.

"Come on, get up," I said, kicking his foot with my boot.

Before I met Fiore, I would have stepped on his ankle with my boot. A good stomp in the ankle will put a spring back in their step. EMS will usually rub their sternum until it annoys them awake, I find that takes too long, so I gave him another kick in the foot.

"Hey, buddy, come on, wake up." He moved a little, so I nudged again. "Hey! Let's go."

"What? What?" he moaned, his head still on his arms.

"Hey, oh come on, wake up."

"What?" He picked his head up and looked at me, bleary-eyed. When he saw we were cops, he said, "Oh come on." He tried to sit up and slowly got his upper body off the grating, resting on his hands. He fell back down, rolling over onto his arms again.

"Police, let's go, you can't lay here." I love repeating myself.

He sat up again, trying to focus his eyes on me.

"You can't stay here, you gotta get up." He stared at me, but I didn't think anything sank in.

"Come on, Joe, let's get him up," I said to Fiore.

We hauled him to his feet, each of us taking an elbow. "What are you doing? No, let me sleep," he slurred.

"He's not steady on his feet," Joe said.

I gave his arm a little jerk and said, "Come on, you gotta walk, wake up."

We would have taken him home to sleep it off, but he was too wasted.

"He's not gonna be able to walk out of here," I said. "I think he lives in one of the apartments on 9th Avenue, but I don't know which one." We lowered him back down to the ground, where he passed out again.

"He can't lay out here, he needs to go to the hospital," Joe said, getting his radio.

"South David to Central."

"Go ahead, South David."

"Is a bus responding?"

"Yes, two-minute ETA." (Estimated time of arrival.)

In a couple of minutes EMS, or Emergency Medical Services, was on the scene, a male and female we've answered jobs with before. The female smiled when she saw the drunk. "Charlie!" she yelled. The drunk looked up and smiled at her. She was nice, always friendly to whoever she's picking up. She looked to be in her late thirties. She was a little chubby with short, black spiky hair.

"You know him?" Fiore asked her.

"We see Charlie all the time, right, Charlie?" He looked up and smiled at her again. Her partner was a little older than she was, maybe forty. He was about five foot ten, heavyset with brown hair and square, wire-rimmed glasses.

"I think he lives on 9th Avenue," I told them.

"Yeah, he does," the male said.

"Charlie," she called as she rubbed his chest. Charlie kept pushing her hand away. "Come on, Charlie, let's get up." He sat up and smiled at her again, then his head rolled back with a bonk.

"We'll take him," she said, grabbing him under the elbow. "If you guys want to make it 55, go ahead." A 55 means ambulance case, no RMP required, so we wouldn't have to fill out an aided card or go to the hospital.

Joe and I thanked them and waited while they got Charlie onto a chair. We had no other jobs, so we parked in the empty lot on 37th Street. Joe took a nap, and I sat smoking and reading the paper.

We went back to the precinct at 5:00 for our meal. We slept on the benches in our uniform pants, having taken off our belts, guns, vests, jackets, and turtlenecks. Joe set the alarm on his watch for 5:55 and spent ten minutes trying to wake me up to go back out.

We stopped at a bakery on 8th Avenue and 30th Street and got coffee and Babyface cheesecake. We sat in the car outside the bakery while we ate. It was quiet, no commuters were out, and only the 24-hour delis, bagel stores, and bakeries were open.

"So what's on the agenda for today?" Joe asked.

"I'll stop at the jeweler on my way home," I said. "I'm not coming out to go to church today. Michele's driving in later to go to my grandmother's for dinner."

"Gonna be traffic."

"I know, I told her to expect to be in the car for a few hours. The Long Island Expressway is a nightmare on a holiday."

"The Long Island Expressway is a nightmare on any day," Joe remarked, then added, "So you're just picking up earrings, or are you gonna surprise her with a ring?"

"It's still too soon, my family would freak," I said, picturing my father shaking his head and telling me I'm crazy.

"What does your family have to do with this? It's your life."

"I only know her six months." It felt longer than that, but my family wasn't giving her the warm welcome I'd hoped. I wanted them to get to know her and like her a little more before I got engaged.

"Rooney said he married his wife a week after he met her," Joe pointed out.

"Yeah, he was on a binge in hedonism and didn't remember getting married." By the time they sobered up, they figured they'd give it a shot and see how it went. That was a couple of years ago and they're still married, so I guess it worked out okay.

"Rooney's not Italian. If I ever did something like that, my family would never talk to me again," I said.

"I'm just saying it's not like you met her a month ago and got married. If you want to get engaged, it should be your decision, not influenced by what they'd think."

"I don't know if she's ready yet either."

"That's different, as long as it's you two who aren't ready and not your family."

We finished up the night without any more jobs. After we

got changed, I gave him a ride to Penn Station. I wished him a Merry Christmas and gave him two wrapped packages, one for him, one for his father.

"Wait till Christmas morning," I said.

"You too." He smiled, pulling a gold wrapped box out of his gym bag.

I got Joe *100 Years of Major League Baseball*, in hardcover. I got his father two ESPN videos from the Brooklyn Dodgers series. One was "The Jewel of Flatbush: The Duke Snyder Story," and the other "The Quiet Ambassador: the Pee Wee Reese Story." Pee Wee Reese was Lou Fiore's favorite all-time ballplayer, and as far as Joe or I knew, Lou didn't have any of the series.

He waved me off, and I drove north to the diamond district at 46th Street. I put the present under my seat so it was out of sight. I parked on the corner outside Lichtenstein's Fine Jewelry.

My old partner, John Conte, showed me the place when he got engaged to his wife. Over the years, I've come here when-ever I've bought a piece of jewelry. The owner, Sol Lichtenstein, has always done the right thing by me.

Sol was behind the counter and already had a couple of customers. He was somewhere in his sixties, trim and profes-sional in a conservative blue suit. He was Jewish, he wore a yarmulke but didn't have the curls and hat like a Hasid. He had short gray hair, blue eyes, and a clean-shaven face.

The store had waist-high, glass jewelry cases along the right wall and a glass island in the middle, with an attractive older woman waiting on a customer.

"Tony, how are you?" He smiled as we shook hands.

"Pretty good, Sol, how about you, been busy?"

"Thank God, business is good. Let me show you the ear-rings." He held up one finger before he went into the back of the store. I stole a look at the display with the engagement rings.

He came out with the half-karat diamond studs I picked out last week. He took them out of the box by the backs, handing them to me to look at.

"These are beautiful, Sol, thanks," I said. Michele was gonna love them.

"Let me wrap them for you, Tony, we do a beautiful job."

He handed them to the woman in the center island, asking her to wrap them in white and gold.

"Soooo," he smiled. "When are you going to see me about an engagement ring?"

I shrugged, "Hopefully soon."

"Is she a nice girl?" He had a strong accent, it sounded Eastern European to me.

"She's nice, she's beautiful, and a God-fearing woman." I figured he'd like that in a woman considering he's religious and always says "Thank God." The way he says it, it comes out in one word.

"So what are you waiting for?"

I thought he was kidding, then I realized he was waiting for an answer.

"I only know her for six months," I explained.

He waved me away, "Six months, six years, what difference does it make? A matchmaker matched my wife and me, and we've been married for forty-two years—we have nine children and forty-nine grandchildren!" His face lit up when he said it, the skin crinkling around his eyes.

"Nine kids and your wife's still alive?" I joked. I knew his wife was alive, she worked there.

"Esther!" he called toward the back room of the store. Esther came out, looking too good to have had nine children and too young to have forty-nine grandchildren.

"Come here, tell Tony about our children and grandchildren. He's met a nice girl."

"Should I be showing him the engagement rings?" She smiled at me, and I felt myself turning red.

"He says he only knows her for six months," Sol said, smiling at her.

"Six months is only too short if you have doubts. When it's right, it's right." She gave me an indulgent look. "Is it right?"

I nodded yes. "Just not right now," I said. "But soon."

"Then I hope you come back and let us find a beautiful ring for her," she said, smiling again.

"I wouldn't go anywhere else," I said honestly. "Have a good holiday, Happy Hanukkah." I hoped Hanukkah was the right holiday, but I had the feeling I didn't get that right. They thanked me anyway and wished me a happy holiday and a good appetite. They were nice people. They were similar to Italians when it came to family and business, only Italian food was better. Let's be honest, if you had to choose between a matzo ball and a meatball, what's it gonna be?

I took the West Side Highway, getting all the way downtown without any traffic. The Staten Island bound side of the Verrazzano Bridge was unusually clear, except for the E-Z pass lanes where everyone has to move over to the pay tolls. The Staten Island Expressway was already bumper-to-bumper as far as the eye could see.

I took the South Beach Exit, drove to Greeley Avenue, and parked outside my apartment. I moved in here in September, after my family's house was sold. It was an old colonial that sat at the end of Harbor Road, right on the Narrows of New York Bay. My parents got divorced when my father ran off with a civilian who worked in the precinct where he was a detective. My parents had what was called a "verbal agreement"—that he would keep his pension and my mother got to keep the house. My mother was stupid enough to trust him to keep his word, but he and his barracuda wife took her to court and a judge forced her to sell it. I heard he called from the courtroom and listed it with a real estate agent. My brother, Vinny, and I had renovated the house and tied up a lot of our money doing it.

To give her credit, my mother gave us both what we put into it when they sold it, but I was hoping to buy it myself.

So now I live in a basement apartment that Vinny found for me. His boss's brother owned the house, and the brother's son lived there until last summer when he got married. It sat at the end of the block, next to Miller Field, the old airfield that's now part of the Parks Department. My block is a dead end street with an opening in the fence that runs along Miller Field, giving me access to the park.

The house is a white brick ranch, with a staircase on the left side that leads down to my apartment. There's a huge garden, now cleaned up for the winter. There are two fig trees, cut back and wrapped in flannel-backed tablecloths. The trees are tied tightly with twine, and buckets are placed on the tops of them to keep any water out. There's a grape arbor, now bare, over a small patio. My landlord makes his own wine and gave me a bottle of last year's vintage, which I poured down my sink and told him was delicious.

The house to our right is only a couple of feet away. A couple in their fifties lives there. The husband is a big shot with the MTA, and they have three grown kids. They're a nice enough family, but their bathroom is across from my bedroom, and I can hear the drainage pipe when they flush their toilet. I can also hear one of them, I don't know if it's the husband or one of the sons, hocking up phlegm in the morning. It's pretty gross.

I unlocked the door to the apartment and flipped on the light. I tossed my keys on the counter and plugged my cell phone into the charger. I had gotten a cell phone about a month ago so Michele could get in touch with me while I'm at work. I forgot to charge it before work, and my battery had died halfway through my tour. I looked through my refrigerator for something to eat. I defrosted a roll and put a cold chicken cutlet on it with some ketchup. I drank a glass of water, brushed my teeth, and went inside the bedroom to sleep. I set my alarm for 4:00 and closed the blinds to darken the room.

I heard the alarm at 4:00 but hit snooze twice, getting up at 4:18. There was a message from Michele on the answering machine.

"Tony, it's me." She sounded nervous. "I'm leaving now, it's three-fifteen. Please be awake, I don't know what I should wear. Tony?" She sighed and waited a minute. "I guess you're still asleep. I'm on my way."

I showered and shaved by 5:00. I made coffee and waited for Michele. By 6:00 I was starting to get a little nervous. I had tried to get Michele on her cell phone, but it was shut off and I got her voice mail. The phone rang at 6:15. It was my grandmother asking if I was okay. I told her Michele was stuck in traffic and they should start without me.

"Can't you just tell her to meet you here?" Grandma sounded annoyed.

"No, Grandma, if you want to start without me, go ahead, but I'm waiting for Michele."

I hung up the phone and tried to tell myself that my grandmother being annoyed had nothing to do with her not liking Michele. This would be the third or fourth time that Michele was with my family, and each time the reception they gave us got a little cooler. I didn't think my grandmother would ever actually be rude to Michele, but I had the feeling she didn't approve of her.

The truth was Michele had a couple of things going against her as far as my family was concerned. First, she wasn't Catholic, second, she had a kid and wasn't married, and third, she was only half Italian.

Michele knocked on the door at 6:30, carrying a stack of presents and looking stressed.

Michele and Stevie were dressed up for the holiday. Michele wore a long, black silk skirt, black heeled shoes, and a sleeveless silver top. Michele was tall and slim, almost five foot seven, with light brown hair and big brown eyes. She has that clean ivory soap look, a natural beauty that doesn't need makeup. Stevie wore blue pants with a blue and red plaid shirt under a blue Izod sweater. His blond hair was spiked up on top, showing off his big blue eyes. I dressed casually, beige dockers, black sweater, and my black leather jacket.

"Traffic was horrendous," she said as she set the presents down on the kitchen table and kissed me hello. Stevie was wound up, glad to be out of the car after his long ride.

"Where's your Christmas tree?" He ran through the rooms, looking for it.

"I don't have one," I said, grabbing him as he did a running leap at me. "Can I use yours?"

"Okay."

"I'm sorry, now we're late. I should have left earlier. Traffic was bumper-to-bumper all the way here."

"Here," I said, giving her the wrapped white and gold box with her earrings in it. "I wanted to give this to you before we went to my grandmother's."

Stevie got all excited, "Where's mine?"

"You'll open some up when we get to Grandma's," I told him. "These are for Mommy."

"Let me help!" he said. His little hands were clumsy with the paper, but Michele let him rip it off.

"Oh, Tony, these are beautiful," Michele said, trying to get them out of the box. "What did you do? These must have cost a fortune."

"Don't worry about it. I got a good deal on them," I said. She was staring at me, smiling.

"What?" I barked.

"Nothing, I love you," she said.

"I love you too, but we better get going, my grandmother already called," I said, and then her smile faded.

"What's the matter?" I asked.

"Nothing. I guess we better get going," she said. "We don't want to hold up dinner."

"Thanks for wrapping those," I said as I took the presents for my family off the kitchen table. We took Michele's car. We got caught in traffic on Clove Road and wound up getting there at 7:20.

Everyone was already there when we arrived. My grandmother had made dinner for 7:00. It felt like it was a hundred degrees in the apartment. It has the old steam radiators, the kind that leave condensation on all the windows. The oven had been on most of the day, adding to the closeness of the apartment. Stevie was getting tired. He usually goes to bed at 8:00 and had been in traffic for three hours with Michele on the ride in from Long Island.

I could feel the undercurrents of tension when I walked in—it was like I knew they were discussing us before we got there, and then they tried not to show it. My sister, Denise, got up when we got there, grabbing Stevie in a hug and kissing him while he tried to squirm away.

"Let me see!" Denise said, asking to see the diamond studs I gave Michele.

"They're beautiful."

"Thank you," Michele said, smiling as she touched the earrings.

My brother, Vinny, and his fiancé, Christie, were sitting on the couch. They were both dressed in jeans and sweaters. Christie's was a Christmas sweater with St. Bernard dogs on it, Vinny's was dark green. Christie gave me a subdued greeting. She's cute, about five foot two, with dark brown hair and brown eyes. She looked uncomfortable in the company of Michele and Denise, they both looked like models. Marie, my father's wife, is a looker too, but once she opens her mouth she gets ugly.

My grandmother went into the kitchen without saying anything, bringing in the platters of food. They'd obviously been waiting for us to eat. Grandma had her hair done. It was curled on top of her head, tinted that unlikely peach color, and sprayed till it was stiff. She was wearing black pants and a black sweater with little mirrors on it. She had on her shiny gold shoes that she wears for special occasions.

My father didn't look up when we came in, not a good sign. I could smell his cologne as I got closer to him. He gave me a kiss and quick hug without actually looking at me, and he nodded and gave half a smile to Michele and Stevie. He was dressed in black pants with a cream-colored sweater. He always reminds me of Robert DeNiro in the movie *Midnight Run*. He has piercing blue eyes and dark hair greased back to camouflage the gray. He works out to keep himself in shape. At fifty-two he's in better shape than a lot of guys my age.

Marie looked like she was on the prowl. Her dark hair was longer now, straightened to frame her face. She was heavy on the makeup: dark gray, almost black eye shadow, with black eyeliner. Her lips were painted with light brown and looked wet and glossy. She wore black pinstripe pants and a white sweater that showed off cleavage that hadn't been there last time I saw her. This had to be surgically enhanced, she was straining against her sweater so much that I resisted the urge to cover Stevie's eyes. I said hello to Marie, and she nodded. I almost asked her to introduce me to her two friends, but thought better of it.

"Just sit down so everyone can eat," my grandmother said a little sharply. I looked at Grandma, surprised at her tone.

Michele looked at me, stalling as she took off her coat. She looked like she wanted to bolt, and in the midst of such a tough crowd I couldn't blame her. She took Stevie's jacket off and held his hand as she went to the table.

The glass oval dining-room table has those swivel captain's chairs that I remember spinning around in when I was little. Stevie sat down and started to spin a little, hitting the table and jarring the dishes. My grandmother, my father, and Marie all jumped on him at once.

"Oh, don't do that, honey," Marie said curtly.

"Come on, Tony," my father said instantly, "don't let him do that."

"Those are my good dishes," Grandma clucked disapprovingly, checking the dishes to make sure none were cracked.

"Nothing broke, Grandma," I said shortly.

I saw the color creep up into Michele's cheeks, and she pulled Stevie onto her lap, putting her arms around him protectively.

My grandmother's apartment is so different than Michele's tasteful ranch home. Grandma's reminds me of a Bensonhurst five-and-dime, complete with a red velvet couch and plastic slipcovers. There's a green area rug under the couch and coffee table that gives the room a year-round Christmas feel. There's an oblong, smoked glass coffee table on a gold base, with a centerpiece of red plastic roses. The end tables match the coffee table, except that they have wrought iron lamps with hanging smoked crystals dangling across the top. On the wall across from the couch is a fake marble fireplace, guarded on either side by three-foot-high ceramic lion statues.

There was a two-foot white Christmas tree with red balls hanging from it, the kind that are made of string tightly woven around them. A couple of them were partially unraveled and had shredded somewhat since last year. An ancient piece of gold garland wound around the tree and bunched neatly at the bottom. There were colored lights around the inside of the window that faced the parking lot of the apartment building, and a plastic Santa Claus was tacked into the molding with push pins.

There was a white wrought iron fence, like the kind used for outside railings, separating the living room from the dining area. The centerpiece on the table was a white ceramic bowl full of plastic fruit. It's been there as long as I can remember, and I used to love pulling off the grapes and using them like suction cups on my tongue.

My grandmother may live on a fixed income, but she spares no expense on food and wine. I saw a bottle of 1994 Brunello Di Montalcino that probably cost forty bucks, two bottles of Merlot, and a bottle of Cabernet Sauvignon. She made the traditional fish dinner that she makes every Christmas Eve. Shrimp cocktail, fried fillet of flounder, fried calamari, broiled lobster tails, scallops sauteed in garlic, lemon, and butter, and fruita di mar. The fruita di mar is a cold fish salad with calamari, shrimp, crab, and scungilli, marinated in garlic, celery, lemons, parsley, and olive oil. The pasta was linguine with clams, mussels, and shrimp in a white wine and garlic sauce. There was a platter of roasted vegetables, a tray of eggplant parmigiana, a tossed salad with oil and vinegar, and Italian bread.

Stevie, being four years old, wouldn't eat any of it. He sat there with a disgusted look on his face, saying things like "yuck," "eeewww," and "what is that?" Michele put a piece of bread and some salad on his dish, but there was so much vinegar in the salad that his face puckered and his body shuddered. I could see my father was getting angry, shaking his head while he ate, looking like he was barely containing himself.

To give her credit, Michele tried to make polite conversation. She complimented Denise on her outfit, a pair of camel-colored suede pants and a red sweater. Denise dresses provocatively when she knows my father will be somewhere because she knows it annoys him. Denise's outfit was nowhere near Marie's as far as being offensive, and I thought she looked nice. She has dark, almost black hair that she had curled at the ends. She has my father's blue eyes, lined in smoky gray. She's beautiful enough for a magazine cover, but she has no self-esteem whatsoever.

I could see everyone getting uncomfortable when Michele said it, so I said, "What?" to everyone around the table. "What's wrong with Denise's outfit?"

"I got my belly button pierced, Tony, and Dad doesn't approve," Denise said matter-of-factly. "But I guess he doesn't have a problem with Marie's new implants."

"Of course not, he paid for them," Marie said sweetly.

"Why would you mutilate yourself like that?" I asked. Both Denise and Marie looked at me, I guess both of them mutilated themselves.

"What's moot-moot a wait?" Stevie chimed in, trying to pronounce it.

"I didn't mutilate anything, see," Denise said, lifting up her sweater to reveal a rhinestone belly ring. "It's just like an earring for your belly." Stevie looked at it in wonder.

I hoped Marie didn't lift up her sweater to show him her new bra size.

"The kid doesn't need to see that," my father barked, his fork echoing when it hit his plate.

"Which, the implants or the belly ring?" Denise asked, deadpan.

I felt Michele stiffen when my father called Stevie the kid, and I felt like jumping the table and bashing him. I squashed the anger, refusing to let him get to me. Part of me wished I still drank so I could chug down the bottle of wine that winked at me from across the table.

"His name is Stevie," I said quietly. "Don't call him the kid." My father didn't acknowledge that I'd said anything, just continued to eat.

Everyone was quiet after that. I'd been through this enough times to know it was not going to end well. If my father's in a bad mood, no one can get him out of it. It usually runs its course, and he's okay the next time we see him. I normally would ignore him, but since Michele and Stevie were there, I wanted to eat as quickly as possible, open up the gifts, and hightail it out of there.

Denise had to open up her trap and say, "I don't know about anyone else, but this is really uncomfortable. Why don't we just get everything out in the open, you know, discuss the issues—"

"Denise is in therapy again," Marie said, her voice flat. She didn't bother to look up from her plate when she said it.

"Why don't you stop going to those headshrinkers and grow up, Denise?" my father snapped. "Stop blaming everyone else for your problems. Go get married or something. What happened to Sal?" he said, talking about Sal Valente, Denise's boyfriend.

"He went back to his ex-wife," Marie said smugly.

"No he didn't," I said. "He'd never go back to that psycho." Sal would never go back with her. The only reason he spoke to the woman was because she had custody of his children.

I waited for Denise to deny it, but she didn't. She was glaring at Marie, then she got this crafty smile on her face and said, "How do you know that, Marie? Did Bobby Egan tell you?"

That seemed to shut Marie up, but my father said, "How do you know Bobby Egan?"

"Who's Bobby Egan?" I asked, suspicious.

"He's a detective in Chinatown," Denise said. "A friend of Sal's. Apparently he's a friend of Marie's too." Denise threw a knowing look at Marie.

Something was going on. My gut was telling me that Marie was up to her old tricks and had a little something going on the side that Denise knew about. That's probably what the surgery was for. Good. Maybe she'd divorce my father and we'd never have to see her again.

This seemed to make my father angrier; he was chewing his food and guzzling wine at a rapid pace. Stevie, oblivious to the whole thing, was getting bored. He climbed off of Michele's lap and made his way over to the ceramic lions that guarded the fake fireplace in the living room. They were gaudy statues, five-and-dime stuff that my grandmother loves. He tried to pick one up, but it was too heavy, and he dropped it with a klunk to the floor.

"No! Don't touch that!" My grandmother was out of her chair faster than any eighty-year-old woman I've ever seen. "Get away from there!"

I was so taken aback by the way she spoke to him that I was speechless for a second. Stevie was humiliated, and I rushed over to pick him up. He hid his face against me, and I said, "It's okay, buddy, you didn't do anything wrong." I brought him back to the table and sat him on my lap. He wouldn't turn around to look at any of them, and that was fine with me. Screw that. I stole a look at Michele. She was staring down with a blank look on her face.

Marie raised her eyebrows disapprovingly, turning her head to scratch behind her ear. Christie and Vinny exchanged a look, and my father stewed some more.

"Leave him alone, he's four years old," Denise said, getting out of her chair. "If you're so afraid of him breaking something, give him something to play with." She went into my grandmother's bedroom and came out with a stack of gifts. At least someone was trying to be nice.

"Come here, Stevie." She patted the floor next to where she

sat down. "Want to open the presents I got you?" Stevie nodded tentatively. "Come on, then," she said, patting the floor until he walked over and sat with her. He opened the first one and yelled out "It's Scoop! Mom, look, it's Scoop the bulldozer." Sure enough, it was Scoop the yellow bulldozer from Bob the Builder, who Stevie loves. Denise also got him a Dragon Tales board game, a Yankee hooded sweatshirt (like the one she has), and a Veggie Tales Junior Asparagus night-light, because he's afraid of the dark.

She also got him a videotape of the Dragon Tales that had two of the episodes from the TV show. He sat quietly and watched it, probably glad to be away from the table.

There was an uneasy silence at the table. Michele seemed to realize that Denise was her only ally at the table, so she tried again to start a conversation.

"Have you always lived on Staten Island?"

"All our lives," Denise said.

"Tony was born in North Carolina," my father threw in without looking up.

"Why there?" She directed the question to me, but my father answered.

"I was in the service," he said, still concentrating on eating. "Tony was born on the Marine base in West Cherry Point."

"When were you in the service?" Michele asked him, hesitantly.

"From 1966 to 1970," he said, putting his fork down.

"Were you in Vietnam?" she asked.

"Yup." He nodded without looking up.

"You and Mom got married while you were in the service, right?" I asked, almost kicking myself for it. Never mention my mother with Marie around.

"They had to get married, your father came home on leave and knocked her up," Marie cut in.

51

"You were what, two years old then, Marie?" Denise asked sweetly.

"Shut your mouth, Denise," my father warned.

"Why do I have to shut my mouth? Why don't you get a muzzle for *her*?" Denise tossed her head at Marie.

"That was right in the thick of it," Michele said to my father, but he didn't answer her.

"That must have been hard, leaving a baby behind and going over there," Michele remarked, looking nervous.

There was a confused silence around the table. We never discuss Vietnam. It has always been understood that the subject is off-limits.

"Was it hard to leave your baby?" Michele asked again.

"No. He wasn't born yet, and I wasn't thinking about him at the time," he said stonily. What a guy.

"That must have been hard for you," Michele said, turning to Grandma.

"Oh, I didn't know he was there," Grandma said.

Michele blinked. "Where did you think he was?"

"Hawaii," Grandma said, straight-faced.

"Grandma, there was a war in Southeast Asia in 1969. We had thousands of troops there, and you thought Dad was in Hawaii?" Denise asked, incredulous.

Grandma looked confused. "That's where he said he was."

"Did he ever write to you?" Denise asked.

"Well, yeah," she said.

"Did you look at the postmark on the letters?"

Denise waited for an answer, but Grandma fiddled with the crucifix around her neck without answering.

"Were you drafted?" my brother, Vinny, asked. I guess he figured if everyone else could ask questions, so could he.

"No. I signed up with the Marine Corps instead of being drafted into the Army."

"Where were you stationed?" Vinny asked.

"Da Nang."

"How long were you there, Dad?" This from Vinny again.

"One tour."

"Did you count the days while you were there?" he asked, fascinated.

"No, I never counted the days." His demeanor always softened when he talked to Vinny. "But I knew when it was time to go home."

"Wait a minute," Michele interrupted. "None of you knew any of this?"

"We really don't like to talk about it," Grandma said bluntly.

"That should give you a little insight into the family," Denise whispered to Michele.

"What's that supposed to mean?" my father asked.

"Weren't you afraid you were never going to see your family again?" Michele asked, trying to steer the conversation away from a fight.

"No." My father looked at her. "I set my head. I told myself, *I'm going home, no matter what. I'm gonna handle this.* Guys were lax, I wasn't. I was at the peak of my performance, and I stayed there the whole time I was there."

"Were you homesick?" No one tried to interrupt Michele's questions, we were fascinated by this. We'd never heard anything about it, and we hung on every word.

"Yeah, I was homesick, but I lived day by day. I set my head," he said again. "I wouldn't get depressed like the other guys. I mean, I would talk about the food back home and stuff like that, but I didn't dwell on missing anybody."

"Did you pray? I would have been praying day and night," Michele remarked.

"I prayed. And I went to church."

"They say the country is beautiful. Is it?" she asked.

He seemed to ponder that for a minute. "There were things that looked beautiful, but you couldn't appreciate it. There were some places that I remember being nice, China Beach was one of them. It was hot. Humid, tropical weather. It would rain hard for an hour and be done with it. I thought the whole place smelled like fish heads being boiled in rice. The food was horrendous, I had the runs the first few days I was there. They gave me some white chalky stuff, and I eventually adjusted."

"Were you wounded there?" Vinny asked.

"No. I wasn't wounded, didn't get post-traumatic stress disorder, shell shock, battle fatigue, or any of that other baloney," he said, as if that kind of weakness was beneath him.

"Do you keep in touch with anyone from the war?" Vinny again.

"No. There were guys on the job with me that were in Vietnam, but none that I served with."

"Were there a lot of drugs there?" Denise asked. "I've read there were a lot of problems with drugs there."

"Do I look like someone who would take drugs?" he snapped at Denise. "I don't know why you ask such stupid questions."

"I didn't say you did drugs, Dad," Denise said, like she was talking to a ten-year-old. "I said were there a lot of drugs there?"

He answered the question, but he looked at Vinny when he answered. "There weren't a lot of drugs where I was. I mean, everybody drank. I'm not much of a drinker, but we drank. Black Label, Vietnamese beer, Flagstaff, Bud, Schmidts." He looked lost in thought for a second. "I remember drinking with this one guy, we had watched a documentary film on World War II. This guy's father had been killed in the World War II Air Corps in one of the B17's. He thought he saw his father flying a plane in one of the films. He later freaked out in action."

"Did you see a lot of action?" I asked. He ignored me and directed the answer at Vinny, who was mesmerized by the whole thing.

"We saw a lot of action. I hung with the Italian guys. When it all hits the fan, they're the best guys to have around."

"How did you get through it, Dad?" Vinny said compassionately.

"I didn't think about it until it hit, and then I'd say to myself, *I won't be shot here, I won't die here, I'm going home. I'm from New York. I'm not like these yokels, I'm smart, I'm tough, and I'm going home.*"

That was just like him, so arrogant and sure of himself that he wouldn't die there. I admired him and pitied him, all at the same time.

"Did you kill anyone?" I had to ask.

He didn't answer at first. "That's none of your business what I did there," he said, his voice deadly. "There's stuff I'll take to my grave that I'll never tell you or anyone else about."

I'll take that as a yes.

He shook his head at me. "You live in your little world, and you have no idea what goes on out there. We were in the middle of a war, Tony—what did you think we were doing over there?"

Stevie, who I thought was watching TV, was staring intently at my father. He walked back to the table and onto my lap, as if to protect me somehow. I hugged him close and told him everything was okay.

My perception of Vietnam veterans was of those tormented soldiers who fought a losing war and returned home to the loathing of an unthankful nation. I saw them as the emotionally disturbed and often maimed, wheelchair skells destined to live out their lives in misery. (Skell is our word for homeless, crackheads, prostitutes, whatever we have to clean up off the street.)

I forget a lot of times that they're guys like my father who came back and lived ordinary lives, keeping their memories of war locked away in a place that couldn't hurt them.

Michele realized this was getting too heated and switched to another minefield.

"What did you do when you got back, did you go right into the Police Department?" she asked quietly, knowing he had been a cop too.

"It was about a year after I got out that I went on the job. At first I took a job delivering lumber for an outfit in Great Kills." I thought he would leave it at that, but he surprised me by adding, "I remember making a delivery to a house on Amboy Road in Bay Terrace. I had just gotten back, and I saw a picture of a Marine on the mantel over the fireplace. I asked the woman if that was her son, and she said yes. I told her that I was a Marine and that I'd just come home. She told me her son had died there." He paused. "I never told anyone again that I was in Vietnam."

"How did you feel about the war?" Michele asked. "About the American occupation in Vietnam?"

"Spoken like someone who knows nothing about it," my father said derisively. "*American occupation*." He shook his head. "I never thought about it, it never bothered me."

"How did you feel about Lyndon Johnson?" Denise asked.

"He did what he had to do," my father spat. "I liked him. I loved Nixon and Spiro Agnew too."

"What about the protestors?" Vinny asked.

"What about them?"

"Did they spit at you when you came home?"

"Nobody spit at me," he said, as if they wouldn't dare.

"How did you feel about them?"

"I wanted to kill them. They did more harm than good. I loved locking them up."

"There were still demonstrations when you got back?" I asked, trying to figure out the time frame. My father was still a rookie at the time, and he would have caught a detail like that.

"One time there were like four or five days of demonstrations. The protestors were moving past City Hall, standing on the councilmen's cars, doing damage to whatever they could. This one punk, some rich college kid, burned a flag right in front of me. I knocked him on the ground and put it out."

I could see the rage in my father's face as he talked about it. Then he started laughing.

"They protested their way downtown, right into a construction workers' strike. A little while later they're heading back toward us, running for their lives, bleeding and crying. The strikers beat them within an inch of their lives, and we were so happy. We cheered the strikers, raised the flag up, and sang 'God Bless America.' Then the protestors went into Pace University to hide from the strikers. We went after them and beat them up a little more. A couple of the strikers were gonna throw them off the building, and we were gonna let them. I loved it. As far as I was concerned, they got their due process." He was seething.

"Dad, they were protesting the slaughter of our American soldiers and the innocent people in Vietnam," Denise said.

"Don't tell me about those protestors. They were cowards, rich punk college kids with nothing better to do than cause riots in this country. I served my country, not like those bas—"

He cut himself off when he realized Stevie was watching him, but he had said it with such fire that Stevie said, "What's a bas?" I hoped my father didn't say "Technically you are, kid." Instead he hung his head down and said, "Ah man, I'm sorry."

"What's a bas?" Stevie asked again.

"It's something people say when they're mad, it's not a nice word. Okay?" I said to Stevie, rubbing his head.

Stevie nodded and gave my father an intimidating look. My father didn't scare him at all, he was something.

The table got real quiet.

"I'm sorry," Michele said, looking nervous. "I didn't realize you had to deal with the protestors when you got back."

"Yeah, well the job was different back then. We had a lot to deal with. And some of us didn't spend our entire careers on patrol," he said pointedly.

"Who are you kidding? I've been in more riots than you have!" I said, my voice rising. "You got something to say about me being on patrol? You would have been on patrol if you didn't have a hook!" A hook is getting somewhere by knowing someone, not getting there because you deserve it.

"I didn't have a hook, *you* had a hook! I just lucked out!" he shouted. "I tried to help you! You would have had your shield by now, but you screwed up!"

"I didn't screw up!" I roared, vaguely aware that Michele was pulling Stevie off my lap. This was an old bone of contention between us.

When I had less than two years on, my father worked with someone at the 5th Precinct who used to be partners with the captain of my command. My father had his friend make a call to my captain to have me put into Anti-Crime, a plainclothes unit usually made up of veteran cops. You usually need seven to ten years on patrol to get in. It was a step toward getting your detective's shield. You go to Anti-Crime for a while, then up to RIP, or robbery in progress, where you work with the PDU, precinct detective unit. In RIP you have your silver shield for eighteen months, and then you get your gold detective shield.

About six months before my father made his friend call

my captain, there were a lot of cops in an uproar about four guys who were transferred into Crime. They had bounced four veteran cops who rightfully deserved the spots. Two of them were hooks, one was the son of a chief with only two years on, and the other was the nephew of an Inspector with only three years on.

The other two were patrol cops with foot posts up on 8th Avenue between 42nd and 45th Street. What they did was, instead of writing the required twenty to twenty-five summonses a month, they were writing twenty in a tour, making the rest of us look bad. Most of us do about twenty-two in a month and no more. If you give them twenty in one day, they're going to want twenty the next day. The department loves summonses because they make money for the city.

They were also making all these trivial collars, crack stems with a rock in it, urinating in public, open container of alcohol—arrests that are all misdemeanors.

The arrests took the cops off the Street, leaving it unpatrolled. They did this for like six months, giving the commanding officer big numbers for the precinct.

These two were picking up these rinky-dink arrests, which isn't bad if it deters problems for your post. But now they were off post for an open bottle of booze, while robberies and grand larcenies were happening. This makes it difficult for the next tour walking the foot post, now stuck with a couple of blocks worth of garbage because no one was patrolling earlier. If there is no police presence on the street to move the crowds along, larger crowds gather, making it more difficult to keep order on the block.

When these two made Crime, they bumped two guys who had ten years on and had been waiting a couple of years to go into Crime. Because they didn't have the same numbers as the foot posts, they didn't get in. They had better-quality arrests, felonies versus the rookies' misdemeanor quality-of-life stuff. They also had more experience testifying in court than the two rookies.

So here I was, two years on, shooting my mouth off about the injustice of it all, and my old man wants to do the same for me. I had a chance to beat the system like the other rookies did.

When the captain called me into his office, Lieutenant Farrell was there, smoking his pipe, watching me shrewdly. The captain's name was Horn, an older guy, late fifties I guess. He was clean-cut, in good shape for an old-timer. The captain asked me, "What can I do for you, Tony?"

"I was told to come in and talk to you about going into Anti-Crime," I said.

He knew without mentioning names exactly what I was talking about. He said something like, "Most of the guys who go into Anti-Crime have more time on, more experience."

"Well, basically, I don't think it would be right if I go into Crime with less than two years on." He didn't say anything, just nodded for me to go on. "I know there's guys with ten years on who have the experience that I don't. I think I need more time on before I go into a unit like that."

He seemed relieved, like I took him off the burner. Lieutenant Farrell didn't say anything, but I think I earned his respect that day. It was right after that he started drinking with me.

Part of the reason I didn't take it was because I didn't want anything from my father. I'd rather do it myself. When my father found out I didn't take the spot in Anti-Crime, he was livid. I still remember the conversation to this day.

"Did you talk to the captain?" he asked me at Grandma's one day.

"Yeah, I turned it down. Let someone with more time on take it," I said. "It's not right, I'm not ready to go there."

"Are you kidding me? What is wrong with you?" His face twisted in rage. "Don't you think that someone else who has a hook isn't gonna take that spot?"

"That still doesn't make it right," I said.

"You embarrassed me. I called in a favor for that. I'll never help you again," he said with contempt.

Which was exactly the way I wanted it, I didn't want to owe him anything.

4

*T*his was starting to get really heated, and Michele said quietly, "Tony, maybe I should go."

"Don't go," I said. "Let him leave."

"I'm not going anywhere," my father said arrogantly.

"Ignore him, Vince," Marie ordered in her Brooklyn nasal tone.

"It's okay," Grandma said. "It's good to clear the air." She looked at Michele. "I told you, we don't like to talk about this stuff."

Michele stared at her for a second and said she needed to take Stevie to use the bathroom before they left. I didn't want to argue with Michele about leaving in front of them, so I got up to help clean off the table. My father, Marie, Vinny, and Christie stayed at the table while Denise and I brought the dirty dishes into the kitchen. I heard the mumble of a conversation at the table between Christie and Marie, ending with both of them laughing. For a second I thought that Marie and Christie were talking about us, but I didn't think Christie would do that.

Michele opened the bathroom door, which you can see

from the kitchen, and gave me a small smile as Stevie washed his hands.

"No, don't touch that!" Grandma half shouted as she went down the hall toward the bathroom. I followed after her, thinking he was touching something that would hurt him. He stood there with his hands stalled by the towel rack. "Those are just for show," she said of the black dress towels with the gold roses pinned to them. "Here, use this." She pulled a small washcloth from the linen closet next to the bathroom.

"What's he doing now?" Marie said, loud enough for me to hear.

I bit the inside of my cheek to calm myself down. I wasn't sure how to handle this. I expect this kind of thing from Marie, but I didn't know where this was coming from with my grandmother.

"I'm sorry, there wasn't any other towel in here," Michele said. I could see she was humiliated and wanted to get out of there as much as I did.

"I think I should get going," Michele said again.

"We didn't have cake yet, and Stevie has to open his presents," my grandmother said.

"I have a long ride home," Michele said lamely.

"It won't take long, I already put the coffee on." Grandma smiled at her. "Go sit down."

I looked at Michele. Whatever she wanted was fine with me. We stared at each other for a couple of seconds, and I could see how uncomfortable she was.

"We'll go after the coffee," Michele said, resigned.

I saw Marie and Christie taking Christmas presents and putting them in piles on the couch. Grandma had cleaned off the table and was putting the coffee cups and cake plates out. There was a platter of pastry, cannoli, Napoleans, sfogliatelle, which we also call clams because of their shape, tiramisu, fruit tarts, and eclairs. There was another tray of Italian bakery cookies, still wrapped in the colored paper.

My father had gone into the living room and was flipping through the TV channels with the remote control. Michele stood next to the table, not knowing what to do next.

Grandma said to Michele and me in a conspiring voice, "Don't bring up the war anymore, it upsets your father."

"Grandma, we didn't say anything wrong," I said.

"Then why is your father so upset?"

"He's always upset," I said.

"Who's always upset?" Denise said loud enough to wake the dead.

"I said I don't want any more talk about the war, Denise. It upsets your father," Grandma scolded.

"Sorry, Grandma, the Vietnam War is a fact of life. If you think we're going to pretend it didn't happen so Dad won't get mad, then you're in worse denial than you were when you thought he was in Hawaii," Denise said.

"Your kids have no respect, Vince," Marie said. "Well, Vinny does." She grabbed his cheeks. "He's the best one."

"You'll have to talk to their mother about that, she's the one who brought them up that way," my father said as everyone gathered around the table again.

"Well, they're old enough to know respect," Marie said in disgust.

"What do you know about respect, Marie?" Denise said. "Do you really think you deserve my respect?"

"You're just like your mother," Marie said. "And you'll wind up just like her too, alone and a drunk."

"Their mother was always a lousy drunk," my father said. "Nothing was ever good enough for her."

Denise looked stunned and clenched her fist like she was getting ready to swing, then she caught sight of Stevie out of the corner of her eye. She ran her hands over her face and sighed deeply.

Michele didn't sit. She stood with her hands on the back of her chair, looking down. She took a deep breath and said, "Mr. Cavalucci, I'm sorry I brought up Vietnam. It must have been terrible to be there and see all the things you did. I understand your anger toward the protestors after having served this country. The saddest thing is that we lost so many men and lost the war anyway."

"We didn't lose the war," my father said angrily.

Everyone but Grandma looked at him, even Marie. No one said anything, but of course Denise had to have the last word.

"We lost, Dad. Or am I the only one who saw that famous rooftop scene at the American Embassy in Saigon? In fact, it's no longer Saigon, it's now Ho Chi Min City, clear proof that the North Vietnamese took it over when they stormed the city," she said loudly.

He got enraged and shouted, "The North Vietnamese fought an aggressive war, we couldn't hold them—but we didn't lose. That's it!" He sat down at the table, putting milk and sugar in his coffee.

"Sit down!" he ordered.

"No," Denise said stubbornly. "I won't sit down. We couldn't hold them means we lost."

"We didn't lose."

I wondered if they would regress to "did not," "did too."

"Leave it alone, Denise," I warned.

"No! Are you telling me I should pretend we won the war in Vietnam so Dad doesn't get upset?" She was yelling now, anger blazing in her eyes.

"I'm telling you to shut your mouth," I said.

She shook her head, flipping her hair back in anger. "No wonder I need therapy."

"You need therapy because you're a spoiled little girl who has to be the center of attention all the time," Marie said.

Stevie was inspecting the tray of pastry, lifting up one of the fruit tarts to examine it when Grandma said, "Oh no, don't touch that!" She took the tray away from him. "Don't put your hands on other people's food."

Marie let out a long-suffering sigh and shook her head. "You've got your hands full with him," she said to Michele.

Michele picked Stevie up and brought him into my grandmother's room. I followed her and said nothing while she put his jacket on. He didn't pay any attention to her as she zipped his jacket; he was too engrossed in staring at the artwork on my grandmother's wall. There were two lighted pictures that hung on either side of the crucifix over the bed.

"What's that? Jesus is bleeding!" he said of the picture of the Sacred Heart with the crown and the thorns around the bleeding heart.

"That's an angel!" He pointed to the picture of an angel hovering over two children crossing a broken bridge. The pictures were spooky. When I used to sleep here as a kid, Grandma used them as night-lights. The eyes of the Sacred Heart picture follow you wherever you are in the room. The kids with the angel aren't any better. They used to give me nightmares.

Michele didn't answer him, just put his hat and scarf on in quick, jerky motions. She put her black wool coat on, not bothering to button it, and grabbed her keys and pocketbook. I picked Stevie up and followed her back out to the dining room, which is right next to the foyer.

"Merry Christmas," she said quickly, not looking at anyone in the room. "Thanks for dinner." She turned and took Stevie from me and tried to open the door. She had to undo the chain and the deadbolt, so she moved Stevie to her hip as she opened it.

I followed her out, neither of us saying anything as we walked down the hallway. Our footsteps were muted from the gray carpet, making a dull thud as we walked out to the lobby.

"Wait," I said. "Let me get my jacket and the Christmas presents."

"No, I'm not going back in there." I'd never seen her angry before, and I wasn't sure how to handle it. "Well, let me get my jacket, and we can go back to my house."

"I'm going home," she said with decisiveness. "I really don't want to see you right now."

"So you're gonna leave me here? How am I supposed to get home?" I asked.

"If you want me to drive you home, go get your jacket, but I don't want any of their Christmas presents and I don't want to talk to you—I'm too angry right now," she said.

"What about tomorrow morning? I want to be there when Stevie opens his presents," I said.

"I don't think that's a good idea," she said.

"What?" My voice rose.

"Keep your voice down, Tony, he's heard enough of that tonight," she whispered angrily.

"Are you telling me I can't spend Christmas morning with you?" I could feel anger rise up in me.

She had started her car and strapped Stevie into his booster seat. He was smiling and waving at me from the backseat, and I waved back, giving him a small smile.

"Don't do this," I said as she opened her car door and got in, driving away without another word.

I was ripping when I went back inside to get my jacket. I was gonna call a cab, but when I went back in, Denise was duking it out with all of them.

They were sitting around the table. Denise was putting the gifts she got for Stevie in a shopping bag, her face flush with anger.

"Stevie forgot his presents," Denise said, handing me the shopping bag. I put the bag next to the front door and went inside for my black leather jacket. I heard Marie say, "That was rude—I thought she's supposed to be so religious."

"What's that supposed to mean?" I asked her, coming out from the bedroom.

"It means if she's supposed to be so religious, why did she storm out of here like that?" Marie said.

"She didn't storm out, she said Merry Christmas and she thanked you for dinner," I said.

"Well, if she's supposed to be so religious, why does she have a kid and she's not married?" my father asked contemptuously. I could see the empty shot glass next to his espresso and the bottle of Romana Sambuca on the table.

"That's none of your business," I said, raising my voice.

"In my day, if a girl got in trouble they didn't parade themselves around like that, having a baby out of wedlock," my grandmother spat. "I see it all the time, these young girls acting like it's nothing to have two and three children and they're not even married! Some of them have different fathers!" Her voice rose in indignation.

"At least back then they had the decency of being ashamed of themselves," my father threw in.

"Dad, my mother was pregnant when you got married," I pointed out.

"Yeah, but I married her," he said.

"And what if you didn't? That wouldn't have been Mom's fault."

"No, but your mother would have had the decency to be ashamed of herself."

I didn't understand his logic.

"Why weren't you ashamed of yourself?" Denise yelled. "You cheated on your wife! You left your family! Why is that okay?"

"We were in love," Marie spat. "Your father was miserable with all of you." She turned to Vinny. "Not you, you were just a kid." She turned back to Denise and me. "All you care about is yourself, Denise. You don't care that your father was unhappy, that he had to support your mother because she was too lazy to get a job. You don't care that he was stuck in a marriage because he couldn't leave you kids alone with your mother."

"I hate you," Denise said quietly to my father. He turned sharply to look at her, but before he could answer, she added, "I hope you die, and I'll dance on your grave in a red dress."

"Don't you talk to your father like that!" Grandma was horrified; death and red dresses were a no-no with Italians.

"Why not? I don't care anymore. I never want to see you again," she said. She never said that before, and I guess it got his attention. "You know, it's so ironic." She let out a strangled laugh. "I used to adore you. You were everything to me. I was so sad when you and Mom started having problems. Did you think it didn't matter that you left? Every day after school the first thing I did was check and see if you left. I used to run up the stairs into your room and make sure your clothes were still there, and I'd be okay when I'd realize you hadn't left." He was silent now, watching her. "For the longest time after you left, I'd dream I was running up those stairs, but I could never make it to the top."

"Touching story, Denise," Marie said with derision, and rolled her eyes. If she hadn't looked away and rolled her eyes, she would have seen Denise's car keys before they connected with her head.

My father stood up to go after Denise, but I got in front of him. I was shaking with rage, but I couldn't figure out who it was directed at.

I had a flashback to the last time we squared off like this. I was about sixteen years old. He wanted me to do some yard work for him. He did that a lot. He'd fight with my mother and take it out on us, making us do all kinds of work around the house. I was on the gymnastics team in high school, and we had a meet that day. He told me I couldn't go, and I said I had to. I had gotten to the edge of my front yard when he came up and punched me in the head, full force. It stunned me for a minute, and then I saw red. I remember letting out a roar as I took him by the shirt and pants when he was walking away. I lifted him up over my head while he flailed like a fish out of water. I let him squirm a little while he threatened to kill me. "I don't think so," I said as I set him down on his feet. I didn't throw him like I wanted to, and I picked up my gym bag and started walking away.

"You think you're stronger than me?" he screamed. I didn't even look back at him, just kept walking. "I'll take a friggin' bat to your head when you're not looking," he yelled after me. I turned to look at him, shocked that he would say that to me. We stared each other down; we each had that same look in our eyes now.

I blocked him while Denise picked up her keys and got her coat out of the bedroom. Our eyes were still locked while Marie held her head, calling Denise every name in the book. For all her bravado, I could see Marie was embarrassed. My grandmother handed me a shopping bag, I guessed with leftovers in it. I kissed her cheek but didn't say anything. I waited until Denise got out of the door before I followed her, making sure no one tried to chase us.

I had Denise drive me home, neither of us saying anything on the ride from Clove Road. I sat up watching TV and smoking cigarettes until about 1:00 in the morning. I went to bed, tossing and turning most of the night.

Christmas morning I woke to a cold, overcast day. The phone rang at 9:00, and I snatched it up.

"Hello."

"It's me," Michele said.

"You get home okay?" I asked.

"Yes, it was fine." She didn't sound fine, she sounded mad.

"Listen, I'm sorry about last night. Denise doesn't know when to—"

"Don't apologize for her, you should apologize to her," she cut me off.

"For what?" I asked.

She was silent for a minute, and I thought she hung up. "You there?" I asked.

"Yes," she said quietly. "But I'm furious, and I don't want Stevie to hear me yelling."

About what? The woman never yelled.

"Tony, in the few times I've met your family, Denise has been the only one to go out of her way to make sure Stevie and I know she likes and accepts us."

I guess that was true. "And?" I asked.

"Each time that I've seen your family, your father and his wife have ridiculed Denise and put her down while you, your grandmother, and your weasel of a brother and his rubber-stamp girlfriend say nothing." I was surprised at the anger in her voice. Weasel of a brother?

"Denise was wrong last—" I tried to say, but she cut me off.

"She was right! In everything she said. I could feel her frustration. She's so isolated because the rest of you are incapable of standing up to your father and his horrible wife because you're so afraid of him."

"I am not afraid of him," I said flatly. "I just won't fight with them all the time like Denise. She knows how my family is, but she can't leave things alone."

"Why should she?" Michele said, her voice rising in anger. "They degrade her every chance they get, yet treat the woman who broke up your family like a queen."

"No they don't," I said. "I don't." Did they?

"Oh please, Vinny and Christie are always sucking up to her. And your grandmother's no better."

"I'm sorry for the way my grandmother acted last night—I've never seen her do that before. I think the family gets to her," I said.

"Don't make excuses for her, Tony. It's very obvious that she doesn't approve of me, and because the rest of the family agree with her, she felt she could treat us that way," she said. "Your father was so rude to us, he didn't even try to hide that he didn't like us."

"The rest of the family doesn't feel that way," I insisted.

"Sure they do. With the exception of Denise, whose opinion doesn't matter to them anyway, they all agree with your father."

"Vinny didn't say anything," I said.

"And he won't. He's not man enough to have his own opinion; he goes with whatever your father says. That's why your father likes him so much," she said.

I thought about that for a minute. I always thought that Vinny was the peacemaker, wanting to make nice all the time, but maybe Michele was right. He never disagreed with my father, while Denise and I always did.

"As for you, I was disappointed that you let everyone treat your sister that way."

When I didn't answer, she sighed and said, "I need some time, Tony."

"Time for what?" I asked, dreading the answer.

"Time to figure out if being involved with you is going to be good for Stevie. If it was just me, it would be a different story. You spend a lot of time with your family, and I don't think that's a good atmosphere for him to be in. I don't like that you were raised to have a low opinion of your mother and sister and were taught to respect your father's mistress, even if she happens to be his wife now. Your father and Marie always criticize your mother. Every time I've seen them, they've said mean things about your mother, and none of you have defended her."

"Everything they say about my mother is true!" I didn't want to toss my mother into the pot here. "My mother's a drunk, Michele. End of story."

"I'm not so sure about that. Even if that was true, she's still your mother. Why is it that no one saw your mother for Christmas? Did she spend it alone?"

"She was with my aunt, and I sent her money for Christmas," I said. "What does my mother have to do with any of this?"

"It sends a confusing message to Stevie. He knows you have a mother, more from what he hears your father and Marie say than from you. If she really has alcohol issues, I can understand you not wanting us to meet her, but I don't think that's why."

I didn't answer her; I didn't want to talk about my mother.

"So when you say you need time, that means time away from me?" I asked.

"Yes."

"Why stay away from me? We just won't see them all that much," I said. "I really only see my father and Marie on holidays."

"Staying away from them won't mean anything if you don't think there's anything wrong with the way they act. Their behavior is a result of their mind-set. If you allow them to treat your mother and sister that way, why wouldn't you allow them to treat Stevie and me that way?" she said softly. "And if I'm anywhere near you, I can't think clearly. I'll just be thinking how great it is to be with you, and all this stuff won't seem so important. But it is, it will matter later on."

"You know what, I don't want to hear all this psychobabble about behavior and mindsets. They're friggin' nuts, okay? I never said they weren't. The bottom line is can you deal with that? We won't go there every Sunday for macaroni; we'll see them when we have to. Or are you asking me not to see them at all?" I asked angrily.

"I didn't say that, Tony," she said.

"Then what are you saying?"

"I don't know," she said miserably.

"Why don't you give me a call when you figure it out," I said and hung up.

I didn't want to sit alone in a basement apartment on Christmas Day. There was no one else I could call. I wasn't about to go see my grandmother after the night before. Vinny lived with my Dad and Marie, and I definitely wasn't going there.

Denise called me about 11:00, but I didn't feel like seeing her either.

"What are you doing home?" Denise snapped when I picked up the phone.

"Why are you calling me if you didn't think I was home?" I snapped back.

"I was leaving you a message," she said.

"What's the message?"

"Remember you asked me about Bobby Egan, the detective who works with Marie?" she asked.

"Yeah."

"Well, he's a friend of Sal's—"

"What happened with Sal?" I cut her off. "Did he really go back with that psycho?"

"Yup," she said sadly. "But about Marie, I think she's fooling around on Dad with this detective. Sal went to the precinct one day to visit Bobby, and they told him Bobby went to lunch. Sal said he almost fainted when Bobby came walking in with Marie. Remember Sal met her Fourth of July? He said Marie was real cozy until she realized who Sal was. He said when he asked Bobby what the deal was with Marie, Bobby said she was someone he was seeing."

"She's such a snake," I said.

"I know, but Bobby called Sal later that day to say he hoped Sal didn't misunderstand, that they weren't involved in any way, just good friends," Denise said. "I went up to the precinct and watched them. I saw them leave together around lunchtime, but I didn't want to chance following them. I've been thinking about hiring a private investigator like Marie's ex-husband did. In fact, I think I'm gonna call her ex-husband and find out the guy's name."

"Stay out of it, Denise," I warned. "You already hit her last night. If you start stalking her, she'll lock you up."

"I know she would—that's why I want to hire someone," she said.

"Do you have any idea how expensive that is?" I asked.

"Yeah, that's why I want you to chip in with me," she said.

"Let me think about it," I said. Normally I wouldn't, but it might be a good idea to find out what Marie was up to.

"I can't believe Sal," I said, getting back to him and his man-killer wife.

"Can't believe what? That once again I picked an emotionally unavailable man," she said sarcastically.

"No, I can't believe that Sal went back with his wife. Why?" I asked. Sal's wife was nasty, both in looks and personality. Other than her cup size, I don't know what he ever saw in her.

"Supposedly she got sick. I think she just couldn't stand that he was seeing me and that we were happy. She doesn't want him, but she doesn't want anyone else to have him either. It started out that she was having tests done and she needed him to babysit. He was so desperate to see his kids that he'd do anything to see them. Then when his wife found out I was with him, she said it was too emotionally damaging for the kids to see him with another woman." She sighed. "Then she had to have some surgery, and she asked him to stay in the house while she was in the hospital. Then when she got out, he stayed to help her, and he's been there ever since."

"I'm sorry, Denise," I said, meaning it. I was disappointed. He and Denise were good together. "I hate to say this, but it's better you found out now," I said.

"That's what I keep telling myself. I don't want to talk about Sal. What time are you going to Long Island?" she asked.

"I'm not sure." I said. I didn't want to tell her about Michele.

"I don't know what to do with myself today. Maybe I'll go to Dave's later," she said, talking about Dave's Tavern, the old neighborhood bar where we spent most of our misbegotten youth.

"Don't you have any friends?" I asked, annoyed. I didn't want to think about Denise alone in some bar because she had nowhere else to go. It was ironic, because that's exactly where I wound up.

5

I was showered and shaved before noon. I lounged around in sweats and tried to read my Bible, but I couldn't get into it. I sat on the couch, flipping through the channels on the TV. The classics were on, *It's A Wonderful Life, March of the Wooden Soldiers*, and all those other stupid Christmas movies that I can't stand. I fell asleep about 3:00 and woke up at 5:30.

It was dark outside, and I was feeling groggy from too much sleep. I rummaged through the fridge, pulling out some of the leftovers my grandmother managed to toss at me before we left last night. I put eggplant and spaghetti on a dish and popped it in the microwave. I poured a soda and took my dinner back to the couch.

By 8:30 I was bored out of my mind and told myself that a drive would clear my head. I put on jeans, work boots, and a sweater, grabbing my leather jacket on my way out. I drove around the deserted streets; I guess everyone was already wherever they were celebrating. Except for the occasional convenience stores, all the stores and restaurants were closed. I felt that old loneliness seep in, wondering why I always seem to end up alone.

I turned up Midland Avenue and headed back toward the beach, intending to turn down my block and go home. I saw the bar up ahead on my right, the lighted beer signs beckoned from inside a dive that didn't even have a name.

I parked out front, feeling the chill through my leather jacket as I walked the few steps from the street. The front was cement painted cream, with brown wood shutters on the front glass window. The brown painted door squeaked when I opened it, revealing a dimly lit interior.

It was a dump, an old man's bar with Frank Sinatra blaring from the juke box, singing "Strangers In The Night." The smell of cigarette smoke, stale beer, and hopelessness permeated the room. It was a one-room bar, no pool table, just a dart board on the back wall with a chalk scoreboard. The bar was along the wall on the right, with red-cushioned bar stools. There was a row of booths on the left with the same red cushions and brown formica tables.

Three old men sat at the bar, separately. None of them were talking except the guy at the end. He was doing a playful come-on with an old hag with a bad bleach job. I saw her eyes catch me, and she smiled seductively, revealing a set of yellow, crooked teeth. *Yeah, that'll happen*, I thought. No matter how drunk I got, I'd be leaving without her. I ignored the voice of my conscience warning me that alcohol raised the libido but lowered the standards.

I tried to remember the last time I'd been with a woman. I was feeling sorry for myself because I'd been such a Boy Scout all these months—no booze, no sex, and where did it get me? Nowhere, alone on Christmas at some old man's bar where the only woman was a shriveled-up skank.

I took a seat at the end of the bar near the front door. I signaled the bartender for a beer. He was an old man, probably in his seventies. He walked slowly toward me with a hint of a limp. He was balding and overweight, with tired blue eyes and a gravelly voice.

"What can I get ya?" he asked.

"Give me a Bud," I said.

"Bottle or tap?" he asked, not caring.

"Bottle," I said. He nodded and gave me an ice-cold longneck.

The first sip was just like I remembered it. Cool, crisp, the taste of a thousand other beers that I've drunk, and it went down nice and smooth. I wanted it to remind me of summertime and youth, of days when I could drink without thinking and never go home alone. Instead, it reminded me that I'd broken my record of not drinking for almost six months.

I finished the first beer and ordered a second, watching the others in the bar for entertainment. The one guy and the blonde were getting loud. He was talking about the old days when he was a ballplayer. How he was the best shortstop in the Colonial leagues. I tuned him out and looked at the other two. One was so old he looked like someone pulled him out of a coffin and sat him at the bar. He wasn't moving at first, and I thought for a second that he was dead. Then he picked up his tap beer and took a drag from the cigarette that was burning in the ashtray as he stared at the mirror behind the bar.

The third guy was a little younger, maybe fifty. He was doing some serious drinking, shots of Jack Daniels alternating with beer. He was sitting closest to me, so I could see what he was wearing. Blue polyester pants, black dress shoes, and a cream-colored sweater stretched out of shape. His dark hair was in need of a haircut and was greasy. I could see flecks of dandruff in it, or maybe it was lice. He was watching the blonde with a detached look on his face.

The blonde kept looking my way, trying to make eye contact with me. I could see her staring at me in my peripheral vision, but I wouldn't look at her. Her date got off his stool, unsteady as he walked, and stumbled as he headed toward the men's room. I could hear her cackle as she cracked up when he fell. He steadied himself, holding onto the wall until he made it to the bathroom.

I felt the old familiar buzz when I finished my second beer and ordered a third. The bartender turned a shot glass upside down and told me the next one was on the house as he walked away.

The juke box had switched to "Rockin' Around the Christmas Tree," and I saw the blonde start to do a little dance. I played with the neck of my beer bottle and looked around the room at them. They were so pathetic. I didn't want that to be me in thirty years. The question came to me from deep inside, *Do I get smashed or walk away while I still can?* I knew God didn't want this for me. I mulled it over for a few minutes. I finished my beer, guzzling it in three gulps. I took my money off the bar, leaving a ten-dollar tip, and walked back out into the cold.

I went home, went to bed, and slept like the dead. I woke up to sunshine streaming through the windows. I was thankful that at least it wasn't raining. I spent the day keeping busy. I cleaned my guns, washed my bathroom, watched the Weather Channel and *Lethal Weapon 3* on cable.

I left early for work, eager to escape the quiet in my apartment. There was little traffic on the roads, and I drove through the Verrazzano, the Gowanus, and the Battery Tunnel without slowing down.

I was dressed and had already drunk a cup of coffee when Fiore got to the precinct.

I could see in his eyes that he'd already heard about the fiasco at my grandmother's house on Christmas Eve.

"You okay?" he asked.

"Bad news travels fast," I remarked. "I guess Michele talked to Donna."

I could see he wanted to deny it, but he said, "Yeah, she did," instead. "It'll work out," he said.

"I don't know, it was pretty bad," I said honestly.

Sergeant Hanrahan had approached us on his way to the podium. He cut his hair last week into a short, almost military style, showing off his blue eyes. I noticed he had put a couple of pounds on his six-foot frame.

"Hey, Tony, Joe," he said, shaking our hands. "How was Christmas?" He looked back and forth between us.

"Great!" Joe said. "The kids loved it."

"What about you, Tony?"

"Pretty good, boss," I lied. "How bout you? How's the family?"

"Everyone's good, thanks. Listen," he leaned in closer, and his eyes scanned the room as he spoke quietly, "there's an overtime detail that I think you guys will be interested in."

He said it so secretively that I nodded, leaned over, and whispered, "Who do we have to kill?"

He smiled and said, "Seriously, this is right up your alley."

"I don't know, boss," I said skeptically. "Sounds like work to me."

He waved me away as he walked to the muster room podium and gave the fall in order.

He gave out the foot posts, the sectors, and the color of the day and wound it up with, "The administrative sergeant left me a message," he continued, "that some pretour and end-of-tour overtime is available. If anyone is interested, see me after the roll call." He closed with, "Be careful, and foot posts, make sure you pick up the jobs on your post."

Mike Rooney, McGovern, O'Brien, Fiore, and I approached the boss after roll call.

"About the overtime," he said. "I was told by Sergeant Bishop from the day tour that there is a detail available if anyone wants to volunteer."

If we were being asked to volunteer, then nobody else wanted the detail. There's a system behind the system for the way this works. The administrative sergeant on the day tour, who does the precinct stats for the CO, and the captain get the overtime order. The guys who work upstairs and suck up to him get first crack at the overtime. They buy him dinner for giving them the good details and for the most part just feed his ego. Since the administrative sergeant's name is Charlie Bishop, we call his guys "Charlie's Angels."

At first I thought Charlie's Angels had a better detail, but as Hanrahan explained the detail, I realized why they didn't want it.

"We're paying special attention to the parking garages in the vicinity of Times Square," Hanrahan said.

"Special attention" means the city is on alert. The department never tells us the city's on alert. We usually read about it in the newspaper, or like tonight, we hear at roll call that we're paying "special attention" to something.

This year's overtime detail, like last year's, was checking all the parking garages in the vicinity of Times Square for bombs. It doesn't take a brain surgeon to figure out that if we're looking for bombs, we've been getting some threats again.

If no one volunteered for the overtime, the precinct would have to start mandating it. Since the week between Christmas and New Year's is usually busy, I figured the bomb duty was an easy gig.

"Hey, Tony, you in on this?" Fiore asked.

"Sure. I could use the money," I said, wondering what the hit would be on my Visa this month.

"Did you see Nick?" he asked, meaning Nick Romano.

"He's not here," I said. "He probably took off because he couldn't get Christmas off."

In a way I was glad that Romano wasn't around. I wouldn't have talked to Joe about things if he were here.

I went over to the radio room to speak to John Conte, my old partner. They had him working the radio room; I guess he was covering for Vince Puletti. Vince has so much time on, he probably hasn't worked the holidays in twenty years.

It was John's first day back on limited duty, and he was dressed to be inside. Long-sleeved, blue-collared shirt with blue clip-on tie, rather than the NYPD turtleneck. He had no vest on and was carrying two guns. He had his off-duty Glock on his hip, and I could see the shoulder holster under his shirt. We hugged and slapped backs when I walked into the room, and I could feel the .38 under his arm digging into my side.

"Hey, buddy," he smiled. "Good to see you."

"Hey, John, how you been? How does it feel to be back?" I asked.

"It was either this or get divorced," he joked.

Most cops would have gone out on three-quarters for a line-of-duty injury like John's. If you figure it takes us twenty years to get half pay from a job that never increases, three-quarters tax-free anytime sooner is like hitting the lotto. But John is gung ho; he would sit at a desk with his leg amputated before he'd go out, he loves the job.

John looked healthy. His color was good, not that gray pallor us midnight guys get from lack of sunlight. He was thirty, a little on the skinny side, which made him look taller than he really is. He was about five foot eleven and weighed about 170 pounds. He was Italian but with blue eyes, light skin, and frizzy brown hair. I noticed his skin had cleared up some. When he worked with me, he was always going to the dermatologist to treat his acne. I think the time away from the job helped. It

83

could also be the fact that he lived up in Westchester, away from all the dirt in the city. The exhaust from the cars and buses alone gives you a layer of grime on your face.

I talked to him as I signed out my radio, but someone interrupted us every thirty seconds to welcome him back and ask how he'd been. I stayed for a few minutes while he gave out the radios. I watched him pull the radio from its designated slot labeled in duct tape with the radio number written in black magic marker. He had the cops sign out their name next to the corresponding number.

All the interruptions were making it difficult to catch up on what was going on with him. I hadn't told him a lot about the changes in my life, and I was sure he'd hear some things now that he was back.

"How do you like working with Joe? He's a good guy, right?" he asked. I almost laughed because that's what everyone says about Fiore.

"Yeah, he is a good guy," I said and left it at that.

"You know, you look a little like him," John said.

A lot of people say that, but I don't see it. Fiore is taller than I am, closer to six feet while I'm almost five ten. He's built, but I'm stockier. We're both dark haired, but my hair's straight and his is wavy. He has big, dark brown eyes where mine are hazel, and I'm more heavy lidded. I have what my grandmother calls a "classic Roman nose," whatever that means. Fiore's nose is wider, but it fits his face. Joe came over to say hello to John before we went out.

I had a set of keys made for my RMP, so I didn't have to get them from Rice and Beans. A cold front was moving through, and the temperature had dropped into the twenties. The windchill was supposed to make it to about twelve degrees. It was a biting wind that stung my face as I walked to our car. I was dressed warm, thermal shirt under my turtleneck with NYPD on the collar. I had my gray leather gloves tucked into my gun belt, folded over the front of my buckle. I didn't wear long johns under my pants, it would have been too hot in the car. Fiore was dressed pretty much the same as I was, except he had the longer winter jacket. The newer one that I wore was waist length while Fiore's was pants length. Mine looks better and is easier to move in, but Fiore's is warmer.

We cleaned out our sector car and settled our gear, hats in the backseat, radios in the doors, and handcuffs pulled to the side of our belts.

I drove to the corner of 35th Street and 9th Avenue to pick up coffee. Fiore grabbed a muffin to go with his coffee, but I didn't get anything to eat. I still felt full from all the food I ate over the holiday. I had scarfed down leftover eggplant parmigiana before I came in tonight and couldn't fit any more food. I drove to 8th Avenue and up to 37th Street and found a spot on 37th between 8th and 9th where we could have our coffee.

"So what did Michele say?" I asked as Fiore pulled the muffin out of its paper holder.

He seemed to stall for a minute and said, "She told Donna that she doesn't think your family is too happy about you going out with her."

That was an understatement.

Fiore waited a beat and added, "She also said that she feels there's a lot of hostility there that might not be so good for Stevie."

Michele is always so tactful, she would never come out and say they were a bunch of psychopaths.

"What happened?" he asked. "Why are things always so—"

He stopped, putting his hand up as he listened to a radio transmission that caught our attention. A North car came over the air, saying: "Central, this is North Henry. I've got a late model black Suburban, Ford Explorer, New York plates."

85

He read off the three-letter, four-number plate to Central. "It just left the scene of an accident and is westbound on 57th Street, just past 5th Avenue." He added, "Just past 6th Avenue."

Now, nobody's saying they're pursuing the vehicle, but we know they are. In New York City, the Police Department does not want high-speed chases through the streets—they can end in death to innocent bystanders and lawsuits for the city. If the North Sergeant thinks a unit is in pursuit, he's gonna get on the radio and call it off.

The sector came back over the radio again with "Central, the black Suburban just turned south on Broadway after striking a city bus and leaving the scene just past 56th Street."

Now he's coming down toward us, and he is moving. The North Sergeant comes over the radio and says, "Central, this is North Sergeant, what is the vehicle wanted for?"

Central says, "I've run the plate, and it's not stolen. As far as I know it's for leaving the scene."

The North Sergeant responds with, "Call it off, Central, call off the pursuit."

We put our conversation to the side for now as we moved the RMP to the corner of 37th Street and 9th Avenue. I wanted to find out which direction the black Suburban was headed and position myself in case he comes this far south or west. At this point North Henry is no longer identifying themselves, and we're hearing 55th, 54th, 53rd, 52nd, 51st, identifying the streets the black Suburban is whipping past. Someone else comes over the air, saying, "He's blowing red lights!"

Then we hear the shrill alarm sound that Central uses when they're saying something important. It's only used for higher priority issues to get everyone's attention. It's a loud, high-pitched series of multiple short beeps followed by the message, "North Sergeant has called off the pursuit."

Another voice followed almost immediately with, "Eastbound on 50th Street."

Central hits the doo-doo-doo alarm again and repeats, "Call it off! North Sergeant has called off the pursuit! Is there a unit in pursuit?"

Silence follows on the radio.

"Wanna move?" Fiore asked.

"Yeah," I said, putting the car in drive. Now that he was going east, I drove south to 34th Street. This is the fastest way across town to the East Side, where the Suburban is heading.

It was now midnight. Something was going on at the Manhattan Civic Center, with taxis and limos two deep out front. A few people were coming out of the movie theater across from the Civic Center, and pedestrian traffic was still pretty busy along this end of 34th Street. The Knicks or the Rangers must have had a game at the Garden, because a bunch of people were exiting from there and crossing both 34th Street and 8th Avenue.

As I was driving eastbound on 34th Street, I passed Macy's on my left. It was still decorated for Christmas, so was most of 34th Street. Fiore and I were driving slow, keeping an eye out to make sure this clown didn't come flying down to where we were. The next thing we heard was "Four-eight and 5th," which means the driver has now made a right onto 5th Avenue and is going south. They were at 48th Street. I was one block west of 5th Avenue and 14 blocks south of 48th Street.

Central put over the air, "Is there a unit in pursuit?"

Silence.

"Is there a unit in trouble?"

Silence again. No one was going to admit to a pursuit.

It was quiet for what seemed to be three minutes, then we heard screaming over the radio.

"Someone just hit our car! Central, someone just slammed into us!"

Fiore and I sat up straighter and leaned into the radio, as if it could give us a visual. I looked at him. He shrugged and said, "What was that?"

"No idea," I said as they transmitted again.

"Central, FTU, uh, automobile to Central!" They were yelling so loud it distorted the communication.

"Unit, identity yourself," Central ordered.

"FTU. FTU mobile. A black Suburban just struck our vehicle." As they spoke, we could hear shouts in the background as the radio button was held down, "He's on 5th Avenue, he's passing 42nd Street on 5th Avenue."

"Unit, identify yourself," Central ordered again.

"North Sergeant to Central," the sergeant from the North interrupted.

Central: "North Sergeant."

"Central, the unit is probably the FTU unit in car 4255. What is their location?" The sergeant sounded calm but annoyed.

I should probably add here that the FTU, or Field Training Unit, car held a couple of rookies right out of the Academy. They were clueless what to do here and were probably scared out of their minds right now.

Central: "FTU, what is your location?"

"Heading south on 5th Avenue approaching 41st Street," FTU answered.

"Central, find out if their vehicle was hit," North Sergeant requested.

Central: "FTU 4255, was your vehicle hit by the black Suburban?"

FTU responded with, "Yeah, Central, it slammed into us—and he just hit another car!" They started screaming again.

It was apparent these numb nuts had no idea this was the same car that a chase was called off for.

While this was going on, Fiore and I were driving east toward 5th Avenue, expecting to see this car at any minute. While approaching the southwest corner of 34th and 5th, I spotted the black Suburban screeching through the intersection, then making a left. They slammed into a black livery cab parked at the bus stop on the southeast corner.

"Look at this genius," I said as the Suburban continued on without stopping, then I added, "That'll teach 'em not to park in the bus stop."

"You're not kidding," Fiore agreed.

As the Suburban made the turn onto 34th Street, we could see two people in the front seat, a white male and a hysterical white female. She was screaming and throwing punches at him as they drove past. I didn't think this was gonna help his driving any. Then I saw her put her head between her knees like you do when you're nauseous.

The FTU car was about fifty feet behind the black Suburban. I didn't go into the intersection at this point. If I blew the light and got hit, Fiore and I would be walking for thirty days. At the corner of 34th Street and Madison Avenue, the light was turning red for the east-west bound traffic, including the black Suburban. The northbound traffic had four lanes. Two cars were stopped at the light in the two left lanes. In the two right lanes were two cabbies that approached the intersection by slowing down but not actually stopping. They call this timing the lights, and the cabbies do it for as many intersections as they can before they have to come to a full stop.

As the traffic light turned green for the northbound traffic, the two cabbies came from behind and led neck and neck into the intersection. The cars in the left lanes hadn't even started into the crosswalks yet.

From here on in things seemed to go in slow motion. Dread pooled in my stomach as I heard the black Suburban accelerate as it approached the intersection of Madison and 34th Street. Fiore closed his eyes, shook his head, and said, "Oh no," and I heard the smash of the impact and the exploding of glass as the Suburban hit the rear passenger door of the cab. It knocked the first cab into the cab next to it, pushing it onto the northeast sidewalk. The black Suburban actually went up in the air when it hit the cab, and it finally stopped in the middle of 34th Street.

6

*F*iore grabbed the radio. "Central, I need two buses forthwith at 34th and Madison. The black Suburban has just struck two cabs. Also have South Sergeant respond to the scene at 34th and Madison."

There was an eerie silence after the crash. I heard sirens approaching from the east side of 34th Street, hopefully already responding to the scene. One of the FTU rookies ran over to the Suburban and pulled the driver out. The rookie didn't realize how big the guy was. The guy fell forward on top of the rookie, and both of them hit the ground. The driver was huge, at least six foot five and built solid, like 250 pounds. The other two rookies ran over to give him a hand, turned the driver over, and pulled his hands behind his back to cuff him. He started to fight them, but I figured the three of them could handle him. They were in the westbound lane of 34th Street, and I was in the eastbound lane, before the intersection. From where I stood twenty feet away, I could see this guy was drunk and dazed. His face was bleeding over his left eyebrow, and he kept opening and closing his eyes.

He was clean-cut and looked like what we call black Irish,

black hair, dark eyes. Maybe he was a Westie, one of Hell's Kitchen's Irish mob. He was wearing a button-down denim shirt over a black turtleneck, jeans, and cowboy boots. He was full of powder from his airbag and looked soaked with sweat in spite of the cold.

The female was petite and pretty, with shoulder-length blond hair and a big purple egg on her forehead. She was about five foot four and wore jeans and high-heeled black boots. She was also wearing a black turtleneck, but she had on a long black sweater coat. She looked like money, even with the egg on her head and airbag powder all over her. She had gotten out of the Suburban and was crying quietly as she stared at the crushed cab.

Fiore and I had started toward the cab when I saw one of the FTU rookies whacking his arm up and down on the driver like an axe. It looked like it was taking a lot of effort for the baby-faced rookies to hold the guy down. You could see the fear and excitement in their faces as they scrambled all around him. I almost laughed as the two Irish guys and a Spanish female tried out their Academy cuffing technique. I shook my head and pictured the newspaper with "How Many Cops Does It Take to Cuff a Perp?" splashed across the front page.

In theory, if you're holding your cuffs properly, you hold the chain in the palm of your hand and close your fist. If you do this, one cuff will be coming out the top of your hand, and the other will come out the bottom. The bottom part of the cuff is stationary, and the top part swivels. In one swift motion, you're supposed to hit the wrist with the swivel part of the cuff so it would swing around the wrist and lock the cuff into place. This would give you control of the cuffed hand even if the perp is moving. The more he moves, the more you twist, and the cuffs cut into his wrist.

It was comical to watch the rookies attempt this maneuver. Two of them were sitting on the driver's back, while the other one slammed him over and over on the wrist with the stationary end of the cuff. The perp was yelling and bucking like a horse. "Get off me!" he kept yelling, and the rookie was so excited, he didn't realize he was hitting the perp with the part of the cuff that doesn't move.

I walked over and grabbed the cuffs out of his hand.

"Give me those," I barked at him. "I don't have time for this." I cuffed the perp while the other two held him down.

"Sorry, sir," he said, embarrassed.

"Who are you calling *sir*? Do I look like an old man to you?" I asked, up in his face. *Did I look that old?*

"No, sir," he said, then corrected himself. "Sorry, no." I remembered he was just out of the Academy and had to call everyone *sir*. That'll wear off.

"Watch him," I said to the one whose cuffs I took. I pointed to the female who had been in the Suburban with the perp. She was still standing by the cab, crying. Her nose was red now, and she was huddling into her sweater.

"One of you watch her, and the other start directing the northbound traffic around the cars," I said to the other two FTU cops.

Traffic was backing up in all directions, and rubberneckers were slowing down whatever traffic could get through. The exhaust from the cars was coming out in streams of smoke from the cold, while the plumes of hot air from the subways underneath came through the manhole covers. There was a red and white rubber smokestack on the southwest corner of 34th Street. Con Edison uses them to redirect the steam from the subways as they work underground.

The female rookie babysat the perp's girlfriend while the other rookie stood in the middle of Madison Avenue, facing south, and directed the northbound traffic east on 34th Street toward Park Avenue.

The intersection of Madison and 34th had scaffolding around the buildings on the northeast and northwest corners. The scaffolding that the cab was pushed into on the northeast corner didn't collapse, but I'm sure it weakened the structure. Once the cars were moved, we would have to rope it off so no one walked under it. It would be a fixer, a post that you're stuck on until you're relieved. A fixer can be a DOA, crime scene, hospital with a prisoner, targeted location, any thing like that. Someone would have to sit on it until a city engineer checked it out. Then the scaffolding company would have to come and fix it, but it wouldn't be my fixer or my problem.

The North Sergeant said over the radio that he was coming to the scene at 34th and Madison. He also said that two other vehicles had been hit by the black Suburban, making it a total of seven cars and one city bus that this clown hit.

I zipped up my jacket as Fiore and I went over to the cab. I approached the side of the car that was hit, and Fiore went around to the other side. The passenger sitting next to the door in the backseat was dead. The left side of his face was full of blood, and his head was slumped to the right. This gave me a clear view of the wound, and I would say he probably died at impact since half his head was gone. He must have been facing the other passenger since the force of it hit him in the back of the head. I hoped he never knew it was coming.

The windows had exploded on impact, and the twisted metal door went into the passenger. I tried not to look too much at him, but a superficial once-over told me he was in his late thirties, with short dark hair. He was wearing a long, black wool coat and a light-colored scarf, now stained red. The guy next to him was also motionless.

The cabbie was moaning in a Middle Eastern accent, "The light was green, the light was green."

I opened the driver's door and said "Easy, buddy" while I

shut the ignition off. The cab wasn't running any longer, just a series of clicks from the engine. "Tony, this guy is still alive," Fiore said from the other side of the car. He walked over to the second cab that was hit, and I saw him open the back door, checking on the passengers. I nodded my head and asked, "What's up?"

"They're a little banged up, but they'll be alright," he said.

There were other cars at the scene now. Sergeant Hanrahan and the first ambulance arrived simultaneously. I told the EMT, "The passenger behind the driver is dead, but the other is still alive."

The EMT gave a quick check to the first passenger, confirmed he was dead, and called his partner. He and his partner started to work on the other guy. They gave me his info from his passport and got him into the ambulance, then left the scene within a couple of minutes to take him to Bellevue. Another ambulance arrived, and this pair of EMTs went over to the driver of the first cab.

I walked over to the second cab. The driver was screaming about the damage done to his cab and wanted to know who's gonna pay him for all the money he won't be making tonight. His passengers were three pros on their way uptown. Pros is short for prostitute and is pronounced the same way. EMS got the first two pros out of the cab. The first one was in a powder blue nylon dress with black boots and stockings and a black leather jacket that came to her waist. Her hair was short and spikey, blond on the ends and black at the roots.

The second one was dark skinned with long black hair and was wearing a short, white rabbit fur coat over a thigh-length leopard dress. Her black stockings had a run in them, and her black stiletto heels were scuffed.

The third one was taken out on a backboard. She had a nasty gash on her forehead, and her nose and mouth were bleeding as well. She was wearing a red dress in the same cheap nylon material as her coworkers. She wore a fake fur coat that may have been white once; now it was an ugly shade of gray.

They weren't homeless pros. They had enough money to share a cab, but they were pretty sleazy looking. No escort service here.

Fiore was talking to them, calming them down while he got their information for the accident report. They were banged up and crying. The first two walked to the second ambulance, the third pros they put on a stretcher. I wondered who was gonna pay them for the money they wouldn't be making tonight.

Sergeant Hanrahan walked over toward Fiore and me. "What happened here?" he asked.

"This is the yo-yo they were looking for in the north for leaving the scene. The guy's hammered, he bounced off the FTU car, we saw him hit a livery and these cabs. He played bumper cars for about twenty blocks before nailing the cab. One guy is dead, the other is likely to die." I nodded my head toward the perp. "Look at him," I said with disgust. He was still carrying on, yelling at the rookies.

His girlfriend had stopped crying and was now complaining that she was cold. She was on her cell phone and at the same time telling the female rookie that she wanted to go home.

"Officer!" Hanrahan said to the female rookie watching the perp's girlfriend. "Cuff her." He nodded toward the perp's girlfriend.

"What?" she screamed. "What did I do? Hey, I'm talking to you!"

The boss ignored her as he walked over to the sergeant from the North. The North Sergeant looked like a boozer to me. He was about five foot eleven with thinning red hair and blue eyes. He had a bulbous nose with broken blood vessels in it and deep lines in his face. He looked fifty but might have been younger. He told Sergeant Hanrahan to let the rookies handle the arrest and said something tasteless about them losing their virginity. When the boss smirked, he added, "I'll have the FTU Sergeant respond to the south and help them with the paperwork. We'll let her handle the accident report."

I had gotten the badge number of the EMS guy who took the "likely to die" to Bellevue, I would need it for the accident report later. Even though we were getting everyone's name, address, social security number, license, registration, and insurance, we'd all end up back at the precinct anyway.

"Hey, Tony," Hanrahan said. "Search the DOA (dead on arrival), see if he's got any personal belongings or anything of value to voucher." He meant money, jewelry, passport, ID, cell phone, drugs, anything like that. "Do you have gloves on you?" he asked.

"I should have them in my trunk," I said while I walked back to my RMP.

The initial commotion of the accident had worn off, and I was starting to feel the cold. My ears were stinging, my nose was starting to run, and my fingers were getting numb. I blew on my hands, then pressed them over the tops of my ears to warm those up a little as I walked back to the car. I didn't want to put my leather gloves on because they would make it difficult to search the DOA, plus I didn't want to get blood on them.

I opened the RMP's trunk and found an opened box of latex gloves with a couple spilled out around the box. There was also a spare tire, orange traffic cones, flares, tire chains, a crumpled brown paper bag, a Louisville Slugger baseball bat, and a five-gallon can of house paint. Someone probably took the bat off a perp. I picked up the can of paint and shook it. It felt full. It said "premium interior latex, pastel base" on the front and had a number written in magic marker with a splash of green paint on the lid. I looked at the color, decided

I wouldn't paint anything in my apartment with it, and put it back in the trunk.

I took the crumpled paper bag with me and pulled on the gloves as I went back to the cab. I couldn't open the dead guy's door, so I went around to the passenger side of the cab. I wouldn't sit on the backseat, so I perched myself at a weird angle by putting one foot on the seat and the other in the passenger side footwell. The smell of blood was strong inside the cab, slightly reminiscent of our butcher shop in Dongan Hills. The smell doesn't bother me anymore. When I first came on the job, I almost fainted the first time I saw a lot of blood, but you get used to it after a while.

I pulled up the guy's sleeve on his left hand and took his watch off. I held it up to the light to get a better look. It was stainless steel, with a silver face and a black leather band. It said VERSACE on the face and looked pretty valuable to me, but what do I know? I found the pants soaked in blood and dripping on the seat of the cab. The wound had bled out onto the seat. It was dry in the front, but it was still wet as it ran down the rivets in the leather toward the back between the seat. I pulled an Italian passport, a black leather wallet, and a wad of cash out of his front and back pockets. My gloves were getting sticky as the blood dried on them, and they were adhering to the wallet as I moved it.

I put everything in the brown paper bag at the farthest end of the seat. I had to lift his head to check his neck for chains, and of course he was wearing one. I pulled the fastener around to the front because I didn't want to wrestle with the head to take it off. The gloves were making my hands clumsy, and it took me a couple of tries to get it off. I didn't look at the face, I didn't want to remember it. I knew the eyes were closed, but other than that, I couldn't tell you what he looked like. One less face in my nightmares.

Fiore was talking to the sergeant when I walked over.

"I got his valuables," I said, holding up the bloodstained bag. "I checked all his pockets, wrist, fingers, and neck. He's got an Italian passport." I tried to remember how this would be handled. I was pretty sure it would go upstairs to the detectives, who would contact Intel (Intelligence), and they in turn would contact Interpol.

"Tony," the sarge said, "you and Joe go back to the house and give the info to the North Sergeant on the DOA, the likely to die, the pros, and the cabbies. And do me a favor, type up the voucher report for the DOA's property."

"You got it, Boss," I said.

It was now almost 1:15 a.m. The cabbies and the pros had all been taken to the hospital. Someone from Highway was there to do an analysis of the accident. He was taking pictures when Fiore and I left. One of the FTU would sit with the body in the car until the coroner came to take it.

When we got back to the precinct, the FTU Sergeant, a female from the North, was at the front desk, talking to Lieutenant Coughlin. Vinny Begaducci, or bag of donuts as we call him, wasn't at the desk, but I could hear him telling the FTUs to control their prisoner, who was screaming "Get these cuffs off me!" from one of the cells in the back.

"Hey, Lou," I said. "Sergeant Hanrahan's got us vouchering the DOA's property and wants us to the give the info on the two cabbies that were hit to the North Sergeant for the accident report."

He nodded. "Give the info to the FTU Sergeant here," he said, pointing to the female sergeant, a skinny redhead with freckles, talking on the phone at the desk. "Vinny," the lou called, "get vouchers for the DOA's property."

"Hey, Joe, Tony," Vinny said as he came in carrying a handful of perforated computer sheets, still attached, "I think you guys got a hit." He walked back behind the desk.

"James O'Connor." Vinny read off the sheet. He gave a West 51st Street address. "Twenty-eight years old. Let's see, we got robbery, attempted robbery, attempted murder, eight assaults?" he read off. The guy was probably professional muscle, a leg breaker who collects vig for a loan shark. (*Vig* is a mob term for interest on loans to a loan shark.) He had no warrants.

Joe and I went into the muster room to voucher the property. I put some newspaper down on the old metal desk and pulled two new rubber gloves on, snapping them like a proctologist for effect. I asked Joe to write down the property as I read it off.

The voucher, or property clerk's invoice, is used to record arrest evidence or to record a DOA's property. Joe checked off "decedent's property" while I read off the items I found on the DOA.

"One gold-colored chain, approximately fifteen inches." Joe wrote while I set the chain on the newspaper. The reason I don't say "one gold chain" is because if I go to trial and some lowlife defense attorney puts me on the stand, he looks for something like this. I say it's a gold chain, and it turns out it's only gold plated, or not gold at all. Then the attorney has a field day with me, saying I switched the chains, and I'm a thief and his client is innocent. Or he says "How do you know it was gold, are you a metallurgist?" and wastes two days of testimony making it look like I'm a dirty cop and it was conspiracy against his client.

"One silver-colored watch with a black band," I continued, "with the word VERSACE written in black letters on the face."

"One Italian passport." I gave the number. "With the deceased's name 'Francesco Costo.'" It said that he was from Rome.

I counted off the money. "Three thousand, four hundred and

seventy-nine dollars in U.S. currency." The money was soaked through with blood and would probably have to go to the lab even though it's not evidence. I can't voucher it like that.

"One black wallet. One Italian driver's license." I named his credit cards, four in all, and opened the billfold and pulled out a white, blood-soaked piece of paper.

"It looks like our DOA was a Mo," I said, still reading.

"Why do you say that?" Fiore asked, looking up from the passport he was trying to read without touching it.

"A blood test report." I held it up. It was from a laboratory on Third Avenue and was checked positive for the HIV virus. "He's got the monster," I added.

As soon as I said the word *Mo* I felt heavy, like I did something wrong. Mo is short for homo and is usually what I say to describe someone who's gay. Fiore doesn't say it, but he's never said anything when I do. That's probably because when he first became my partner, I used to use some really nasty adjectives to describe people just to see if I could get a rise out of him.

"What's wrong?" he asked. "You look funny."

"Nothing," I said.

In some ways life was less complicated when I didn't have a conscience. I guess I had one when I was a kid and lost it somewhere along the way. Since I met Fiore, it seems to have come back. Not that it isn't good, it's just that it changes who I've been for a long time.

Now I'm feeling guilty for calling the DOA a Mo. There was a hotel passkey for one of the big hotels right in Times Square. Those rooms are booked for this time of year at least a year in advance. He was probably doing that once-in-a-lifetime trip to experience New Year's Eve in Times Square. Then the poor schmuck gets whacked in a cab by some drunk on 34th Street without getting to see the ball drop. Another New York vacation moment. We got a million of them.

I was still looking at the blood test report. If the driver of the Suburban goes to trial and his lawyer gets a list of this man's personal property, I'm sure they'll try to work it into the defense. I could hear the defense attorney telling the jury the man was HIV positive and his client saved him from dying a horrible death.

Now I had to let the sergeant know and get an exposure number in case down the line something comes up with me. I wasn't worried. I'm not HIV positive and I had gloves on the whole time, but everything is procedure.

Fiore was reading the lab report with his head tilted when I asked, "Joe, do you think this guy went to hell?" That's another new thing for me, wondering what happens to someone when they die.

"I have no idea." He looked surprised by my question. "Why would you ask that?"

"Because he's gay," I pointed out.

"So?"

"Isn't being gay a sin?" I asked, maybe a little sarcastically.

"A lot of things are sin, Tony. People don't go to hell for being gay, or killing someone, or anything else that's a sin. They go to hell for denying Jesus. If you believe in Jesus and repent and ask for His forgiveness, He forgives your sin. It says in the Bible in 1 John 1:9, 'If we confess our sins, He is faithful and just to forgive us our sins and to cleanse us from all unrighteousness.' He cleanses us, and that's what keeps us out of hell."

I cut him off. "But I thought homosexuality is a mortal sin."

He chuckled. "What's a mortal sin?"

"A mortal sin will send you to hell," I said.

He looked confused, so I continued, "It's not like a venial sin."

"I have no idea what you're talking about," he said.

"A venial sin is like a white lie," I explained.

"A *white* lie?" He smirked. "I didn't realize lies had colors."

"A white lie isn't a bad lie. It's a little lie, like a lie you have to tell," I said.

"A lie is a lie, Tony, big or little," he said seriously.

"You're misunderstanding what I'm saying." I thought a minute. "When Donna had the baby, and she still had a couple of pounds on from the birth and asked you 'Do I look fat?' what did you tell her? Didn't you say no?"

He rubbed the back of his neck and seemed to be thinking before he said, "I didn't think she looked fat. I thought she looked beautiful, and I told her that. I don't think she asked me if she looked fat. Are you saying my wife is fat?" He said it sharply, but I saw a little twitch of a smile.

I held up my hands, ignoring his question about Donna being fat. She's great, but a little too chunky for my taste. "What about this, let's say you're in court testifying about a perp you observe doing a hand-to-hand transaction on 42nd Street and 8th Avenue. He sees you and bolts, and you follow him a block up and grab him on 7th Avenue. The defense attorney asks you if you ever lost sight of the perpetrator when you chased him, and you say no. Now, you know when he turned the corner of 7th Avenue you were still behind him, so for a split second he's out of your sight, but the lawyer is gonna try and beat you up and make it look like you were chasing the wrong guy. Even though it's the same guy in the same clothes with the same crack on him."

"If he turned the corner, I'd say he turned the corner," Fiore said.

"And then he gets off because you say that?" I said, getting irritated. "You know he's guilty, and the lawyer is gonna say you had the wrong guy 'cause you lost sight of him!"

"Whether or not he's guilty isn't my problem, making sure I

tell the truth is my problem," he said calmly. "I would say that I still had a positive ID after coming around the corner."

"It's a white lie, Joe. It doesn't hurt anyone, and if we don't lie a little, he's gonna walk away."

He came a little closer and looked me in the face and said, "Tony, the Bible is very clear on this. It's not acceptable. In fact, if you take a look at Proverbs chapter 6, it says there are six things that the Lord *hates*, and seven are an abomination to him. The first thing he hates is a proud look, but the second is a lying tongue. Don't kid yourself here." He was moving his index finger back and forth to punctuate. "There are no lies that are okay with God. There is never a time that you have to lie, and don't think you can ever justify one, because you can't. He *hates* it, and you don't want to be doing what God hates," he finished.

"So you're telling me you never told a lie?" I said skeptically, although with Fiore it was probably possible.

"No, I've lied plenty of times. But I do my best not to, and if I catch myself telling a lie, I go back to the person I told it to and tell them I lied," he said. "I also repent to God."

I wasn't gonna argue with that, 'cause it was true. I've heard him say something and then back up and clarify something if he didn't say it right. I never thought about him not stretching the truth a little while testifying—everybody does it. It was probably a good thing that all cops didn't think like Fiore, no one would ever go to jail.

"Do you understand that when Jesus went to the cross, he was the sacrifice for *all* sin? There wasn't any sin that his blood didn't cover," he said.

"But I thought some sins were worse than others," I said.

"In the context that they do more damage, yes, but the price he paid is still the same. It says in Romans 3:23 'for all have sinned and fall short of the glory of God,' it doesn't say that some sins are worse than others, but that we've all sinned," he said.

I digested that. It's different than what I was taught. I thought that as long as you were a good person, you wouldn't go to hell. I actually thought as long as my intentions were good, even if I sinned, I wasn't sinning. It makes more sense the way Joe describes it, because if Jesus's death on the cross was only for the good people, then we could earn our way into heaven and we wouldn't need God.

Joe stayed with the DOA's property while I went into the back to type up my voucher. The Anti-Crime room was empty, so I went in and used their typewriter.

The room was about twenty feet long and twelve feet wide. The crime sergeant's desk is by the gated window, and on either side of the room two desks face each other. One set Anti-Crime uses, and the other set is for Narcotics.

A gray metal cabinet with double doors holds radios, and there's a utility table with a microwave and a minifridge. Next to the fridge is a row of gym-sized lockers the plainclothes units use. They keep their different-colored wristbands for the color of the day, the shield holders for around their necks, fanny packs, all the stuff they don't want to keep downstairs in their regular lockers.

The room already stunk of smoke, so I lit a cigarette and grabbed a half-full bottle of Coke with butts floating in it as an ashtray. I index-finger typed the voucher, made a copy, and gave the original to the FTU Sergeant.

We had a 4:00 meal, and Joe went down to the deli on 9th Avenue to get us some sandwiches. By now I was getting hungry and could use a nap. He came back with two oversized egg-roll-looking things sliced on an angle with the wax paper still on them and a couple of bottles of water.

"What is this?" I said, eyeing the food suspiciously.

"They're wraps. Which do you want, the veggie or the grilled chicken?" He saw me staring at him and said, "What?"

"Veggie wraps?" I shook my head. "What, are we on a diet? What am I supposed to do with this?" I turned it around to look at the other side, and it still looked like a big egg roll. "Since when are we eating girlie food? I can't eat this stuff." I shuddered.

"Gimme the veggie, you eat the chicken, I don't want your chest hair falling off," Fiore said as he grabbed the veggie thing and swallowed it in four bites. "Eat it, it's good for you," he said.

I ate the chicken, surprised at how good it tasted. It had a white dressing; I think it was Caesar with strips of grilled chicken and romaine lettuce.

"Not bad, eh?" he asked.

"Bird food," I countered.

We washed it down with the bottles of water. Joe passed out on one of the cushioned plywood benches in the lounge. I sat up for a little while, thinking about Michele. I swung back and forth with a sick feeling in my stomach from missing her and wanting to choke her for blowing me off.

I finally fell asleep for about five minutes when I heard Fiore's watch alarm go off at 5:00, and we went back out on patrol.

7

When we went back outside, the night sky was still black, and the temperature had dropped. The wind was blowing down from the north, adding to the chill factor. The paper said we were going down into the single digits tonight, and my nose hairs froze as soon as I walked outside. The air was so cold it almost took my breath away, and my eyes started to tear by the time we got to the RMP.

It took a while for the car to heat up, so I let it idle on the corner while I went into a bagel store on 9th Avenue. The first morning's bagels were coming out, and I grabbed an everything bagel, nice and fresh with butter. I got Fiore a pumpernickel with walnut raisin cream cheese to go with his coffee. I'd already read the early edition of the *Post*, so I grabbed the *Daily News* and I pulled into a small parking lot on 37th Street to eat our breakfast.

The bagel was still warm, and the melted butter pooled in the wax wrapping paper. I dipped the bagel into the melted butter as I ate it, alternating with sips of coffee. I finished the bagel and opened my window so I could smoke a cigarette.

Fiore doesn't smoke, so I kept my left arm out the window until my fingers started getting numb.

I've been trying to quit for a couple of months now, and every day I make and break my promise to myself that this will be my day to quit. I've tried smoking ultralight cigarettes, but there's not enough nicotine in them and I smoke twice as many. I banged it down to Marlboro lights, and that was a little better. I tried the patch, but I kept grubbing cigarettes and smoking with the patch on. Rooney said that could kill me, so I nixed the patch. I switched brands, but I kept grubbing cigarettes because I couldn't stand anything but Marlboros.

Rooney told me he only smokes every two hours. He said he's down to less than half a pack, and eventually he'll go to three hours in between, then four, until he quits. I tried to wait two hours, but then I smoked three cigarettes after the first two hours were up. Cigarettes are so expensive in New York, and each time they raise the price, everyone says they're gonna quit. So far it hasn't worked for me; I'm still puffing away.

As I blew on my fingers to warm them up and get the blood circulating again, Fiore said, "I'm amazed at how much a smoker will go through just to have a cigarette. You're freezing, but you still continue to smoke, not to mention all the other stuff smoking does to you."

He was quiet for a couple of minutes, scanning the *Daily News*. "We're getting a storm, a nor'easter, on Friday," he said as he read.

"Great, right in time for New Year's." I could just picture trying to clean up Times Square for the ball drop.

"So what happened at your grandmother's?" Fiore asked. "You started to tell me before we got the DOA."

I sighed, "Joe, you need to understand how my family is. They're the old-fashioned Italians, they're set in their ways," I explained.

"Your grandmother's the only old one, right?"

"Yeah," I said cautiously.

"So what's the deal with everyone else? From what Michele said, it was a brawl," he said.

"Actually it really started cooking when she left." I laughed at the thought of Michele seeing the real deal.

"If it's that bad, why do you still go there?" he asked.

"They're my family," I said, as if that explained everything.

A call came over the radio, it was now 5:20. Central read off the job code. "South David, we have a 54 at 320 West 30th Street, apartment 3D as in dog. A male," she hesitated, "is, uh, puking blood."

"Puking blood?" Fiore responded.

She hesitated again and said, "That's what it says."

I shrugged at Joe. "10-4," Fiore responded.

We pulled the RMP in front of the building, and Fiore radioed back 84, on the scene. It was a tan brick building, not Park Avenue, but not bad. A camera was anchored to the right corner above the doors. The doors were locked, but the buzzer sounded just as we pulled on them. We stepped into a small entranceway, and there was another set of glass doors in front of us. Just inside the lobby next to the doors was a desk with a security guard seated behind it.

The guard was a clean-cut male, black, midtwenties. He was friendly enough, dressed in a white shirt with the security logo on his left sleeve, and blue pants.

"Is everything alright?" he asked.

"How you doing, guy?" Joe shook his hand.

He nodded. "What's up?"

"We got a call for an aided up in 3D, supposedly some guy is throwing up blood," Fiore explained.

He showed us to the elevator, and we took it to the third floor. Apartment D was at the end of the hall. I tapped my nightstick on the gray metal door with a peephole under the stick-on 3D letters. Fiore and I stood on either side of the doorframe and heard someone approach the door. I knew he was looking through the peephole at us, but he still said, "Who is it?"

"Police," I said. "We got a call someone is throwing up blood."

"Everything's okay," a muffled voice said and started coughing. I heard a dimmer voice say, "Open the door."

"I said I'm fine," the first voice said, a little more forcefully before going off into a spasm of coughs.

I tapped the door a little louder this time and said, "Come on, let us in. We have to make sure everything's okay."

I heard the clink of bottles, while at the same time the sound of the chain sliding and the dead bolt unlocking. Someone said, "Why did you have to call them?"

The door was opened by a dopey-looking white male about thirty years old. He was about five foot nine with a medium build, brown hair in need of a cut, brown eyes, and a mustache. He was dressed casually in black jeans and a beige sweater. He let us in, gesturing us into the living room.

The smell of stale beer, cigarettes, and something sour hit us as we walked in. The apartment was old, with high ceilings and the old pulley windows that looked painted shut. There was no real furniture, just a couple of folding chairs around a big wooden spool, the kind that's used to hold cable wire.

The other guy, who I guessed was the puker, was cleaning up beer bottles and red plastic cups off the wire spool, which also held an overflowing ashtray and two boxes of Marlboros. He was a chalky-looking white male in his early thirties, wearing worn, tattered jeans, no shoes, and a faded black T-shirt with a red plaid flannel shirt over it. He had shaggy blond hair, and his eyes were light green with dark circles under them.

Next to the spool table was a medium-sized black waste-basket half full of liquid.

"Who called us?" Fiore asked.

"I did," Dopey said as the other guy brought the beer bottles into the kitchen. I could hear them clanking as he threw them in the garbage.

"Who are you?" Fiore said.

"I'm his friend," he answered.

"What's the problem here?" I interjected.

"He's puking blood, and he won't stop drinking." He sounded upset as he pointed to the basket. I looked into the basket and realized the liquid in it was blood.

"That's nasty," I said.

"It's no big deal," the puker said as he came back over to us. "I don't know why he had to call you. I'm not going to the hospital." He sounded annoyed, and it annoyed me that they were talking to us about each other like they weren't both in the room. As he got closer, I could see a couple of days' worth of stubble on his face. It was obvious he hadn't showered; his hair was greasy and he smelled sour, like sweat, alcohol, and vomit. There were stains on his T-shirt, some white, others were wet, turning the shirt darker.

"This isn't the first time he's done this," the friend said. "He knows he can't drink anymore or this will happen."

Fiore walked back toward the front door and told Central we're gonna need EMS. "They're three minutes out," he said quietly to me, and I said, "Joe, if he doesn't want to go to the hospital, let his friend deal with him."

Fiore shook his head. "No, let EMS take a look at him first."

The puker got a little loud now and said, "I'm fine, why do you have to worry all the time—" he started coughing and retching. He walked toward the basket and barfed out a stream of bright red blood.

111

His friend yelled, "If you don't stop, you're gonna die!"

I stepped back so I wouldn't get any on me and said, "Buddy, you got problems."

We heard a knock on the door a few minutes later, and Fiore opened it to a couple of EMS workers we've met before. These two had been around a while, they had that worn-out look they get after they've had more than five years under their belt. One was a female, heavyset with short dark hair. The other was taller and thinner, with balding blond hair and a mustache.

"What's going on?" the female asked.

"He's puking blood in the bucket," I said. I had my back to the guys, so I tipped an invisible glass to my mouth to let her know he was a boozer.

"How long has he been vomiting?" she asked.

"A couple of hours," the friend said, hovering nearby and looking worried.

"This isn't the first time you've done this," the other EMS guy said. "How long have you had a problem with your stomach?"

"A couple of years. It's only when I drink."

Was it me?

"Hey, Einstein," I said. "Maybe you should stop drinking before you kill yourself."

"Ah come on. I just ran out of pills for my stomach. I got ulcers," he said, dismissing me.

The female EMS worker was getting the pertinent info from the friend, address, telephone number, date of birth, and information in case we needed to contact someone. Fiore was with her, writing down all the information we needed for the aided card. The male EMS worker was taking his vital signs and said, "We're going to have to take him to Claires," meaning St. Claires/Roosevelt Hospital.

"No! I'm not going." He coughed again and let another stream of blood loose into the basket.

The basket was getting full now, and I was thinking, *We better get this guy out of here.* He's bleeding from somewhere and pukes every time his stomach fills up with blood.

They put him on a fold-out chair and strapped him in. The friend grabbed a pair of sneakers for him, no socks, and a wool jacket. We all crowded into the elevator and went back to the lobby. They had given him a small plastic basin to hold, and so far he hadn't used it. The guard waved to us in the lobby, holding the doors open as we took him outside.

The ambulance was double-parked next to our RMP. Fiore found out his name was John Russell and was talking to him as we walked outside.

"You okay there, buddy?" he asked.

He nodded. He was shivering now, almost uncontrollably, and he looked ghostly in the shadow of the streetlight.

They pulled the chair over to the back of the ambulance. The male EMS worker opened the door and stepped backward into the ambulance, holding the back of the chair. The female EMS worker took the right side of him, I took the left, and we hoisted him up into the ambulance. They strapped him to a gurney as he started to retch again.

Joe climbed into the ambulance with him and the friend, and he radioed Central to tell them we were taking the aided to St. Claire's. I drove to 50th Street, just before 9th Avenue and parked outside Claire's emergency room and followed Joe and the two EMS workers with the gurney. The blast of heat from the blowers hit us, a welcome change from the cold outside.

We walked down a ten-foot hallway to where the triage nurse sat. They brought him right inside, and he was in a bed within two minutes. He was looking really bad now, and he had a gray cast to his skin. They started hooking him up as the doctor came in, and I heard the doctor tell the guy they'd have to pump out his stomach. He was complaining that he didn't want them to do it. "I'm fine, I'm telling you, just give me something for my stomach."

The doctor insisted, and after a few minutes of bickering the puker let them pump his stomach. They used a tube attached to a cup on the wall behind him that works as some kind of vacuum. As soon as they put the tube in his throat, I saw the stream of blood flow from the tube into the cup on the wall.

"What's wrong with him?" I ask the Doc.

The doctor was a male Asian, kind of compact. "It's common with alcoholics," he said, not looking at me. "The blood vessels in the esophagus bleed."

Fiore was watching them suction him. I guess the suction was working because he became quieter, and his eyes were heavy. I heard Fiore say "Doc" as the man's eyes rolled back in his head. Then a long beeeeeeeeeeeep as the alarm went off when he flatlined. I turned to Fiore to say "Everyone's buying it tonight." But his head was down, and I saw he was praying. I wondered why he's always thinking to pray for somebody and I never do. I bowed my head and prayed to God that he would let this guy live, and I thanked him that we didn't blow this off back at the apartment.

We stepped out of the way as seven or eight people descended on him. I heard the "Clear!" as they zapped him, and his body came up off the table. They had to zap him again, and then they got a heartbeat.

It took a little while for him to be conscious again. They had oxygen on him now, along with an IV and a mess of other things. They had shot him up with something through the IV, and I guess it woke him up. He had a "What happened?" look on his face and was frightened for the first time tonight. He was staring at Joe and me, his eyes going back and forth between us.

"Yeah, you're fine, buddy," I said sarcastically. He looked

confused, so I added, "You just died, and they had to zap you twice to get you back. Make sure you thank the Doc for saving you."

He nodded and didn't say anything. Central called "South David" over the radio, and Fiore walked out of the room. I heard him answer "South David." He went over to the nurse and asked if he could use the phone at the desk. When he came back over, he said, "I just talked to Sergeant Hanrahan; he wanted to know if we were coming back anytime soon."

The clock over the bed said 7:50. We finished up at the hospital, Joe notified the puker's friend, who was out in the waiting room, that he was now stabilized in the ER and they'd be getting him a bed. We went back out to the RMP. It was light out. The sun had come out, but it was still freezing. Rush hour was starting, and the streets were filling up as we made our way back to the house.

Sergeant Hanrahan was by the front desk when we got back.

"Joe, Tony, I'm glad you made it back," he said. "Take Rooney and go over to the parking garage at 243 West 43rd Street. Relieve the guys that are there, let them take the car back. You'll get relieved by the four-to-twelve guys." He rubbed his hand over his face and stretched his neck from side to side. He looked tired as he continued. "I'll be out there later to sign your books. Split up your meals. When I come out there, let me know what time you're taking your meals."

We called Rooney away from Kathy Brodsky, a female cop from the day tour that he was talking to in the muster room.

"I'm serious, my grandfather had five wives," he was saying. "All of them dead. The last wife was thirty-eight years old."

"How did they die?" she asked, her big blue eyes widening. She smiled at Fiore and me as we walked over, a woman used to getting attention from men. She was about twenty-five, tall and thin with shoulder-length blond hair.

"No one knows. I think he poisoned them," Rooney said. "He was loaded. I think he didn't want any of them to get his money."

"Didn't anyone question that all five of his wives died?" Kathy asked doubtfully.

"Not that I know of," Rooney said. "He lives way upstate in the boonies. They don't even have a Police Department where he lives."

"Mike, we're heading out, you coming with us?" I asked. I'd heard this story before, another one of his many tall tales.

He left with us, telling Joe the story of his grandfather and the five dead wives on the way. The streets of Midtown were packed as we took 8th Avenue to 44th Street and drove around the block. We parked in front of the garage next to the Times building.

Rice, Beans, and Carl Beers were there. Carl Beers, who we call Six-pack, works midnights but is in a different squad than us. Last night was his RDO (regular day off), but he worked it for the overtime.

"Six-pack my man!" Rooney yelled as we entered the garage.

Six-pack and Beans were searching a car as we came in. They had the doors and the trunk open, and Beans was on the floor, looking under the car. They joined us when they were finished, shaking hands all around.

"How was it?" I asked about the overtime detail.

"It's been dead most of the night," Rice said. "But it's cooking up now."

"We did a perimeter check," Six-pack said. "We checked all the cars that were parked in the garage when we got here."

"Good enough," I said.

"We split it up into teams. Two of us work for an hour, then we each get a half hour break. There's a heater in the office, works pretty good. Three guys work here. The older guy is in the office, and the two younger ones park the cars," Rice said. He had his own set of keys to the RMP, and he waved to the older guy, who nodded at them as they left.

The three workers were all Spanish. The two younger ones didn't speak much English. The older one who stayed in the office was about fifty years old with curly salt-and-pepper hair; he was overweight and cranky. He took care of putting the parking stubs in the cars while the other two moved them. He kept barking out orders at the other two in Spanish and moved with a lot more speed than his age and size would have suggested.

The garage was four stories and worked with elevators instead of ramps. There's two elevators that they drive the cars into to take them to the other floors. A hanging black cable is suspended from the ceiling and connects to a box. The box has two buttons to move the elevator up or down. There's a scissor gate that is opened and closed manually when the elevator's in use.

The front of the garage was wide open, giving us no sunlight and a lot of wind. There were signs posted giving hourly, daily, weekly, and monthly rates. The daily rates were broken down into day, night, and weekend prices. The garage offered storage parking and discount cards for long-term users, but everywhere you looked signs were posted: "We Are NOT Responsible for Articles Left in Vehicles." They requested that keys be left in cars because I'm sure plenty of bozos drive up in their cars and walk away with their keys, leaving their car blocking the entrance to the garage.

Joe and I took the first car coming in, a black BMW. We checked under the seats, then we checked the rear seat for a false backing. We did a cursory look at the glove compartment and console, can't fit much explosive in that, and checked the trunk. We got down on our hands and feet push-up style to check under the car, and then we let the guy go in. The owner of the car didn't even question why we were checking, he was talking on his cell phone the entire time.

Rooney came back with our breakfast. A bacon, egg, and cheese on a roll for me, two ham, egg, and cheese on a roll for him, and a turkey with egg whites on a roll for Fiore.

"Are you sure you're not on a diet, Joe?" I asked. "First a veggie wrap and now egg whites."

"I'm trying to eat right, cut the cholesterol, and keep the protein," he said defensively.

"My grandfather," Rooney cut in, "the one with all the wives. He smokes, drinks, eats butter, bacon, all kinds of crap, and he's still alive at eighty-three." He shoved his second roll in his mouth a half at a time. Joe looked at me and shook his head.

"It must be killing all those women that's keeping him young," I said.

He shrugged. "I think it's good genes. Everyone in my family lives long. My other grandfather is ninety-two, lives down in Florida. Still healthy."

Rooney and Joe took the first shift while I napped in the office on an ancient swivel chair with a slit on the seat and the foam exposed. It was a rickety old thing, and if I leaned back enough, it would've tipped. Rooney knocked on the glass at 9:30 to get me up, and I smoked a cigarette and drank the rest of my now cold coffee to wake me up.

Rooney and I took the next hour while Joe took a break. By this time the lot was filling up, and there was a line to get into the garage because we were stopping all the cars. The cement was cold through my gloves as I checked under the cars, and I could smell the oil and exhaust from the cement floor.

I could hear the cars honking their horns for us to hurry up, but I ignored them.

People were surprised that we were checking the cars and asked us things like "What's going on?" and "Is everything okay?" We told them nothing was wrong and we were just checking for explosives all this week for New Year's Eve. For the most part, everyone was good-natured about things and didn't complain. The ones who said "What if I don't want you to search my car?" were the ones we played with. A woman in a power suit, complete with briefcase and cell phone attached to her ear, huffed that this was "inconvenient and unnecessary."

"If you don't let us search your car, you can't park here," I said professionally.

She got out of the car, but she sighed loudly and looked annoyed, so when I went down to look under her car, I yelled to Rooney, "We've got wires under here." She looked surprised and a little scared, and I saw her bending down to try and peer under the car.

"Step back please," I said to her. "Mike, take a look at this."

He knew what I was doing and came around to look. He pretended to write something in his memo book, glared at her, and told her to go ahead.

"What about the wires?" she asked.

"I'd get that looked at if I were you." He waved the next car in, trying not to let her see him smirk.

About ten minutes later, this guy in a dark blue Infinity starts joking with us.

"Should I call my lawyer to see if this is legal?" he joked.

"Go ahead, give him a call," I said.

"If you find my wife's body in the trunk, am I in trouble?" He laughed.

"Not if she deserved it," Rooney countered.

We had the doors and trunk open, and I stood behind the

open trunk and took my Glock out of my gun belt. I picked it up by two fingers and held it up to him. "What do we have here?" I said seriously, pretending I found it in the car.

I saw the blood drain from his face as he said, stunned, "That's not mine!"

"Is this your car?" I asked.

"Yeah," he said, his mouth open in surprise.

"Did you lend the car to anyone?"

"No." His voice cracked. I could see him panicking as he thought who he might have lent his car to.

"Oh look, it must be mine," I said easily as I turned to reveal my empty holster. Rooney and I cracked up.

His shoulders slumped as he whooshed out a breath in relief, and he said, "You guys are funny." He started to chuckle as we waved him on.

"Good one," Rooney said.

"I know. Did you see his face?" I laughed.

Joe took Rooney's place at 10:30. Sergeant Hanrahan came out to sign our memo books and make sure we were on post. Things started to slow down by 11:00 and stayed at a good pace for the rest of the day. The four-to-twelve detail would get busy when everyone picked up the cars later in the afternoon.

Although we were checking each car that entered the garage, there was something more specific we were looking for. We weren't too concerned about the business people or the reporters from the *Times* who questioned us the most. I think they smelled a story and wanted to make sure they knew what was going on. We were looking for Middle Eastern men in rented trucks or vans like the one they used to try and blow up the World Trade Center in February of 1993. That's when a Ford F350 Econoline van rented from a Ryder agency in Jersey City exploded in the second level of the parking basement in the North Tower of the World Trade Center. The rear cargo of the van was loaded up with fertilizer-based explosives and blew a 150-foot hole, blasting through five floors of the tower. Six people died, almost a thousand were injured, and fifty thousand had to be evacuated. The blast busted two main sewer lines for both towers and the Vista hotel and poured out two million gallons of water and sewage.

The schmuck who rented the van had the brass to call Ryder in Jersey City and ask for his deposit back. "Sure, no problem," they told him and had the FBI waiting for him when he got there.

If any vehicle came in and refused to be checked, we would document the description of the driver, the tag, the make and model of the vehicle, and identification of all persons in the van. It turned out we didn't have any problems, and for the most part the day went without incident.

Fiore and I found a hot dog cart in the corner of the third floor and took it apart looking for explosives. We were careful not to key our radios while searching anything suspicious. The frequency of the radio is said to be able to trigger an incendiary device.

At 1:30 when Rooney and Joe were changing shifts, we were talking in front of the office window when we heard a witchy voice cackle, "Hey! Does your friggin' radio have to be that loud?"

"Whoa," Rooney said, actually taking a step backward.

The Spanish guy in the office was leaning toward the window, trying to get a look at the getup this woman was wearing. She was about four foot eleven, wearing a black floral house dress with a brown tweed men's suit jacket. Her hair was set in bright yellow curlers with a hot pink kerchief holding them in place. She had a face full of psych-ward-quality makeup, complete with eyebrows drawn on crooked. She was wearing black padded slippers and white Champion knee socks.

"Hey, lady," I called. "What'd you lose a bet with that outfit?" We all cracked up, even Fiore. If we weren't so tired, it probably wouldn't have been that funny. She must have come out of the welfare hotel next door, because the rest of the block is commercial. The other Spanish guy who was parking the car stopped to look at her, made the sign of the cross, and mumbled something in Spanish, pitching us into hysterics again.

Joe turned around to keep her from seeing him laugh.

"I said turn down those radios!" she yelled.

I turned up the volume and said, "What? I can't hear you, my radio's too loud," sending all of us into another fit of laughter. Fiore tried to ask her how she could hear our radios over all the other noise in Midtown Manhattan, but he kept cracking up. Rooney was just holding his side, telling us to stop. I probably shouldn't have goofed on her, but we were tired and she was busting our chops.

She shuffled away in her slippers, cursing us until she was out of earshot.

It was almost 4:00 when the four-to-twelve detail arrived to relieve us. Joe decided to come back to my apartment to shower so he didn't have to battle the fungus in the shower stalls at the precinct. We would probably only get a few hours sleep, but my couch is a lot better than the precinct's lounge downstairs.

By the time we left the precinct, it was 4:20. It was still cold, but the temperature had risen to about thirty degrees. The sky was light blue with airbrushed streaks of white. The late afternoon sun warmed my steering wheel and showed all the salt and dirt on my truck. I took 9th Avenue down to 34th Street and made a right, and by the time I hit the West Side Highway, Fiore was asleep. There would usually be more traffic at this time of day, but the schools were closed for the holiday and a lot of people took off from work this week.

There was no traffic until Liberty Street, where there are two left turn lanes by the World Trade Center buildings and traffic usually bottlenecks. Of course, there was bumper-to-bumper on the lower level of the Verrazzano Bridge, where they will be doing construction for the rest of my life.

I drove to Greely Avenue and got us home by 5:00.

8

The light was blinking on my answering machine when we came in. I hit the Play Messages button, hoping Michele had called.

I heard my grandmother's voice over the machine. She's getting more deaf by the day, and I heard heavy breathing for a couple of seconds before she said, "I didn't hear a beep. Tony, it's Grandma. Aunt Rose fell and broke her hip this morning coming out of 7:30 Mass at St. Michael's. She's in the hospital, and she's having a hip replacement tomorrow. Call me and I'll give you her room number so you can go see her. I love you very much, and call me back. It's Grandma," she said again before she disconnected.

My grandmother talks in short bursts with the authority of a drill sergeant. I picked up my cordless as the machine beeped and the next message came on.

"Tony, this is Denise," she said, talking loud and fast. "I'm sure you got the call from Grandma about Aunt Rose. Grandma just wants us to go see Aunt Rose because it makes her look good having thoughtful grandchildren. She wants to show Aunt Rose that we're better than her grandchildren. Remember when Cookie's kids only showed up for five minutes at Grandpa's wake and then went across the street to Dee's Tavern and came back wasted? That made Aunt Rose look bad, and now Grandma wants to put her face in it by showing what good grandchildren we are. Grandma and Aunt Rose hate each other. Don't go just to score a point for Grandma and feed the insanity that has been perpetrated in this family for three generations." She stopped and took a breath. "Call me when you get in."

Where does she get this stuff? I thought.

Cookie is Aunt Rose's daughter, my father's cousin. She has two brothers, Uncle Henny and Uncle B, which is short for Biaggio. Henny's a bookie, and Uncle B runs numbers for him out of the bar he owns on Clove Road. Cookie's pretty nice, but her husband's upstate in jail for attempted murder. She swears it was a bar fight that got out of hand, but it's been my experience that stabbing someone in the chest with a broken bottle is usually attempted murder.

Fiore was looking at me with a puzzled look on his face when the machine beeped again.

"Tony, it's Mom." She cleared her throat. "Uhmm, I was wondering if you had any time this week. I'd like to talk to you if it's possible. If you're too busy to come up, I can come down there. Maybe we can have dinner." She paused. "Call me when you get in and let me know. Thanks," she added and hung up.

I took my phone book out of the drawer next to the refrigerator and looked up the number. I glanced at the clock while I dialed, then I remembered that the schools were closed this week. She works as a cook in a small elementary school in the West End of the Pocono Mountains. I heard her say "Hello" on the second ring.

"Hey, Mom, it's Tony," I said.

"Hi. Thanks for calling back," she said and waited a beat. "So, how are you?"

"Good," I said. "Is everything alright?"

"Yes, everything is fine. Did you get my message?"

"Yeah." *What is this about?*

"It's supposed to snow on Friday, and I thought I'd come down tomorrow night and talk to you."

"Uh, okay," I said, puzzled. "I'm working double tours for the next couple of days. I get home around this time, but I'm gonna have to get some sleep." I tried to think of how I could swing this.

"What time do you sleep until?" she asked.

"About 9:00 or 9:30."

"I'll only need about an hour—what if I pick up some dinner and get there for 9:00?"

"Sure. That's fine," I said.

"I'll stop at Giardino's and pick up some ravioli."

"Sounds good," I said.

"I'll see you then," she said. "Be careful tonight."

I called Denise back, but got her machine and left her a message. I called Grandma back and told her I couldn't get to Aunt Rose for a couple of days, but I promised to send some flowers. I jotted down the room number, along with the phone number for Hylan Florist, so I could call in the morning.

I got a pillow and blanket for Joe. He took the couch and I slept in my room, setting the clock for 9:30. I woke up first, groggy and disoriented. I hit snooze but remembered I had to leave for work in an hour and shut the alarm off. I called Angie's Pizzeria and ordered a pie with meatballs and ricotta and jumped in the shower. I woke Fiore up at 9:50 and told him the pizza was on the way.

Fiore was running late; he talked to Donna for about fifteen minutes before he jumped in the shower. He ate two slices of pizza and took the third with him, munching on it as I drove down Father Capodanno Boulevard toward the Verrazzano Bridge.

It was 10:30. The sky was cloudy, and a fine mist shrouded the air. The temperature was still above freezing, probably in the high thirties, but if it dropped, black ice would cover the roads.

"This is good," Joe said around a mouthful of pizza.

"Goodfella's is better, but they're expensive," I said. "They make a vodka sauce pie with fresh mozzerella that's delicious."

"Vodka sauce? That's different. There's a pizzeria in Sayville that makes a good buffalo wing pie. Hot wing sauce, breaded chicken cutlet, fresh mozzy, and blue cheese dressing. I love it, but my mouth burns from the hot sauce," he said.

"Burns your stomach too; that hot sauce runs right through me."

"So what happened Christmas Eve?" he asked. "We got some time now, no interruptions." I was driving up Lily Pond Avenue, heading toward the Brooklyn-bound ramp of the Verrazzano.

"You sure you want to hear this? You just ate." I said.

"I'm fine."

I started with Christmas Eve dinner.

Joe and I were on the West Side Highway now. We went through the Gowanus Expressway without hitting any traffic. One lane was closed in the Brooklyn Battery Tunnel, and we got behind someone actually doing the speed limit, which slowed us down some. Fiore didn't say anything at first, just sat staring ahead looking at the dashboard.

"Have you spoken to Michele since then?" he asked.

"She called me Christmas morning. I was supposed to go out to the Island to spend the day with her and her parents after we opened gifts," I said. "She said she had some things

127

to think about, and she needed time. I haven't heard from her since."

"Well, you can't blame her," he said.

"Joe, it's not my fault the way my family acts," I said indignantly.

"I didn't say that. You can't control how they act. But I can understand Michele not wanting to be involved with them," he said honestly. "If it was me, I wouldn't bring my kids over there."

"So you're saying you wouldn't see your family?" I asked.

"I wouldn't put up with that," he shook his head. "I definitely wouldn't make my wife and kids put up with it." He paused. "How'd you get home?"

"Denise took me home," I said. Then I told him about Denise yelling at my father and throwing her keys at Marie.

"She hit her?" Fiore said, shocked.

"Nailed her right in the head," I said. "Hey, we put the fun in dysfunctional."

"Good," he said. "What am I saying?" he added, shaking his head.

We had parked the car and were walking across 9th Avenue, toward 35th Street.

"I don't understand why you and your sister keep going to all these family dinners, they always end up this way," he said.

"What am I supposed to do?" I asked.

"Don't go," he said. "Why put yourself through that?"

"What about my grandmother?" I asked.

"What about her? She's not innocent either, Tony—what's in your heart comes out your mouth. It's very obvious she had a lot to say about Michele, and she treated Stevie terrible."

"She's never acted like that before," I said.

"You should have stuck up for the both of them," he said. "And for your sister."

"I did stick up for them. And Denise starts in all the time. She knows how they are, yet she baits them every time," I said, fuming. "She should know better."

"Why should she know better, but not them?" He stopped walking. "You got this backward, buddy. They're the ones who are wrong." He started walking, leaving me standing there. "Come on," he said when he saw me standing there. "We still have to change and get upstairs."

He sounded like Michele.

We ran into Jimmy Murphy outside the precinct, smoking a cigarette. He worked the four-to-twelve Madison Square Garden detail.

"Hey, Tony," he said, shaking my hand. "How's Denise?"

He met Denise on a Wednesday night a couple of weeks ago at the Rangers-Montreal game at the Garden. She had gotten a couple of nosebleed tickets from a pharmaceutical rep she knows. Murph helped us out, moving us all the way down behind Montreal's bench. After the game, he took us back by the locker rooms so Denise could get some of the players to sign the little Ranger hockey stick she bought at the concession stand.

"Your sister's a knockout," he said, smiling. "Can you hook me up?"

"My sister's a knockout? I'll knock you out," I said. "Stay away from my sister. I thought you were married," I added, remembering a wife and kids.

"I've been divorced for three years. Where you been? My wife's remarried. She married the CEO of some communications company and lives in a mansion out in East Hampton. Probably pays more in real estate taxes than we make in a year."

"Then you should know how women are and stay away from them," I said, hating all women, especially long-legged schoolteachers with cute little four-year-old sons.

Murph was a nice guy, good cop. We see him pretty often while we're on our way in and he's finishing his tour. He had about ten years on the job. He was about six feet tall, brown hair, blue eyes. I didn't know he got divorced. I met his wife a couple of times, good-looking girl. Denise commented that he was a nice guy. She wanted to know why I didn't work the Garden detail so I could get her in to see the Knicks and the Rangers all the time.

"No, seriously," Murph said. "I liked your sister. Is she seeing anyone?"

"Forget it, Murph, I'm not setting you up with my sister," I said, walking toward the stairs.

"Why not?" he asked after me, sounding insulted.

I waved him away. Fiore gave me a puzzled look and said, "What's wrong with Murph going out with your sister? He's a nice guy."

"Yeah, imagine what he'll be like when she gets done with him," I said. "That's all she has to do, bring home a divorced Irish cop. I could just hear my father saying that his grandchildren would be half Italian, half ashamed. Besides, I don't want anyone at work knowing about my family, or my business."

Roll call was uneventful except for when the new XO (executive officer) addressed us. Most precincts have captains as their CO (commanding officer) but our command, because it's so busy, has an inspector, which is a higher rank. The XO is second in command and carries the rank of captain. He's been here a couple of months, but the XO works day tours, so we rarely see him.

Sergeant Hanrahan was sharp enough to scan the room before starting the roll call. If someone who was expected in wasn't there, he didn't say their name. The captain doesn't know who's supposed to be there anyway, so no one gets in trouble for being late.

He was young for a captain, maybe late thirties, stocky build with dirty blond hair. He had a round, friendly face and he introduced himself as Captain Lysorgowski. He had a brisk manner, walking quickly to the podium and addressing the roll call. He went through the usual blah-blah-blah, I'm new here, honored to be working with you, all the bull they give you right before they nail you.

"It's no secret that the morale within the department is at an all-time low." He scanned the room for nods, he got a couple of half nods. "I think a lot of the problem is how the public perceives us. They need to see that we're here to help. We need to treat the public better. If we treat the public better, they in turn will show us more respect, bringing up morale among cops."

He waited for support, but all he got were blank faces around the room. He seemed more naïve than arrogant, like he really thought if the public showed us more respect, we'd be happy.

"Oh gimme a break, are you kidding me with this garbage?" Rooney bellowed, but the captain interrupted him.

"Does someone have something to say?" the captain asked. "Do you want to come up here and say it?"

"I said it," Rooney announced.

"Then come up here," the captain said.

"No problem," Rooney said, stomping up to the front. He stopped at the front, standing in line next to McGovern and O'Brien.

"No, come up." The captain gestured to the podium. I guess he thought Rooney would be intimidated, but he wasn't. He went right up to the front and faced the roll call.

"I don't think the problem is us treating the public any better; we treat the public fine. That won't bring up morale. Paying us a decent salary for a day's work would bring up morale." A cheer came up from the roll call, with whistles and boot stomping.

"Come on, Mikey!"

"Wait a minute." Rooney held up a hand, quieting the ranks. "If I was to ask how many people here had to work a second or even third job to pay their bills, I bet almost every hand in this room would be raised. We're tired and beaten down, and all we get is grief from you guys."

Calls of "Yeah," "Give us a raise," and the old reliable "This job sucks!" came from around the room.

Fiore surprised me by piping up and adding, "I think everyone here does their best to treat the public with respect. We do our jobs and we try to do them right, but every time we come here, all we hear is what we're doing wrong. I'm not saying public opinion isn't part of it, but most of it comes from the fact that we do everything you ask of us and we don't even have a contract. Our last contract the department gave us zeros, which shows us how much they think we're worth." Fiore surprised the captain by asking him, "Do you have kids?"

He looked taken aback, but shook his head yes.

"What happens to a kid when you keep telling him he's no good? He starts keeping his head down, shuffles his feet, loses his confidence. That's the same thing that happens here. All we hear about is what we do wrong, and you know what? We do a lot right, but we never hear you talk about that. And it's not like the sergeants are always browbeating us—this comes from the Brass." Fiore seemed embarrassed when everyone started clapping, but everything he said was true.

The captain was nodding his head like he understood what we were saying. He probably just got back from some meeting at the Ivory Palace (Police Headquarters) and he was told by the Brass that low morale was our own fault. And this is how to straighten us out. He left it alone after that, talking about the upcoming year, how New York is expected to have a record number of tourists in the city in 2001.

According to him, more than 40 million visitors are expected to spend more than 17 billion dollars this year. The majority of it would be concentrated in our command and the North command. They projected a 3.1 percent increase in growth in the visitors market, and the hotels in Manhattan were expected to be at 85 percent capacity. I pictured all the walking 61s out there, complaint reports waiting to happen. All it meant to us was more robberies, pickpockets, grand larcenies, and scams.

I've seen so many scams over the years. The old three-card monte, I can just hear them: "I see red, I see black." They have ten people in the crowd working with them to entice the tourists walking by into the card game.

The parking lot scams are hysterical. Some skell will stand outside a parking lot and collect twenty bucks from the cars coming in and give the drivers ticket stubs he found on the street. Then the skell runs away before the parking attendant comes out to warn the drivers they were duped. The skells do the same with taxis. They ask your destination and tell you to give them twenty bucks because that's the fare. They put your luggage in the cab, put you in the cab, and take off with your money. Sometimes the cabbies will chase the skells off if they see what they're doing, but most times people don't realize what happened until they get to their destination and the cabbie demands their money.

My all-time favorite is the beer bottle bump, where an unsuspecting tourist is bumped into by a skell, breaking the bottle on the sidewalk. The indignant skell starts getting loud, demanding money for the beer that he waited all day for. It's usually water in the bottle, but the tourist is usually too scared or embarrassed and just throws the skell a five or ten to cover it.

The captain ended the roll call by thanking us for doing such a good job. I guess his morale speech didn't turn out the way he planned, and he looked uncomfortable as he dismissed us. I stopped at the radio room to sign out my radio and talked to John Conte for a couple of minutes before I headed out.

We stopped for coffee on the corner of 9th Avenue and parked in our usual spot, an empty parking lot on 37th Street with a nice view of the Empire State Building, still decked out for the holidays in red and green lights.

Central called us with a job from South Adam's sector. We knew from listening to the radio that they were handling an accident with injuries on three-nine and Park.

"South David," Central called.

"South David," Fiore responded.

"We have an open door alarm at 89 East 43rd Street, cross streets Madison and Vanderbilt." Which is across the street from Grand Central Station.

"Do you have a firm name?" Fiore asked.

"Negative, it just says open door alarm," Central responded. An open door alarm means the door was accessed and tripped the alarm.

I took Madison Avenue and drove north to 44th Street, coming around the block. When I got to 43rd Street I drove slowly, looking for any open doors or broken windows with gates up.

About thirty feet from the corner on the north side, Fiore said, "Wait, we got an open door here."

It was a big steel door, partially opened, with a u-shaped handle and a bolt lock on it.

"Let me just check the rest of the block," I said, thinking that if it's a back exit, someone already came out that way.

We drove up the rest of the street, which is only the size of about half a city block. We didn't see anything else that was suspicious, so I turned the turret lights on and backed the car up to the open steel door. I put the lights on in case anyone was running out from between the cars, they'd catch the lights and I wouldn't run them over.

I shut the lights and double-parked the RMP. We took our flashlights out, police issue black mag lights that can also double as a weapon in a pinch.

It was a white brick commercial building, but the open door wasn't the front entrance. There were no signs or advertisements, nothing to give us any indication what kind of business it was. There were no lights or any audible alarms, and the street was empty of pedestrians.

Joe radioed back 84, on the scene. Next to the open door were metal shutters that were blowing warm air but gave no entry to the building. When we opened the door all the way and looked inside, there was a dim light up on the cinderblock wall. We stepped onto the landing of an oversized stairway.

The stairs went down, with no access to any upper floors. Thick metal tube railings painted yellow ran along the metal stairs to a landing below. I went to the edge of the rail, and I saw that the landing below us was lit, but beneath it was dark. We could hear clinking and banging of machinery below us and what sounded like a compressor in the far distance.

We walked down to the third landing and could now detect a foul stench that I can only describe as homeless. It's a mixture of urine, feces, unwashed feet, perspiration, and bad breath magnified a thousand times. We could feel the change in temperature as we descended, and the heat from below closed around us.

It would make sense that homeless would congregate here. Not only was it protection from the elements, but they wouldn't be preyed upon like out in the street. It was getting darker now; the only light was from our flashlights. We were losing radio contact, and I could no longer hear Central transmitting, just intermittent bursts of static.

We walked quietly, holding our cuffs so they wouldn't jingle as we walked. We stopped at each landing, shining the beam of the flashlight downward, only to see stairs as far as the light would reach.

We walked another four stories down. I was starting to sweat in my winter jacket.

"I don't know where this is going," I said quietly.

"We can't receive transmission, and I doubt we'll be able to transmit," Joe said in hushed tones.

We try to avoid any spots where we don't have radio contact. If we ran into a problem here, no one would know where we were. There were probably a bunch of skells down there in the dark, and that wasn't what I was here for.

"Let's get out of here. There's nothing going on," Fiore said.

"I don't want to find out what that smell is that we're getting closer to," I answered.

We walked back up the stairs. When we got closer to the top, we could hear Central again. It was oddly comforting to hear the impassive voice that I'd recognize anywhere giving South Charlie an aided case on the corner of West 33rd and 7th. Apparently there was a heavy bleeder in front of Madison Square Garden.

The cold air was almost refreshing when we stepped out of the stairwell. We pushed the door shut, checking that the push bar locked in. We stood for a couple of minutes, listening for sounds of trouble.

"It probably leads underneath to Grand Central," Fiore said.

"It could be anything," I said. "All the trains come through here."

The New York City subway system is a world in itself. Some parts of the subway line are eight stories deep. I once read that if you include underground, elevated, and open cut lines, the mainline track for passengers is over six hundred miles. If you add the New York City Transit yards, shops, and storage areas, the entire system would be over eight hundred miles. If you put it all in one stretch, it would go from New York City to Chicago.

The busiest subway stations in New York are here in Midtown. Times Square is the busiest, with more than 35 million people using it annually. Grand Central is second, with about 31 million, then 34th Street and Herald Square with about 23 million, and Penn Station with about 19 million.

Joe called Central back 91, unfounded alarm, and we started back, patrolling our sector. We started at 5th Avenue, driving down to 42nd Street. We took Broadway south and made a right on 41st Street down to 9th Avenue. We do it this way, east to west, then south, west to east, then heading back north, going the long way through the whole sector.

We were looking for broken windows, smash and grabs in stores and cars. We checked darkened doorways and alleys, looking for characters lurking there. It was cold out, so that would keep the streets somewhat quieter, but something's always going on in Midtown.

"I gotta ask you, Tony, did you drink?" Joe said, not looking at me. I had turned onto 40th Street and was driving east toward 5th Avenue again.

"Why would you say that?" I asked, stalling.

He shrugged. "Just a hunch."

I didn't say anything at first, just kept driving, scanning my side of the street.

"It's not what you think," I said.

He looked over at me. "Did you?"

"Yeah," I said. "Not like the old days. I had a couple of beers, thought better of it, and went home before I got drunk."

I told him about Christmas Day, how Michele called in the morning to dump me. Well, not dump me, but "take some time," which is something women say to torture us. If I didn't know Michele better, I'd think she was playing games, but she's not like that. I understood how she felt about having Stevie with my family, but I didn't understand why she thought it had anything to do with us.

"Are you craving a drink?" Fiore asked, looking more concerned than disappointed.

"No, I drank more out of habit," I said honestly. "I was feeling down, and that's what I used to do when I felt down. I don't want to go back to that, even if things don't work out with Michele."

"You feeling guilty?" he asked.

"Pretty much," I said. "But I want to stop using it as a vice."

"Don't feel guilty about it. The good thing is you made a choice not to get to the place where you couldn't stop," he said.

"I guess. I think being hung over would have made everything worse," I said.

"Sometimes when things are put in our face, God is telling us he wants us to deal with them," Joe said.

"Like what?" I asked.

"Your family," he said.

"It seems to be getting worse," I said. "I can't believe Denise hit Marie."

"Things like this always escalate, Tony. You know how it is with domestic disputes. In the heat of it people don't care."

"I don't think they're gonna kill each other," I said, making it sound ridiculous. "They're not that bad."

"Tony, when you live in the middle of something and it's all you know, it seems normal. You've changed your life over the last few months. You've come to God and decided to live his way. Let him show you what his way is," Joe said.

"Do you think he wants me to leave my family?" Aside from Joe and Michele, they were all I had. Not that they did me any good, but family's family, good or bad.

"I think he might want you to handle them differently than you have been. You need to pray about it, see what the Bible says about family. It has a lot to say about how we should live," he said.

"But I can't change them," I said.

"Good thing you know that right out of the gate."

9

I was driving westbound on 39th Street by the big needle and button statue that lets you know you're in the garment district. I was almost past the ATM near the corner on my left when I saw a man being held around the neck next to the machine on the end.

I slammed on the brakes. "Hold on," I said, putting the RMP in reverse.

A tall male black had a middle-aged white guy in a gray business suit around the neck with what looked like a knife at his throat. The perp's left arm was around the guy's waist, holding his left arm down. I didn't get a clear view of the weapon, but I saw the guy in the suit's eyes bulge when he saw us drive past.

"He's got him by the throat," Joe said. "It looks like he's got a weapon."

I threw it in park and grabbed the keys while Fiore radioed Central that we had got a possible robbery in progress at three-eight and Broadway.

The ATM is a glass-enclosed lobby strictly for cash machines; it isn't a bank. It has a round counter in the center, with pens attached to chains and envelopes for deposits. There are two big columns to support the building in the middle of the room, and a row of six cash machines against the far wall.

Joe was fishing his wallet out of his pocket as we trotted up to the door. We weren't concerned about the perp getting out—this was the only exit.

"Don't leave home without it," Joe said, swiping his ATM card as we waited for the light on the door to turn green. We heard the beep and click of the lock opening and went inside, with Joe putting his card in his jacket pocket.

At this point we could hear the other sectors asking Central for our location and the type of job.

The inside was well lit. The victim was sitting in the corner on the floor. His coat lay next to him, and his tie was loosened around his neck.

The perp was hiding behind the farther column, and Joe and I circled him. I went toward the bank of ATM machines, and Joe went by the front window. Our guns were out of our holsters at our sides. Our fingers weren't on the triggers, but they were resting on the trigger control.

"Police! Don't move!" Fiore yelled. "Come out from behind the pole!"

He came out from behind the column on Fiore's side by the street. I was aware of the victim in the corner, but my eyes never left the perp.

"Hey, calm down. I didn't do nothin'," the perp said, arms out in front of him. He was wearing a long black trench coat, dark pants, and black rubber-soled boots.

"Up on the wall," Fiore ordered, the two of us coming up on him.

He complied, like a pro, someone who'd done this before. He turned against the wall between the windows and the cash machines. His arms were out, his back arched with his head looking down, and legs sprawled out spread eagle against the wall. I held my gun ready while Joe holstered his, taking his cuffs out simultaneously. Joe put his left hand on the perp's back and told him to put his right hand behind him, which he did. When I heard the sound of the cuffs locking, I holstered my gun.

"This is South David, slow it down, we've got the perp in custody," Joe said to Central.

I walked over to the victim while Joe patted down the perp, checking his pockets and shoes.

The victim was still crouched in the corner, looking dazed. He looked to be in his midthirties, with thinning blond hair. As I got closer, I could see he had bloodshot eyes, and his clothes were all rumpled. He had red marks on his neck from being held, and he had a small cut on the left side of his neck that was bleeding. It wasn't dripping blood, just congealing in the spot it was cut.

"You okay, buddy?" I asked him.

"I think so." He looked dazed. "I was just getting money out of the ATM machine, and all of a sudden someone grabbed me from behind and put something sharp to my throat. He told me to give him my money and my ATM card."

He reeked of booze, and I couldn't tell if he was dazed from the booze or if he was in shock. The cut on his neck wasn't serious, and he didn't seem to be injured anywhere else.

"Tony," Joe called. He held up a miniature meat cleaver, like the kind that come with a cutting board for cheese.

"What is that, a cheese cutter?" I asked, shaking my head. "First the machete, and now this—doesn't anyone use knives anymore?"

"Come on," the perp said. "I was helping the guy. Look at him, he's wasted. He fell down, and I was helping him up."

"It looks like you were trying to shave him," I said, grabbing the victim's chin to inspect the gash on his neck, purposely letting the perp see it.

"I found the money," Joe said, picking it up from one of the cubbyholes where the deposit slips are held. There were five twenties, along with the bank card and receipt.

We heard the beep and click from the door, and I saw Sergeant Hanrahan putting his ATM card back in his wallet as Noreen, his driver, opened the door.

"What do you have?" Sergeant Hanrahan asked. We heard the beep and click of the door again, and Rooney's bulky frame filled the doorway. He came in, putting his wallet in his back pocket, while Garcia held the door for McGovern and O'Brien, who were also making their way in.

"I got a guy here practicing to be a barber. He left his tip over there by the counter."

"I never said I was a barber," the perp said indignantly.

Hanrahan looked confused, so I spelled it out for him.

"This guy," I pointed at the perp, "was yoking this guy," I pointed to the drunk, "with that weapon. He got his ATM card and cash, about a hundred bucks."

"I did not, I was helping him up when he fell," the perp said, but quieter this time, looking at his feet.

The choke hold alone made it a robbery because of the force used. But he used a weapon, so it raises the charge to robbery one. Technically the cheese cutter is not a weapon, but it is a dangerous instrument, although it isn't categorized as one of the seven deadly weapons.

"Is that a cheese cutter?" Rooney asked, inspecting the little cleaver.

"It looks like one of those Hickory Farms things," O'Brien said.

"Check him for sausage," Rooney added.

"Yeah, the summer sausage," O'Brien said. "I love that stuff."

"I like the petit fours," McGovern threw in.

"I'll give you a friggin' petit four," Rooney barked.

"You don't like those little cakes with the chocolate icing?" McGovern asked. "Then it has the different color icing to make it look like a ribbon." McGovern was making a little square with his thumb and index fingers.

"Is that what they call them?" O'Brien asked. "I always thought those were candy."

The perp was getting mad. He was shaking his head and working his jaw, so the sarge broke it up.

"Do you want the collar?" he asked Fiore and me.

"Yeah, we'll take it," Joe said with a nod.

"I'll find someone to take your place at the bomb detail in the morning," he said.

"I'll take the complainant back to the house; you guys take the perp," the sarge said, then added, "I'll raise Central to send a bus (ambulance) to the house to take a look at his throat."

We had helped the victim to his feet, but he was still looking confused. The boss took his arm and steered him out toward the RMP.

We got back to the precinct by 12:50. Joe and I talked about it in the car and decided he would take the collar so he would get some overtime and not have to work a full tour. He was missing his family and wanted to go home and see them.

The complainant was sitting in the muster room, looking lost and exhausted. Lieutenant Coughlin was at the desk, his reading glasses perched on the bridge of his nose.

"Whaddaya got?" he asked without looking up.

"A robbery," Joe said.

"Aw, come on man, you see what I get for trying to be a nice guy? This guy's wasted and I help him up, and you're locking me up for a robbery," the perp said, shaking his head.

The lou looked up at the guy, looked at Joe, then looked back down. Terri Marks was working the desk again.

"Terri, can you do me a favor and run this name?" Joe asked.

She beamed at Fiore. "If it was anyone but you, Joe, I'd tell him to get back here and do it himself."

"I appreciate that, Terri," he smiled at her.

"Hey!" I said indignantly. "You wouldn't run it for me if I asked?"

"No way, Cavalucci," she countered.

"Why would you do it for Joe and not for me?" I asked, insulted.

"He's better looking than you," she said, smiling again at Joe.

"He's married, and I'm not," I pointed out.

"You asking me out on a date?" she asked.

"No!" I said quickly, then corrected myself. "Not that there's anything wrong with asking you out on a date, but I was looking to get you a cup of coffee," I said.

"I don't put out for a cup of coffee," she said, causing the lieutenant to raise his eyes and smirk at me. She started walking away from the desk.

"Do you want coffee or not?" I called after her.

"Make it a regular, and get me a buttered roll," she called back.

I took Joe's gun and locked both of our pieces in the gun locker behind the desk. I walked back to the cells with Joe to make sure he got the perp to the cell without a problem.

Once we got him in the cell, I asked who wanted coffee (including the perp to make sure I'm treating the public good, bringing up morale for police officers everywhere). I got my gun back and went down to the corner for five coffees (me, Joe, Terri, the perp, the complainant) and a buttered roll.

I gave Terri and the complainant their coffee, and Terri gave me the rap sheet on the perp. I scanned the old dot matrix perforated sheet to see what our guy's been up to.

Aside from the information at the top of the page that we fed into the computer, I could see our perp had arrests dating back to 1984. He had variations in his address, and the spelling of his name was different a couple of times. The date of birth was off a couple of times, with the year changed to make him a year younger or older.

His specialty was robbery. He had four of those mixed with grand larceny, petit larceny, and two assaults. He'd done time, going upstate twice. This would send him back there. His sheet was marked recidivist.

I locked up my gun again and went to the gated metal door that led to the back by the cells, holding the rap sheet and the two coffees for Fiore and the perp.

I stopped in front of the door, by the red sign that said "Stop. No Firearms Beyond This Point" in white letters. There were three other printed signs: "All Prisoners Must Be Handcuffed When Leaving Cell Area," "All Prisoners Must Be Handcuffed When Entering Cell Area," and "No Weapons Are Allowed Beyond This Point." It seemed like overkill, but what do I know?

"Terr, can you buzz me in?" I asked.

"Only if you say please," she said.

"Terr, can you buzz me in please?" I said dryly.

I went through the doorway. Ahead was the fingerprint scanner with a bulletin board over it giving instructions on how to use it. There was a bottle of Windex and some wipes on the machine to clean off the smudges, and a box of latex gloves so we didn't have to touch the prisoners and catch who knows what from them.

I made a right through a small room, which is where we

keep the paperwork for fingerprinting and arrest processing. It's mostly for misdemeanors because they don't go through the system.

There's a desk and a chair, with a phone on the wall next to the desk. Next to the phone is a stairway that leads up to a row of cells. There's about twenty cells up there that used to hold the overflow of prisoners from The Tombs downtown. We would hold them there until they were ready to be arraigned. They're mostly empty now and are used by Narcotics, Peddlers, and Street Crime when our regular cells are too full.

Straight ahead are two sets of doors. Above one door is the "Welcome to Oz" sign, the last thing the perp sees before the cell door clanks shut.

Joe was sitting at the table across from the cells, filling out the paperwork on the arrest. I gave Joe both coffees. The perp had fallen asleep in the cell and was snoring loud enough to wake the dead.

Joe made a call to Manhattan Robbery to see if they wanted to come down and do an interview. If they had any open cases with his MO (modus operandi), they'd come down and talk to him. They can also check to see if there are any warrants that aren't in the computer and any court dates this guy may have missed. We call them anytime we get a robbery, I've hit before with them. They took the info on the perp, but they didn't want to interview him.

"I'll do the complaint report, aided card, and the supporting dep, and I'll type up the voucher," I said, taking the supporting deposition from the complainant to go with the weapon and the money the perp took from the ATM.

"Thanks, Tony," Joe said. He yawned. "I could use the coffee."

The supporting deposition is used for robberies, burglaries, and grand larceny where the complainant is signing that the property taken from the crime is theirs and stating the approximate value. If five computers were stolen from a store, the store owner would sign that yes, they're mine, and they're worth fifteen hundred bucks each. This has to be signed by the complainant in front of the desk officer.

I went back out to the muster room to find EMS was finished working on the complainant. I got the EMS and bus number before they left. They said he'd be fine, and I went over to where the complainant still sat rumpled and bewildered. I did the aided card first, taking a couple of Polaroids of the cut on his neck and the bruises on his throat. I did the complaint report next. He told me he had been drinking after work at one of the Irish pubs on Broadway. He was on his way down to Penn Station to catch the train home. He said there was no one in the ATM when he entered and he didn't notice anyone outside, so the guy must have come in behind him. He said he was grabbed from behind; the guy's arm came around his chest, pinning his left arm down. The guy's other hand had the knife to his throat.

"What were his exact words?" I asked, copying it down verbatim.

"Give me your money and your card."

"What happened then?" I asked.

"He took the one arm off me, keeping the knife at my throat, and grabbed the money, stuffing it in his pocket. He grabbed me again, that's when you saw him." He was getting choked up.

"Did he say anything else?"

"He said, 'Shut up, don't say nothin' or I'll cut you.'"

I was still writing when he asked, "Will I have to testify?" That seemed to scare him.

"If he doesn't plead guilty, you'll have to. You definitely have to testify before the grand jury. The ADA will give you a call," I said.

I took him to the desk and had him sign the supporting deposition in front of Lieutenant Coughlin.

"Officer, thank you," he said, shaking my hand. "I'm so embarrassed by this."

"It's not your fault," I said, thinking what a moron he was for being drunk in an ATM late at night. He should have just painted a bull's-eye on his back.

"You okay to get home?" I asked.

"I'm getting a cab home," he said.

"Good idea," I said.

I typed up the property vouchers for the cheese cutter knife, a copy of the complainant's ATM card, and the five twenty-dollar bills the perp stole. I put them in the property clerk's envelope and gave them to Joe. The money is evidence now, but the DA's office will cut the complainant a check for the stolen money.

I was done, so after I gave Joe the paperwork, I went downstairs to the lounge to get some sleep. I had nothing but broken sleep for the past couple of days, and it was catching up with me.

The lounge was empty. I shut off the lights and took off my shirt, vest, shoes, and gun belt, hanging all but the shoes on the pegs above the cushioned foam benches. I muted the sound to the ESPN channel and closed my eyes.

I slept soundly until Joe shook me and said, "Ton, it's time to go back out."

I looked up at him, disoriented for a second. I sat up, groggy, and stared at the floor.

"Come on, Tony, get dressed; we'll get some coffee," Joe said, looking exhausted himself.

The clock said 4:55. I went through the motions of putting on my shirt and vest. I put the clips on to hold my gun belt stationary to my belt. I tied my shoes and shuffled up the stairs after Fiore.

It was still dark outside. I alternated between shivering and yawning in the cold RMP. I put the heat on while Fiore ran into the deli on 9th Avenue for coffee, but it just blew cold air on me.

Fiore came out with two coffees and the *Post*, and I drove to 37th Street to park. I drank my coffee and smoked two cigarettes before I felt alive again.

Fiore was reading the paper, and I sat there scanning the block, thinking about Michele and Stevie. I was thinking about calling her when I got home, but I didn't know what to say. It's been my experience with women that when they want you to see something their way, they don't bend on it. If I called her and said she's making a big deal about my family, it would only make it worse.

"My father's gonna love this," Fiore said, still reading.

"What is it?" I asked.

"Listen to this: 'The first professional baseball teams to play in Brooklyn in forty-three years will be named the Brooklyn Cyclones.' This will be the first team in Brooklyn since the Dodgers left back in the fifties. They had a contest to see who came up with the best name."

"What are they, the rivals of the Staten Island Yankees?" I asked.

"Yup, the Mets own them. They're a class A team in the New York-Penn League. Their inaugural season will be 2001. They're building a sixty-five-hundred-seat stadium in the old Steeplechase Park in Coney Island."

"Not bad. The Staten Island Yankees' park is beautiful," I said. It was on the waterfront in St. George, with an awesome view of the harbor and Manhattan.

"I'm gonna see about getting some tickets for Father's Day. It says the season is mid-June to Labor Day. I'll take my boys, maybe we'll take them to Nathan's after the game," Fiore said.

"Bring your gun," I said. "The place is dangerous—at least it was when I was there."

"You did your FTU there, right?" he asked.

"Yeah, I wouldn't bring my kids there," I said. My father never took us to Coney Island. He didn't like it, and maybe that clouded my judgment when I got there as a rookie. I remember my father saying, "You'll definitely get an education there; the place is a friggin' cesspool."

"It's been rundown since we were kids," Fiore said. "My father still brought us there. He loves Nathan's."

"You can get Nathan's hot dogs anywhere," I said.

"He says it's not the same. He's right, they taste better there," Joe said.

"Yeah, take your life in your hands for a freaking hot dog." I shook my head.

"My father didn't go just for the hot dogs. He used to get their chicken chow mein on a roll. You ever have that?"

"Nope, I don't eat Chinese food in a hot dog joint."

"Neither do I," he said.

"Joe?" I asked.

"Yeah," he answered, half listening as he read.

"I want to call Michele today, but I don't know what to say. I don't want to upset her," I said.

"You asking my advice on your love life?" He chuckled.

"You're in better shape in that area than I am," I said, feeling pathetic.

"Tony, just tell her the truth." He put the paper down. "Tell her you never had to deal with your family before with anyone but yourself. And even then you drank yourself through it. The truth is you don't know how to deal with them." He shrugged. "You're willing to step back and let God guide you, aren't you?"

"Well yeah, I guess so," I said, picturing an old man with a shepherd's hook waving me on behind him.

Joe continued, "There's nothing wrong with stepping back until you're ready to deal with them. You need wisdom, so look in Proverbs 3, verses 5 and 6. It says, 'Trust in the LORD with all your heart, and lean not on your own understanding; in all your ways acknowledge Him, and He shall direct your paths.' Your own understanding isn't working here. You need God's help."

I wondered for a second how God would do against Marie, forgetting for a minute that he could handle himself.

"Has anything changed there in all the years you know them?" Joe asked.

"Honestly it wasn't this bad before Marie came into the picture. I'm not saying my family was perfect, but we got along better." I paused. "So you think I shouldn't see them at all?" I asked.

"Maybe you should limit the time you spend with them until you're better prepared to deal with them," Fiore said.

"It just surprises me that I never saw a lot of this before," I said.

"Well, the Bible says the truth will set you free. God's Word is truth, and it tells us in Romans 16:17, 'Note those who cause divisions and offenses, contrary to the doctrine which you have learned, and avoid them.' The reason you didn't see it before is because you kept doing the same thing with your family and expected things to change. Until you do something different, nothing's going to change."

Central interrupted us with a call for an alarm on 39th Street, which turned out to be a wrong address. Then we got a call for a man with a knife on 8th Avenue, but no one was there when we got there, so Joe marked it unfounded to Central.

10

About 7:00 we got a call for a suspicious person. Central gave us an address for a deli on 7th Avenue between 37th and 38th Street. The sun was up now and the sky was clear, the calm before the storm if we got that nor'easter they'd been promising all week.

It was a Greek deli. There was a six-by-three-foot counter with a cash register and rows of gum, candy, and cough drops. To the left of the register was the chip rack, and behind the register, the cigarettes and the lotto machine.

I could smell the food cooking. The breakfast special was bacon, egg, and cheese on a roll for a buck fifty. A Spanish guy in a white apron and black hair net was behind the grill, frying bacon. There was a long deli case separated into three parts. The first part had salads, potato and macaroni, stuffed grape leaves, marinated tomatoes, and grilled vegetables. The grilled chicken with spinach looked good. I could see the chunks of browned garlic and grated cheese on it.

The second deli case was cold cuts; it looked like the full line of Boars Head. The third case was empty. I guess it was for the hot food that wouldn't come out until later in the day. There were stacks of premade Greek salads on top of the glass case. I guess if you wanted to pick up your lunch in the morning, you wouldn't have to wait for it later.

We spoke to a female who was working the register. The deli might be Greek, but the workers were Spanish.

"Did you call the police?" I asked. She was in her late thirties, her hair twisted up neatly behind her head.

"Yeah," she said, her accent pegging her as New York Spanish. "I called." She pointed toward the back of the deli. "I think she needs help."

A woman was sitting on the floor in the corner, in front of a glass refrigerator. She had her arms around her knees and her head down. Fiore and I walked toward the back of the deli. I could see she was dressed kind of shabbily, a waist-length wool coat with lint on it, faded black pants, and black sneakers. Her glossy black hair was long and pulled back in a pony tail. She looked up at us for a second before putting her head back down. I could see from her facial features that she was Mexican. She looked young, maybe twenty years old.

"What happened?" Fiore asked the cashier.

"I don't know, something about her boss touching her," she said.

"Does she work here?" Fiore asked.

"No, I think she works at one of the sweatshops up the block," she said.

"Can she speak English?" I asked.

"I don't think so," she said.

"Can you interpret for us?" I said.

She called someone else to work the register for her. We were getting curious stares from customers. I could see them hesitate when they saw us in the back of the store, then go about their business.

As we got closer, we could hear her crying quietly, weeping

really, a low, mournful sound. I crouched down and tapped her on the shoulder, making her jump out of her skin. She looked up at us with big scared eyes.

"Miss, are you okay?" I asked.

When she didn't answer, I looked over at the cashier and indicated my head toward the girl. The cashier rattled something off in Spanish, and the girl nodded and sniffed out a response. They talked back and forth in rapid-fire fashion, and I could pick out a couple of words like *orden grande, entranous officina, Marisol Suarez*, which I guessed was her name, and *attacko*.

"Okay," the cashier said. "She works in a sweatshop down the street. She went to work early because they have a big order going out. The boss called her into the office and attacked her."

"She needs to explain exactly what he did," Fiore said.

The cashier started talking again and the girl opened up her coat, keeping her head down. I could see her shirt was ripped and her neck was bruised. There was a bloody scratch that had welted up on her chest. She closed her jacket and started crying again.

"Was she raped?" I asked.

"No," the cashier said after they spoke again. "She got away, but he grabbed her and did other gross things, the pig." She shook her head.

"What other gross things?" I asked.

The cashier shook her head. "Grabbing himself, making gestures." She showed us a couple of classics favored by perverts everywhere.

"Ask her how she got here," Fiore said.

The cashier nodded and listened, then said, "She ran to the door, ran outside the office, and grabbed her coat and left. She said she didn't know where to go. She looked in the deli and saw that I was Spanish and asked if I spoke Spanish."

"Ask her how long she's worked there and if she plans on going back," I said.

They spoke again, and the cashier said, "She just started working there two days ago, and she's not going back."

"Can she point him out?" Joe asked.

The young woman looked scared but nodded and said, "Si."

"Tell her not to be afraid—we'll stay with her the whole time," I said. She nodded again at this, and I helped the girl up. We told the cashier to get the address for us. It was on 37th Street, but this is the garment district and there are sweatshops everywhere.

Joe got the cashier's information, name, address, and home and work phone numbers in case she had to testify later on to what she saw and what was said when she interpreted. Joe called Central to give them the address we were going to and put it over as an assault in the past. We put the victim in the car and drove down to 37th Street and made a right. The address was halfway down the block, and we parked two doors down.

I pointed to the building, and the victim nodded, "Si, Si." I motioned her out of the car, holding the door open for her.

It was a twelve-story, light sandstone building situated in between a sewing machine store and a fabric wholesaler. We walked into the building through the vestibule and down a short hallway. Two elevators were on the right, and when I hit the button, a door opened. I pointed to the panel, asking her which floor, and she pointed to the eleventh floor. I pressed the button for 11, but it wouldn't light. I realized it had been locked off. I stepped back out of the elevator and looked at the key panel above the elevator button on the wall.

"He keyed it off," I said to Joe.

"I guess we're not going up this way," Joe said, motioning her out of the elevator.

We tried the stairwell door next to the elevator, but it was locked. Now we were starting to get mad.

"Maybe there's a freight elevator," Joe said.

We walked back out of the building, motioning her along. To our left was the sewing machine place, but to the right, in between the fabric shop and this building, was an extended wall and an opening with two metal doors. On top of the door on the archway it said "Freight."

The doors were open and we walked through them, almost colliding with the super of the building. He was an Italian guy, about fifty, that I'd seen before in the precinct for burglaries in the building. He was grubby looking, balding, with tufts of gray hair sticking out along the sides and back of his head. He had a stained JETS sweatshirt over his beige workpants. If I didn't know him, I would have thought he was a skell.

"Hey, guys, what's going on?" he asked us, eyeing the victim.

"Listen," I said, "we're trying to get up to the eleventh floor, but the elevator was keyed off. Is there a sweatshop up there?"

"Uh," he started to stammer. "Yeah, why do you want to know?" He was looking at the girl, not at us.

"Do you remember her being here earlier?" I asked.

He hesitated. "Yeah, I remember her coming in early. They have a big order going out, and I saw her go on the elevator. What's this about?"

"We just need to talk to the owner," Joe said easily.

"Can you take us up?" I asked, not as nice as Joe.

"Uh, yeah," he stammered again.

We walked into the freight elevator, signaling the girl to come with us. She looked scared again, and I wondered what it must be like to be in a place where you don't understand what anybody's saying. The super pulled down the strap to close the gate, and I asked him if he remembered seeing the

157

girl leave. He looked at Joe and said, "Why, did something happen?"

Joe didn't answer him, and I cut right in with, "Do they normally lock out the elevator once the employees are up there?"

He hesitated and said, "Well, Mr. Kim told me to lock it up and not let anyone else up. Why, what's wrong?"

"Does he tell you to do that every day?" I snapped. "Or was it just today?"

He didn't answer the question, but he told us what a great guy Mr. Kim is. I'm sure Mr. Kim takes care of the super, slipping him cash to keep his mouth shut.

We reached the eleventh floor, and he pulled the gate up by the leather strap, with the bottom half of the gate going down and the top half going up. There was a locked door off the elevator, and he fished for the key. I could hear the sewing machines inside the door. The super paused and turned. "He told me not to let anybody up here."

"Really?" Joe gave him a harmless smile. "I don't think he meant us, do you?"

He had nothing to say to that, so he unlocked the door. We stepped into a big loft with rack after rack of clothing. I could hear the sewing machines loudly now, and the hiss of the pressing machine as it finished a garment. Pushing the clothes out of the way as we went was like walking through a jungle without a machete.

As we got past the clothes, the room opened up into rows of tables broken up into sections. In one section women were using sewing machines, in another were long cutting tables where men worked. The workers were Spanish and Mexican and ranged in age from very young to very old. They all wore similar work smocks as they drudged through their tasks.

I could see all eyes on Fiore and me, and I resisted the urge to yell "Immigration!" and watch the room clear.

It was cold in there—that's how they run these sweatshops, no heat in the winter, no air conditioning in the summer. Most of the workers wore sweatshirts under their smocks, and some had fingerless gloves on while they worked.

"Where's the boss?" I yelled out.

No takers here. Everyone did their best to look busy, but they knew something was up. I scanned the room and spotted an office in the corner to my right. I looked at Joe, and he nodded toward it.

"Want me to go?" Joe asked.

"Nah, I'll go," I said.

"I'll make sure no one leaves," he said.

As I walked toward the office, an older Korean woman who looked to be in her late fifties, short and plump with chin-length glossy black hair, looked up from some sketches she was looking at with a younger Oriental man.

I turned to the victim and pointed to the Oriental guy with the woman, but she shook her head no.

I continued walking toward the woman and saw her eyeing me shrewdly.

"Where's the boss?" I barked out to her.

"I boss. I owner," she said sharply.

"Is your husband here?" I was guessing now.

She turned toward the office and yelled in Korean. A short, wrinkly, greasy-haired Korean man walked out of the office in slippers and a cheesy plaid sports jacket over blue pants. He looked to be in his sixties. He was skinny, with a frail look about him. I looked back at the victim and saw her eyes widen.

Mom and Pop shot back and forth in Korean, which was annoying. I looked back at the girl and pointed to the old guy. She nodded, her head bobbing up and down, while she lifted her hand and pointed at him.

The wife stopped talking and stared at the girl with a deadly look. The old man walked back to the office and slammed the door.

I followed him, walking toward the office, when the wife shouted, "You no go there!"

I kept walking.

Joe intercepted the wife, and I could hear him asking her if she remembered the victim working here.

"No, she no work here. You leave!" she yelled.

I went into the office, pushing the door hard enough to slam it into the wall behind it. There was an old battered desk with a computer and telephone on it. Above it was a calendar with an Oriental girl in a pink sweater holding a kitten. To the left of the door was a black leather chair, and I saw a smock on it. I picked it up. It was a pink floral print, like the ones the other workers were wearing, and it was torn on the right where the victim was cut. The collar had been split, and the buttons were ripped off. On the label, scrawled in black ink, was the name *Marisol*.

"You can't touch that," the old man yelled. I held it up and looked in the pockets. I didn't care what he said, she'd already ID'd him, and I was locking him up.

"Hey, Papa San," I said, "get over here." I was still holding the smock, looking at it from every angle. He followed me out into the sweatshop again, and I held up the smock to the victim. She pointed to the smock with one hand and pointed at the old guy with the other.

Mama San started yelling, "You can't take that! What go on? Why you here?"

I could see in her eyes she knew exactly why I was here.

"This woman made an allegation that your husband attacked her when she came into work this morning," Joe said.

"Who she? She no work here. I never see her before," she cackled. "She no legal anyway."

"She can still prosecute your husband," I said angrily.

"The super saw her come into work this morning," Fiore said calmly, but I could see he was angry. "And your husband made him lock the elevator after she left and told him not to let anyone else up here."

Through all this, the super was standing behind Joe and the victim, listening intently. When Joe said that, I could see the super turning red, like he shouldn't have told us that.

"You get out. Get out!" she screamed again.

"Shut up," I said to her. I turned to Joe. "If she opens her mouth again or tries to stop me from cuffing her husband, we'll lock her up for obstruction." She shut up, but she was seething.

"Oh come on, guys, he's a good guy," the super said to us. I gave him a "don't even try it" look, and he backed off.

I threw the cuffs on the old man, and he kept saying, "No, no, I good guy. I good guy." The wife didn't come any closer, but yelled at the victim, "You liar, liar, liar!"

The super saw my eyes flash over to her and he told her to calm down, she doesn't want us locking her up too.

"Come on, let's go," I said to the super. "Take us back downstairs."

We went back to the freight elevator, and I did a fast toss of the old man to make sure he didn't have a weapon. He had a small bottle in his front pants pocket, but I wasn't concerned about it. I noticed he wasn't looking at the victim, who had stepped back from him and was cowering in the corner.

"Where are you bringing him?" the super asked.

"Back to the precinct. Why?" Joe asked him.

"Can I come with you guys?" he asked. I guess he was concerned about losing whatever it was the old man did for him.

"Are you kidding me?" I asked angrily. "I'm not taking you back with him."

"He wouldn't do something like this, he's a good guy," the super argued.

"Look at her!" I pointed at the victim. "Does she look like she's lying?"

I didn't talk to the super again for the rest of the ride down. Now I had the perp and the victim together, but it was getting late and I didn't want to call and wait for another car.

It was now 7:50. Fiore called Central to tell them we had one under and gave the address on 37th street.

"I'll sit in the back," Fiore said, getting in between them in the back of the car.

On the drive back to the precinct, the old man was chanting over and over, "I good guy, everybody know me, just ask them."

I looked in the rearview mirror at Fiore and said, "Can you believe this guy? Shut up!"

"Listen," Fiore said, "we heard you the first time, and no one is asking you if you're a good guy." Fiore probably wanted to sit back there because he's a much more mature Christian than I am, and I would have smashed the old man's friggin' face into the partition that separates the front seat from the back.

When we got back to the precinct, Joe took the victim into the muster room. I took the collar over to Hanrahan, who was standing behind the desk.

"I guess you're not doing the bomb detail either." He sighed and scratched his head, probably thinking of who else he could ask to fill my spot.

"Nope," I said.

"Whaddaya got?" He eyed the old man curiously.

"Sexual assault," I said.

"I no do nothing, I good guy." The old man smiled at Hanrahan.

"I wasn't talking to you," Hanrahan dismissed him. "Is that

the victim over there, Tony?" He pointed to the female with Fiore.

"Yeah, that's her," I said.

"Do the pedigree on him and take him in the back," Hanrahan said.

I stood by the desk and took his pertinent information, using the wallet he had on him with his driver's license and social security card. I was surprised to see that he was seventy-one. He looked younger; I thought he was about sixty-five.

I made him empty his pockets so I could count up his money and give it back to him. I counted out $54.78 he had in his wallet, a stack of business cards, and the bottle of medicine. I picked up the bottle and looked at the label, figuring it was some heart pills or something like that.

"Look what we have here," I said contemptuously. I held the bottle up to his face.

"They're not mine," he said, his English pretty clear now.

"Your name is on them, the prescription's made out to you," I said. "Nothing to say now?"

"What is it?" Hanrahan asked. I handed him the bottle of male performance enhancement drugs.

"Why does he need these when he's at work?" Hanrahan said angrily. "Friggin' perv," he mumbled.

"No, he good guy," I said. "Just ask anyone."

"Make sure you voucher them as evidence," Hanrahan said.

"I also have the smock he ripped off her," I said.

"Take pictures of any bruises she's got," he said, then added, "and call for a bus to look at her."

I nodded.

"Come on," I said as I took the old man into the back.

I took him in the back to the cells. As I was taking his cuffs off he tried to pull away, saying, "You no lock me up, I good guy."

"Sure you are," I said. And I put the cuffs back on him so he'd be uncomfortable while I put him in the cell. I left him there with Tommy Flipowitz, or Flip as we call him, the arrest processing officer. I went back out to the muster room to get a statement from the victim.

She was sitting in a chair in the muster room with Joe. She was holding a cup of coffee; I guess Joe had gotten it for her. She was looking down at her legs, which were pressed tightly together, and she was rocking back and forth. Garcia was there interpreting for us. He was going on the bomb detail but stayed to help us talk to her.

I found out she was twenty-two years old, married with three children. Both she and her husband worked and were trying to move out of East New York, Brooklyn. East New York is a tough neighborhood to raise three kids in, and them being illegal made it almost impossible for them to get decent jobs.

She told us what happened again, her story the same from when the cashier in the deli interpreted it for her. We knew she wasn't lying, between the scratches and welts on her chest, the male performance drug, and the super verifying that she worked there, we knew we had a case. Fiore had run his name, and the guy had no record. Even though we'd charge him with attempted rape, it would get banged down to sexual abuse third degree, a B misdemeanor, which is nothing.

I wasn't sure she'd come back and testify because the fact that she was illegal would come out. At one point she looked up at us with these puppy dog eyes and asked a question, starting to cry again.

"What'd she say?" I asked Garcia.

"She wants to know if she should tell her husband. She said he'll come back and kill the guy," Garcia said.

164

I didn't know what to tell her. We felt sorry for her. Here she was trying to get ahead and she gets attacked on her job; now she'd be afraid to work anywhere. She said she needed a job, she had just started this one two days ago and wouldn't even get the pay for those days.

Garcia called his wife and wound up giving the victim his wife's phone number. His brother owned a factory in Prospect Park, and maybe they could find her something there.

Joe finished up with the ADA (Assistant District Attorney) for the ATM robbery by 10:30 and went home. I got in touch with the ADA by 9:30. I vouchered the bottle of pills and the smock and finished processing the arrest by 12:15.

11

I stepped into the bright sunlight. The air was clear and cold without much wind. I walked over to where I had parked my car on 36th street and let it warm up for a couple of minutes before I drove off.

The West Side Highway was moving straight through to the tunnel, but the tunnel had an outbound lane closed, slowing me down some. There was an accident on the Gowanus Expressway, and it was stop-and-go traffic from 48th Street through to the Verrazzano Bridge. The bridge bottlenecked on the right lower level, like it always does until the right lane clears for the E-Z pass lanes.

The boardwalk was on my left, and the ocean shimmered in the sunlight. The seagulls sat on top of the traffic lights along Father Cappodanno Boulevard, facing east toward the sun. There was a hockey game going on in the South Beach parking lot. None of the kids' jerseys matched, so I guess it was just a neighborhood game.

I took Father Cappodano Boulevard to Greeley Avenue and made a left toward Miller Field, parking at the end of the block. I let myself in, going right to my answering machine to see if Michele had called. The steady red light annoyed me, and I was starting to get fed up with Michele. If the whole family thing was bothering her so much, why couldn't she just talk to me about it?

I took out my phone book and looked up my mother's number. I didn't know what she wanted to talk to me about, but since I was home earlier than I expected, I called her to change the time for dinner. I figured whatever drama she was going to bring would just give me agita, and I wanted to get it over with before I had to leave for work. I dialed the number, and she answered on the first ring.

"Hey, Mom, it's Tony."

"Is everything okay?" she asked cautiously.

"Yeah, but I got home earlier than expected, and I thought you could come by a little earlier, maybe seven?" I asked.

"Uh, sure," she hesitated. "Seven's fine, I'll just leave a little earlier." She was quiet for a minute. "If I leave here by five, I'll be okay. I'll take the streets instead of the expressway so I don't hit rush hour traffic."

"Do you want me to call Denise or Vinny to come over?" I asked. I couldn't tell you how long it's been since I was alone with my mother, and I didn't want to do it now.

"If it's okay with you, I'd like to speak to you alone," she said.

I couldn't think of what to say to that, so I just said, "No problem, I'll see you tonight."

I changed into sweats, noting that if I didn't do my laundry soon, I wouldn't have any clothes left. One of the perks of living in a house is having a washer and dryer. I missed being able to stay home and wash my clothes. I've been using the laundromat on Sand Lane; they just renovated it, so it's pretty clean. I just hate sitting there waiting for my clothes; it feels like a waste of time.

I set my alarm for 6:16 and fell into a dead sleep. It was 6:24 before I heard the alarm, and I slapped snooze for another nine minutes and dragged myself out of bed at 6:33.

The shower woke me up a little, and I was shaving when I heard the knock on the door.

"Hold on a second," I yelled, wiping my face clean with the towel. I hung the towel on my bedroom door. I threw on sweats and a T-shirt and grabbed a pair of socks off my bed, putting them on as I unlocked the door.

The wind hit me and blew the storm door backward, jarring the chain at the top. I grabbed it and pulled it in, letting my mother walk in ahead of me.

I didn't recognize my mother at first. Her hair was dyed red, I guess a dark auburn, and was cut short. It was a cute style that she had tucked behind her ears. She looked uncertain as she stepped inside. I stood there for a second, taking in the changes.

She had lost weight, a good twenty pounds. She was never fat, just kind of bloated the last time I saw her. She looked fit, like she'd been exercising. She was dressed in rust-colored dress pants, a white shirt, and a brown wool jacket. She had makeup and jewelry on. I saw silver earrings and a silver chain necklace, and she wore a snowflake pin on the lapel of her jacket. Her skin had a polished look to it, and she had eye shadow and mascara on. It wasn't overdone, just noticeable.

I stood there staring at her, not sure if I should give her a hug and kiss.

"Hi," she said cautiously. "I think that storm is coming early. It's been snowing since I was on Route 280 in Newark."

"Yeah, I thought it wasn't gonna snow till tomorrow," I said, staring at her. "You look different—good," I corrected myself.

"Thanks," she chuckled. "Am I early?"

"No, it's fine. I just got out of the shower."

I noticed she was carrying two shopping bags, and I took them from her. I could hear glass clanging as I carried them over to the kitchen table.

"What's this?" I asked.

"I cooked," she said. "I was going to stop at Giardino's, but I figured you eat enough takeout."

She cooked? I couldn't remember the last time we had a meal together that she cooked.

"What'd you make? There's a lot here," I said.

"Let's see, 'scarole (escarole) and beans, garlic bread, but I didn't cook that yet. There's stuffed mushrooms, chicken with spinach and prosciutto, rice with peas, and I baked some zucchini bread." She looked embarrassed.

"Wow," I said, "you've been busy."

I got out the bowls, dishes, glasses, napkins, and silverware while she took off her coat and used the bathroom. I wondered what was up, but I figured I'd let her tell me in her own time. I never know what's going to set her off, but I didn't think that was the case tonight. I put the bowl of 'scarole and beans in the microwave and put the rest of the stuff, except for the zucchini bread, in the oven on warm.

"I guess you're curious why I'm here," she said when we sat down to eat. I said a silent thanks for the food and waited for her to tell me.

"A little," I said.

She took a deep breath and said, "I went to rehab."

Wasn't expecting that.

"When?" I asked, my spoon stalling in midair. "I didn't hear anything about this."

"Last summer. July 20 actually—I stayed there for twenty-eight days," she said, looking me straight in the eye.

"Did anyone know about it?" I asked. She had gone just

after the Fourth of July massacre, which is what Denise calls the last family gathering my mother was at.

"Just Aunt Patty," she said. "And she promised to let me tell my children myself."

"I didn't realize you needed something like that," I said cautiously.

"Either did I, at least not until I went."

"Where was this?"

"In Pennsylvania, a place out by Bethany."

"What made you go there?"

"My boss. She didn't make me go, just made the suggestion, and I took it."

"What, she thought you were an alcoholic?" I asked, irritated that someone else besides me thought she was a drunk.

"I am an alcoholic, Tony. I have been for a long time," she said with dignity. "Part of my recovery is to make a list of the people that I've harmed and be willing to make amends to them all. That's why I'm here. I've harmed both you and Denise, other people too, but mostly you two." She looked vulnerable, like she thought I was gonna yell at her.

"You mean you got so drunk you needed to detox?" I asked, still back by the "I went to rehab" statement.

"No. They send you to the infirmary for withdrawal to detox, but I was only there a couple of hours to make sure I was stable. After that, they let me go to my room to put my stuff away, and then I went to a meeting," she explained.

"What was it like?" I asked, curious.

"It was—" she paused as if trying to find the right words, "exactly what I needed. It was strange, there were about thirty men and maybe eight women. I had a roommate, a girl about Denise's age who reminded me of her." She chuckled. "We actually got along pretty well."

I nodded.

"You can't have any chocolate or caffeine. I've cut back on both of them, but I still like my coffee in the morning." She smiled.

"How did you find this place?" I asked.

"My boss got me in; she'd been there. I had just found out that your father and Marie sold the house out from under me, and I was in a bad way. My boss, her name is Dotty, a big Pennsylvania Dutch woman, saw me coming out of the liquor store on Route 209 and stopped by to see me. I really owe her." My mother stopped to compose herself. "She's helped me a lot."

"What do you do there?" I've never been to a rehab. The cops that go to the farm, as we call it, never talk about it.

"You get up early and make your bed." She smiled. "I had a basic room, two single beds, one bathroom, a desk, and a dresser. It's peaceful. You clean your room, go to an AA meeting, and say your prayer for the day. Simple things like that. Then you go down for a cafeteria-style breakfast with the trays of food. The days are full of meetings, group counseling, individual counseling, the dentist, and gym. They make you exercise." She smiled again. "Since then I've kept it up."

"You've lost a lot of weight," I said. "You look great."

"I feel great. I was pretty shaky for a couple of months, but I feel better than I have in a long time." She got up and took her bowl to the sink, rinsed it out, and put it in the dishwasher. "You done with that?" She nodded toward my bowl of soup.

"In a minute," I said, eating what was left in the bowl. I got up to put it in the sink, but she took it and rinsed it.

"You said making amends is part of your recovery—what's the other part?" I asked.

"Well, there's steps to it," she said.

"What steps?" I asked. I've heard of the twelve-step programs, but I never paid any attention to them.

"Like admit that I have a problem and I'm powerless over

alcohol. That my life has been unmanageable due to my drinking. That a power greater than myself can restore me to sanity." She rattled them off like she had them memorized. "That I have to turn the care of my life over to my higher power."

"You mean God," I said matter-of-factly.

"Yes, *I* mean God. But the program is for all religions, so they make it the person's individual higher power. I didn't like referring to God as a higher power." She shrugged. "It seemed disrespectful."

"What else did they teach you?" I urged.

"That I have to take a moral inventory of my life. I've had to admit to myself and another human being the nature of my wrongs."

"Is that where you are?" I asked. "Making a list of people you've harmed and making amends to them all?"

"I've hurt a lot of people," she said sadly. "But mostly you and Denise."

"What are you sorry for?" I asked.

"For not being there for you. For abandoning both of you emotionally. For being angry at you for loving your father. I've come to understand that it's okay for you to love him, I was wrong to expect you not to."

"I understood why you were so mad at Dad," I said. "But I never understood why you were so mad at me and Denise but not at Vinny."

She smiled. "I'd like to say it's because he loves everyone the way they are and accepts us for it. The truth of the matter is I think he just tells me and your father what we want to hear. He hates fighting, he always did. I guess he just wants to avoid it."

She sounded like Michele.

"You reminded me of your father," she continued. "You looked like him; you became a cop like him. I've realized over these past few months that you're nothing like him. He never felt any pain, and you always felt so much." She looked sad again. That probably shouldn't have felt like so much of a compliment, but it was. I wasn't used to seeing anything but anger and bitterness when I looked at my mother, and I felt an unexpected rush of emotion.

"Why were you so mad at Denise?" I asked, changing the subject. "I never understood it."

"Denise was so angry at me. She thought if I was different, better somehow, that your father wouldn't have left. She loved him so much. She didn't want to stay with me. She wanted to go live with him when he left, but he wouldn't have any of it." She got up to take the food out of the oven, putting it on our plates and carrying them back to the table. She turned the oven on broil and unwrapped the garlic bread. She let the top brown for a minute and brought it to the table.

The mushrooms were stuffed with bread crumbs, cheese, and garlic. I wolfed them down and went for the chicken cutlets rolled with prosciutto, mozzerella in a brown sauce, and the rice with peas, onion, and garlic in it.

"This is delicious," I said. I had forgotten what a good cook she was.

"It's part of my recovery. I do three unselfish acts every day that I get nothing out of. I'm not always sure what to do, so I cook. There's a girl next door, a young woman whose husband left her with three small kids, and I drop off dinner there a few times a week. A man down the street from me, his wife is sick, so I cook for them too." She shrugged. "Keeps me from thinking about myself."

"How did the drinking get so out of hand?" I asked, then added, "I haven't drank since last summer either. Actually I had a couple of beers Christmas night, but I don't have the heart for it anymore."

"I know. Vinny told me you quit drinking and found God?" She said it like a question.

I nodded. "Pretty much. It's changed my life."

"I've been going to church too, not a regular church, one that my sponsor goes to."

"What do you think of it?" I asked.

"It's different than what we grew up on. But Dotty, my sponsor, said if I was going to change my life, why not take a different look at God? She's a strong woman—I call her a blue book Nazi. The big blue book is from Alcoholics Anonymous. Anyway, I went to church with her a couple of times, and then went by myself. I go twice a week now, Wednesday night and Sunday. And every time I leave there, I feel—" she searched for the right word, "like I've learned something important, not that I fulfilled an obligation so God wouldn't strike me dead."

"I know exactly what you mean," I said. "I go because I want to, because I love God."

She smiled, and something passed between us that said we were both on the same page.

"Where were we? Oh, how did the drinking get out of hand? Well, you remember growing up, your father and I had company almost every weekend. We drank then, but I guess after the thing with Mrs. Baxter, I started to get out of hand."

"Mrs. Baxter from our old block?" I asked, confused. "What about her?"

"You know, the thing with your father and her," she said carefully. "I thought you knew about that." I thought for a second. I remember Mr. and Mrs. Baxter being friends with my parents for a long time, then they weren't friends anymore and the Baxters moved away. I must have been about twelve at the time. They had two sons, John, who was my age, and Jeremy, who was two years younger. Mrs Baxter was pretty, and she always made us tuna fish sandwiches for lunch with those Rice Krispies treats for dessert.

"What happened with Dad and Mrs. Baxter?" I asked, guessing the truth.

"Tony, I'm not here to talk about your father. That was the time that I started drinking more, not just on the weekends, but during the day."

"Dad was fooling around with Mrs. Baxter," I stated. "That's why they moved."

She didn't try to deny it. She got up and started cleaning off the table, but I took her arm and made her sit back down.

"I thought the only time he cheated on you was with Marie," I said.

She barked out a laugh. "Tony, it's water under the bridge, and it doesn't matter anymore. I'm trying to make amends here, and I won't be able to do that by dredging up the past."

"Okay, just one more question, and not about other women. Will you answer it?" I asked.

She nodded.

"How could you let Dad get half the house?" I asked.

She sighed. "There was nothing I could do about it. Our agreement was verbal: He took the car and his pension, I got the house."

"I know all that," I said. "But why would you give a verbal agreement and not put it in the papers? It's not like it's the first time Dad and Marie screwed you over."

"Just stupid I guess," she shrugged. "I never thought he'd do that." She chuckled, "Should have seen that one coming."

"You're not kidding," I said.

She squared her shoulders and sat up straighter, "And if I think about all the things they've done, I'll just get angry again. I've decided to leave them in the past where they belong." She took a deep breath. "So I want to say that I'm sorry, Tony. For all the anger and resentment, for all the times I was mean to you, and when I wasn't there when you needed me. I'm asking you to forgive me—you don't have to answer now," she said, holding up her hands. "I want you to think about it, take your time. I'd like to be a part of your life, but I won't push you. After everything I've done, you have the right to say no."

"You're my mother, I'm not gonna say no," I said.

She was quiet for a minute and said, "Just because you love someone doesn't mean they're good for you. I've learned that. I thought that because I was married to your father and we had three children together, that we should stay married, but I was wrong. I should have left him long before he left me. I should have had more respect for myself than to let someone treat me that way. And if you need time before you forgive me, I'll understand. I haven't been good to you in the past."

I found myself telling her about Christmas Eve. I told her how everyone treated Michele and Stevie and that Michele wasn't sure about us because of my family.

"She sounds like a smart girl," she surprised me by saying. "Your grandmother hated me, and she made my life miserable."

"Did she?" I asked. I didn't remember that.

"Oh yeah. She criticized everything I did. So did your grandfather. I didn't cook good—"

"You cook good," I cut in.

"Well, they didn't think so. They didn't like how I kept house, how I decorated, how I raised my kids—they constantly put me down. We had to spend every Sunday with them. I used to fight with your father about it, but he'd say they were his parents, as if that in itself was an excuse for the way they acted. He never stuck up for me, and I always resented him for it." She got up again to clear the table. I got up too, rinsing the dishes while she put them in the dishwasher. I put the coffeemaker on while she sliced pieces of zucchini bread.

"I told Michele the same thing Dad told you, that it's just the way they are," I said when we sat down again. "I didn't let them put her down, but I just let it go because I just wanted things to be peaceful for once. I don't fight it, not like Denise does."

I told her about the fight Denise had with my father and Marie. That she told my father she hated him and threw her keys at Marie.

"What did Sal say?" she asked. "I bet he got right in front of Denise."

"He went back to his ex-wife," I said.

"Ouch," she said, shaking her head. "I liked him," she chuckled. "He stood up to me when I went at Denise. Is she upset?"

"Yeah."

"Maybe I'll go see her," she surprised me by saying.

"I don't know if that's a good idea," I said. "Denise might not want to see you."

"Well, I won't know unless I try. My daughter's hurting; I'd like to be her mother for once and help her out with it. If she slams the door in my face, that's okay. If she doesn't," she shrugged. "Who knows?"

"I guess it can't hurt to try," I said.

We finished our coffee, talking until about 9:30. The snow was falling steadily now, and I could hear the wind whistle as it blew against the window.

"Maybe you shouldn't go over to Denise's. If you leave any later, you may wind up in the middle of a blizzard," I said.

"I'll be okay. Living in Pennsylvania, you get used to driving in the snow," she said.

I looked out the window. "I don't know, Mom, we're supposed to get hit with a big storm."

"If it gets too bad, I can always get a hotel room," she said.

"Wait a minute," I said. I took my extra key from the drawer next to the refrigerator. "Here." I handed her the key. "If you get stuck, you can come back and stay here—just don't give Denise the key. She'd move in while I was at work."

"Thanks," she said, putting the key on her key chain.

I gave her directions to Denise's apartment and walked her out to her car.

She leaned in to hug me. It felt awkward, but I let her do it.

"I love you, son," she said.

"I love you too, Mom," I said quietly, and walked back inside feeling better than I had since Christmas.

12

I turned on the television and put on the weather channel. The nor'easter New York was expecting was working its way up the East Coast. The storm was a huge, comma-shaped swirling mass, 150 miles wide and 500 miles long. The news people love this stuff and looked almost giddy as they predicted that the snow could fall for 24 hours, at one inch per hour. It would be moving up the Atlantic Seaboard through the night and all day tomorrow. It was a powerful storm, the biggest we've had since 1996, when we got over two feet of snow.

Along with the snow, we were due to get strong winds, thunder, lightning, and storm surges, with tides flooding the beach areas. I calculated the distance from the beach to my apartment and figured my truck would be safer up in Midtown with me.

I packed some extra clothes and warmed up my truck. The snow was already starting to fall hard, and I figured I'd give myself some extra time to get into the city. I took the Verrazzano Bridge to the Gowanus Expressway. The wind was kicking up good, and the snow was causing a whiteout effect. There wasn't much traffic on the road, and I followed the taillights of a tow truck on the Gowanus because I couldn't see the lines on the road anymore. The snow was building up fast on my windshield, and I had the defroster blasting so the windows wouldn't fog up. I have four-wheel drive on my truck and it can handle the snow, but visibility was nil.

I angle-parked on 36th Street between 9th and Dwyer, halfway on the sidewalk. I brought a shovel with me so I could dig myself out tomorrow after the snow trucks plowed me in.

Joe wasn't in yet when I got to the precinct. I went downstairs and changed in the locker room, saying hello to Nick Romano, who was back in. I got a cup of coffee and waited by the front desk for the rest of the squad to straggle in.

Cops commute to Midtown from all over the five boroughs and the outlying areas. Some come in from Long Island, some from Rockland, Westchester, Orange, and Putnam Counties, in Upstate New York. The snow would slow down the roads and the trains. It would have to be some storm to keep all but the upstate cops from getting in. Unlike other jobs, the NYPD runs 24/7, and calling in too often because of weather is a no-no. I guess since Joe wasn't in yet, the Long Island Railroad was running late.

Sergeant Hanrahan approached the podium and looked at his watch. "I'll give everyone a little more time before we get started. The roads are pretty bad, and I guess the trains are running behind schedule."

"Hey, Tony?" Nick Romano came up to me.

"What's up, Nick?" I said.

"What does the flag of Italy look like?" he asked.

"Why?"

"Because Bruno Galotti got a tattoo of the flag of Italy, and it doesn't look right to me," he said.

"Mama's boy Galotti?" I asked of the rookie who came on with Nick and reminded me of an Italian Baby Huey. When he first started working here, his mother called the precinct and told the lieutenant at the desk that Bruno was sick and he couldn't come to work that night. She had called during roll call, and you have to call no later than two hours before tour to report out sick.

Lieutenant Coughlin was working the desk that night, and we heard him yelling, "Who are you? Whose mother?" We saw him listening, and his face was getting red with fury. "He told you to call me because he doesn't feel good and he can't come to work?" Coughlin was quiet for a minute, and then he started yelling again, "I don't care if he's throwing up, you tell him to get his butt out of bed and call me right now."

Coughlin didn't say butt, but I'm trying to watch my language. He slammed down the phone and stared at the startled faces in the muster room. "Do you believe this guy?" he said as the phone rang again. He listened for about two seconds and started screaming again, "Don't you ever have your mother call me again! If you're sick, you call yourself! What are you gonna do next? Bring me a letter that says 'Please excuse Bruno from work 'cause he's got a bellyache'?"

The lou got off the phone and told everyone at roll call if their mother ever calls him, they'll be on a fixer, standing in the middle of nowhere for thirty days. We all laughed hysterically, and Bruno hasn't lived it down since.

"When did you see the tattoo?" I asked Nick.

"In the locker room, he got MOM on top, and the flag of Italy with ITALY FOREVER under it, but it looks funny to me."

About ten minutes later, the guys who ride the Long Island Railroad came in. Since I was standing near the front doors, I could hear the whoosh of wind as the outside doors to the precinct opened. There are two sets of metal-framed glass doors with a vestibule in between. Both sets of doors are kept closed, but you could hear the rush of air between them every time the outside doors open. The vestibule between the doors has a pay phone on each side and black carpet runners over the old marble flooring.

I could hear light boot stomping, and then Carl Hart opened the door. He got to the precinct first like he always does; he never waits to walk with anyone. He's pretty much a loner and keeps to himself to begin with, and a blizzard isn't gonna make him any friendlier. He nodded as he walked past me and headed downstairs to the locker room.

The doors opened again as the rest of the Long Island Railroad riders got there. It sounded like a small army marching in place as they stomped the snow from their shoes. Joe came in, along with O'Brien and about eight others who ride in with them. Fiore was dressed for the walk from 34th Street in a black wool hat, gloves, a blue down jacket, and construction boots. O'Brien was wearing an army trench coat, green rubber boots, and a gray wool cap. Linda Ryan was the only female in the group, and she pulled a scarf from around her neck as they shook the snow from their clothes.

"Hey, buddy," I said to Joe. "Finally made it in?"

"Yeah, it looks like it's gonna be a big one," he said. He took off his hat, and his hair was plastered to his head. He went downstairs to the locker room with the rest of them to change.

Fiore came down by 11:30. Most of the four-to-twelve tour was back in, and about three-quarters of the midnight tour was there talking and laughing. I saw Bruno Galotti come into the muster room.

"Hey, Bruno," I said. "I hear you got a new tattoo."

"Yeah, the guy did a good job," he said, happy that I would talk to a rookie like him.

"Let me see it," I said. I could see he was getting excited, unbuttoning his shirt. I was gonna have him show me in the middle of the muster room, but something told me not to.

"Come here," I said, directing him toward the stairwell. He unclipped his tie, unbuttoned his shirt, and rolled his T-shirt up, revealing a big patch on his upper arm. He peeled off the patch and there it was, the flag of Italy, backward.

"Were you drunk when you got that tattoo?" I asked him.

"No, why?" he asked.

"Because it's backward, you moron," I said. "Cover that up before you can never show your face here again."

"Are you sure?" He looked horrified.

"Yup, Italy is green, white, and red. Yours is red, white, and green."

"No, it's green, white, and red." But he was starting at the part of his arm that's closer to his body, not the outside. I pointed it out, showing him where the colors go.

"What country did I get?" he said, looking like he was gonna cry.

"I don't know, Portugal or something," I said. I had no idea what country he had.

"Can they fix it?" he asked.

"Sure, they can fix anything these days," I said, doubting it.

I walked back in, feeling like I did the right thing not humiliating Bruno in front of the whole squad.

Everyone was still talking and laughing in the muster room. Mike Rooney's voice could be heard above everyone else's as Sergeant Hanrahan's "Attention to the roll call" announcement quieted the room.

He gave out the sectors and the foot posts, and the color of the day was white, I guess because of the snow. He gave Romano a DOA fixer at a hotel on 43rd Street, and wrapped it up with, "The snow is starting to pile up out there, so everyone take it easy. I saw a couple of accidents coming in, and I don't want anyone getting hurt. No rushing to jobs, and try to refrain from doing 360s in the parking lots." His mouth twitched. "There should be chains in the trunks of the RMPs." He raised his eyebrows and tilted his head in a "Yeah, that's likely" look. "Since we'll be getting more than four inches of snow, you're gonna need them. If you don't have any chains, come and see me. I don't want you going out without them. Check your sector, check your foot post, we don't want any homeless freezing out there."

We have to watch the homeless in weather like this because if they're loaded, they can pass out and freeze to death. Nobody wants a frozen dead body on their post—how do you explain someone frozen on your post? A body would have to be there awhile to freeze, but it has happened. In the winter we usually bring the homeless to the hospital on a night like this. Most of the time they won't go to a shelter, and personally, I've never taken one there. The fact that it was freezing outside would justify calling an ambulance.

Hanrahan called Joe and me over after the roll call.

"You guys up for some OT in the morning?" he asked.

"Yeah, I brought clothes in anyway. I figured you're gonna be short on the day tour," I said.

"Yeah, me too, the railroad's gonna be delayed anyway. I might as well make some money," Joe added.

"Alright, I'll give you your posts in the morning for the bomb detail." He wrote down on the roll call, putting an asterisk next to our names.

Vince Puletti was still on vacation, and my old partner, John Conte, who was covering for him, was out. Garcia, Mike Rooney's partner, still wasn't in, so they had Rooney giving out the radios. At least he was supposed to be in the radio room, but instead he was over by the desk, blabbering with Rice,

Beans, and Yolanda Santiago from the four-to-twelve tour. He was so loud and obnoxious, trying to impress Yolanda with some baloney about how much money he won betting on the illegal football tickets some numbskull in the squad was running. You'd think Rooney would have the brains to shut up about it in the precinct.

I got my keys to the RMP out. When I walked over to the radio room, Rooney told Yolanda to hold on a second and swaggered over to the radio room twenty feet from the desk.

He popped his head into the room, holding onto the door frame as he leaned in. I was first in line signing out my radio, with about fifteen people behind me when he came in.

"Hey!" he growled, "Make sure you sign out your radios."

"*You're* supposed to be signing out the radios," I said, but he was already gone.

He stuck his head back in and yelled, "You hear me, Cavalucci?"

I smiled. He was such a schmuck. I turned back to look at him, and I saw him say something to Yolanda and walk outside, probably to throw snowballs at the four-to-twelve cops still coming in.

Everyone signs the radio log with their name next to the number that matches the radio. I signed out our radios "276 Rooney" and "277 Rooney" next to where Joe's and my names should have gone. Then I pointed it out to McGovern so he could see it and follow suit. He smiled and nodded, signing "278 Rooney" underneath mine, and gestured to the guy behind him to do the same.

"Joe, where's our car?" I asked, handing him his radio.

"Across the street. Why?" he asked.

"Let's get out of here," I said, laughing.

"Why, what'd you do?" he asked suspiciously.

"I'll tell you when we get in the car." I nodded toward the front door so he would get moving.

"Want a ride to post, Nick?" I asked Nick Romano, who was on the front steps smoking a cigarette.

"Sure, I'll take a ride, thanks," he said. Technically he's supposed to walk to his post, but no one will say anything if we give him a lift. Some old-timers could be real hard about it and would make you walk.

I kept my eye on Rooney as he walked back inside toward the radio room that now had a line of only two people.

"What'd you do, Tony?" Fiore asked again.

"Ah, Rooney was being cocky about signing out the radios and singled me out in front of everyone. So I signed out our radios with his name, and everyone else followed."

Joe smirked and shook his head. He knew that Rooney would have no idea who signed out what radio and that he would have to straighten it out before the night was over.

Our car already had chains on it, so we dusted off the snow that had accumulated on the windows. We tossed our hats in the backseat with Romano, adjusted our gun belts, and put our radios in the door handle. I backed the car out and saw Rooney come running out of the front doors of the precinct.

"Cavalucci!" he roared. He was working himself up into a frenzy, scrambling to gather up some snow as I started driving toward 9th Avenue. He swung his arm back too hard as he started to throw a snowball at the car, and his feet went out from under him.

We cracked up at the sight of him slipping as he tried to get up.

"Shouldn't we see if he's okay?" Romano asked, still laughing.

"Are you kidding me?" I said. "Knowing Rooney, he'll find

a way to get out on three-quarters for this. He'll be thanking us later."

The plow trucks had gone down 9th Avenue, but the precinct block still wasn't cleared. Why would the city plow a block where emergency vehicles need to get in and out?

We stopped on the corner of 9th Avenue and 35th Street for coffee and drove around to 34th Street past the Lowe's Theatre and up 8th Avenue. The shrubs along 34th Street toward Macy's twinkled with Christmas lights and gave the empty streets of Midtown Manhattan the feel of a small town. The light turned red as I approached the intersection of 42nd Street and 8th Avenue. I looked down to take my coffee out of the cup holder, and something caught my eye across the street on the northeast corner.

A bunch of skells had a boom box set up on the curb. It blasted out an old Four Tops song while the snow collected on top of it. They were dancing chorus line style to the song. Fiore, Romano, and I stared for a couple of seconds in amazement as they danced in the westbound lane of 42nd Street.

They were a sorry bunch, teeth missing, holes in mismatched filthy clothes. I'm sure they stunk of booze and homeless, but I had to admit they danced pretty good. Alcohol was definitely at work here; I saw a few paper bags next to the radio.

"Are they doing the bus stop?" Fiore asked, still staring.

"I think it's the electric slide," I said, surfing the radio, trying to find the song they were playing.

"Nope, it's the cha-cha slide," Romano said, wiping the fog off his window to get a better look.

I hit pay dirt on 101, the oldies station, and put the Four Tops song over the PA system of the car. A cheer came up from the skells, and they danced away, waving at us and wishing us a happy holiday. I drove up 8th Avenue with the music still playing.

I made a right on 44th Street, going around the block. I stopped in front of 245, the hotel where Romano had the DOA fixer. Joe and I left our coffee in the RMP and walked Romano upstairs so we could take the four-to-twelve cop who Romano was relieving back to the precinct.

The hotel was a white building on the corner of 43rd and 8th. To the left of the entrance was an ice-cream store, a deli, and a cell phone/beeper place. The front of the hotel had three wide steps that rounded around the front of the building, leading up to a wide set of glass doors.

It was an old hotel, used mostly by senior citizens and welfare recipients. It was the remains of what was once a grand hotel. The outside still had the original detail of the building—ornate scroll work, large oversized windows, and on the upper floors I could see the cement gargoyles perched on the ledges around the building.

The lobby was spacious, with groupings of old couches, chairs, and coffee tables set up in different places. To our left was an old bellhop desk. In front of the lobby doors, set back about twenty feet, was the security desk. Big marble columns could be seen throughout the room; they looked to be part of the structure rather than decoration. There was a smattering of people in the lobby. Two old men were playing checkers while a third looked on. It was just before twelve, so most of the old folks were in bed.

We threw a wave at the security guard and turned to the left, past the empty registration desk toward the elevator.

"So how was the holiday, Nick?" Fiore asked.

"Pretty good. I had my daughter most of Christmas Day," he said. Nick had a baby with a woman he was involved with up until about a year ago. She got pregnant but didn't want to get married, and she dumped Romano after the baby was born. He took it hard for a while, but he's better about it now.

"Oh!" he said loudly, getting excited. "I had my first interview with the Fire Department." He was on the list to go over to FD. He hated being a cop and couldn't wait to trade bullets for fire hoses.

"How'd it go?" I asked.

"Pretty good, I think," he said, biting his thumbnail. "I mean, the guy who interviewed me seemed up-front, not like the Police Department interview where they try to mess with your head. It was pretty straightforward, personality profile, family background, current job, hobbies, those kinds of things."

"Where was the interview?" This from Fiore.

"Down in South Brooklyn near Jay Street, 9 Metrotech."

"Any idea when you'll get called?" Fiore asked.

"Hopefully soon. Next is the psychological profile and the medical. Once I pass those, I wait for the call for the Academy. If nothing holds up the list, it shouldn't be too long," he said.

"Good for you," Joe said.

"So, you're gonna be a hose head?" I laughed.

"Better than a flat foot," Nick countered. "At least the hours are better."

"Can't argue with you there," Joe said.

We got off on the 23rd floor into a dimly lit hallway. There was a musty smell to the place, probably more pronounced because of the damp weather. I'd been to this hotel before on jobs, mostly for nut-job EDPs (emotionally disturbed persons). It's a sad place that makes you wonder what happens to people that they end up here alone. We walked east, toward room 2321. The DOA was a couple from the end, and there was a chair outside the door where the four-to-twelve rookie had been sitting.

He was an Irish guy, O'Malley his name tag said. He was young, early twenties with short blond hair and blue eyes. He was pretty big, over six feet tall, with a solid frame. He stood up and stretched when he saw us, putting the newspaper on the chair.

I saw lights flickering in an open doorway a little farther down the hall.

"What's up?" I asked O'Malley as I pointed to the open door.

O'Malley said, "You gotta see this." He tiptoed over to the doorway, waving us over to follow him. "Check this out," he whispered, pointing to the interior of the room.

It was a small room with a shrine of some sort. I couldn't tell what it was from where I stood. It didn't look like voodoo; I've seen enough of that to know it. A table holding about fifty candles in red glass containers was set in the middle of the room. Sort of like the candles you see in church. They were all lit, set up on tiers, flickering in the middle of the dark room. There were statues that I didn't get a close enough look at, because O'Malley pointed past the candles to where a man was lying in an open casket.

The casket was light wood, and the satin lining was black. I've never seen anything like this at a wake, so it must have been custom-made. The guy was ghoulish looking, pale white skin and long, stringy black hair. He had some kind of Alice Cooper thing going on. His arms were folded across his chest, and his nails were painted black. He wasn't gothic, just dawn-of-the-dead looking. He was wearing a black satin robe, making his face look like it was floating among the black fabric.

We were standing there whispering, but the guy didn't look up. He wasn't dead, and I doubted he was sleeping with the door open. I was sure he could hear us talking and wondered what he was up to. We watched him for a few minutes as he lay there motionless.

"Let's get out of here," I said. The room was creepy, like it had an evil presence in it. I was gonna go in and blow out the candles, but I didn't want to step into the room.

"Is that the fixer?" Romano asked, looking shaken.

"No, he's over here," O'Malley said, pointing back to the door that he had been sitting outside of.

We moved away from the door, then Fiore said, "Nick, don't go near that room."

"Why?" Romano asked, almost panicking.

"Because the guy is evil," I said.

"How do you know?" Romano whispered.

"The casket and the candles are pretty good indicators that the guy likes the dark side," Joe answered.

"What if he comes out here?" Romano whispered.

"What are you whispering for?" I slapped him on the side of the head. "Shoot him if he comes out."

"No, seriously, Tony," he said, ducking his head away.

"Seriously, shoot him," I said, blankly. "You should be more concerned about the DOA—now if he moves, he's already dead, so you could shoot him."

When I was a rookie, something like this would have freaked me out too. Over the years I've gotten used to seeing freaks like the guy in the coffin.

I opened the door to the DOA's room and walked inside. Fiore and Romano came in behind me. It was a small room, with a bathroom. There was a single bed against the far wall, a broken-down night table, and a shabby dresser. The guy didn't have many possessions. I saw some medicine bottles on the dresser, with a wallet and an eyeglass case. There was a glucose monitoring machine and a small vial of test strips. A stack of papers was on top of the dresser, and I saw Medicare statements, some legal papers from Social Security, a Publishers Clearinghouse envelope, and some bank statements. There was a large-print word search book on the night table, a glass with teeth in it, and an overflowing ashtray full of butts. One butt had a long ash; I guess that was his last cigarette.

There was a strong smell of cigarettes in the room with the underlying smells of urine, feces, and mustiness. An old museum print with a dented brass frame was leaning against the wall on the floor. I could see the hole in the wall where the nail was.

The room was warm. There was an old steam radiator under the window, the kind my grandmother used to dry socks on. The window was open about an inch, blowing a dark green curtain. I could hear a plow truck pass below us on 43rd Street.

The DOA was in the bathroom. It was a small bathroom with the original porcelain tub and sink. A radiator about half the size of the one in the other room hissed under the bathroom window. The sink had a constant drip, leaving a reddish brown stain in the path of the water. The tub had the same stains in the drain, with a little aqua blue color mixed in. The grout was molded around the tub and in between the little white tiles enclosing the bathtub.

He must have gotten out of the tub and fallen. He had a towel wrapped around his waist. He had one black slipper on his right foot; the other lay haphazardly near his left. Urine and feces were on the floor, melting into the condensation that covered the room.

He was an elderly man, unshaven and in need of a haircut. He was heavy around the middle, with the chest scars of heart surgery. His hand had nicotine-stained fingers and long yellowed nails. There was a small tumor on his left temple, but other than that nothing notable.

There was no family and no one to notify, or the case wouldn't have gone to the detectives to see if they could find any next of kin. The guy must have had money to live in a hotel in Midtown, no matter how cheesy it was. The welfare residents are subsidized, but the old folks have to pay. It's sad to see someone die like this, alone without anyone but us to acknowledge his death. I said a quick prayer for the old guy, asking God to have mercy on his soul, and we went back out into the hallway where O'Malley was waiting.

Romano looked at Fiore. "Why don't you guys hang out here awhile?"

"We gotta take O'Malley back to the precinct. We'll come back later and check on you," Fiore said. "If the coroner comes and takes the body before we get back, give us a call and we'll come get you."

"Okay." Romano nodded. "Thanks, Joe."

My coffee was cold when I got back to the RMP. The snow was really swirling now, and we took it slow on the way back to the precinct.

"Wow, it wasn't even snowing when I went to the fixer," O'Malley said, watching the blizzard around us. "I hope I can get home."

"Where do you live?" Joe asked.

"Long Island, Massapequa," he said.

"Good luck," I said.

"The trains are running late, but you'll get home. I don't know about in the morning—it's supposed to snow all night into tomorrow afternoon," Joe told him.

We dropped him off in front of the stairs at the precinct, with a message. "Tell Rooney to make sure he logs in your radio."

"Why?" O'Malley asked, puzzled.

"Tell him Tony said make sure you log in the radio, and then duck." I laughed.

"I'm not saying anything to Rooney, I don't have any time on yet," he said as he closed the car door.

"What's up with babying Romano?" I asked Joe as soon as O'Malley got out of the car.

"I'm not babying him. I think there's a lot going on underneath the surface with him. I just want to make sure he's okay. He's a kid. If you were a rookie, that guy in the coffin would have spooked you," Joe said.

"No, I would have gone in, lit a cigarette, and blew out the candles," I laughed.

"You're full of it, Tony, that would have bothered you," Joe said.

"Yup, and it's gonna bother Nick, and he's gonna get through it. That's how you learn," I said.

13

We stopped on the corner of 9th Avenue for another cup of coffee, tossing the cold ones in the garbage can outside the store. I drove through our sector, then went up to Times Square. I parked on the north side of 44th Street, just west of 7th Avenue next to MTV Studios.

We sat in our car, drinking coffee and watching the light show. The super signs, NBC, Astrovision by Panasonic, the Dow Jones zipper, Budweiser, Cup O Noodles, and Coca Cola advertised their goods oblivious to the snow. The thousands of other smaller signs joined in and lit up the night with every color imaginable. The snowflakes picked up the colors from the signs until they fell out of the touch of lights.

I sat there thinking about the dinner I had with my mother, the stuff she said about how my father was about the family. I don't know which bothered me more, that Michele agreed with my mother on the family stuff, or that I thought like my father about it. I almost brought it up to Fiore, but his cell phone rang and he was talking to Donna about his daughter having a fever.

I looked over at Barbara Walters smiling down from the

giant reader board at ABC Studios, where they broadcast *Good Morning America*, *Nightline*, *20/20*, and *World News Tonight* from the Times Square Studios. The electronic headline that wraps itself around the building spelled out the news from around the world in moving letters. It warned us that a powerful winter storm would be arriving in New York City in the early hours of the morning. I wondered if actual scientists work for the weather bureau, since it was after midnight and it had already been snowing for three hours. The weather people are never right. We already had three inches on the ground, and it looked like the snow had no plans to stop.

The weather report went on to say that we would have gale-force wind, heavy snow, rough seas, and strong onshore winds.

The house that I grew up in, which was sold a few months ago, was right on the Narrows of New York Bay. When I lived there, I would've loved a storm like this and probably would've watched most of it from out on my deck.

"South David," Central radioed.

"Hold on, honey," Fiore said to Donna, then, "South David."

"10-1 the house." Which means call the precinct.

"10-4," Fiore said and chuckled. "I guess Rooney's trying to figure out the radios."

"Ignore him," I said. We knew it wasn't the lieutenant because he would have just transmitted as "South Base, have South David 10-1 the house." This was Rooney waiting by the phone at the desk, panicking because he has no idea who has what radio.

Joe shut his cell phone, put it in his jacket, and asked, "How was dinner with your mother?"

"Interesting."

"It usually is with you." He laughed. "Want to talk about it?"

"Don't you ever get tired of listening to my crap?"

"Nah, it breaks up the monotony. What'd your mother want to talk to you about?"

"She went to rehab." I barked out a laugh and rubbed the back of my neck. "It wasn't funny really, I mean, she seems to be taking it serious. She went in last July, and she's been sober ever since."

He nodded. "This is a good thing."

"I know. She said she's been going to church too. She was telling me about the rehab place she went to. She said it was helpful, I guess it was 'cause she hasn't drank since. She looks good. She lost weight and cut her hair." I shrugged. "She did the AA bull."

"AA bull?"

"You know, 'I want to apologize for all the rotten things I did to you while I was drinking,' blah-blah-blah."

"You think she's legit?" Joe asked.

"She sounds legit, and I was glad when she said it, but I don't know how much I trust her. I figure I'll give it some time, see how it goes." I said it lightly, like it didn't matter. The truth was I wanted her to be legit, but our track record goes back a long way. I guess I find it hard to believe that someone could be a mean and nasty drunk for twenty years and be all better after twenty-eight days of rehab. She was mean all the time, not only when she was drunk.

"Time will tell. Did you tell your sister?" Joe asked.

"No, my mother was actually going over there tonight when she left my house."

Fiore's eyebrows shot up.

"Yeah, I know—I gave my mother the key to my apartment for when Denise tosses her out in the snow." I rolled down the window and lit a cigarette. "I figured I'd call Denise in the morning and find out who came out alive."

"My money's on Denise," Fiore said.

"Mine too."

"God is really moving in your family."

I looked at him, puzzled. "What's that supposed to mean?"

"I mean, look at all the good stuff that's happening." He counted off on his fingers, "Your mother is sober and going to church, Denise is in therapy, and you're taking a step back from the family so you're not caught up in all the drama anymore."

I guess this is the perfect example of the glass half full versus the glass half empty. Fiore sees things going good with the family; I see it that the family is insane and my girlfriend left me because of it. The jury's still out on my mother, so I'm not gonna start celebrating.

We heard Central radio South Charlie to 10-1 the house.

A scraping sound, which I dismissed as a plow truck coming down 7th Avenue, was coming south toward us. As the sound got closer, I realized it wasn't a plow truck but a guy dragging a cross through Times Square.

I've seen him before, usually in the nice weather. He was a male black, I guess in his late thirties, early forties. He was in good shape, about six foot with a solid build and short-cropped black hair. He's homeless, and he's not all there.

The cross was big, over six feet, made out of treated four-by-fours. I usually see him in the summer, when the streets are packed with pedestrians. He usually wears shorts and a muscle shirt and sneakers with no socks. Today he dressed all in black, with a black bubble jacket over his clothes.

Fiore was watching him intently as he got closer to us.

"Don't even think about talking to him. He hates cops," I said. "Not a happy camper."

"You know this guy?"

"I've seen him around. He's always dragging the cross."

"It looks heavy. Where'd he get it?" Joe said. We could hear the heaviness of the wood by the scraping sound it made against the street.

"I have no idea."

He had a rope tied around his chest, almost like a harness. The rope was tied around the "T" of the cross. He had a drawstring sack tied around his waist, over his jacket. His hands were inside the rope, and the weight of the cross rested on his shoulders. He walked with his head down, and I could see the path the wood left through the snow.

The sound of the wood was getting louder now, and the few people walking around Times Square stopped to stare at him.

"Why would he do that?" I asked.

"He's nuts," Fiore said, and laughed. "Just kidding." He shook his head. "I'm hanging out with you too much—I'm starting to sound like you."

"What's the deal with him, what's he trying to prove?"

He shrugged. "Sometimes people take the Bible out of context. There's a Scripture in Mark 8:34 that says, 'Whoever desires to come after Me, let him deny himself, and take up his cross, and follow Me.' It doesn't mean what this guy's doing."

"Then what does it mean?"

"It means that if you follow Christ, you have to deny yourself, your own fleshly desires, and your own agenda and get with God's agenda. It doesn't mean we have to be crucified, He did that for us."

"For our sin, right?"

"Yeah, for our sin," he said.

"South David," Central interrupted.

"South David," Fiore answered.

"We have a 10-13 at West 34th and 7th in the subway."

"What line?" Fiore asked.

"The #1 line," Central said, giving us the location for the 1, 2, 3, or 9 trains, letting us know where in the subway.

199

"10-4, Central."

A 10-13 is an officer needing assistance. It was in the subways. More than likely a transit cop put it over the radio, but all available officers respond. I drove South on 7th and made a right onto 34th Street. I parked at the southwest corner of 34th and 7th, which is the entrance to Penn Station and the Long Island Railroad.

I turned off the car and locked it up. I didn't want someone stealing the car or hocking up a lunger on our seats while we were down in the subway. I left my car unlocked once in the winter and came back to find a skell sitting in it with the heater cranked up to keep warm. On our way into Penn Station we heard Central radio South Adam to 10-1 the house, and we laughed out loud.

We took the escalator down, taking the stairs two at a time. The Long Island Railroad was in front of us at the end of the corridor, so we were doing a quick jog. We had radios in our left hands, and our gun belts squeaking, and our keys jangling. Penn Station wouldn't normally be this quiet at this time of night. I guess the storm must have sent everyone else home, it was like a ghost town.

We made a left just before the Long Island Railroad, and there were five transit cops, all male, standing in a circle outside the 1, 2, 3 line. They looked up as we came around the corner right outside the turnstiles.

"Everybody alright?" we asked.

"Yeah, everyone is accounted for, it's unfounded," the Transit Sergeant answered. "Thanks for showing up."

Sometimes the "Officer needs assistance" calls are 911 pranks, or people see something and they overreact, thinking a cop is in trouble. You never know if it's legit, so you always hurry to get there. We stayed with them for a few minutes, talking about the storm and the delays on the Long Island

Railroad. Joe radioed Central to give it back 90X, unfounded by Transit.

We got a call for an alarm at 250 West 39th Street. It was an office building that was locked. We didn't see any footprints leading to the front door, or any broken windows. We called it back 90 Nora 3, or premise secure.

At 2:30 we got a call for a car accident at West 42nd and Park. No one was there when we got there, so we asked Central if there was any other info. Central replied there was nothing further, so we marked it unfounded. We drove around the immediate area, but the streets were deserted.

I parked in a lot on 37th Street. Joe was starting to nod off, so I cranked up the heat and rolled down the window to smoke a cigarette. I thumbed through the paper, reading an article about Mayor Lindsay, who died earlier in the week. The article was about the city's fondness for the mayor who believed in New York. It said he used to pick up litter in the streets, yell at doormen for letting limos double-park, and once walked into a bar and ordered garbage men out of the bar and back out to their trucks. Sure, they talk nice about him now that he's dead, but I'm sure the press tortured him while he was in office.

I scanned the movie section. Michele and I had taken Stevie to see *Rugrats in Paris* a couple of weeks ago, and my stomach felt sick when I saw the advertisement for it. For a week after we saw it all we did was sing, "I see London, I see France, I see Coco's underpants."

The next thing I knew, someone was tapping on the window of the RMP. I jumped at the sound; I guess I fell asleep. I looked at the clock, 3:45. Joe was snoring, his head back against the headrest. I lowered the window to a preppy-looking guy walking a medium-sized black dog.

"You guys okay?" he asked. He looked concerned. Who knows, maybe he thought we were dead.

"Yeah, just working late. Thanks," I said.

I got a better look at the dog. It was an ugly dog. The guy looked like a do-gooder, the kind who would go to the pound and save the ugly beast from annihilation. As he walked the dog out toward the street, the dog squatted to do his business. The guy pulled a paper plate out of the plastic bag he was carrying and put it under the dog's backside. When the dog finished, he bagged up the goodies and tied them up in the plastic bag. What a model citizen; they should all be like him.

Fiore was still snoring away when "South David" came over the air. Without skipping a beat, Fiore put the radio to his lips and answered "South David" into the receiver.

"We have a dispute at 330 West 30th Street, Apartment 214."

"10-4."

The building was between 8th and 9th Avenue, a residential block and the site of the old French Hospital.

"Those are the French apartments," I said, "the old French Hospital where Babe Ruth was. I think he died there."

"Really?"

"Yeah. I wonder if your Dad knows that?" I said. Fiore's father knew more about baseball than anyone I know.

"I'm sure he does, but you could try and ask him."

Fiore's dad and I have this ongoing contest where I try to come up with a question about baseball that he doesn't know the answer to. Over the last few months I've spent a lot of time at Fiore's house. Fiore's close with his dad, so I see him a lot. He's a Mets fan, and Fiore and I are Yankee fans. He's obsessed with baseball and the Brooklyn Dodgers. We talk baseball all the time, and he's amazing with what he knows. I found a book on baseball trivia at a newsstand on Broadway. I went through the whole book, everything from batting averages, World Series, All Star games, and career stats, and I couldn't get him on one question. I even started going to the library to find something to stump him.

"I think I found a question your father doesn't know the answer to," I told Fiore.

He laughed. "Sure you do."

"Seriously, I ran into this old guy at Montey's last week. We were getting sandwiches, and he and Montey were talking about the Yankees signing Mike Messina from Baltimore. Anyway, this guy reminded me of your father, and I told him I was trying to come up with a question he didn't know the answer to. The guy was a Yankee fan, and he gave me something good about Babe Ruth."

"Tony, my father knows everything about Babe Ruth."

"Maybe not," I said.

I pulled up in front of the building. It was a long, white brick building that at one time was connected to the building next door. It was five stories high, a security building with a guard in the lobby.

The security guard buzzed us in. He was an older white guy who looked to be in his early sixties.

"How you guys doing?" he asked as we brushed the snow off ourselves.

"Pretty good. We got a call for a dispute in apartment 214," Joe said.

"Take the elevators over there," he pointed across the lobby, "and make a right when you get off the elevator."

"Thanks," we said.

The elevator was waiting at the ground floor, and we took it to the second floor. The hallway was carpeted, muting the sounds of our footsteps as we walked. It was quiet in the building, and aside from the occasional TV I heard as we passed an apartment, there were no signs of a dispute.

"So what's the question about Babe Ruth?" Fiore asked.

"It's not about Babe Ruth, but it's about the curse of the Babe. When Harry Frazee sold Babe Ruth to the Yankees, I think he mortgaged Fenway Park to finance a play on Broadway."

"Tony, he knows all that."

"What was the name of the play?" I held my hands out. "Hah—don't know, right?"

We stopped outside the door to listen, positioning ourselves on either side of the door frame. We didn't hear any sounds from inside the apartment, so I tapped the door with my nightstick and called "Police!"

Anywhere else in the world, people would open their doors to see what's going on, maybe be concerned for their neighbors, but not here. This was New York City; no one wants to know.

"Who is it?" a female voice called from inside, as if she didn't hear me the first time.

"Police. We got a call for a dispute here," I said.

"Everything's okay," the voice said. That's what they all say.

"You still gotta open up," Fiore threw in. "We got a call for a dispute, so we have to check it out."

We heard the dead bolts unclick and the chain slide. She pulled the door open about halfway.

She was in her late twenties, about five foot five with long, black frizzy hair falling out of a clip on top of her head. She had olive skin, I would guess Italian or Spanish. She was one of those women whose every move is orchestrated to seduce. She wasn't good-looking enough to do it without props, so she had to resort to other things, like answering the door naked.

"Ma'am, can you put some clothes on please?" Fiore said politely. He kept his eyes above her neck.

Not me, I checked her out. Michele needs some time? Fine, all bets are off.

She turned around and walked back inside, so I got the whole deal.

It's not uncommon for us to answer jobs and find people in various stages of undress, but this was the first time someone actually answered the door completely naked.

Fiore was looking inside the apartment, his eyes fixed on the pair of legs sticking up in the air as a pair of boxer shorts was put on.

The small kitchen was to the left of the front door. Straight ahead was the living room, with a hallway to the right that I guess led to the bedroom.

A bunch of blankets were on the floor of the living room, where a light-skinned Spanish man who looked to be in his midthirties was sitting on the floor, holding his pants. He had short brown hair and a medium build. He turned down the Toni Braxton tune on the stereo and stood up.

"Who called us?" I asked. No one looked like they were in trouble. She walked over to the blankets on the floor and bent over to pick up a white nightgown. She pulled it over her head. It barely skimmed the tops of her thighs and was see-through—not much help there.

"I called," she said, facing us now.

"If you knew we were coming, why weren't you dressed when we got here?" Joe said.

No answer from either of them.

"So what happened?" I said a little sharply. It's a friggin' blizzard out there, and I get called in for some psycho's head game.

"We had a fight, and I told him I wanted him out," she said, looking at me.

"Is this your apartment?" I asked.

"Yes," she nodded as her boyfriend stepped into his pants.

"What was the fight about?"

"It's personal," she said as she lit a cigarette and blew out a stream of smoke.

"Did he threaten you or hit you?" Fiore asked.

"She started hitting me, and I threw her onto the couch," the guy answered, pretty low-keyed.

"I told him to get out, and he threatened me." She sounded bored.

"Well, what did he say?"

She looked up at the ceiling as if trying to remember what he said. This was getting us nowhere.

She shrugged. "He threatened me, that's it."

"What did he say to threaten you?" I said louder.

"Uhmm," she was drawing the words out. "Heeeeee said he was going to hit me."

I looked at the boyfriend, who rolled his eyes as if to suggest she was lying.

"Well, it didn't look like you were kicking him out when we got here," Fiore said. "How do you know him?"

"We're friends, okay?" she said through gritted teeth.

"It looks pretty friendly." I smiled at her negligee.

She gave me a disgusted look and blew out some more smoke.

I smiled. "This is what we're gonna do." I pointed at him. "You're getting dressed and leaving. Do you have a way home?"

"I have my car outside," he said quietly.

"Finish getting dressed, get your keys, and let's go." I pointed to the door.

She sat down on the couch and crossed her legs. She took the last drag off her cigarette and put it out in the ashtray. He put his shirt, shoes, and jacket on and bent down to pick up some CDs off the floor.

"Those are mine," she snapped.

"Whatever," he said, putting his hands up in the air.

We walked him out. He left without a word to her. On the way to the elevator, Joe asked him what was the deal with her.

"We're just friends," he said as we got on the elevator.

"Come on," I said. "You're both naked when we get there. Married people don't even battle naked, do they, Joe?" I asked Fiore.

I could see him thinking. "No," he shook his head, smiling.

"She just gets crazy sometimes," the guy said.

"You married?" I asked, "Is this something on the side?"

He shrugged and didn't answer. We walked out of the elevator and back to the lobby. We threw a wave to the guard and went back out into the snow.

"Listen," I said, "if she calls you, maybe you should think about staying away from her."

"Yeah, I guess you're right," he said, but he didn't look happy about it.

He crossed the street and got into an older blue Honda Accord. He started the car and got back out with a scraper. Joe and I got back into the RMP and watched him clean the snow off his car. We saw him stop and pull his cell phone out of his jacket and start talking on it.

"I bet he's talking to her," Joe said.

He threw a look at us and got back in his car. He wouldn't go back in because we were sitting there. About five minutes later, the girlfriend came downstairs wearing a long, black wool coat and pink fuzzy slippers. I could see her legs, and I guessed she was still wearing the peekaboo nightie underneath the coat, probably freezing her tail off.

He rolled the passenger-side window down, and we saw them talking.

"Let's go check on Romano," I said. "This clown doesn't know when to go home."

We drove back to Romano's fixer and found him sitting on the chair outside the room, reading the *Post*. He jumped up, happy to see us. "Hey, Joe, Tony."

"How's the ghoul?" I nodded to the doorway where the coffin sleeper was.

"He hasn't come out, I don't hear anything coming from there." The candles were still flickering in the room.

"I called the coroner's office," Romano said. "They said it would be a while, backed up because of the storm. They'll probably show up when I'm relieved by the day tour." He looked miserable.

"At least you're not out in the snow." Joe said.

"Yeah, what are my choices? A dead guy and a vampire or a blizzard—I hate this job."

"You want coffee?" I snickered, thinking his choices were pretty funny.

"Yeah, can you get me something to eat?"

"What do you want?"

"I don't know, I didn't eat dinner. Get me a sandwich, Boars Head baloney, American cheese, mustard, and tomato on a roll." He handed me five bucks. "And get me a Kit Kat bar. Bruno's gonna relieve me at five, so I can go back to the house with you for my meal."

I went downstairs and crossed the street to the 24-hour deli on the same block of West 43rd Street. I got the sandwich, three coffees, and the Kit Kat bar. When I got back upstairs Bruno Galotti, frozen like a popsicle, was in the hallway with Fiore and Romano.

"What, were you outside the whole night?" I asked him.

"Yeah, I think I got frostbite," he said, blowing on his hands and stomping his feet. "My toes are numb."

"You need to hang out with these two," Romano said, nodding his head toward me and Fiore. "They'll teach you the three things a good cop never is."

"Whaddaya mean?" Galotti said, shivering.

"A good cop is never cold," he counted off one finger, "wet," he counted off another, "and hungry." Romano held up his three fingers. "Right?" he asked me.

"That's right," I said. "But you look frozen, soaked, and hungry," I said to Galotti.

"How am I supposed to do that?" Galotti asked.

"How many places on your post are open?" I asked. Galotti's post was 8th Avenue between 42nd and 45th Streets.

He shrugged, "I don't know."

I named one of the porn places on 8th Avenue between 42nd and 43rd. "You could stand under the overhang and not get wet, and if you get cold, go inside and stand by the front door. They like having a cop there. It's good for business, makes the customers feel safe."

"But I'm supposed to be working," he said.

"You're working—working at staying warm." We all laughed, but he looked confused.

"I don't want to stand in the porn place," he whined.

"Then stand in one of the hotel vestibules. The Milford Plaza's nice," I said.

"I've hung out there," Romano said. I was glad to see the kid was listening, learning how to make the job work for him.

We left Galotti at the hotel to thaw out and took Romano back to the precinct with us. The radio room was closed; I guess Rooney finished figuring out the radios. We went downstairs to the lounge, and I stood over Rooney, who was asleep on one of the benches.

He must have sensed someone was there, because he opened one eye and looked up at me.

"Shouldn't you be upstairs making sure everyone signs out their radios?" I mocked.

"Wise guy," he mumbled. "I'll get you back."

"Sure you will," I chuckled as McGovern and O'Brien said, "Shhhh, we're trying to sleep here."

14

It was ten to five when we shed our gun belts, jackets, vests, and shoes and stretched out on the benches. I was asleep almost immediately. The last thing I remembered was hearing the beep on Fiore's watch as he set the alarm for 5:55. I didn't hear the alarm go off, and the next thing I knew, Fiore was shaking me awake.

"Tony, come on, wake up."

I sat up and nodded.

"You awake?" he asked. He's done this before and walked out of the room, and I've gone back to sleep.

"I'm up," I snapped.

"We'll meet you upstairs," he said as he and Romano left the lounge.

I sat there orienting myself, trying to figure out what day it was, pretty sure it was Thursday.

I used the bathroom and washed my face. My hair was smashed in a little on one side, and I had five o'clock shadow. I shuffled upstairs, wanting coffee and a cigarette before I had to deal with anyone.

Romano was standing by the front doors, yawning and

stretching. Fiore was annoyingly chipper, waving to Terri Marks, who was beaming at him like she was madly in love.

"Man, it's coming down harder than before," I said, holding my hat over my eyes to keep the flakes from hitting me in the face. We stopped to talk to Hector, the maintenance worker at the precinct. He's a Spanish guy, about fifty years old. He's short and skinny with receding black hair and an attempted mustache. He's got extensive tattoos with elaborate artwork on his arms, hands, and neck. He's a hard worker, always smiling and happy. I don't know what he's so happy about, but hey, whatever works for him. He had shoveled the front steps of the precinct and was whistling as he worked on the sidewalk when we came outside.

"Hey, Tony, Joe," he said as we shook hands. "Is this beautiful or what?" He looked up at the blizzard and smiled. "I love the snow." Like I said, he's a happy guy.

"Yeah, it's beautiful," I said dryly. "Give it an hour. It'll be a nice shade of grime."

Hector smiled. "That's what I like about you, Tony, you're always looking on the bright side."

"Hector, do you know Nick Romano?" Fiore cut in. Maybe he thought I was gonna say something to Hector.

"Nice to meet you, Nick. I've seen you before," Hector said, shaking Nick's hand.

Hector went back to his shoveling, and we could hear him start to whistle again as we cleaned the snow off our car, using our hands and jackets 'cause the city's too cheap to give us scrapers.

There was about half a foot of snow on the cars that were there all night. The street had been plowed once about three inches ago and was due for another scrape.

We drove over to a bagel store on 33rd and Madison. The windows were steamed when we came in, and I could smell the coffee and the bread baking. We went over to the coffee counter, and Fiore and I made ourselves a 16-ounce cup. Nick got coffee and added French vanilla syrup in his. It smelled good, but I like my coffee regular.

There were no everything bagels ready, so I got a toasted bialy with butter. A bialy is a cross between a bagel and an English muffin, with onions baked into the center. Nick had a poppy seed with butter, and Fiore had pumpernickel with cream cheese.

We dropped Romano off at the hotel, telling him to send Bruno down so we could drive him back to post.

We dropped Bruno off on 8th Avenue, giving him a couple of tips on staying warm and dry, and drove back to our sector. We parked on the corner of 7th Avenue and 35th Street behind Macy's, past the loading docks.

The sky was lit up from the city lights reflecting off the snow coming down, and the streets were still deserted. The occasional bus or cab driving by with its chains clicking made up the morning traffic. The radio was quiet; I guess all the bad guys were snowed in.

"I'm gonna miss church this week," I commented as I lit a cigarette.

"Yeah, me too," Joe said.

"If I'm not seeing Michele anymore, maybe I shouldn't keep going to that church."

"What does that have to do with it? Who are you going there for, God or Michele?"

"What do you think?" I snapped at him. "But she was there first."

"So what? Is that your church? Is it the church that you're supposed to be at?"

"I guess so. There's no place else I want to go."

"If this is your church, then this is where you have to be.

When you feel God guides you to a church, you stay, even if you don't want to."

"I don't want to run into her, or Stevie. I knew I shouldn't have gotten involved with him. He loves me, and now he's gonna get hurt when I'm not around."

"Whatsamatta with you? Why are you talking like this is already over?" He looked surprised.

"'Cause I'm a friggin' wuss, upset about someone I'm not even getting any from and worrying that I won't be in *church* on Sunday." I laughed at the irony of it.

He laughed too. "Don't worry about it," he said. "Just pray, and read your Bible—"

"And let God guide you," we said at the same time, only my voice was mimicking.

"Are you making fun of me?" he looked a little insulted.

"No, but you're perfect and always pray and read your Bible."

"And I get it on a regular basis." He said it so normal that I almost missed it.

I barked out a laugh. "Captain America has a sense of humor? What's next? Dancing?"

"You're a funny guy," he said.

"I'm pathetic," I said.

"No you're not. At least you're not drinking."

"But then I'd be drunk and wouldn't care."

"Eventually you'd have to sober up," he looked at me. "Do you feel like drinking, or are you joking?"

"I'm joking—don't I sound like I'm joking?" I held my hands up.

"I can't always tell with you."

"I'm not gonna drink, don't worry about it."

"Seriously," he said. "Don't get off track. I've been through times where I'm bummed out about something and I don't feel like praying or reading the Bible. But those are the times you need it most. Read through the Psalms. David wrote most of the Psalms when he was under pressure, being hunted by people who hurt him and wanted to kill him. He turned to God, and God called him a man after his own heart."

"Didn't he get in trouble for doing someone else's wife?" I asked.

He shook his head and smiled. "Yes, David did do that, and he had her husband sent into the front lines of battle so he'd be killed. But David isn't our example, Jesus is. So don't go pointing your fingers at him, thinking what he did was okay."

"Getting back to reading the Bible," I said. "I'm not avoiding it on purpose. I'm trying to get into it, and then I get distracted and put the TV on."

"It's easier to escape into TV or a book than to press into God. Pray about calling Michele to ask her what's going on."

"We've been working every day, and when I had time off this week, my mother was there. In fact," I looked at my watch, "too early to call. I want to see how my sister made out last night."

"She won't be working today. What does she do again?" Joe asked. My sister, Denise, changes jobs so often it's hard to keep track.

"I think she's selling motorcycles," I said. "There's a Harley-Davidson place on Bay Street that gave her a job. I don't know how many bikes you sell in December, so how bad could she screw it up?"

"I don't know why you always give her such a hard time. She's not a screwup, she just hasn't found her niche yet. When she does, she'll stay with it."

"If you say so," I said doubtfully.

We sat talking and drinking coffee in the car until about 7:20. The sky was brighter now, but the snow was still falling steadily. The radio was unusually quiet, with only one alarm for South Charlie the whole time. We drove back to the precinct and parked across the street. The front steps and sidewalk were shoveled and salted, and a couple of day tour cops were outside smoking.

We stopped to talk to the day tour guys on our way in. When we walked in, Hector was inside the front doors with a mop and bucket, wiping up the dirty snow near the entrance. The desk was busy now. Phones were ringing, keys were being dropped off at the desk, where they would be hung beneath the designated number of the RMP they belonged to. The radio room was busy, with the day tour signing out their radios and the midnight tour returning theirs. Fiore and I didn't return ours, but we did get new batteries since we'd be going back out.

Romano wasn't back yet. He would get stuck on that fixer. He was supposed to be relieved by the day tour, but if we were short cops, he wasn't a priority. Later on, they'd hold someone over from the day tour to do the four-to-twelve and relieve him.

Sergeant Hanrahan was at the desk, talking to the sergeant from the day tour.

"Hey, Joe, Tony, are you still doing the parking garage detail?" he asked.

"Yeah, Boss."

"Good, we'll go out after we see the training officer."

Victor Santiago, the new training officer, was holding his paperwork and talking to some of the midnight guys. He had props with him, a four-foot rolling TV stand with a 36-inch television and VCR combo set up on top of it. The stand was high enough to be seen from the whole room.

Sergeant Hanrahan gave the fall in command as he walked into the muster room.

"If anybody is interested in some OT, they're looking for bodies to stay," he said. "After training is over," Hanrahan continued, "I'll have the roll call for everyone to sign out once I know there's enough coverage for the day tour."

Hanrahan would be staying; he was running the parking garage detail. Most of the volunteers for OT were there for the parking garage detail and any fixers not covered.

Sergeant Hanrahan backed up to give Santiago the platform. Calls of Aaaarreeebbaa! and other Latino type slurs filled the room.

O'Brien started singing the Mexican hat dance as good as any mariachi player. Then he took his hat off his head and tossed it on the floor to dance around it while snapping his fingers on the side of his head. Santiago was getting embarrassed, half laughing and looking intimidated.

"How's everybody doing this morning?" he said as Rooney used an orange traffic cone as a megaphone, puckering his lips and ripping out gas sounds so we couldn't hear what Santiago was saying.

Rooney put the cone behind him as the room erupted in hysteria and Santiago turned red. Sergeant Hanrahan, who had been writing, looked up to see who did it, and I saw a smirk playing at the corner of his mouth.

"The reason we're here this morn—" Santiago tried again as Rooney let out another long and juicy one, making us laugh even harder.

Santiago tried one more time as Rooney did it again, and he gave up and started laughing himself. He tried to just keep talking, going neck and neck with Rooney on the megaphone. The squad finally settled down, hearing only half of what Santiago was saying. A couple of seconds later Rooney was at it again, singing the Mexican hat dance song. The rest of us threw our hats on the floor and danced around them, snapping our fingers until Hanrahan laughed and said, "That's enough, this is important."

The training was about bomb threats and incendiary devices. Santiago went into it a little about what to look for over the next couple of days with New Year's Eve coming up. He mentioned those of us working the garage details, and what to do if we found such a device. He went into suspicious property first, any containers, luggage, duffle bags, or packages not immediately discernable by appearance. Like if someone leaves a suitcase in the middle of Penn Station, we'd call the bomb squad. It's usually nothing, but we can't take the chance with New Year's upon us. We have to try to determine the owner, see if anyone saw who left it, hold whoever discovered it for questioning, and evacuate a thousand feet around the unattended article. Once we evacuate the area, we get to a landline and call Central, with a separate number for Central that's not 911. We are not to use our radios or cell phones under any circumstances as they could trigger the incendiary device to explode. We'd most likely call the desk at the precinct first, and let them call Central.

If we ever do find what we know is a bomb, the first thing we do is look for a secondary device. That's how these psychos work. They use a second, hidden device to throw us off and try to blow us up while we stand away from the first one.

He turned on the video, and we heard it say that a supervisor will respond and begin a level-one mobilization. A command post is set up in the evacuated area and prevents entry of persons into the area.

Until a supervisor gets there, the person in charge is the senior member of service, or whoever has the most time on.

Usually we'd walk out of a training video, but it was New Year's Eve week and we knew the city had been getting threats. Most of this stuff we know, but in recent years the city has picked it up a notch. Terror threats were becoming more commonplace, and since our command packs the most people into a couple of city blocks, we should know what to look for. The video lasted about fifteen minutes, then we filed out.

"Wait for me and I'll give you a ride over to the detail," Hanrahan said as Rooney, Joe, and I came out. Hanrahan went back to the desk and spoke to the sergeant and lieutenant, asking if they needed any extra bodies from the midnight tour.

When we got outside, the snow was still coming down hard and fast. A couple of store owners on the block were shoveling snow into the street, but a lot of businesses were closed.

Today's garage was across from the one we were working the other day, on the south side of 43rd Street. Hanrahan dropped us off to relieve Rice, Beans, and Carl Beers again. They talked to us for a couple of minutes, saying the garage was dead most of the night, with just a couple of cars this morning.

When they left, Rooney stayed at the garage entrance, Joe went down the block to check on Romano and see what he wanted for breakfast, and I did a perimeter check.

When I got back upstairs, a woman in a wool cap and peacoat was talking to Rooney. As I approached, I heard him say, "I can't leave my post. If you want I'll call someone."

"What's up, Mike?" I asked.

"The woman over there," Rooney pointed to a woman about twenty feet from us near the corner of four-three and eight, "is confused. She's asking her," he points his thumb at the woman next to him, "where she works."

"She asked me if I knew where she worked and do I know where her job is. When I asked her where she worked, she said she didn't know."

"I'll go talk to her," I told Rooney.

The woman in the peacoat came with me as we approached a white female, late twenties with red hair and blue eyes. She didn't look skelly; she was dressed in black jeans, a red turtleneck sweater, and a multicolored scarf under a black wool coat. She was clean but looked a little out of it. She paced back and forth, walking in one direction, stopping, then turning around and going back the other way.

"Can I help you, Miss?" I asked, leaning in a little so I could see if she smelled like booze.

"I don't know where my job is," she said, looking confused.

"Do you know where you are?" I asked.

She looked around and shook her head. "I don't think so. I think I work around here."

She was pale, and she looked like she was sweating. She wasn't having seizures; I've seen enough epileptics to know what a seizure looks like. I wasn't sure if it was drugs, or maybe she was an EDP.

"What do you want me to do for you?" I asked as a thought hit me. "Are you diabetic?" She nodded yes as she went down like a rag doll. Rooney, who had been watching from the parking garage, took a couple of steps toward me.

"Mike, get me some orange juice," I called to Rooney as I picked her up. I leaned her up against the building, trying to keep her out of the snow as Rooney trotted into the deli next to the garage. He came back about three seconds later with a small carton of Tropicana.

We made her drink about half the carton, and within five minutes she was fine. We found out she was a receptionist at 1501 Broadway, and she was running late and rushed out of her apartment without eating. She had planned on grabbing something when she got off the train, but it was too late. She thanked us profusely and asked for our full names. People do that sometimes, then write in to the *Daily News* or the *New York Post* to mention we helped them out.

It was after 9:00 now, and she was supposed to be in by 8:30. I walked her to work and spoke to her boss, telling him why she was late. She thanked me again as I left. She looked better now. Someone had given her a roll, and there was some color back in her skin.

"Officer Cavalucci?" she said as I waited in front of her desk for the elevator.

"Yeah?" I turned around.

"Are you married?" she said as she smiled at me.

"No."

"Got a girlfriend?" She tilted her head.

"I'm not sure," I said honestly.

"Well, if you find yourself sure you don't have a girlfriend, maybe we could have a drink sometime."

"You got it." I smiled. She was pretty, but I don't know about the passing out thing.

Fiore was at the garage with Rooney when I got back.

"I'm going to get breakfast," he said. "Nick's stuck on that fixer, so I'll pick him up an egg sandwich and some coffee. What do you want?"

"What's Romano crying like a girl 'cause he's gotta stay?" I chuckled.

"Nah, he's alright. I explained it to him." Fiore started talking with his hands. "I told Romano he should be thankful he's making OT sitting in a chair doing nothing when he could be outside with us, freezing his tail off. He can always raise us on the radio if he needs something."

"How's the freak in the coffin?" I asked.

"The door was closed. Nick said he came out about 7:30, dressed all in black, and left."

"Nick's probably gonna get stuck there all day," I said.

"He'll be fine," Joe said, then added, "So what do you want for breakfast?"

We all had egg sandwiches and coffee, and Joe went back to the hotel to give Romano his breakfast. After breakfast, when

Rooney took a break and went into the office to sleep and Joe did another perimeter check, I called my sister.

"Hello." She sounded upbeat.

"Hey, it's Tony," I said.

"Where are you?"

"I'm still at work. I'm at a detail on 43rd Street."

"Oh, everything okay?" she asked.

"That's what I wanted to ask you. Did Mom come there last night?" I thought maybe my mother changed her mind and drove back to Pennsylvania instead.

"Yeah."

"So what happened?" I wondered what was up since I never have to pull information out of Denise.

"Nothing. We had a long talk, straightened some things out, and now we're doing our nails."

Doing our nails?

"She's still there?" I asked.

"Yeah, in case you haven't noticed, there's a blizzard outside. We would have gone to the Korean place on Bay Street where I usually get my nails done, but I'm sure they're closed," Denise said. I heard my mother saying something in the background, then Denise said away from the receiver, "Under the sink in the bathroom."

"So it went good? What did you talk about?" I asked.

"A lot of things. Listen, Tony, can I call you later? We're in the middle of doing our nails, and I just put a movie on."

"Sure, no problem," I said. I went to say something else, and Denise said, "Okay, bye," and disconnected before I had the chance. I hit the end button on my cell phone, feeling a little blown off. I was about to shut the phone off to save my battery when it rang. The display showed Michele's number out in Long Island, and I looked at it for a second before I hit the send button.

"Hello?" I said.

"Hi, it's Michele," she said cautiously.

"I know." I smiled, glad that she was the first to break down and call. "I was gonna call you today."

"How are you?" she asked.

"Good, a little tired. I've been working a lot of OT this week."

"Is Joe with you?"

"Yeah, he's here." There was an awkward silence. "About Christmas Eve," she started.

"I wanted to apologize to you about it," I cut in. "I shouldn't have made excuses for my family—they were wrong."

"And I shouldn't have put you in the middle of me and your family. I was wrong about that," Michele said. "I'm sorry too."

"Before you, I never had to deal with them about anyone else," I said.

"They've never met any of your other girlfriends?" she asked dryly.

"They've met a couple; I guess Kim was around them the most."

"Did they have a problem with her?"

I had to think about that. Kim and Marie actually got along pretty well, but I didn't think I should mention that. "Denise didn't like her. I don't know about the rest of them. Honestly, I've never seen them act like that before. I've been talking to Joe about it, and he pointed out a few things I never noticed about them before. I mean, I noticed them, but they didn't bother me," I said.

"Sometimes it's hard to see things when they've been in front of us all our lives. I'm not trying to make you mad at them, Tony, but I felt like you were dismissing what they were doing as harmless, and it isn't. I was surprised that the only person you gave any responsibility to in this was Denise."

"That's because she knows how they are and she lets them suck her in every time. She always lets them get her mad, and they love it. It makes her look wrong because she's the one who's screaming and throwing things."

"She didn't scream *or* throw things when we were there," Michele said a little sharply.

"No, she waited till after you left," I laughed.

"Who did she throw something at?"

"Marie—she hit her in the head with her keys," I said, my voice rising.

"Good for her! Marie had it coming."

"I can't believe you said that, Miss Time-Out advocating violence?" I mocked.

"Miss Time-Out also believes in a whack on the bottom when it's appropriate, and trust me, Marie was due."

"My mother came over to see me last night," I said, not wanting to talk about Marie anymore.

"Really?" she said, surprised. "Why?"

"She wanted to tell me she went to rehab last summer and she's been sober since."

"Wow. That's a twist."

"Yeah, I know. She came to give me the twelve-step 'I'm sorry for everything I've ever done to you' speech."

"Well thank God, this is good news."

"I guess. She looked good. She seemed sincere enough," I said. "Time will tell."

"I can understand you being hesitant after her track record, but you have to admit it's a step in the right direction." She paused and said, "Things are changing, Tony, but they can't all change at once. I just didn't expect it from her end."

"What about us?" I asked. "Three times with my family and you throw in the towel? I thought you were tougher than that."

"I am. But I have Stevie to think about. Trust me, if it were just me, it wouldn't matter. He was getting anxious there. They were criticizing everything he did, and he wasn't doing anything wrong."

She was getting angry, so I cut her off. "I know he wasn't doing anything wrong. I'm sorry. I love him, and I love you. I'd never hurt either one of you—you know that, don't you?"

"Where are you?" she asked.

"Don't change the subject, and answer the question," I said, my voice getting sharp.

"I know that *you* wouldn't hurt us, Tony, but *they* would. And that's why they have to be a consideration."

"Listen to me," I said, my voice rising, "if you're not comfortable going there, we won't go there. I'm gonna talk to them about how they acted, but they're not gonna listen. Maybe my grandmother will, but Marie and my father are how they are."

"I know they are. I'm trying not to get my feelings hurt that they don't like me or my little boy. I can't put Stevie in that position again, Tony, I won't let them hurt him."

"He won't be anywhere near them, at least not until they learn how to treat the both of you, okay?"

"Okay. So where are you?" she asked again.

"Doing some overtime at a parking garage."

"Why there?"

"We're checking the cars as they come in, keeping the garage secure for New Year's."

"I was watching the news—there's some concern about terror threats again. Do you have to work New Year's Eve?" She sounded worried.

"Yeah, I can't get out of it. It's my RDO (regular day off), so I'll be at one of the details."

"Which one?"

"I'll find out tonight; they have to give us advance notice."

"I don't like this," she said.

"I'll be fine. Joe will be with me. If it looks like anything's gonna go down, I promise we'll get out of there."

"Can you do that?"

"Sure," I lied. "We can leave whenever we want." She didn't say anything, and Joe's words "There are no lies that are okay with God" came back to haunt me. So I told her, "I can't leave the area, but I can go off post if I need to." Which is basically true.

We talked for a little while longer. Stevie got on the phone for a couple of minutes, asking why I haven't been out to see him. I promised him I'd be out after New Year's. Realistically I'd be working till then. I promised Michele I'd call her later and hung up as Rooney was coming out of the booth.

"Hey, Tony," he growled. "Don't think I forgot about what you did with the radios last night. I saw you laughing when I fell." Rooney gets nasty when he doesn't have his coffee.

I busted out laughing. "You should have seen your face. It was hysterical!"

"You're lucky I didn't catch you—"

"With what, a snowball? You can't even throw anymore; we're gonna need a new pitcher for the softball team."

"I pitch just fine. I threw out my arm," he said as he lit a cigarette.

"Next time don't bust my chops about signing out my radio to impress Yolanda. I always sign out my radio," I said.

"I wasn't trying to impress Yolanda!"

"Don't worry, after the fall you took, I doubt she was impressed."

We spent the rest of the day taking turns napping in the parking attendant's office. Dominick DiSanto, Craig Jensen, and Jimmy Flaherty, the day tour guys, relieved us at 4:00. We took their RMP back to the precinct. The snow was falling slower now, the flakes fatter and fewer than before.

We stopped at the deli, picking up chicken cutlet heros and minestrone soup. I got the chicken cutlet with mozzy and sliced hot cherry peppers; Fiore got his the same but with roasted peppers. Rooney got the cordon blue, chicken with ham and melted swiss.

We went downstairs to the locker rooms to change. I put on jeans and a sweatshirt and sat down at the table in the lounge to eat. I picked the lima beans out of my minestrone before I ate and watched Miami Vice reruns until I passed out on one of the benches.

I woke up at 10:15 to the sound of Fiore's watch beeping.

"You taking a shower?" he mumbled, shutting the alarm off.

"Yeah," I said.

"Wake me up when you're done."

"Sure, no problem."

I went into the locker room to change. I wrapped a towel around my waist and dug my old blue flip-flops out of a bag in the bottom of my locker. I grabbed soap and shampoo and headed to the bathroom, my shower shoes clicking against my feet as I walked. We all keep a supply of necessary items in our lockers: shampoo, soap, Q-tips, deodorant, toothbrush and paste, blow dryer, brush, and extra clothes in case on days like today we're stuck here.

The bathroom is a white-tiled room, now a dingy shade of gray. It has two stalls, two urinals, two sinks, and one shower on the other side of the wall next to the sink. While Hector cleans the bathroom, he won't touch the shower.

I put my stuff on the shelf on the wall outside the shower and hung my towel on the hook next to it. There's an ancient green and mold shower curtain that goes straight across the front of the shower. The shower has a white base, and the walls are enclosed with small tile encrusted with black mold. On the floor was half a bar of gold soap and the wrapping from a bar of Dial. I took my soap from the plastic travel case I use and tried not to look at the hair, mold, and melted soap around me. The shower was so disgusting that I stood under it without moving, trying not to touch the floor, wall, or shower curtain with any of my exposed skin.

There's a guy from the four-to-twelve who cleans the shower sometimes. He gets so disgusted with it that he bleaches the whole thing. A week later it's just as dirty as it was before, so I don't know why he bothers.

I woke Joe up when I was done, and he trudged over to the shower in brown shower shoes and blue gym shorts, with his towel around his neck. He carried his essentials like I did.

Joe came out about ten minutes later, and we were dressed and upstairs before roll call.

15

I had finished my coffee and had a cigarette before Sergeant Hanrahan's fall in announcement. He was looking a little worn out, walking around the muster room, giving out the New Year's Eve detail assignments before the roll call. Our squad had our RDO (regular day off) on New Year's Eve, and the department has to give us 48 hours' notice before they change our tours. Either way, we knew we'd be working New Year's.

"Hey, Tony, Joe," Hanrahan said as he approached us. "I need you to sign next to your name." He held out the white detail roster to Joe and me.

"We'll be meeting at four-seven and Broadway at 1345 hours, and the detail starts at 1300." Which means we have to be suited up at 1:00 in the afternoon, ready to go over to 47th and Broadway to muster up at 1:45. In reality we'd be mustering up by 2:00, getting our assignments.

The week before New Year's is always busy, and the overtime was taking its toll on a lot of us. He gave out the sectors and the foot posts, checking to see if we had enough bodies to cover the tour. The roads were still a nightmare, and both the Metro North and Long Island Railroads were running on limited schedules.

"Does everyone know what their assignments are for New Year's Eve?" he asked, scanning the room to make sure. He didn't mention not to bang the day on New Year's—it's an unspoken rule that if you call in sick on New Year's, you better be in a coma.

While Hanrahan was doing the roll call, Sergeant Yu walked around the muster room and gave out notification slips, probably for court. He paused when he saw Joe and me, and I saw him craning his head around Garcia to see my name tag. He's not our sergeant, so he didn't know us personally.

"Cavawucci?" he asked. He seemed to have problems pronouncing *L*s.

I nodded and waved. He tapped Garcia and had him hand Joe and me the notification slips.

"Look at this, RDO Grand Jury notification." I smiled. It was for January 2, which meant we'd be getting OT before working that Tuesday night.

Sergeant Hanrahan wrapped it up with, "Be careful driving out there. The temperature is below freezing. Some of the melted snow is probably frozen over, and I don't want any accidents. Remember, it's Friday night, New Year's weekend, and a lot of people are in town for the holiday. They're already partying, so be careful, it's probably gonna be busy."

The snow had stopped hours ago, leaving us with clear, cold skies. The temperatures had dipped into the twenties, freezing the snow that was still left on the ground. In 48 hours Midtown would be packed with a million people, and the snow would have to be removed by then. The mayor gave a press conference from the city's emergency bunker in the World Trade Center, telling everyone that the city is ready, and come enjoy the New Year's weekend.

The tow trucks were already out towing parked cars from snow lanes. Sanitation had 350 salt spreaders dropping 200,000 tons of salt on the streets of the city, and 1,275 garbage trucks had plows mounted on them. The airports called in reserve workers, keeping the runways clear with thousands of gallons of anti-ice chemicals. The mayor went on to say that the Police Department would be keeping officers on overtime duty beginning tonight if we get anymore snow and replacements can't report in. It was news to me. I was hoping to get at least some sleep in my bed before New Year's.

The main thing, the mayor said, is New York is not letting a little snow stop the festivities—we got through Y2K last year and had the best New Year's celebration in the world.

That may be true, but there was still snow everywhere. Store awnings, newsstands, mailboxes, traffic lights, and marquees had it piled on top of them. It was frozen to the turret lights and the roof of our RMP. Sidewalks were still not shoveled, and cars were buried under a foot of snow. The wind was blowing now, sending showers of powder off buses and cabs onto the cars around them.

We had stopped for coffee and buttered rolls and drove up 8th toward 42nd Street to take a look at the Deuce before patrolling our sector. As we stop at the 42nd Street and 8th Avenue light, I see one of my favorite felons crossing westbound on 8th Avenue. I let the car go into the intersection to scare him a little. He jumps back and puts his hands out in an angry "What's up?" stance. Then he saw me smiling at him and he bopped over, smiling.

"Officer Cavalucci," he said as he came over to the driver's side of the car. He shook my hand and nodded at Fiore. He was a male black, late twenties, about six foot two, with short black hair. He was expensively dressed, new black leather jacket, baggy jeans, designer Yankee hat turned to the side, and gold earrings in both ears.

"Hey, Mr. Thompson, what's going on?"

"Nothing, just chillin'."

"Where've you been? I haven't seen you," I said, hoping he hadn't been upstate doing time. I locked him up once. He snatched some money out of someone's hand he was supposed to be getting a cab for. He wasn't a bad guy, I hoped he was staying out of trouble.

"I've been working clubs."

"Bouncing?" I asked.

"Yeah, I'm working uptown."

"What are you doing down here?"

"I'm meeting someone over at Port Authority."

"You staying out of trouble?" I raised my eyebrows at him.

"Yeah," he said as he smiled and leaned toward the window. I smelled leather and his cologne. He pointed to me as he said to Joe, "This guy's a good guy."

"This guy?" Joe nodded his head toward me. "You sure?"

"Yeah, I'm sure. Listen, Officer Cavalucci," his voice dropped lower. "I'm gonna do you a solid."

"What's up?" I leaned my head out the window.

"There's a car parked on 44th Street, right around the corner. A black Maxima. There's two guys," his voice lowered again and he looked around, "let's just say it's hot, and they're trying to sell it."

"Around the corner just off 8th?" I asked.

He nodded. "Just off 8th, but don't mention me."

"Mention who?"

"Yeah, that's it." He smiled and shook my hand.

I threw him a wave as I continued on 8th Avenue. I turned left on 45th Street and went around the block to 44th Street. I drove slowly down the street, spotting the Maxima close to

8th Avenue. We drove past the car without pausing, while Joe copied down the license plate number. I took a right on 7th to 43rd, made another right, and parked on the southeast corner of West 43rd and 8th Avenue, a block down from where the car was.

There was no computer in our RMP, so Fiore called the desk and had them run the plate number for us. It came back 16, which is stolen. We sat and waited on the corner. We couldn't see the car from where we were, but whoever drove it would have to pass through the intersection.

As we were sitting there waiting, I saw two guys and their dates crossing the opposite corner from us, going northbound on 8th Avenue.

"Look who it is," I chuckled. "You remember him, Joe?" I pointed to the bigger of the two guys.

Fiore studied them, "No." He shook his head, still studying him. "Who is he?"

"You don't remember him? That's John Wilson. We locked him up last summer, and he had you gagging out the window after he let loose in his pants in the backseat." I laughed harder now. "You almost puked from the smell."

"He looks different."

"He's fatter for one thing, and his hair was blond." I watched him as he waved his hands around homeboy style, showing off to the girls.

"Oh no, I hope he's not the one who stole the car," Fiore said. "Ya think?"

"Nah, not his style. He's just a dealer."

As I said that, he and his buddy started walking faster, in front of the girls, and turned left at 44th Street, out of sight. A minute later the black Maxima pulled into the intersection of 44th and 8th, driving eastbound. Wilson was driving, his buddy in the passenger seat and the two girls in the back.

"I'm not up for this," Fiore said with feeling. He grabbed his radio and said, "South David to Central."

"Go ahead, South David."

"We're following a possible 16 vehicle, New York plate." He gave the number. "We'll need another unit, no emergency."

"Central, this is South Eddie. We're five blocks out," Rooney responded.

The Maxima was driving eastbound on 44th Street and made a right on 7th Avenue, through Times Square. They drove southbound past 42nd Street, and I saw them stop at 40th Street on 7th Avenue, in front of the New Fashion School. I gave them a little distance, falling three cars back with no lights on. As I was driving on 7th Avenue, I told Joe, "Find out where South Eddie is."

"South David to South Eddie," Fiore put over the radio.

"South Eddie," Rooney answered.

"Where are you right now?"

"Westbound, from four-one and six."

Fiore and I were coming up to 40th. As we approached 40th and 7th, I saw the Maxima stopped at the light.

"Don't look at them," I told Fiore. "I'm gonna pull up in front of them at the light and pretend we're looking for someone."

I pulled up on the left in front of them, into the crosswalks. Joe looked west, and I looked east, like we were looking for someone else. In my peripheral vision I saw Wilson sit up straight.

"I think he might need a diaper change now," Fiore said, his expression blank.

Now technically when we spot a stolen car parked, we're supposed to impound it and wait with it until it's towed to the precinct. That way the car can be returned to its owner intact. But grand larceny auto is a good collar, and Wilson just doesn't learn.

Joe had his radio down next to his leg so it looked like

he was talking to me and said, "Sector Eddie, where are you now?"

"Westbound on 41st, passing Broadway."

I kept my head straight ahead, but my eyes were on the rearview mirror. I saw Rooney coming down the block behind me. "It's about time," I mumbled to Joe as I watched Rooney approach the Maxima.

"Just pull up behind them," Joe told Rooney over the radio.

As Rooney pulled up behind them, I put my lights on. I pulled our car to the right and in on an angle, blocking the front of their car. Rooney put his lights on at the same time I did, but he didn't pull his RMP up close enough to the Maxima for us to box them in.

Now Wilson knew we had him, and he panicked. He backed the Maxima up and turned the wheel, with his tires hitting the curb. He punched the gas, going around us with his tires spinning on the ice. He fishtailed as he pulled away and took off through the now green light. Rooney took off after him, whooping his siren down 40th Street.

I couldn't go forward because there was a pole in front of me, so I slammed the car into reverse and it stalled out on me.

"Oh come on," I said as I hit the steering wheel. "What a piece of garbage."

"Just put it in park and start it up again," Fiore said calmly.

"Ya see, this is the kind of crap I hate," I said, aggravated.

By the time I started it up again and backed the car out, Rooney was moving eastbound on 40th Street, approaching 6th Avenue.

I heard Rooney on the radio telling Central he's following a stolen vehicle, giving them his location.

"South Sergeant to Central," Hanrahan radioed.

"Go ahead, South Sergeant," Central responded.

"What is the vehicle wanted for?"

"It's a 16 vehicle, Sergeant."

"Central, is that unit in pursuit?"

I heard Central raise Rooney, "South Eddie, are you in pursuit?"

Silence.

"South Eddie, are you in pursuit?" Central asked again.

Silence again.

"South Eddie, this is South Sergeant, what is your location?" Hanrahan sounded all business, but I could tell he's wondering if he should call this off before someone gets hurt. The streets had already been plowed and salted, but there's always ice patches.

I turned north on 6th Avenue and went eastbound on 42nd Street. Bryant Park sits behind the Manhattan Library, which is on 5th Avenue. The park is two blocks long, and 41st Street doesn't cross through.

Rooney radioed in, sounding pumped up.

"South Eddie to Central. The Maxima just lost control of the car and crashed into a cement bastion by the guard house at Bryant Park." He waited a beat, then added, "They're running northbound through the park!"

As we headed east on 42nd Street, we were looking into the park, which was now lit up from all the snow. John Wilson and his buddy were running toward us, while the two females attempted to follow them.

I stopped the car, and Fiore and I got out. We took our cuffs out and stood by the car. We could see the smoke from the other side of the park, where the Maxima was now folded up like an accordion. The sidewalks in the park were semishoveled, with a thin coating of snow on them. These two knuckleheads were cutting across the park through the deep snow.

"They're making this too easy," I said, leaning against the car.

"Should we go after them?" Joe asked.

"Nah." I lit a cigarette. "Rooney and Connelly are on the other side."

The two females gave up and were attempting to hide behind some bushes midway through the park. We were twenty feet away from Wilson and his buddy, and we could hear them breathing. The snow was making them pull their legs up with each step.

"He looks like he's using the stairmaster," Joe remarked as Wilson fell down. I heard the other one say, "Come on, keep moving," and Fiore and I cracked up laughing.

The other guy was taller and thinner than Wilson, about five foot eleven, maybe 180 pounds. Wilson was wearing a yellow down bubble jacket with black trim, making him look like an oversized banana. His buddy was wearing jeans and a green hooded fleece jacket. He leaned on his knees to catch his breath while waiting for Wilson. Wilson got up and started running again, bumping into his friend as he shot past him.

They ran another ten feet and looked up to see Joe and me smiling at them. I took a drag off my cigarette and waved to them. I saw the look of panic cross their face and saw Wilson's eyes dart to the left to see if they could cut over, away from us.

"Don't even think about it," I called to them. "You got no-where to go."

Wilson looked to the left again, then put his head down. They tromped the rest of the way through the park. When they got to us, we threw them up on the wrought iron fence that surrounds Bryant Park. We gave them a fast toss; I took Wilson, Joe took the friend.

"What were you thinking?" I asked Wilson.

"I didn't know the car was stolen," he said. He wasn't crying this time. The last time I locked him up, he cried like a baby and crapped in his pants. He was alone then. I doubted he'd do that with his buddy here.

"If you didn't think it was stolen, why'd you take off?" I asked.

"I didn't take off. I was taking my boy downtown to some clubs when you guys started chasing us," his voice quivered a little.

"Not only were you driving a stolen vehicle, now you smacked it up," Joe threw in.

Wilson put his head down with nothing else to say.

Joe radioed Central, "Central, this is South David. No further, we have two under at the north side of Bryant Park."

"South David, that's gonna be 0107 hours," Central said, indicating it was 1:07 a.m.

"10-4."

Rooney and Connelly were on the other side of the park, with the stolen car. Rooney radioed us, "South David, you guys need a hand?"

"No, Mike, we're gonna bring 'em over there," Joe answered.

Hanrahan pulled up on the other side of the park and radioed Central that he was 84, on the scene with South Eddie.

We put Wilson and his buddy, Alan Bronsky, in the car and drove around to 41st Street, where Rooney and Connelly were.

"What about the two females that were with you? Did they know the car was stolen?" I asked them.

"No, we just picked them up. They wanted to go to clubs with us," Alan said.

"What are their names?" I asked.

"I don't know." Wilson shrugged and looked at his buddy. "Tara and Danielle, I think."

I pulled up behind where the Maxima had crashed. Hanrahan was there with Noreen, his driver, and Rooney and Connelly were walking back into Bryant Park toward where the two females had been crouching behind the bushes.

"Mike, Jimmy," I yelled to them. "What are you doing?" I asked when they turned around.

"We're gonna try to find the other two," Rooney yelled.

"Forget it, we got our two keepers. Let the other ones go," I said. Technically we should be locking up the two females for being in the stolen vehicle. But probably they didn't know the car was stolen, and in this situation, stupidity isn't a crime.

I crouched down and looked back to where they were hiding behind the bushes, but I didn't see them. "They're gone. How hard do you want to look for them?" I told the boss.

"You got the driver?" Hanrahan asked.

"Yeah," I said.

"Alright," he nodded. "Take the two of them back to the house." He looked over at the smashed Maxima and said, "Is anyone injured?"

"Nah, just their pride," I chuckled.

"See if they want to go to the hospital."

I walked back to the RMP and stuck my head in the driver's side window. Wilson had his head down, and his buddy had his head back, staring at the roof of the car and taking deep breaths.

"Hey, Einstein," I said to Wilson. "Do you need to go to the hospital?"

He shook his head no. "I can't hear you," I cupped my hand behind my ear.

"No," he mumbled.

"What about you?" I said to the other guy.

He looked up at me. "No," he said miserably and smacked his head back against the seat.

"No, Boss, neither one wants to go to the hospital," I told Hanrahan.

"I'll meet you back at the precinct then," Hanrahan said, getting in his car.

I got back in my RMP and heard Hanrahan calling for a department tow to bring the stolen car back to the precinct. Fiore called Central to tell them we were going back to the house with two under.

It was 1:40 when we brought Wilson and Bronsky back to the precinct, stopping at the desk to check in with Lieutenant Coughlin.

"Whaddaya got?" he asked without looking up, in his usual jaded tone.

"Two for grand larceny of an auto," I said.

He peered over his glasses. "Where's the vehicle?"

"Sergeant Hanrahan's having it towed from Bryant Park."

He nodded and grunted, looking back down at his paper-work.

Joe and I did the pedigree sheets, then locked our guns up behind the desk before being buzzed into the back where the cells are.

We took the cuffs off Wilson and Bronsky, searching them again to make sure we didn't miss any drugs or a weapon. Joe got the info on the car for me, when it was stolen, where it was stolen from, and who the owner was.

We found out the car had been reported stolen thirty hours ago from Napier Avenue in the Bronx. Because of the time frame and where it was stolen from, I can't prove Wilson actually stole the car. I was gonna charge him with grand larceny of an auto, but it would probably get banged down to criminal possession of stolen property.

"Officer Cavalucci, do you think they'll hold us downtown past New Year's?" Wilson asked from the cell.

"Probably not," I said. Even if he'd be there till February, I wouldn't tell him. I didn't want to hear him crying about it.

I finished the paperwork about 3:30 and got verification back on the prints from Albany by 4:00. We put Wilson and

Bronsky back in the RMP to take them downtown. Joe radioed Central, telling them we had two to MCB (Manhattan Central Booking), which we call The Tombs.

We went crosstown, taking the FDR Drive to the Brooklyn Bridge exit. We whipped around Center Street over to Baxter Street, which leads to the back of The Tombs.

We parked on Baxter Street and took the two perps over to the automatic metal gate. The gate is big enough to drive a bus through and opens into an area that is sealed off with a second metal gate in front of us.

The guard hit the button, and the gate went up and closed behind us once we were inside, sealing us in the gated courtyard. The guardhouse was to the left of us, so Joe and I went one at a time to lock up our guns and mace.

The guard buzzed the second gate, and we marched the prisoners through. We walked down a flight of stairs and came out into a long hallway. Cells ran the length of the hallway on the left, and the right was a cement wall all the way down to the end of the hall, where the Corrections Officer (CO) sits. There is a white line down the center of the hallway that the perps aren't supposed to cross.

We said hello to the CO and processed our paperwork. A second CO came out wearing rubber gloves and had Wilson and Bronsky empty their pockets. He also had them remove their belts, shoelaces, and jewelry and place them on the floor in front of them.

He put them on the wall and searched them again. While they were on the wall he went through their property on the floor. He told them to pick up their property, and they followed him to the back of the cells.

We said good night to the CO at the desk and walked back out the way we came in. We drove back uptown, getting to the precinct by 6:00 for our meal.

We slept for an hour and stayed inside for the last fifty minutes of our tour. Joe went out with the day tour for the bomb detail; he said he'd rather get a full tour of overtime since he wouldn't be going home anyway.

Since I had to wait until 9:00 for the ADA, I changed into my street clothes and went into the lounge to take a nap. My cell phone rang at 8:30, and I saw my sister Denise's number flash on the display.

"Hello," I said.

"Hi, Tony, it's Mom," I heard my mother's voice.

"Still here, huh?" I said, amused that she and Denise lasted this long together without killing each other. I heard Denise saying something in the background.

"I want to ask him first," my mother said, her voice away from the receiver.

"Ask me what?" I asked.

"Denise wants me to meet Michele and Stevie. She said they left Christmas Eve without Stevie's presents. She wants to pick them up at your grandmother's so she and I can drive out to give them to him," she said.

I'd forgotten about the presents. They were the last thing on my mind that night.

"Denise doesn't even have Michele's phone number, let alone know where she lives," I said, panicking at the thought of my mother going out to meet Michele.

"Denise called information for the address and phone number, but I wanted to call you first to see if it was okay."

My mother sounded sincere enough, and I appreciated that she called to ask me first, but I didn't think it was a good idea for Michele to see any more of my family this week. Maybe in a couple of years.

"You there?" she asked.

"I'm thinking," I said. I was quiet for a minute and said, "Let me call her first and see what she thinks."

"I think that's a good idea," my mother said. "Why don't you call her and give us a call back?"

I sat there thinking what to do. If I called them back and said Michele didn't want to see them, they'd be insulted, plus my Jiminy Cricket conscience was telling me not to lie. On the other hand, if I let them go out to see her, I wouldn't be there to make sure things didn't get out of hand. I dialed Michele and figured I'd see what she wanted to do.

"Hey," I said when she answered.

"I'm beginning to forget what you look like," she joked.

"Same here."

"Where are you?" she asked.

"Still at the precinct. I had a collar, and I'm waiting for the ADA to get in."

"What was the collar?"

"Grand larceny of an auto," I said.

"Better than the bomb detail."

"You ain't kidding. Listen," I dove right in, "my mother just called me. She's still at Denise's, and she wants to meet you."

"Okay," she said cautiously.

"You don't have to meet her," I said. "I told her that I'd call and ask you. She and Denise want to bring Stevie's Christmas presents out to him so she could meet the both of you."

"So she's still at Denise's?" She sounded surprised.

"Yeah. Last time I talked to them, they were doing their nails."

"I want to meet her," she said with conviction.

"I'm not sure that's a good idea," I said. "If she doesn't act right, is it gonna cause more trouble between us?"

"Tony, the way your family acted isn't what caused trouble between us—you thinking there was nothing wrong with it

243

was the problem. I don't want to get into this now anyway. I think we should talk face-to-face about it."

"You really want them to come?"

"Yes, I do."

"Alright, hide the knives and I'll tell them how to get there."

"When will we see you again?" she asked, softer.

"Probably not till after New Year's."

"That's too long," she said.

We talked for a few minutes more, giving each other the goo-goo "I miss you," "I miss you too" crap. Sometimes I think it's better that we don't see each other too much. Otherwise I'd be tempted to talk her out of those morals she's so bent on sticking to. Not that I don't agree, but I'm still tempted.

I called my mother back and gave her Michele's number and directions out to Long Island. I fell asleep in the lounge until 9:20, when Lisa Mazza, the assistant desk officer, barreled in.

"Cavalucci, ADA's on the phone," she yelled in. She's a big Brooklyn girl, divorced with a couple of kids, and nobody I'd mess with. I never tangle with a woman I'm not sure I can take in a fight.

"Thanks, Lisa, I'll be right up," I said.

When I got upstairs, the phone at the desk had the receiver lying on its side next to it.

"Cavalucci," I said as I picked up the phone.

"Officer Cavalucci, hi, this is ADA Ahearn," he said.

"How you doin'?" I asked.

"Fine. So tell me what happened?"

I went into it about following the car from 44th Street and recapped the story for him. I left out the part about Thompson giving them up earlier.

"How long ago was the car stolen?" Ahearn asked.

"We got it on the printout that it was thirty hours previously, out of the Bronx."

"Did any of them make any statements?"

"Wilson did, just that he didn't know it was stolen."

"What about the two girls, there were two girls in the backseat?"

"Basically it sounds like they didn't know anything about it. They thought they were going clubbing with those two yo-yo's and the car belonged to Wilson. They took off anyway; we never got them," I said.

"I think we'll probably knock this down from GLA to unauthorized use. How much do you think the car was worth?" he asked.

"It was a late-model Maxima, definitely more than three thousand," I said. "They smashed it up, so I don't know what it's worth now."

"Then we'll probably keep the criminal possession," he said, meaning criminal possession of stolen property. "Just fax me down the paperwork, and I'll fax you an affidavit to sign. What's the fax number there?"

I rattled it off to him.

I finished up about noon. The day was bright and clear. The sky was cloudless, but the temperatures were in the teens. I walked out to my truck to find it plowed in with half a foot of snow frozen to the windows, hood, and bumpers. I started the truck to warm it up and used my shovel to dig myself out. There was an icy wind blowing, and my face and ears were stinging as I worked. It took me almost a half hour to get the snow off my truck and burrow a path into the street. I took the West Side Highway downtown, and except for a lane closure outside the Battery Tunnel, there was no traffic all the way home.

16

The message light was blinking on my answering machine when I got home. I tossed my keys on the counter and charged up my cell phone while I played it.

"Tony, it's Grandma," she said. She waited a beat and said, "I guess you're not home, but I need to talk to you. I want you to come for dinner tonight. I'll make breaded steak." She paused again. "Call me and let me know if you're coming. I love you."

Normally I wouldn't blink if my grandmother called me, but after the way she acted Christmas Eve, I wondered if I was walking into an ambush. On the other hand, it might give me a chance to find out what the deal was with everyone about Michele. I decided as I dialed the phone that if my father and Marie weren't going, I'd go talk to her. I already knew Denise wouldn't be there, so that slimmed the chances of a brawl.

"Hello," Grandma picked up on the first ring.

"Grandma, it's Tony," I said without much enthusiasm.

"Is everything okay?"

"Everything's fine," I said. "Who's coming for dinner?"

"No one, just you. Can you come?"

246

"Okay," I said. "Can I do a load of my clothes there?" If I didn't do something soon, I'd be wearing shorts.

"Sure, I'll run downstairs with them when you get here," she said. "About what time?"

I looked at the clock. It was now 1:30, I wanted to get at least five hours sleep.

"How about seven?"

"That's fine. I'll see you then."

I set my alarm for 6:30 and passed out. I hit snooze once and headed for the shower, grabbing a towel off my doorknob that I'd used twice already.

I was shaved, dressed, and out the door with my laundry bag by 7:05. I took the back roads over, Todt Hill Road to the expressway, and cut over to Clove Road. I parked in the spot reserved for 4A like I always do and buzzed 1C for my grandmother.

She was waiting for me in the hall, wearing a cotton shift dress in a floral print, knee-high stockings, and brown slippers. She had a kerchief over her hair to keep her hairdo intact until her weekly trip to the beauty parlor.

"Give me the clothes and go get a cup of coffee," she said, trying to take the laundry bag.

"I'll go down with you to do the laundry," I said. That's all I needed to do, send my eighty-year-old grandmother to get mugged doing my laundry in the basement.

We walked back out to the lobby and took the elevator down to the basement. The laundry room was across from the elevators. I brought change with me, and we loaded two machines, one for towels, socks, and underwear, and the other for dark clothes.

We went back inside, where I had a cup of coffee while she put out bowls for soup.

"I made lentils," she said. She ladled the soup into the bowls and pulled a loaf of Italian bread out of the oven.

We sat in silence while we ate our soup. She had the table set with wineglasses for the both of us, and next to her was an opened bottle of Chianti Classico. We finished our soup, and she went over to the stove and turned on a frying pan. She drizzled some olive oil in it and added a pat of butter. She took a plate out of the refrigerator with three breadcrumb-encrusted rib eye steaks chilling on it. She cooked the steaks three minutes on each side until the breading was golden brown. She transferred the steaks to a platter and took two dishes out of the oven.

She brought everything to the table. The vegetables were broccoli, sautéd with garlic and oil-cured black olives, and baked potatoes.

She poured us each a glass of wine and set mine in front of me. She looked down at her plate and started to eat. I moved the glass of wine away from me, and she said, "Drink the wine, Tony, it's good for you."

"I don't want any wine. I don't drink anymore."

She looked up at me, her face set in anger, and said, "You are not an alcoholic. Are you trying to tell me if you drink this glass of wine you can't stop?"

"No, I can stop." I knew I could. I had a couple of beers Christmas night, and I was able to stop.

"Then why don't you take a drink of wine? Who is filling your head with all this stuff that you can't drink?"

"Is this what you want to talk to me about?" I asked.

"Tony, you know I love you," she said, and her face softened. "And you know I only want what's best for you. But that woman you're seeing." She shook her head. "I got a bad feeling about her."

"Grandma—" I started.

She held up her hand. "Let me finish, and then you can talk. She started so much trouble here Christmas Eve." She held up her hand again when I tried to interrupt. "I said let me finish."

I sighed. "Go ahead."

"She almost broke up the family. Now Denise and your father aren't talking. Denise came here today and said your mother was going to Long Island with her to bring the presents to the little boy. I'll bet she thinks she can get your mother on her side."

"Her side of what? Michele didn't start any trouble here on Christmas. Dad and Denise never talk—how can you blame her for that?" My voice was rising now.

"She's a *putana*!" she spat.

"*What?*" My grandmother just called Michele a whore. "Grandma, what is wrong with you? Don't you ever call her that again!" I said angrily, the closest I've ever come to yelling at my grandmother.

"She has a child out of wedlock, and she's not Catholic! Now, I don't know what kind of religion she belongs to that says a woman can have a baby and not be married and act like she's done nothing wrong. She's going to hell, and she'll take you with her if you marry her!" She made the sign of the cross.

"Grandma, do you know how many women I've slept with?" She shrugged. "I could have had kids with any of them. Does that mean I'm going to hell?"

"It's different, you're a man," she said matter-of-factly.

"No, it's not different. And what about Dad? He cheated on his wife. That's in the top ten of 'Thou shall nots.'" I couldn't believe what she was saying.

"He went to confession and he got an annulment, so in the eyes of the church, that sin of divorce is absolved." She slapped her hands in a "case closed" gesture.

"Michele made a mistake. She could have had an abortion, and no one would have known about Stevie. But she didn't, and I'm glad. He's a great kid and I love him, and if I marry her, I'm gonna adopt him." I almost picked up the glass of wine by reflex but stopped myself at the last second, wondering if that's what Grandma had in mind.

"He will never be your blood, or our blood," she said, slamming her hand on the table.

I didn't even know how to respond to that, so I got up and walked to the door.

"Where are you going?" she asked, startled.

"To put my clothes in the dryer." I had to get out of there before I exploded on her.

I took the stairs down instead of the elevator. I put my clothes in the dryer, added enough quarters for a half hour, and sat down on one of the plastic chairs. I sat there praying for a couple of minutes, asking God to help me calm down and asking him what to say to her.

This was the first time in my life we've ever disagreed on anything. I didn't understand why she didn't like Michele and Stevie. I mean, if she could accept Marie into her family after everything she'd done, why would she have a problem with Michele? And what about Stevie? He was an innocent kid in all this.

Michele was right—they'd never see Stevie as their own, and it would matter down the road. She was also right about my family feeling the same way about her. I could see it in their eyes Christmas Eve, but I didn't want to admit it to myself. It was ugly, but it was true.

I went back upstairs and tried to finish eating. Breaded steak was one of my favorites, but it tasted like cardboard in my mouth. Grandma wasn't looking at me. She was concentrating on her food. I put my fork down and wiped my mouth with the napkin.

"I'm not going to hell, and neither is Michele," I said.

"She's not Catholic, you are," she said.

"Not only Catholics are going to heaven," I said, but she didn't look convinced.

"Why don't you go to Mass anymore? Why do you go to her church?"

"Church or no church isn't what gets you into heaven. Being Catholic doesn't matter to me anymore." She made another sign of the cross. "Knowing Jesus does. For the first time in my life I feel like I know God, and He's not trying to send me to hell. He died for my sins to keep me out of there."

"Don't do this to your family," she pleaded. "She'll ruin us."

I stood up and brought my plate to the kitchen. "Leave that," she said, taking it before I could scrape the uneaten food into the garbage. She scraped it, then washed and dried it and put it away.

"I have cake," she said and pulled a bakery box out of the refrigerator. She filled two mugs with coffee and placed them on the table along with spoons, forks, and cake plates.

The cake was a blueberry meltaway. Cheesecake with blueberries and a crumb topping. She cut us each a slice and sat down.

"So is this how everyone feels about Michele?" I asked.

She shrugged. "Everyone's worried about you. She's changed you."

"No, the way I've changed has nothing to do with her. It was my decision before I met her."

"She's clouded your judgment. That's how women ruin men—they tempt them until they can't see straight. That's what happened to your father. Your mother wasn't so young anymore, and Marie wouldn't leave him alone," she said tiredly. "He wouldn't have left his family otherwise."

"Marie wasn't Dad's only thing on the side. He'd done it before." I could tell by her face that I wasn't dropping any bombshells here.

251

She pointed her finger at me, "But he never left his family, and he always went back to your mother and you kids."

"Lucky us," I mumbled.

I stayed another ten minutes to finish my coffee and cake. I went back downstairs for my clothes. Grandma came with me, and we folded them together in strained silence and put them back in the now clean laundry bag. We took the elevator back up to the lobby, and I walked her to her apartment. I kissed her cheek and said good night.

"Wait, let me wrap up some food for you," she called as I walked down the hallway toward the lobby.

"Don't," I said. "I'm not gonna be home for the next couple of days anyway."

She nodded, looking old and tired as she let herself in.

I went home and put my clothes away. My phone rang at 9:30, when Michele called.

"Hey, good-looking," she said cheerfully.

"Hey yourself, legs. Still alive, huh?"

She laughed. "Yes, I am. Actually, we had a nice day."

"Really?" I said, surprised.

"Really. I like your mother, and Stevie loved her."

"He loves everybody."

"I know, but she was very good with him."

"What did you do?"

"We stayed here, and I made us lunch. Then Denise took Stevie to get a movie and took an hour doing it, so I got to talk to your mother by myself."

"How was my mother with Denise?" I couldn't picture it.

"They seemed fine, very relaxed with each other. Your mom said the blizzard forced them to spend a couple of days together and get things settled."

"Good, I'm glad for them," I said.

"So what did you do today?" she asked.

"I got some sleep, then my grandmother called me to come for dinner. She said she wanted to talk to me," I said casually.

"Talk to you about me." Her voice got sharp.

I didn't want to get into it now. I still hadn't told her about going to the bar on Christmas Eve, mostly because I didn't want to say it over the phone.

"Yeah, we talked about you. I'll tell you about it on Monday when I come out there," I said.

"Okay. I had a nice day, and I'm sure whatever she said will aggravate me anyway."

"Is Stevie up? I want to say hello to him."

"He's unconscious. We were out in the snow for three hours, and he was exhausted," she laughed. "Your mother was cute. She made cookies with him from scratch and hot chocolate from cocoa, not the instant kind, and she made whipped cream. It was delicious."

I remembered that from when I was a kid. Real hot chocolate, then she made her own whipped cream and put a dollop of it in each mug.

"Let me guess, peanut butter crisscross," I said about the cookies.

"That's the one. Denise told me your mother always made them for you guys when you were little. Stevie rolled the dough into balls and flattened them with a fork to make the design on them," Michele said.

"If you dunk them in the hot chocolate, they taste like Reese's peanut butter cups," I told her.

"I know, Denise showed us."

We talked for a couple of minutes more about my mother. Apparently they made plans for us to go see her in Pennsylvania. I wasn't sure how chummy I wanted to get with my mother but didn't say anything about it. My mother had asked me last fall to come up there with Michele and Stevie. I told her I would but never did. I know my mother has changed; I just want to take it slow before I jump off the bridge with her.

I packed a couple of days' worth of clothes and the charger for my cell phone. Chances were I wouldn't be back until sometime New Year's Day.

I left my apartment at 10:00. On my way in to work I saw that security was beefed up at points of entry into the city. I saw a helicopter in the harbor, coming toward the bridge as I went over it. Extra cops were posted at the Verrazzano Bridge and Brooklyn Battery Tunnel. Trucks were pulled over, and I saw their cargo being inspected at the Verrazzano. There was a K-9 unit at the tunnel, standing by with his dog while a trunk was being searched.

There was snow along the curb lines as I made my way up the West Side Highway. Sanitation was everywhere, using an arsenal of payloaders to fill the dump trucks up with all the snow.

I parked on 36th Street, finding a spot on the corner near Dyer, and sandwiched myself between a mountain of snow and Terri Marks's Volkswagon Jetta.

I went downstairs and changed into my uniform, then talked to John Conte in the radio room while I waited for Fiore to get in. I smoked a cigarette until the fall in sounded.

The ranks were exhausted and roll call was quiet, the usual banter replaced by yawns and scratches. Hanrahan was looking worn as he gave his attention to the roll call order. He gave out the sectors, foot posts, and the color of the day (yellow) before getting down to business.

"It is now 24 hours before New Year's Eve," he said, as if we didn't know. "There's gonna be a detail inside Times Square tonight for all the nut jobs camping out. Check all your posts for any suspicious packages. Any calls for suspicious packages found—I want them taken seriously. Follow the guidelines, and don't use the radio or your cell phones. If you find anything or get a pickup of one, call me on my cell phone, but use a land line. I'll call Central and the desk to let them know." He gave us his cell phone, which we wrote in our memo books. "Any jobs in Times Square, I want the foot posts to handle them. I want the sector cars on patrol. If the Times Square detail picks up any jobs or has any collars, I want the foot posts to handle it."

The detail in Times Square is made up of cops from other commands. They're supposed to handle the aided cases and complaints. Since they're standing on a detail, they don't have aided cards or complaint reports. If they do get a job, the reports have to go to our precinct. The detail usually calls us anyway to handle it, so if the foot posts took care of it, the sectors could continue patrolling.

The sarge wrapped it up with, "I need to see Sector Eddie and Sector David after the roll call. Make sure you pick up your jobs, and make sure you're on your posts—there's a lot of Brass around tonight."

"What's up, Boss?" I asked as he approached Fiore and me.

"I have some 'No Parking' signs I want you to put up," he said and handed us a stack of the blue signs that say "No Parking Today" in bold letters and "By order of the New York City Police Department" below it. "You and Joe take 42nd down to 40th between 6th and 8th Avenue. Let Romano help you with it."

He handed Rooney a stack and said, "Mike, you and Jimmy take 43rd up to 45th between 6th and 8th Avenue, and let Galotti take some of it."

Even with Romano helping us, it was gonna take us a while. Romano was complaining before we even got in the RMP.

"How am I gonna work twenty hours between tonight and tomorrow? I'm exhausted already," he griped.

"Stop crying, everyone's exhausted," I said. "Wait till next week when you get your check, then you'll be happy."

"It's blood money!" he yelled.

Joe and I laughed at the same time. "You've been listening to the old-timers too much," I said. They always call it blood money because it's not easy overtime. It's usually at least a seventeen-hour day. For Romano, between his DOA fixer, this midnight tour, and six hours sleep tomorrow before the New Year's detail, he did have a legitimate complaint. But I wasn't gonna tell him that; we all had to do it.

We stopped at the Sunrise deli on 40th and 7th to get coffee and drove up to the Deuce and parked outside Applebee's. It was still clear and cold, around twenty degrees.

A group of sailors passed us. We see them every year in their whites and peacoats with their sailor hats, just asking to get yoked. By the time the week is over, they'll be robbed, scammed, beat up, and broke.

We let Romano take a couple of sips of his coffee and threw him out of the car to put up the signs, starting at 8th Avenue and working his way back toward us.

"How was the overtime detail?" I asked Joe as we drank our coffee.

"Busy. They cleared the streets, and the only parking is in the garages, so they're packed," he said. "It was nonstop all day."

"They're getting serious with these terror threats," I told Fiore. "They had a lot of cops at the bridge and the tunnel checking the trucks and cars. They even had a dog there."

"I know. I read in the paper the Coast Guard is in the harbor, watching the bridges and Liberty and Ellis Islands as possible targets for terrorists," Fiore said.

Romano had jumped back in the car and caught the end of the conversation.

"Do you think they're gonna blow us up tomorrow night?" he asked, looking worried.

"Did you finish those signs?" I growled at him.

"Yeah, look," he pointed his thumb down the street, where we saw the signs lining the poles.

"How'd you do that so quick?" The signs had metal clasps with rubber bands that had to be punched through the paper and wrapped around the pole.

"I ran, and I put the rubber holder through while I was running to each pole."

"I'm impressed, Nick," Joe said. "Tony usually rips three or four of them before he gets it right."

"Joe, I'm serious, are we gonna get blown up here tomorrow?"

"Nick, no one is going to get in Times Square with a package bomb. The whole area is searched," Joe said.

"What about those suicide bombers, or car bombs?" Romano asked.

"They can't get a car bomb in here. We put salt trucks at every block so they can't drive a car through here. As far as a suicide bomber, he'd blow up at the checkpoint or get shot there," I said. "They'd have a better shot at blowing something up during rush hour, but not on New Year's Eve. The whole inner perimeter is secure."

"Don't worry about it, Nick. It's been eight years since anyone tried to bomb us," Joe said. When Romano didn't look convinced, Joe emphasized, "Listen to me, Nick, everyone's gonna sign out tomorrow night. Nothing's gonna happen."

"What about the Oklahoma City bombing?" he asked.

"It was in Oklahoma, you hose head," I said. "Plus it was one of those white supremacist groups."

"They still bombed the building," he insisted.

"That was different," I said.

"Last New Year's that guy came over from Canada with a car full of explosives," Nick said.

"So what? They caught him," I snapped. "Are you done with your coffee?"

"Yeah," he said, taking his last sip.

"Then go put your signs up and stop worrying."

"My hands are freezing. I can't even wear gloves with these stupid signs," he said as he got out of the car.

"Actually, Joe, there were serious terror threats last year," I said.

"I know, the city was on alert, I was here."

"Well, you remember how last year everyone was worried about the Y2K thing?"

"Yeah."

"Lieutenant Farrell gave Rooney and me the inside scoop on what was going on," I said.

"What'd he say?"

I filled him in on what Lieutenant Farrell had told me. He said, last year with all the ominous warnings about the Y2K threat, everyone was sure that as the clock hit 12:01 on New Year's Day, there would be complete pandemonium throughout the city. There was real concern about the city's vulnerability to the 2000 computer glitch.

While the Police Department plays the major role in keeping order on New Year's Eve, the Fire Department, Sanitation, and Con Edison all have their part. Sanitation handles the cleanup of tons of debris as soon as the crowds leave. Con Edison keeps the city lit and makes sure the ball drops and the lights don't go out in Times Square. The Fire Department and EMS are trained for large-scale casualties.

For the millennium, Con Ed assured us they were not worried about a computer failure or a blackout from an overloaded power system. Considering all the blackouts the previous summer, nobody believed them. RMPs escorted the Con Ed trucks around the city. In case of a blackout, the trucks would be able to get anywhere they needed to go. Con Ed said we wouldn't be using enough juice to overload the system; they said the security of their power plants posed more of a threat than a blackout.

A computer defect or power failure would affect New York City on New Year's Eve more than anywhere else on earth. If you take into account that we have eleven thousand traffic lights, plus power lines, phones, elevators, toll booths, subways, bridges, tunnels, banks, hospitals, police computers, and court records, a defect in just one of those could cripple us.

Since the 1993 bombing of the World Trade Center, the city had been implementing new procedures for the threat of terrorism. Last year's millennium celebration generated so much speculation about a possible terrorist attack that people were getting hysterical about it. The press kept talking about terrorists getting into Times Square, but the mayor was saying there was no specific threat against New York City.

Last year, before I became partners with Fiore, I went out drinking with Rooney, Garcia, and McGovern from our squad.

It was the week after Christmas, and like this year, a lot of overtime was available. We had gone to the bar on 9th Avenue after working some OT following our tour. Lieutenant Farrell was there talking football and drinking shots with us. Since it was a Sunday, we went to the bar to watch the Giants play Minnesota.

McGovern and Garcia went back to the precinct to get some sleep, leaving Rooney and me to keep an eye on the lou, who was half in the bag. Eventually the conversation came around to the job, and the lou began to fill Rooney and me in on what the Brass was saying about New Year's Eve.

259

According to Farrell, the Times Square gig was almost called off. He said the city was gravely concerned about some kind of terrorist attack within Times Square. He told us that hospitals had biohazard suits and decontamination showers. They also had antibiotics for anthrax and ventilation rooms for chemical attack. Something like fifty ambulances were on standby, as opposed to the usual twenty. He also told us that body bags were being stockpiled up at the Javits Center on the West Side and at Bellevue Hospital. He also told us there were twenty buses at each location to transport the injured, or the dead.

If it was anyone but Farrell, we would have questioned it, but the lou's not that kind of guy. He'd be the one to know what's going on in Midtown. He's worked here for thirty years and is probably the smartest guy they've got. The reason he's never gone further up the ranks is because as a lieutenant he still makes overtime. He's still able to run a whole detail, and if he makes captain, there's no hands on. He doesn't delegate, he likes to do things himself.

He's the one who told me the Coast Guard would be patrolling the harbor. The Statue of Liberty, Ellis Island, and under the bridges would be possible targets. We knew how extreme it was in Times Square; we'd been working the details.

Last year, by the evening of the thirtieth, people had already set up camps on Broadway. A detail the city had put together to manage the early crowd that didn't get there on time. They pulled us off bomb duty because five hundred people had already congregated in Times Square, blocking the sidewalks up and down Broadway. By 4:00 in the morning on the thirty-first, the barricades were already being set up, as opposed to the afternoon, when they usually cordon off the area. By the time I got there at 2:00 in the afternoon, the people were already in barricades as far as 47th Street. By 9:00 there was a sea of people all the way up to Central Park at 59th Street.

I heard that the people who spilled over from the barricades wound up inside Central Park.

The millennium was a global celebration, with festivities starting in New Zealand at 6:30 in the morning of the thirty-first. The campers planned to stay in Times Square until the following morning, when the final toll of the new century would be in French Polynesia, in the Midway Islands.

The streets were almost impassable as the crowds thronged into Midtown. People had bags and backpacks with food and clothes that we checked as they walked into the inner perimeter cordoned off around the core zone. If they wouldn't let us check their bags, they took their Constitutional rights with them when we tossed them out of Times Square.

If we found booze when we checked them, we dumped the booze and got rid of the bottles so they couldn't throw them at us later. Once they got inside the interior of the barriers, they picked their spots and tossed their belongings in a pile. They donned their 2000 glasses and funny hats that they paid too much for on the street and waited for the ball to drop.

Most people don't realize that the best spot to see the ball drop is a couple of blocks up from where it sits on top of One Times Square.

There was no way for us to check the contents of every bag that came into Times Square, so the best we could do was clear the perimeter. Cars were towed, manhole covers were welded shut so they wouldn't blow up into the crowd during an explosion. Mailboxes were locked and garbage cans were removed so bombs couldn't be planted in them. Bomb-sniffing dogs patrolled under the streets to search for explosives, and helicopters patrolled the area from the sky.

For the first time I saw sniper teams leaving the ESU (Emergency Service Unit) trucks and going into buildings with their Remington 700 8-mm bolt action rifles.

Salt trucks were parked crosswise at the corners of each street coming into Times Square so no one could drive a car bomb into the crowd.

On the whole, the city did everything it could to secure the area. When the clock struck twelve, the ball dropped, the lights stayed on, the computers didn't crash, and the old century ended.

17

Romano was on the other side of the street now. He went down to 8th Avenue and was working his way back toward us. We planned on letting him do 42nd Street and then stay on his post while Joe and I finished up 41st and 40th Streets.

"I remember the big thing last year was Y2K. People were getting nuts about it, piling up on food and bottled water, worrying that the world was gonna end," Fiore said, still talking about last year.

"Were you worried?" I asked.

"No. I mean, I took extra money out of the bank and filled the cars up with gas. Donna wanted me to drive in that night in case the computers went down and the Long Island Railroad wasn't running, but we didn't panic. We had enough food and water for a couple of days in case the power went out, but I was okay about it. How about you?"

"I wasn't sure what would happen. Half the things you heard said it'd go off without a glitch, and the other half said to find a hole to crawl into and bring enough food to last you six months. I was too busy the week before New Year's to worry about it." When I wasn't working I was drunk and picking up women, but I didn't mention that.

I moved the car up toward 7th Avenue. A barrier truck was on the corner, and a couple of plainclothes cops were unloading barriers, stacking them up in piles. They were the blue barriers with "Police Line Do Not Cross" in white letters across them. We threw them a wave, and they waved back, we're all cops.

As the last barriers were placed and the truck pulled away, an ESU truck pulled up across the street, on 42nd just off 7th Avenue. An old, battered white utility truck pulled up behind it, one of those trucks with drawers on the side and a back compartment to hold larger tools.

Two ESU cops got out of the truck and pulled on leather gloves. One of them was holding a metal hook, the other a handheld searchlight.

The cop with the hook knelt down and pulled the manhole cover up with the metal claw. It made a loud scraping sound as he dragged it off the hole and clanked it on the street. The cop with the light climbed down into the hole and disappeared below the street. A guy in overalls climbed out of the utility truck. He went in the back for his welding gear and placed it on the ground next to the open hole.

"Looking for bombs again, huh?" Fiore asked.

"Yup, let's go check it out," I said, getting out of the car.

We walked over to them. "What's going on, guys?" I asked.

The cop turned. "How you doing, guys?" he said, shaking our hands. He leaned back over toward the open manhole. Fiore and I looked down into the hole and saw the faint beam of light and heard the hollow sound of footsteps on the metal staircase below.

"We're searching underneath to make sure there's no explosives down there before we seal off the manhole covers.

There's another unit that has a dog sniffing out the areas with underground walkways through them."

"They did this last year too," I said.

"We'll probably do it every year," he said.

We saw the light coming back toward us now as the second cop reached us and climbed up out of the manhole. As he popped his head out, he said, "Everything's clear."

When he climbed out, his partner grabbed the metal hook again and dragged the manhole cover back in place. The guy in the overalls fired up his torch and said, "Don't look at it," as he pulled the visor on his helmet down over his face.

We turned away as he began welding the manhole cover closed. We stood there talking to the ESU cops. They were talking about their bomb searches around Times Square, and I was starting to feel insignificant until I realized we'd been searching for bombs too. But they are the elite.

Emergency Services are the cop's cop. If we have a situation we can't handle, we call them in. If we're outmatched or outgunned, they come on the scene and even up the odds. They're better trained for jumpers and hostages and are better equipped for the more sophisticated emergencies. They have the saws, the jaws of life, the sniper rifles, and the machine guns. It's a nice gig, but hard to get. They're the first to respond to all the extreme situations like killer animals, building collapses, and catastrophic events.

One of them was telling us about their New Year's Eve detail, when we heard an explosion to the north of us. We all stood there for a second. I knew the sound was from up near 43rd Street, but I thought for a second it might have had something to do with the guy welding the manhole cover.

As we looked up toward 43rd Street, we saw people running toward the back of a Con Edison truck with a protective area closed off around where they had been working underground. A small cloud of smoke rose up from the work area, and one of the workers was screaming while looking down into the hole.

The four of us looked at each other and took off together toward 43rd Street, leaving the welder and his flame behind. As we were running toward them, I heard over the radio, "South substation to Central, there's been an explosion on four-three and seven."

When we reached the truck, a small crowd had gathered and the Con Ed worker was still yelling down into the hole. Cops were coming from everywhere, most of them the Time Square detail and our foot posts.

"What happened?" Romano yelled, looking scared out of his mind as he came running up behind us.

Reporters from the *New York Times* were coming toward us now, and I heard South substation asking Central for two buses forthwith.

We could hear coughing and screams coming from below. Within a couple of minutes, EMS was on the scene with two ambulances. Hanrahan pulled up along with South Eddie and rushed out of the cars.

"What's up?" Hanrahan asked, looking serious.

"I don't know, some kind of explosion underground," I said.

"Everyone alive?" he asked.

"They're screaming, that's a good sign," I said. "If we didn't hear anything, then I'd be worried."

They took the first guy out. He was cut up and knocked around but looked okay.

"What happened?" his buddy asked.

"Cable shorted out."

You could almost feel the relief that it wasn't any kind of explosive. When they brought the second guy out, he looked a little more serious. He must have been the guy to catch the juice from the cable. From where I was standing, I could see burns on his legs. EMS got them right out of there, and other Con Ed trucks were pulling up and going down to the site.

We walked back down to 42nd Street with Romano and the two ESU cops.

"What happened?" the welder asked, turning off the flame as we approached.

"Con Ed was working and a cable shorted out," Fiore told them.

"Everybody okay?"

"A little banged up," his ESU buddy said. "They'll be fine."

He nodded and began packing up his welding gear.

We said good-bye to them and went back over to the RMP.

"You okay?" Fiore asked Romano.

"Yeah. I thought a bomb blew up," he said. Both Romano and I lit cigarettes. We were smoking with our gloves on. We'd been outside for a while now, and while we were warm enough with our thermals on, we were feeling it on our hands, feet, and faces.

"Nick, what would you do if you got in a situation where you were in danger?" Fiore asked.

"I don't know." Romano shrugged, "Why?"

"Would you pray?" Fiore looked at him.

Romano seemed to be thinking about that. "Probably," he shrugged. "Twelve years of Catholic school will do that to you."

"What would you pray?" Fiore asked.

"I don't know," Romano sounded annoyed. "I'd probably ask God to help me. Why?" he asked again.

"Because God tells us we can call on him to protect us," Fiore said, taking out his little Bible.

"Where does it say that?" Romano said, leaning into Fiore.

"In Psalm 91," Fiore said, flipping through the Bible.

"Listen to this: 'He who dwells in the secret place of the Most High shall abide under the shadow of the Almighty. I will say of the LORD, "He is my refuge and my fortress; My God, in Him I will trust." Surely He shall deliver you from the snare of the fowler and from the perilous pestilence. He shall cover you with His feathers, and under His wings you shall take refuge. His truth shall be your shield and buckler. You shall not be afraid of the terror by night, nor of the arrow,'—or bullet," Fiore added, looking up at Romano—"'that flies by day, nor of the pestilence that walks in darkness, nor of the destruction that lays waste at noonday.'"

"What does that mean?" Romano interrupted. He had been listening intently but looked a little confused.

Fiore was quiet for a second. "It's about God's protection," he said. "It talks about the person who lives in the secret place of God's protection. The one who says, 'The Lord is my refuge and my fortress, my God, in him I will trust.' It says God will deliver them. Do you understand that?"

"A little," Romano said. "Like the other stuff you were telling me about. I understand what you're saying, but if God protects us, why didn't he protect my father?"

Romano's father had been killed when he was shot in the face in a domestic dispute. Romano was about ten years old at the time.

I prayed for God to give Fiore some quick thinking 'cause things were getting a little heavy here.

"I don't know, Nick," Fiore said honestly. "But I know the Bible says I can call on God to protect me, and I believe he will. In fact, I know he will. He's done it before."

Romano stomped away from us, walking about ten feet

down 42nd Street. He walked back over to Fiore. "Let me see that." He held out his hand for Fiore's Bible.

Fiore handed it to him, still open to the 91st Psalm. "Read verse eleven. 'For He shall give His angels charge over you, to keep you in all your ways.'"

Romano used his finger to find the spot and was reading it to himself.

"Where can I get one of these?" Romano held up the Bible. He sounded angry and glared at Joe.

"Take that one," Joe said.

"Thanks," he said, putting it in his pocket. "You know, Joe, if it was anyone else but you, I wouldn't listen. Not even you, Tony—no offense." His tone was sharp.

"None taken," I said.

He came over and shook our hands. "I'm gonna finish these," he said as he held up his no parking signs. "Can you pick me up for my meal at five?"

"Sure," I said.

"You okay?" Joe asked him.

He nodded and walked across to the north side of 42nd Street with his signs.

Fiore and I took the sector car and drove down to 41st Street and parked on 6th Avenue.

"What was that about?" I asked as we walked from pole to pole putting up the signs. "You been talking to Romano about God?"

"Yeah. He's coming over for dinner on New Year's Day. You and Michele are invited," Fiore said.

"Was this a last-minute thing?" It was the first I was hearing about it.

"Pretty much. I was talking to him in the lounge before you came in last night. He's all churned up inside. He says he always feels better when I talk to him about God, and when you bust his chops," Fiore laughed.

"Did he say that?"

"Yup, he says when you bust his chops he knows you like him, and he doesn't feel so detached from the cops. He said that you and I are good cops, and he appreciates that we let him hang out with us."

I laughed. "He's a pretty good cop," I said. "It's a shame he's going over to FD."

"It's probably better. Any dispute he gets called to is gonna remind him of his father. At least with FD there's no history there," Fiore said.

At 1:00 we got a call for an alarm at 29 West 38th Street. The light in the lobby of the building was on, but the door was locked and no one was inside. We gave it back to Central, unable to gain access, and went back to 41st Street to finish the signs.

Some of the stores on 7th Avenue were already boarded up with plywood, like they were waiting for a hurricane to blow through. New store owners find out that plywood is cheaper than plate glass windows, and the couple of minutes it takes to screw the plywood into the metal frame around the windows is worth the effort. I've seen plate glass windows shatter from the pressure of the crowds pushed up against them.

We finished 41st Street and were headed down to 40th Street when we got another call for an alarm from Central. This time it was a fabric storefront on 37th Street. The gates were down, and everything was locked up for the night. We could hear the alarm from inside the store but had no access to the back entrance. We used our flashlights to look through the gate inside the store, holding the lights away from our bodies as we checked the store. There was nothing going on there, so we gave it back premise secure and went back to the no parking signs on 40th and 6th, working our way toward 7th Avenue.

We finished up and spent an uneventful night sitting in the car talking, the calm before the storm tonight, when Midtown would be a madhouse.

I told Fiore about my dinner with Grandma.

"Whoa, did she really call her a *putana*?" His eyebrows shot up.

"Yeah, and then she said Michele was going to hell and taking me with her. She also said Stevie's not my blood, or her blood."

"What did you say to her?"

"I tried to explain to her that Michele wasn't going to hell and neither was I but she didn't listen. I didn't stay long; I didn't want to hear anymore. It's obvious I can never go there again with Michele and Stevie, not that Michele would go," I said.

"What are you gonna do? Let them say this crap about Michele and Stevie and you go visit them and leave Michele home?" he said. "If you marry her, are you going to your grandmother's for Christmas so they can call your wife a *putana*?" He was getting angry.

"First of all, she's not my wife," I said. "Second of all, I didn't say I'd go there without her if I got married. I don't know what to do. I told you my grandmother's never been like this before."

"I find that hard to believe. You mean to tell me she always got along with your mother?"

"I always thought she did. Then when my mother came over for her little twelve-step talk, she said my grandmother made her life miserable. I don't know what to believe," I said, meaning it.

"Yeah, well my money's on your mother. Granny's got a mean streak, whether or not you want to believe it," Fiore said.

We picked up Romano before we went in for our meal at 5:00 and slept in the lounge for an hour. Romano was out cold. It took us a couple of tries to wake him up when we went back out at 6:00.

We stopped at a bagel store on 33rd and Madison for coffee and bagels. I got a bacon, egg, and cheese on a plain bagel, Fiore got egg whites and turkey breast on a pumpernickel, and Romano got an everything with cream cheese. The bagels were soft and fresh; mine was still warm.

"Hey, how you doing?" Fiore asked the Korean woman behind the counter. "I didn't know if you'd be open today."

"We always open," she said. "We close early today, three o'clock."

I guess they got a lot of business from the Empire State Building and the apartment buildings up and down Madison and Park Avenue.

We took Romano back to his post on 42nd and 7th and ate our breakfast in the car. Sunday morning is usually dead, but today there was a lot of activity.

Police and Fire Department Mobile Commands were driving into Times Square and parking along 7th Avenue and Broadway between 42nd and 43rd Streets. The Fire Department was on the east side on Broadway, and the Police Department was on the west side. The Police Department's Communications Division Command Post was there. They give out the radios to the chiefs and Brass working the detail. The command posts had a lane closed off around them, using metal barriers to keep people off the streets.

The NYPD tow trucks were out picking up the last of the cars parked on the street and taking them to the impound. The fee for getting your car back was nothing compared to what you'd get back if your car was left there. Any cars left near Times Square that the crowds have access to get demolished. The crowds climb up on the car to get a better view of the action. There's so many people there, you can't tell they're standing on a car except that a bunch of people are up a little higher than the rest. When the crowds go home, the roofs of the cars are crushed down to the seats, and the hoods and trunks are caved in. Many a Police Department car has been ruined that way.

Sanitation trucks were collecting the garbage pails inside Times Square, and the postal workers were out locking the mailboxes. A stage was being set up around the substation in One Times Square for lights and cameras. Workers were going up and down the scissor lift next to a box truck and constructing the platform.

There weren't many cars out there yet, and traffic was flowing nicely through the streets. We started heading back to the precinct at 7:30. We wanted to get as much sleep as we could before the detail.

"I can't believe I gotta be back here in six hours," Romano moaned.

"Listen, we'll get some sleep, we'll do the detail, then we're off for two days," I said.

The way our tours work, we have two days off one week and three days the next. Because of the New Year's detail, we'll only have two days off, but with twelve hours time and a half.

I changed into sweats and a T-shirt before I went to sleep. Romano was already asleep, and Joe was still talking to Donna when I passed out. I was groggy and disoriented when Joe shook me awake at 12:20. I got clean clothes, a towel, and my soap and shampoo and used the shower in the basement. Rooney was yelling for me to hurry up, calling me a greaseball, so I peed on the shower floor before I got out.

I smiled at him when I left and said, "It's all yours."

"'Bout time," he mumbled.

Joe and Romano went up to the third-floor showers, which are just as disgusting as the one in the basement, and the three of us were showered and dressed by 1:00. I was warm with the thermals under my uniform, but I'd need them later. We went across the street for coffee and ham, egg, and cheese on a roll and ate by the desk at the precinct while everyone waited to go to post.

We piled into two vans and parked on 44th Street between 8th and 9th. We walked over to 48th and 7th to muster up. We would be posted on 44th and 7th, but this is where they fall us in before we get to post.

The streets were closed now, and the earlier detail cops were already putting people in pens. The pens were filled up from 45th Street down, and people would continue being crammed in as the day wore on.

Rooney, Connelly, McGovern, O'Brien, Romano, Garcia, Bruno Galotti, and Fiore and I stood together talking and cracking jokes. Rooney was talking about his next-door neighbor.

"I'm telling ya, he's a nice guy. Every time it snows, my steps and front walkway are already shoveled by the time I get home," he bragged.

"Sure he shovels your steps—he's sleeping with your wife," O'Brien said, causing Fiore to choke on his coffee while everyone laughed.

We stood and watched as the workers did the practice runs with the ball, lowering it down then bringing it back up.

"Did you know that there was only one year that the ball didn't drop?" Rooney asked us.

"That was during World War II," Fiore said.

"Yeah, it was blacked out in 1943 and 1944, but that was because of the war. In 1956 there was a mechanical failure, and the ball didn't drop. A circuit breaker blew and cut off the power. They got it working like fifteen minutes later," Rooney said.

The day was cold, but the heat from the sun warmed us up a little. The thermals and turtlenecks would keep us warm enough for now. We carried our memo books without the bulky holders, and our jackets were open, with our radios in our inside pockets, closer to our ears so we could hear them.

McGovern was wearing his department issue ear muffs, he's skinny and was already freezing. Rooney whipped out a black vinyl bomber hat and put it on, the ear flaps hanging down.

"What is that?" I laughed, pointing at Rooney's hat.

"What?"

"Your hat. You look like a psycho," I said.

"It keeps me warm," he said.

"No wonder his wife's sleeping with the next-door neighbor," O'Brien said, making everyone laugh.

"Hey, O'Brien, at least my wife didn't leave me for a woman," Rooney yelled.

Laughs and ooohhhs were heard all around. O'Brien turned red but still laughed.

"Mike, what are we in Siberia? This is New York," I said.

"Yeah, wait till later when you're freezing," Rooney said.

"I don't care if my ears fall off, I wouldn't be caught dead looking like that."

As we stood together before we went to post, the questions started as people walked by. We answer as best we can, then we get tired of the whole thing.

"Where does the ball drop?"

"See the Cup O Noodles sign? Right above that."

"What's going on?"

"It's New Year's Eve."

"Why are all the cops here?"

"There's a protest going on. Hundreds of thousands of people are protesting the ball dropping."

"Oh."

"Where does the ball drop?"

"See the Cup O Noodles sign? Right above that."

"What's going on here?"

"There's been an Elvis sighting."

A confused look and forced chuckle.

"Where's MTV?"

"On 7th Avenue between 44th and 45th."

"Where's Dick Clark?"

"Home watching MTV."

"Where does the ball drop?"

"See the Cup O Noodles sign? Right above that."

People wouldn't ask Rooney. They'd pause by him and turn to one of us to ask us a question. "Where does the ball drop?" is the favorite question, and we're asked it thousands of times while we stand there.

When they were getting ready to move us out, two captains were talking to five lieutenants, who in turn walked over to the sergeants. Once they all knew what they were doing, a couple of Brass yelled, "Fall in, five to a line." We lined up, and someone walked through to count the bodies: 5, 10, 15, 20, but there's never just five. You get 4 or 6, and they tell them to slide over or move up or down.

After they count, the sergeants take about eight cops each. Hanrahan had nine. He grabbed Rooney, Connelly, McGovern, O'Brien, Garcia, Romano, Fiore and me, and Noreen, his driver. Bruno Galotti was standing with us, trying to get in.

"Sorry, Bruno," Hanrahan said. "Try to get in with Sergeant Yu."

Bruno looked hurt and disappointed as he walked away.

"Bruno," I called, feeling sorry for him. "Just be careful tonight," I said quietly when I caught up with him.

"Why, you think something's gonna happen?"

"No, not at all," I said confidently. "I'm just saying, be aware of what's going on around you." I shook his hand before I walked back to the squad.

"What'd you say to him?" Fiore asked.

"I told him if he moves out of his mother's house and gets his own apartment, he can stay with us next year."

"Did you really say that?" Fiore looked doubtful.

"No, I told him to be careful."

When we're going into something like this and you know something might happen, you really do care about the people around you. You want everyone to sign out and go home at the end of the night.

As far as Hanrahan not picking Galotti, I didn't blame him. You pick the people you want with you if something happens, cops you know and trust. If something happened, I pictured Bruno running for his life toward the West Side Highway without a backward look.

"Come on," Hanrahan said. "We got 44th and 7th. We'll head over there."

As we walked down, we could see there were already people in the pens below us between 46th and 43rd. The noise was higher now, excited talking and picture taking with the crowds on the sidewalks. People were wearing their 2001 glasses and already blowing those annoying noisemakers that I hate.

People were dressed for the long hours ahead; hats, scarves, gloves, and blankets were seen everywhere.

They're still pumped up about being here, because it's only been about an hour since they got their prime spots in the pens. They'll get tired of it later on, then the closer it gets to midnight, they'll get excited again.

"This is our post," Hanrahan said. "The north part of 44th Street and 7th Avenue. This pen is ours to stay around. If anyone has to use the bathroom, there's a port o' potty right there," he pointed to it, "on the north side of 44th Street, just off 7th Avenue. If someone needs to use the port o' potty, escort them there and make sure they come right back where they were. If anybody wants to leave the pen to get something to eat or drink, they're not allowed back in."

There are four pens per block, with an emergency lane down the middle. The pens are large enough to hold three thousand people, but we'd only get to know people right near us in the pen. We make sure nobody comes in or out. It used to be that once the people were inside the pens, they couldn't leave, not even to go find a bathroom. They had no port o' potties, and people were urinating all over, stinking up the place.

"The color of the day is orange," Hanrahan said. "We'll go two at a time for our meals," he added, giving out the times.

"Rooney and Connelly, four o'clock." He stopped and stared at Mike Rooney. "What's with the hat?"

"Enough with the hat," Rooney grumbled.

"You look like Goofy," Hanrahan laughed.

"No, Goofy wore an aviator's hat," Rooney bit out the words, and everyone started laughing again.

"O'Brien and McGovern, five o'clock," Hanrahan continued.

"Fiore and Cavalucci, six o'clock."

"Garcia and Romano, seven o'clock."

"The Times building is having a free buffet for all of us working the detail. Most of you know this already. They put out a pretty good spread, so you can go eat there if you want. Take the phone number for the command post." Hanrahan read it off and we wrote it in our memo books. "We're in Sector 3. If they raise us, it's gonna be 'Sergeant Hanrahan, Sector 3.' If you hear that, let me know in case I don't hear it over the noise. Our radio will be channel 11."

That's the citywide channel normally used for details, and

it wouldn't interfere with Central and the other Midtown commands.

Hanrahan posted two of us on each of the four corners of the pens. We stood right in front of the pen like thousands of cops have done for almost a hundred years before us, and waited for history to happen.

18

At 2:30 we relieved the post that had been at the barricade since early this morning. We talked to the cops for a couple of minutes before their sergeant pulled them out of there.

Before we settled in, I went across the street to a deli on Broadway and 44th to get coffee for Fiore, Romano, and me. There was a line to the door, and I waited fifteen minutes to get to the counter.

"Three regular coffees," I said.

"That'll be nine dollars," the clerk said.

"Nine bucks? Are you kidding me? That's triple the price! You're a thief." He stood there with a blank look on his face, apparently having had this conversation with everyone else today.

"That's the price, take it or leave it," he said.

"Forget it, I'm not paying that," I said, stomping out.

"Where's the coffee?" Joe said when I got back.

"Forget it, I'm not paying three bucks for a friggin' cup of coffee," I said.

"They do that every year," he said, shaking his head.

Joe and I scanned the area. We were one block North of

One Times Square where the ball drops. Huge Astrovision screens are on either side of the building, taking up most of the street. To the east of us is ABC studios with the electronic news running underneath it. Dick Clark would be warm and toasty on the second floor of the studio until much later. He comes down periodically, and then close to midnight he's at a stage that would be diagonally across from us in the middle island by the Armed Forces recruiting booth.

The MTV stage is right in front of us, and the MTV studios are above us on the second floor. Every street around us has the Sanitation salt trucks used as blockers at the entrances into Times Square.

The area we are now in is secured, and no spectators are allowed. There is no pedestrian movement down here, the people are already in the pens. Workers for the sound and stage with ID tags are allowed to move around, along with Police Department, Fire Department, and EMS personnel.

It is impossible to walk around. Credentialed press are allowed on sidewalks but not the streets, those are emergency vehicle lanes. The sidewalks are open to employees in the buildings, but they have to be escorted in and out by the cops.

Every sign in Times Square is lit, flashing and moving trying to catch your eye. The first ten stories of the buildings are covered in the super ads, and none of the architecture can be seen. Colors billow, the Cup O Noodles soup steams, and the Panasonic screen displays a picture of the Waterford ball.

A group of Anti-Crime cops were going up 44th Street toward 8th Avenue, some in their bright orange hats that could be seen from a block away. They use the bright colors, either hats or wristbands, so they can pick each other out in the crowd.

They were probably going to work the crowds in the outer perimeter of Times Square for pickpockets, assaults, robberies, quality-of-life type things. The only pickpockets in the inner perimeter would be in the pens, and there's plenty of cops here to handle it.

My cell phone rang in my pocket. "Hello." I put my finger in my left ear to block out the noise.

"Where are you?" my father yelled.

"Where do you think I am?"

"You're already there? I tried you at home," he snarled.

"I haven't been home," I said.

"You gonna be there all night?" he asked.

"Yeah, I'll be here for the duration."

"Make sure you dress warm," he said. I looked over at Rooney in his hat.

"It's a little late for that; I'm already outside."

"Who are you with?"

"My partner, Joe, and the rest of my squad."

"Good, good," he said. "Okay, I just wanted to wish you a Happy New Year and tell you to be careful."

"Thanks, Dad," I said. "You too."

I wondered if he's nice periodically just to throw me. It'd be so much easier if he was the same all the time. When he's nice, it confuses me and makes me feel guilty for hating his guts.

Joe was on his cell phone. He had his back to me and his finger in his ear like I did to blot out the noise.

"That was Donna," he said as he ended the call.

"Everything alright?"

"She misses me, and she's concerned about a terrorist attack. She was upset that I didn't go home yesterday to say good-bye."

"Nothing's gonna happen," I said.

"I know that, and she knows that too. She just hates me working New Year's Eve. I told her to get together with Michele. Let the kids play, get something to eat, watch movies. I told her to pray for us and I'll be home as soon as I can."

"She'll be fine," I said. Fiore hates when Donna is upset. It throws him all off. He also gets funny when he doesn't see them for a day or two; it's like he gets homesick.

There were golf carts driving by us in the emergency lane. The golf carts brought the chiefs and other Brass to check the operation. They made sure the barriers were in place, the emergency lanes were cleared, and the blockers and emergency vehicles were in position exactly the way they were supposed to be. They went up toward 59th Street and worked their way back down.

I kept my hat on and didn't smoke. I didn't want a chief to single me out and scream at me for smoking or say something to Hanrahan for me not wearing a hat.

Things were still pretty tame, so we passed the time listening to Rooney entertain us with his little trivia tidbits about Times Square.

"Did you know before the 1930s, only men came out on New Year's Eve?" he asked.

"Why, weren't the women allowed?" Romano asked.

"It's not that they weren't allowed, it was just known as a man's holiday," Rooney said. "There was probably a lot less trouble that way."

"Who are you kidding, Mike?" Noreen Casey, the sarge's driver, yelled from the other side of the barrier. "Are you saying we lock up more women than men on New Year's Eve?"

"How did she hear me say that?" Rooney mumbled.

"Because your ears are covered with that stupid hat and you're talking loud," I said.

"No, it's because you can't trust women. It's like they know what we're thinking."

At 4:00 we started taking our meals. Rooney and Connelly went first, so we had to spread out to cover their post. Joe periodically walked to their post and then back to ours while I stayed put. Romano would do the same thing, walking from his post to ours. Since I didn't have Joe to talk to anymore, I turned my attention to the people in the pen.

A couple of women from Japan asked if they could take my picture. I smiled for them and then let them borrow my hat to take pictures of each other. They spoke English. Their mother was with them, but she didn't speak the language, just smiled and nodded the whole time.

I started to talk to the others and asked them where they were from. That always breaks the ice. There was a couple from Vietnam. Two guys, who I called Hans and Franz, were from Germany.

"What are you doing here?" I asked them, amazed. I thought they were idiots to sit here all day. If they didn't pay me for this, I'd never come here.

"It's the place to be," one said in a boing-boing kind of accent. "I always wanted to be here. It's the best party on the planet." He yelled, whooping up his arms. He was hammered.

"What are you drinking, Jagermeister?" I asked.

"Ya, Jagermeister," he pulled out a flask and offered me some.

If I thought he was gonna be a problem, I would have taken the flask, but he seemed harmless, just keeping warm.

"No way," I waved my hands at him. "I don't want to be feeling like you guys later." There was a time I might have taken a slug off it, but I didn't like it anyway; it tasted like cough medicine.

There were two women, probably in their early twenties, from Brazil. They were pretty and exotic looking. They flirted with me, tried my hat on, asked if I was married.

A guy who looked like he was from New York was there. He was originally from Brooklyn and moved down to North

Carolina. His wife wanted to see Times Square on New Year's, so they made the trip up.

They were telling me where everyone was from. We had Panama, Australia, California, Ohio, San Diego, and a couple of kids from Yonkers, which is above the Bronx.

A couple from Mississippi was feeling no pain. You could tell it was their first time in the big city, and they were pretty excited about it. It must not get too cold in Mississippi, because they were underdressed. They were wearing jeans and sneakers, and sweatshirts with lined flannel jackets over them. They had no hats or gloves and would be freezing later.

Most of the people had dressed right. The daytime temperatures are deceiving—an afternoon temperature of thirty-eight degrees can drop down into the teens by midnight. Plus the buildings make wind tunnels of the streets and the avenues where we were.

It looked like one of those summit meetings for the UN. They weren't your huddled masses. Half of them were smashed out of their minds, having drunk so much booze beforehand because they wouldn't be allowed to drink later.

They'd been cleared for bottles, but I knew there'd be some flasks and other nonglass containers with some sauce. They'd be hurting later on. Now they were juiced up and well fed. Six hours from now they'd be hung over and starving. The booze was keeping them warm. Once it wore off, they'd be feeling the cold. But for now they were festive, excited to be here.

"Who do you think is gonna puke first?" I asked Fiore and Romano. "My money's on the Jagermeister man," I said.

"No way," Romano said. "Mississippi's gonna blow first."

"Five bucks says it's Jagermeister," I said.

"You're on," Romano said as we shook hands.

It drags on while you wait for the ball to drop. Most of the festivities don't start until 8:00, and then it's another four hours till midnight. The initial excitement of getting a great spot was wearing off for them, and the crowd was slowing down now as boredom set in.

I was warm enough. I had a spot where the sun was shining. The buildings block the sun, but as the sun moves, so do the shadows from the buildings. My feet were sweating; I had two pairs of socks on, one pair of nylon dress socks and wool socks over them.

It was twilight when O'Brien and McGovern left for their meal. Joe and I left the post at 6:00. I lit a cigarette and smoked it as we walked over to the entrance of the Times building on 43rd Street between 7th and 8th.

The employee cafeteria was on the eleventh floor. We went down the assembly line, stopping to get trays, napkins, and silverware on our way to the hot food. The spread was roast turkey with stuffing and mashed potatoes with gravy, string beans, corn, rolls, soda, and chocolate cake. They also had a cold buffet with sandwiches and salad, but most people got the hot stuff. They do this every year for us, and the food's pretty good.

Mike Donahue, a cop who used to work at our precinct, put down the newspaper he was reading and waved us over. He was dressed in plainclothes, wearing thermal overalls and black boots. He moved a Timberland hooded sweatshirt and a bright orange hat off the chair next to him and made room for us to sit down.

"Where are you working?" I asked him as we shook hands. "You made sergeant, right?"

"Yeah, I'm doing Anti-Crime up at the four four," he said. The four four was up in the Bronx.

"Easier commute?" I asked, knowing he lived upstate.

"Much easier. I should be going over to ESU soon," he said. "I got a hook that's gonna get me in there."

"Is that what you want?" I asked. Anti-Crime Sergeant's not a bad deal.

"Yeah, are you kidding me? It's nice now being out of the bag (out of uniform), but I still have to make numbers. At least with ESU, you take what comes and don't have to worry about numbers."

He stayed for a few minutes more, catching up on who left the precinct and who's new there.

It was warm in the cafeteria, and Joe and I had taken off our jackets and turtlenecks. We finished our food and sat drinking coffee at our table.

I picked up the copy of the *New York Times* that Mike Donahue had been reading. I scanned an article and then looked up for the date on the paper 'cause I couldn't believe what I was reading.

"Do you believe this?" I asked Joe.

"What is it?"

"Where bin Laden Has Roots, His Mystique Grows," I read the headline with disgust. "Mystique? The guy's a friggin' terrorist."

"Who's bin Laden?" Fiore asked.

I scanned the article about bin Laden, how we had a $5 million reward on his head for the 1998 truck bombings of two American embassies in East Africa. He was the leader of the terrorist group Al Qaeda, which is financed for the most part by bin Laden's inheritance of $300 million. Apparently this psycho was one of fifty-one children, which explains his need for attention.

I put the paper down and wondered for the millionth time why the papers would put this crap in the paper on New Year's Eve when they know people are nervous enough about terrorists.

"What's with Romano coming over to your house?" I asked, changing the subject. I hoped Romano wasn't in some kind of trouble like I had been when Joe had me over the first time. Joe had me stay with him a couple of days last summer when I was having a hard time.

"I think he needs his friends right now," Fiore said. "Donna's making a bunch of food: lasagna, rice balls, lobster soup, stuffed escarole . . ." he looked like he was trying to think of what else.

"I get it, she's making food. Maybe you and Donna should talk to him alone."

"No, you're his friend too. You should be there."

I wanted to sleep and go see Michele. I hadn't seen her or Stevie since Christmas Eve, but Fiore was right, something was up with Romano.

"What about Michele?" I asked.

"She's coming," Fiore said.

"She didn't tell me that," I said. At least I didn't think she did. "We gotta work the next day; we got court notifications."

"So? Court's always an easy day. We'll sleep there," Fiore said.

"Okay, I'll be there," I said.

About fifteen or twenty cops walked off the elevators and out of the lobby of the Times building with us. As we stepped out onto 43rd, the street was empty. I looked toward 8th Avenue and there were thousands of people there, with police standing at the barricades, telling them they couldn't come in this way, that they had to move north. I lit a cigarette when we stopped outside the front doors. We threw the bull with the other cops before heading back.

The radio had been droning all night with, "This is Captain so-and-so to Sergeant blah-blah–blah. Have your men move from West 44th to West 45th."

Or "This is Inspector Joe Shmo to Captain Yada Yada."

"Go ahead, Inspector Schmo."

"Take four of your men and move the barrier on 48th Street and Broadway and make a box for the VIPs."

The radio crackled as someone yelled, "They're breaking through the barriers at four-three and eight!"

We all looked toward 8th Avenue and saw the cops on the right corner trying to hold the barriers in place and stop the people from going over and under them.

As all the cops around them converged to help, twenty or thirty people went crashing through the barriers on the left side and headed toward us.

We all took our nightsticks out and started running toward the crowd. I heard over the radio, "85 forthwith at four-three and eight," which means officer needs additional units.

We ran toward the left side of the street, where the crowd was running up. When they saw us coming at them with our nightsticks, most of them stopped, unsure of what to do. They looked both ways, up at us, back at the barriers, and headed back the other way. I guess it looked easier to get thrown out than go at twenty cops with batons in their hands.

We followed the crowd back toward the barriers. Half the cops put the barriers back up, and the other half helped them struggle with the crowd.

The ones who broke through were trying to get back behind the barriers. One tried to hurdle it, and his left foot got stuck on the top. He went down face-first, with the barrier tumbling after him.

I ran over to help the cops on my right, and I saw a cop holding the wrist of a guy who looked about twenty years old. The cop was holding the barrier with his left hand and the guy with his right. The guy was crouched down, pulling as hard as he could to get away. The cop couldn't hold both the barrier and the guy, so he let go of the guy's wrist and grabbed the barrier.

I lunged at the guy, trying to grab his arm as he took off up 43rd Street. He was running at full speed, looking back at me. He took another ten steps and turned his head back to see where he was going.

I heard the *gong* as his head connected with the "No Standing, Trucks Loading and Unloading" sign. He hit the sign, bounced back about two feet, and held his face as he went down.

The sign was still wobbling when I reached the guy, and I choked on a laugh. I heard someone behind me say, "Oh man, did you see that?"

"Well, he shouldn't have run," someone else threw in.

I could see white teeth on the street. They looked like Chicklets against the asphalt. I picked up two teeth, noticing the green paint stuck to them from the sign. He was holding his face and moaning, and when he looked up at me, I saw the imprint of the sign on his forehead and down his face.

I leaned down and put his teeth in the pocket of his flannel shirt. There was a broken bottle of blackberry brandy in his jacket pocket, oozing all over his clothes.

"Your teeth are in your left shirt pocket," I said. "Next time, don't break through the barricades."

I heard someone say behind me, "Didn't your mother ever teach you to look both ways when you cross the street?" followed by laughing.

One detail in Times Square is there just to take the collars on New Year's Eve. They were on the scene now, along with Task Force in their hats and bats. The Mounted Unit came sweeping in to knock the people away from the barricades. They go in sideways so the horses' bodies can knock the people out of the way. The schmuck who doesn't move gets leveled as the horse connects with him.

I saw Joe pushing people back so they could put up the

barriers. This girl about eighteen years old was too drunk to walk, so she leaned on her arms with her feet stretched out in front of her and crawled like a crab up behind Joe. As he leaned over, she tried to kick him so he'd go headfirst into the fallen barriers. Two Task Force cops grabbed her by the arms, spun her around, and cuffed her with the plastic ties they use when they're cuffing large crowds.

Fiore got the barrier up, clueless as to what just happened behind him. The crowd was so frenzied, he couldn't hear a thing.

Once we got control of the crowd, I turned to see the damage. There were ten people cuffed, including Mr. Chicklet. They were sweeping them up and moving them toward the end of the block to the substation, where they'd hold them in the pen. It was 7:40 when things quieted down, and Joe and I walked back to post.

We could hear the noise now, both from 7th and 8th Avenues. We walked through the darkened street, feeling the chill in the air. As soon as we reached 7th Avenue, the blazing lights hit us from everywhere. The buildings had cushioned the sound that now seemed magnified from when we left.

"Hey, where were you guys?" Hanrahan said, annoyed. He looked at his watch. "I sent Garcia and Romano fifteen minutes ago to go to meal."

"Did you hear the 85 at four-three and eight?" Joe asked.

"You guys called that over?"

"No, we were standing right there when it came over. We ran over to help them, and they locked up like ten people," I said.

The demeanor of the crowd had changed since we left. They were more docile now, sober and shivering. The sun was long gone, and the temperature had dropped to below freezing. The wind that New York is known for whipped between the buildings in Times Square.

Hans, the German guy, looked at me and said, "Officer, I don't feel too good." He proceeded to throw up over the side of the barricade.

"Romano owes me five bucks," I said to Joe.

"You called it," he said.

"Oh come on," I said, stepping back as he emptied his stomach again. "That's disgusting."

"Sorry," he moaned.

"What did you do, eat hot dogs?" From where I was standing, it smelled like sauerkraut and NyQuil from the Jagermeister he was drinking.

"Yeah. Before we came in here we had hot dogs."

A small circle opened up, and I could see them getting out of the way inside the pen. Someone else was barfing. It was the guy from Ohio.

The guy from Mississippi sat on the ground with a blanket wrapped around him, oblivious to the vomit behind him. He was hurting now, and I'm sure the cold ground wasn't helping him any. His wife was standing against the barrier, resting on her arms.

The Japanese women were still smiling, but more subdued. The Brazilian ladies looked disgusted as they got themselves to the very edge of the barrier. The kids from Yonkers were yelling at the guy from Ohio for hurling inside the barricade. "Do it over the side like the other guy!" one of them yelled.

At 8:00 they turned the searchlights on and booted up the surround sound. Some of the searchlights go up into the air, bouncing off the buildings and the advertisements. The other searchlights spanned the crowds, psyching them up for the shows to start.

"Welcome to Times Square 2001," Dick Clark's voice rang out into the night. The crowds went wild, suddenly alive again.

The people in the pen now had red tubular balloons with

gold streamers on the end, and some of them had red and gold pom-poms.

"Where'd you get those?" I asked them.

"Someone gave them to us. They told us to wave them."

"Times Square BID," Rooney said, meaning the Times Square Business Improvement District.

There were hats in the pen now, the cardboard ones that look like birthday hats with the elastic around your chin that always pinches you. They were black, with Happy New Year's in gold letters and gold spikes on top. The guy from North Carolina had an I Love New York hat on (the one with the heart), and his wife had a Statue of Liberty crown.

The performers started. Bon Jovi went first, playing on MTV's stage, the sound amplified all across Times Square. Dancers in skimpy outfits with streamers performed, probably freezing their tails off. Puppets came down the emergency lanes and up to the stage. Something like ten thousand bell ringers were there, while someone sang "Ring My Bell."

We don't get to catch too many of the performers because we have to keep an eye on the crowd. I got a VIP pass from someone at ABC. I usually get one every year from one of the TV stations, and I save them. I have like six of them in a drawer at home.

The Japanese women were the only ones in the pen with any oomph. They had a sign that said "I Love Dick Clark" and were holding it up, trying to get the attention of a cameraman.

The other pens were going wild, but my bunch was dead.

"Are you kidding me?" I yelled at them. "You got a prime spot here, and you're standing around looking like corpses! Look around—everyone is going wild. You guys are embarrassing us." I had their attention now.

"I should throw you out of here and get myself some people who at least have a pulse!" I was using my hands now, punctuating my words with my index finger. Romano looked at me like I'd lost my mind, and Joe's face was blank. They didn't realize that if I tired the pen out now, they'd be less trouble later.

"You guys came here from all over the world," I continued. "You got farther in here than most people who tried to get in. Now let me see some *noise* here!" I screamed.

"He's right," Hans said. "Yaaahhh!" he screamed. The rest of the pen followed suit; even Mississippi threw off his blanket and stood up screaming.

I saw the cameraman pan toward us. I pointed at him. "Look, they're filming you right now. Everyone is watching, wishing they were you!" This launched them into another bout of hysterics. I had no idea if the camera was filming them, but at least they were jumping around and screaming, knocking themselves out.

They used their horns and balloons, pumping their fists up in the air.

The energy was starting to build, and it rippled through the crowd as the shows started. It would lull again, probably in an hour, around 9:30. But for now, everyone was pumped.

Michele called about 9:00. It took three times for me to hear her say she had gone over to Fiore's to spend New Year's with Donna and the kids. I put my head almost inside my jacket to block out the noise.

"How's it going there?" she asked.

"Good, it's pretty quiet," I said.

"You can barely hear me," she yelled. "It doesn't look quiet on TV. We're looking for you in the crowd."

"We're a block down from the ball. If I see a camera, I'll wave. Is Stevie there?"

"Hold on, I'll get him."

"Tony!" he yelled excitedly. "Happy New Year! My mom's letting me stay up till twelve o'clock." He blew a horn into the phone.

"Happy New Year, buddy, it sounds like fun over there," I said. I could hear the phone moving away from him.

"A lady came to my house that knows you," he said, and I heard him call "What?" in the background.

"Oh, your mother came to my house. I didn't know you

had a mother," he giggled. "She was nicer than your father, and she baked cookies."

I laughed, "Put your mother back on."

"I miss you, babe," I said. "I feel like I haven't seen you in so long."

"I know. What time are you coming out tomorrow?"

"I don't know, Joe tells me we're going to his house." I didn't sound thrilled with the idea.

"Is that okay?"

"Yeah, it's okay. I'll catch some sleep and try to get out there by two."

We talked for a couple of minutes more, saying "I love you" and "Miss you." I disconnected the phone, and it rang two minutes later. This time it was Denise.

"Where are you?" she yelled.

"Take a wild guess," I said.

"Times Square?"

"Where else?"

"Is it busy?"

"Not too bad," I said. "What are you doing tonight?"

"I'm going up to Dave's. I'm meeting Jessie and Stacey," she said, talking about two of her friends from the neighborhood.

"Be careful. Take it easy driving home," I said.

"I will, Happy New Year, Tony," she said. "I love you."

"Happy New Year, Denise, I love you too."

I put my phone back in my pocket. I heard screaming across the street at the pen on 43rd and Broadway. We saw a couple of guys going at it, their fists swinging and connecting with each other. They were belting each other pretty good until six or seven cops ran over and pushed the barrier out of the way to get them.

They pulled five males out of the pen and put them down on the ground to cuff them. As they pulled the barricade back in place, I heard it come over the radio, "We got a fight at four-three and Broadway."

The last guy they took out before they closed the barricade took off before they could get him cuffed on the ground. He pulled loose and started running toward us. He didn't look scared; he looked almost amused to have a whole barrage of cops chasing after him. As he made it over toward our pen, he cut to the right toward the middle of the pen. Romano, Joe, and I started running toward him. As he approached the barricade, he held up his arms over his head and did a free fall into the pen. I don't know if he thought this was one of those concert moves where the crowd catches him and moves him along on their hands, 'cause it wasn't. They scrambled out of the way so fast he hit the pavement with a thud and a whoosh as the air got knocked out of him.

The cops who were chasing him grabbed him by the boots and pulled him out from under the barricade that surrounds the pen. He was facedown, and when they stood him up, you could see he was wasted and feeling no pain. His face was scratched, and he had a couple of pebbles imbedded in the skin on his face and hands. He'd feel this in the morning; they always do.

By 10:00 the crowd was only screaming when the cameras hit them. Other than that, they were just trying to make it till midnight. The radio was busy with chiefs and inspectors calling to move sergeants and cops around. At one point, a chief called Central to handle a job that he was right in front of.

"Chief Roche to Central." It was pronounced Roach.

"Go ahead, Chief."

"I've got a pickup of an aided on 48th between 7th and 6th. Have someone respond here to fill out an aided card."

An aggravated voice came over the radio and said, "You're a cop, you fill it out."

"Uh-oh, here it comes. This is gonna be good," I said as the ranks descended upon the airwaves.

"Call an exterminator!"

"Help! I'm stuck on a glue pad!"

"Captain Cocker to Chief Roach."

"Sounds like they're swarming, I'll be right there!"

"This is Mr. Orkin to Chief Roach."

"We have some mouse droppings here!"

I was laughing so hard my stomach was hurting, and I could see cops all over Times Square were rolling.

"Central, mark this radio," the chief said, outraged.

"2205 hours, Chief," she said, indicating it was 10:05, and cut off laughing.

Someone came over with, "That's all, folks!"

He'd never find out who said it. Eight thousand cops were at the Times Square detail, and all of them were on this channel. He should have ignored it and saved himself the embarrassment.

The chief radioed Central again to disregard his request for the aided card. He said he had someone there to do it.

The night dragged on. We had a couple of aided cases. A man had a heart attack in the pen just south of us. A kid overdosed. I don't know if it was drugs or alcohol, but he was taken out of the pen behind us. EMS came up past us and came back with a woman in one of their fold-up wheelchairs. Her arm was in a sling and her face was bleeding. Someone said she got crushed in one of the barricades.

At 10:30 we saw an inspector with a couple of sergeants walking toward our pen with a white female. She was walking in front of them, leading the way as she pointed to us. She was good-looking, brown hair with blond streaks, blue eyes, maybe late twenties, early thirties. She pointed to the middle of the pen as

Hanrahan came around from the north corner of the pen and Joe and I came around from the south. We met in the middle.

The inspector approached Hanrahan, "Hey Pete, how you doing tonight?"

"Good, Inspector, how are you? What's going on?"

"This woman said she left your pen to get something to eat. When she tried to get back in, they wouldn't let her back. She said she left her son in the pen and is trying to get back to him." The woman looked a little worried. Not like some of the hysterical mothers I've seen who won't stop screaming their kid's names when we're trying to get information from them.

"How old is the kid?" Hanrahan asked.

"He's ten," the inspector said.

Joe and I were standing back a little, listening to the conversation. "Joe, Tony, do you remember seeing her or her kid in here?" Hanrahan asked.

"Boss, we've been here all night. There's no kids here," I said.

"We're gonna put it over the radio, with a description of the kid," the inspector said. "He's a male white, ten years old, wearing a blue jacket, blue jeans, white hat, and white sneakers."

"No, he wasn't here. Are you sure this is the pen you were in? 'Cause I don't remember you being here," I said. Maybe she got confused on where she was.

"This is where I was," she said adamantly.

Both Joe and Nick didn't remember seeing her either.

"We're gonna bring her to the substation, so if anyone finds a lost child, they can bring him there," the inspector said. They started walking down toward 43rd Street.

We asked everyone in the pen if they remembered seeing that woman or a ten-year-old child, and they all said no, she hasn't been here. We would have remembered seeing a kid.

We heard him come over the radio, "Inspector Thompson to Central."

"Go ahead, Inspector," Central responded.

"At the Times Square detail we're looking for a male white, approximately four and a half feet tall, eighty pounds, last seen in the vicinity of four-four and seven." He gave the description of the clothes the kid was wearing.

Central put out the high priority "doo-doo-doo" signal over the citywide channel and the description of the missing child.

"How do you lose a ten-year-old kid here?" Romano asked.

Joe looked unconvinced, and I said, "There's two possibilities here: Either someone took the kid, or there is no kid. There's too many cops here for someone not to find him."

Throughout the night, we'd been hearing over the radio that people were trying to break through the barriers, but nothing like we had on 43rd and 8th. Periodically we'd hear Central putting over the description of the missing kid.

Around 11:00 cops up on 57th and 8th were calling for an 85. The crowds had broken through the barriers. There was yelling on the radio for an 85 forthwith at five-seven and eight, and we heard sirens moving northbound as they started toward the break.

A series of golf carts with some big Brass shot past us on their way up. A chief called for Task Force to move north to 57th and 8th.

This would be the hour that the intensity climbed and the crowd worked themselves into a frenzy.

"Now it starts," I said to Joe.

"Did you hear what's going on at 57th and 8th?" Romano asked.

"Yeah, they broke through four-three and eight before while we were over there," Joe said.

"You think it'll start happening over here?"

"Maybe, but we'll be alright. It's not the people *in* Times Square that are breaking through, Nick," I said. "It's the people *trying* to get in Times Square."

We listened to the action up at five-seven and eight while keeping alert to what was going on around us.

By 11:30, 57th and 8th was under control, and the mayor and Dick Clark took the stage.

Everyone was trying to listen to what they were saying and cheered every time they paused. They also cheered when the spotlights hit them, and they cheered when the camera swung by them.

In the last half-hour before midnight the noise level was steadily rising, and we couldn't hear each other talking anymore. Because you can't hear over the noise, you tunnel into what's going on around you.

At 11:40 Hanrahan came over to Romano, Joe, Garcia, and me. "Make sure you stay together and that you can see each other at all times," he yelled. "In case anyone starts breaking through the lines, don't run into the crowds. I don't want you getting trampled."

I looked into our pen. None of them looked like they would break through. As crowds go, they were pretty good.

Hanrahan walked back over to the other side of the pen, where Rooney, Noreen, McGovern, O'Brien, and Connelly were. I'm sure he was telling them the same thing he told us.

"What do we do if they start to come through?" Romano yelled into my ear.

"Just get on the sidewalk and put your back against the building," I yelled back.

In the back of my mind I thought if there was an explosion, it would all be over. The truth is, if anything happened and the crowds broke through, we'd never be able to control them.

By 11:45 the noise reached a deafening pitch and would stay that way until after the ball dropped.

Balloons and pom-poms were all in constant motion now. There were no lulls anymore. It was all sound and movement, lights and people. The surround sound was drowned out by the roar of the crowd, and the countdown flashed on the Astrovision screens. The lights on the ball flashed brighter now, and if possible, the crowd grew louder.

The sound became surreal, so dense it was like no sound at all. Animated faces seemed to freeze as we were enclosed into the energy that surrounded us and were caught in time.

Everyone looked like they were having the time of their lives. We were watching so that the whole thing didn't come crashing down around us. I wanted to put my hands over my ears from the pressure, but I didn't.

I looked at Joe and back to the clock to see how much time we had left. We weren't intimidated by the frenzy, we just weren't consumed by it yet.

Romano looked unsure as he watched everything around him. I caught his eye and looked over at the clock. I held up my finger, one minute left I showed him.

During the final minute, while the ball made its way down the flagpole, the crowd seemed to swell and strain against the barriers. Time was suspended as the constant frenzy worked its way toward midnight.

I was aware that the clock read thirty seconds. There was nothing discernable until twenty seconds, when part of the crowd started to count. At fifteen seconds more joined in, and by eleven seconds, five hundred thousand people in Times Square and a billion others around the world counted with us.

"Ten-Nine-Eight-Seven-Six-Five"—the confetti flew—"Four-Three"—the balloons dropped—"Two"—and the crowd rose.

You don't hear the "One," just a chorus of "Happy New Year!" filled the air around us, and the fireworks exploded on top of One Times Square.

A blizzard of confetti and balloons floated around us as the surround sound blasted Frank Sinatra. I could hear the music over the din and the first words to the song, "Start spreading the news, I'm leaving today, I want to be a part of it, New York, New York."

With an eye on the crowd, in the middle of the pandemonium I wished Fiore a Happy New Year. As we went to say Happy New Year to Romano, we noticed a small crowd was using the corner of our barrier to boost themselves onto the traffic signal pole on 44th and 7th.

They were stepping on the barrier and grabbing the signal box. Two of them had gotten on top of the signal post and were climbing onto the metal part of the pole that hangs the signal light, which was over the middle of the barrier.

Three more had climbed onto the signal boxes and were pumping up the crowd below them. The poles weren't meant to hold this kind of weight and were starting to give way. The crowd was cheering and taking pictures of them, not realizing the pole could come crashing down on top of them.

Joe, Romano, and I rushed over and moved the barrier out of the way to get to them. We used our nightsticks to poke the three on the "Don't Walk" sign, hitting the part of their feet that was sticking out. As we were trying to knock them off there, we heard a hollow thud behind us and a rise in the cheers from the crowd. We turned our attention back to the guys on the pole and gave them another jab with our nightsticks.

"Okay, okay," one yelled as he started to climb down. The other two climbed down after him and ran westbound down 44th Street. The other two knuckleheads were dangling from the overhang part of the pole. One of them was using it as a chin-up bar, inciting the crowd below him. The other guy wasn't that strong. He hung there for a couple of seconds before he fell and his buddies grabbed him. The chin-up guy showed off for about fifteen seconds, then let go. He was more athletic than his buddy and fell with more agility.

Hanrahan was in the barriers now with Rooney and Connelly. He was screaming, "If anyone tries to pull a stunt like that again, lock them up!"

We didn't even try to chase them. We turned our attention back to the crowd that had gathered while we were up on the pole. We heard the hollow thud again and watched as a throng of merrymakers entertained themselves by upending the port o' potty about twenty feet away from us. They had it rocking now, and we heard "One" as it rocked forward, "Two" as it rocked back, then they yelled "Three" as it toppled. Whoever was inside there went one of two ways, face first or backward.

The crowd was cheering now, arms up and whooping as someone jumped up on the overturned potty and put his fists up in the air. There were about a hundred of them, and we have no way of knowing which ones tossed it.

Hanrahan was already storming over, dodging the surging masses that were wishing him a Happy New Year. He zigzagged through them as we followed him, until we all gathered around the port o' potty. We heard a thump and a muffled "Help!" from inside the upturned bathroom.

"Unlock the door!" Hanrahan yelled as he pulled on the door.

"I can't open it," the muffled voice said.

"I have to shoot the lock!" I yelled.

"No! I'll open it!" the guy sounded frantic as he fumbled with the lock.

We heard faint grunts as he strained, and he bumped around a little before we heard the click of the latch.

Hanrahan pulled the door open submarine style, and we saw one arm come out and hold on to the side, then the other. The right arm had wet blue toilet paper stuck to it, and we saw his head emerge like he was coming out of a manhole. He was about twenty years old, drunk out of his mind and stumbling to get out.

"Did you see who did this?" he demanded.

"Oh yeah," I said. "We already cuffed him."

"Good, 'cause that was so wrong," he shook his head.

"You ain't kidding," Romano said, reaching under his arm to help him out.

We all gave him a hand getting out, careful not to touch his hands, which seemed to get the worst of it.

"What a way to end the night." He looked depressed now.

"At least it wasn't anything serious," Fiore said.

He nodded, "Thank you, Officers. Happy New Year." He walked toward 44th Street, shaking out his hands as he went.

At 12:15 Hanrahan gave the order, "Start moving everybody down 44th Street to 8th Avenue."

We moved a couple of the barriers and started directing people westbound on 44th toward 8th. As our pen emptied, people were coming from every direction now.

"Come on, show's over," we said as we waved them out of Times Square.

"Happy New Year!" they'd yell.

"Yeah, Happy New Year, keep it moving."

After a couple of minutes of trying to direct people down 44th, we were overcome by the crowd. We made our way to the building line and put our backs against 1515 Broadway, which is actually on 7th Avenue.

We watched the crowds as they filtered out, with most of them walking in the middle of the street down 44th.

As the crowd thinned, a group of females walked over and

started yelling, "Happy New Year, Officers!" There were about eight of them in various stages of inebriation crowding around us. One came up and kissed my cheek, while another planted one right on Romano's lips, wrapping her arms around his neck.

"Get a room!" Rooney yelled.

Joe held up his hands. "Hey, I'm married," he said as a nice-looking blonde approached him.

Someone yelled "Smile!" as the women stood around us to take a picture.

Romano looked embarrassed, and I rubbed my hand over my mouth, showing him he had lipstick on him.

They moved on, and we stood against the building and watched the mob disband. They yelled to us as they walked by, "Happy New Year! You guys did a great job tonight."

"Yeah, thanks, keep moving," we'd answer.

A few of the drunk ones gave us kisses, although nobody kissed Rooney—he was still wearing that stupid hat.

"Come on," Hanrahan said. "Let's go break down the barriers."

We walked back to the barriers and started breaking them down, grabbing the leg with one hand and the police line with the other.

We stacked them on the corner of 43rd and 7th while standing ankle deep in garbage and confetti. We went back to the building line and leaned against the building to hold us up. We lit cigarettes now, which Hanrahan ignored. He knew we were all exhausted, and he wasn't about to bust our chops.

"Did you know the first time they used the pedestrian signal boxes was on New Year's Eve?" Rooney asked us.

"What are you talking about?" O'Brien snapped at him. "We're exhausted here, and you're still blabbering with this crap."

"No, really, the first time they used them was in the 1940s.

They put them on the four corners of 45th Street and timed them with the traffic lights," Rooney said.

"Fascinating—now can you shut up?" McGovern asked.

It was now 1:30, and most of the crowds were gone. We heard the brushes on the Sanitation sweeper trucks as they came down Broadway and 7th. They came into view about a minute later, sweeping along the side of the street while eight guys with brooms swept alongside them. We heard the occasional clink of them sweeping up a bottle; there's always a couple that get through.

"Keep a heads-up for the captain to relieve us," Hanrahan said, meaning the captain would call him over the radio when it was time to go.

"Hey, Boss," Fiore asked, "did they ever find that missing kid?"

"I don't know. I didn't hear anything that they found him. She should be back at the house. We'll find out when we get there."

We stayed there until 1:40 when the captain radioed Hanrahan and four other sergeants to meet him at 46th and 7th. Hanrahan walked up there, then came back about ten minutes later.

"The detail's over at zero two hundred hours," he said. "Your travel time is until 2:45," which is when we'd stop getting paid.

We stood there trying to get the energy to move. "Come on," Hanrahan said. "Let's go back to the precinct and sign out."

We walked down 44th Street toward 8th Avenue. The street was dark as we made our way back. The lights of Times Square gleamed behind us as we walked.

When we got back to the precinct, I went up to the detectives unit on the second floor. I talked to Lenny Mancuso, one of the detectives working the missing kid case.

"Did they find the kid?" I asked.

"No, actually she never had a kid," he said, running his hands down his face, looking tired.

"What?" I said, my voice rising.

"Yeah, her girlfriend comes to the precinct looking for her 'cause she never came back into the pen. We told her everyone was out looking for her friend's little boy, and the friend told us there was no little boy. Ms. Gibbons here left the pen to see if she could get closer to the action, and when the cops wouldn't let her back in, she told them her son was in there." He shook his head in disgust. "The cop took her back into the pen and asked her where the kid was, and she said he was missing." He nodded his head over to where she was now sitting in handcuffs, crying.

"You're locking her up?" I asked.

"Absolutely," he said, calling her a few appropriate names.

"Are you for real, lady?" I asked, furious. "We had so many other things to deal with tonight and you caused all this panic, taking cops off their posts so you could get a closer shot of the ball drop? You deserve to get locked up."

I was still seething when I went to the locker room to change. The adrenaline from the night was wearing off, and the guys were pretty quiet. The only sounds we heard were the rustling of clothes and gun belts, the metal latches on the lockers as they gave, and the vibration of the doors when they opened. There were about twenty of us down there.

"Get a load of this," I announced as I came in. "Remember the woman who lost the kid?" I paused until I had their attention. "There was no kid. She left her pen, and when they wouldn't let her back in, she made up the whole story about the missing kid to get back in Times Square."

This worked everyone into a frenzy and they ripped her apart, calling her every name in the book. I listened to them as they trashed her, and I started feeling bad about it. I was thinking, how would I like it if I did something wrong and someone broadcast it all over the place? I guess God was letting me know I was wrong, either that or I was turning into a friggin' bleeding-heart liberal, feeling bad for the perps instead of the people they hurt. It was her stupidity that caused a massive search for that kid involving hundreds of cops.

Fish, who usually works inside in the cells, said he was up at 57th Street when the crowd broke through the barriers. He said Frankie Amendola, who works at our precinct, was injured when he tried to hold the barrier in place to control the crowd. The barrier was knocked on top of him, and he got stomped as people ran over him.

"Is he okay?" I asked, concerned.

"He's down at Bellevue right now. He cut his head, and I think he broke some ribs," Fish said.

"You know it only takes fifteen pounds of pressure to break a rib," Rooney told us.

A shower of pennies came over the top of the lockers from where McGovern changes. We keep pennies in our lockers to throw at people for this kind of thing.

"How about fifteen pounds of pennies, Mike, will that break a rib?" McGovern yelled as he sent another shower of pennies over. You could hear laughing and the ping of the pennies hitting lockers and rolling onto the floor.

"McGovern, you're a dead man," Rooney threatened.

"At least if I'm dead, I won't have to hear any more of your crap," McGovern countered.

After I changed, I said good-bye to Fiore. He was heading up to Penn Station to catch the 3:00 train. I started to walk out the front door and turned around and went up the stairs to the second floor. The woman was still sitting there, crying and looking miserable.

"Tony, can you watch her for a couple of minutes while I get some coffee?" Mancuso asked.

"Sure," I said.

"What made you say you lost your kid?" My tone was even now, not angry.

"They wouldn't let me back to where my friends were. I thought they'd just let me back in. I didn't know all this was gonna happen."

"Then why'd you keep lying?" If she told everyone sooner, before it got to the point where there was a massive search, she wouldn't have gotten arrested.

"I wish I never said it, alright?" She was really crying now. "I didn't know it would get so out of control. Then when all the cops got involved, I didn't want to tell them I lied."

"Everybody lies. I've lied plenty of times, the only difference is now I answer to God, and I'm learning how to tell the truth again." I sounded like Fiore now, and she probably thought I was some psycho after I yelled at her before, but she surprised me by saying, "I don't know if God can forgive me for this."

"He can forgive us for anything," I said, wishing Fiore was here so he could talk to her, but I was on my own here. "He's forgiven me for plenty of things, probably worse than what you did tonight, only different."

I wound up talking to her for about ten minutes, until Mancuso came back up. She said a woman she worked with had been talking to her about God, asking her to go to church with her.

"He's reaching out to you," I said.

"Yeah, I think he is," she said, nodding.

"Don't turn him down," I said, feeling better that I didn't leave without talking to her.

I went back downstairs. As I came out of the stairwell across from the muster room, I saw Romano come out from the stairwell by the front doors.

"You going out to Fiore's house tomorrow? I mean later on today?" Romano asked.

"Yeah, I'll be there."

"What a night, huh? At least we didn't get blown up," he said.

We signed the detail roster at the front desk and walked out the doors together.

"You see, Nick," I said. "Everybody signs out."

Epilogue

I went to Fiore's on New Year's Day. Michele and Stevie came, along with Fiore's parents.

It felt like a year instead of a week since I'd seen Michele and Stevie. When I walked in Fiore's house and they were standing there, I felt like I took a sucker punch somewhere in the vicinity of my heart. If it was possible, Michele got better looking and Stevie got taller. I pulled Michele into the bathroom a couple of times to make out, but Stevie wouldn't let me out of his sight and kept knocking on the door.

Romano was there too. He seemed a little uncomfortable at first, but as the day wore on, he seemed to relax. Romano hit it off with Lou Fiore, Joe's dad. We talked baseball for a while, and I thought I finally had Fiore's dad when I asked him the name of the Broadway play Harry Frazee financed when he sold Babe Ruth to the Yankees and mortgaged Fenway Park.

"Hold on, I know this," he held up his hand. I thought I had him when it took him a couple of minutes to answer. Then he looked at me and smiled, "*No, No Nanette*."

"Was that it?" Fiore asked.

"Yeah, that was it," I said. I don't know if I'll ever get him.

Fiore's dad was talking to Romano about going from New York's Finest to New York's Bravest. Somehow the conversation changed, and Romano started talking about his daughter and about his father getting shot. It turned out his father was killed on December 26. He said his mother has never gotten over it, and this time of year is hard for them.

"I'm sorry, Nick," Lou said.

"Mr. Fiore, I know you believe like Joe does," Romano said, looking like he was controlling his anger. "But God should have protected my father."

"You have a right to feel how you feel, Nick, and I understand your anger," Lou Fiore said. "But God is always good, and having a young man taken so brutally from his wife and children is not God's way."

"I know what you're saying," Romano said, choked up. "But I'm having a hard time believing it."

"I know," Lou said seriously, "but just because you don't believe it doesn't mean it's not true."

Toward the end of January, Denise came to see me. She was waiting in her car when I came home from work one morning. She followed me into my apartment, complaining that she still didn't have a key and could freeze to death waiting for me.

She had a cardboard coffee holder and a bag from Starbucks in one hand and a large manila envelope in the other.

"What's this?" I asked, suspicious. She'd been acting weird lately, cool and evasive on the phone with me.

"It's coffee and biscotti," she said, setting it down on the kitchen table. She looked around as she took off her coat. "Not much for decorating, are we?"

"I don't have time to decorate," I said.

"No, I guess that's what the little woman is for," she said sarcastically.

"What's that supposed to mean?" I said tiredly. I wasn't up for one of her man-bashing tirades.

"Nothing. Drink your coffee, I want to show you something," she handed me the envelope.

I opened it up and stared at it for a couple of seconds before I realized what it was.

A private investigation agency with a Coney Island Avenue address was printed on top of a three-page report. There were pictures of Marie and Bobby Egan kissing, holding hands, and going into and out of an apartment. There was also a copy of an apartment lease with Marie and Egan's name on it, dated May 1, 2000.

According to the investigator's report, Marie and Bobby Egan were at it hot and heavy. Egan was older, in his late forties, twelve years older than Marie. I guess she had a daddy complex, since both my father and her first husband were a lot older than she was.

Egan was married, had three kids, and lived in Massapequa. He had a son in college and two daughters in high school. His wife worked for a lawyer in Roosevelt Field.

Eight months ago, he and Marie signed the lease for a studio apartment in Bay Ridge. As I read through the report, I learned they drove in to work together every day. Marie took the bus in to Bay Ridge, and Egan picked her up on 92nd Street on his way in from Long Island. They had lunch together every day at a place in Chinatown and then drove back home the same way.

They went to the apartment after work two of the days they were followed, and Egan brought her back to 92nd Street, where Marie hopped a bus back home.

"Interesting reading, huh?" Denise asked.

"You did this?" I asked.

She nodded.

"Where'd you get the money?"

"Sal gave it to me," she said.

"I thought you weren't seeing him anymore."

"I'm not. I told him I couldn't pay my rent this month, and he gave me a couple of grand to help me out. He probably did it out of guilt. He said I didn't have to pay him back." She shrugged like she didn't care.

I thought about the time frame. Eight months ago when they signed the lease, Marie was busy pushing my father to take the house from my mother. After the sale of the house, my mother and father each walked away with over a quarter of a million dollars. If Marie divorced my father, she'd get half of it.

Her getting half of it wasn't what concerned me, her taking everything out of the account was more her style. I knew she'd never let my father keep the money in anything but a joint account, and I was afraid she would empty it before she took off with Egan.

"Don't tell Dad," Denise said.

"Why not? If you didn't want Dad to know, why'd you do it?" I asked, shaking my head.

"I knew Marie was fooling around on Dad. I just wanted proof," she said, smiling. "And when Marie empties Dad's bank account and leaves him for Egan, I want Dad to know I knew all along," she said with contempt.

"Why? That's putting salt in his wounds," I said.

"Maybe you didn't hear me Christmas Eve, Tony. I hate Dad and I never want to see him again, and if he dies, I'll go to his funeral in a red dress and I'll dance on his grave," she said as she looked at me. I saw anger there, and a coldness I'd never seen before.

"Does Mom know?" I asked, hoping she had nothing to do with this.

"She knows. She tried to talk me out of it. She said she's forgiven Dad, water under the bridge and all that. What about you, Tony? What do you think?"

"I don't know," I said honestly. "If it was me, I'd want to know."

"Me too. He could fall on his friggin' face for all I care. I'm not telling him, and I don't want you to either. I'll tell him when the time is right."

I didn't know how my father would deal with Denise knowing this and not telling him. My father's not stupid, and I had a feeling he already knew about Marie.

On the other hand, if he didn't know, he might lose it if he found out. You never know how it could go in this kind of situation, and I didn't want my father killing Marie or Bobby Egan. I decided to wait, talk to Fiore, and pray about it.

Michele and I are doing great. We haven't seen the family since Christmas Eve. It helps that at this time of year there aren't many holidays, and I have some time before the next round of them. We decided that if we did go see my family, Stevie would stay with a babysitter. She told me to go without her, but then my father would think he got his way. We'll go together, and if things don't get any better, I'll have to make a decision from there. Vinny's wedding is in October and I'll have to go to that, but other than that, I could stay away.

My grandmother's eighty-first birthday is in March. The whole family usually takes her out to a restaurant to celebrate, and I haven't decided whether or not Michele and I will go. Grandma's been calling me, asking me to come for dinner, but so far I've managed to avoid it.

Denise and my mother are spending a lot of time together. Denise has gone up to stay with her a couple of weekends, and she told me they went to some spa for the day in Hershey Park.

Michele and I plan to go see Mom, but I swung out of weekends and it'll be about six weeks before I swing into weekends off again.

Louie Musto, the Anti-Crime Sergeant, approached Joe and me about coming into crime next fall. He said a couple of guys would be going up to RIP (robbery in progress), which is with PDU (precinct detective unit). He said he was looking at Joe and me for their spots. He told us to think about it and let him know. It would involve tour changes; Crime works 10-6 days and 6-2 nights. What's good is we could go in together and get our shields at the same time.

I went to see Sol the jeweler again in the beginning of February, this time to pick out a ring. I didn't realize how hard it would be to pick something out. I drove his wife crazy looking at every diamond in the store until I finally settled on a nice round one that's almost two karats. I went back to pick out the settings, and I have it narrowed down to four, two in gold and two in platinum.

I was gonna give it to Michele for Valentine's Day, but that's too predictable. I don't plan on doing anything crazy to pop the question, probably just the old down on one knee thing. I did go to her father. I called him and asked him to meet me for coffee. We met at a diner out on Montauk highway, and I told him that I bought a diamond and I wanted to let him know ahead of time. He shook my hand, thanked me for the old-fashioned courtesy, and said he couldn't be happier about the whole thing.

I've been talking to Fiore about marriage. Besides his parents, he and Donna are the only married people I know who are happy. I asked him what he thought about me marrying Michele. I was concerned I wouldn't be any good at it, and he seems to think I would. I thought about all the things people have told me about life and women over the years. My parents, other cops, friends that I've had, all had their perspectives. Most of them were self-serving, and none of them included God. But Fiore's different. He's solid and steady, and he lets God lead him. I don't really understand it yet, but I'm getting there.

Acknowledgments

The authors would like to thank the following people:

Mike Valentino of Cambridge Literary for his continual support. Enjoy your bragging rights, Mike. We'll see you in the Bronx in October.

Lonnie Hull DuPont. Opa baby, we love you.

Sheila Ingram, Twila Bennett, Karen Steele, Kelley Meyne, Aaron Carriere, and everyone else at Baker Publishing Group, thank you so much for this opportunity.

Al O'Leary our publicist and friend, thanks for all your hard work and patience.

Joe Amendola, Vinny Benevenuto, and Scott Hennessy, who really are New York's finest.

Sal Ventimiglia, our favorite hosehead. Despite the good natured rivalry, we love FDNY, but they're still New York's noisiest.

Sandy Pedersen for her friendship, then and now, and her brutal honesty about alcoholism and the lost decade.

Denise Hopely, good friend and research partner who always brings the bagels.

Pastors Jim and Janet Petrow from House on the Rock Family Church (the one in Wind Gap, Pennsylvania, not Long Island) and Pastors Steve and Roseann Brower (the ones from Christ the Redeemer Church in Long Island) for their guidance and friendship.

Louis Musto, who loved the Brooklyn Dodgers and wasn't Ward Cleaver, but deep down he wanted to be. We'll see you in heaven.

Louis Musto, who loves the Yankees and knows almost as much as Dad about baseball. Thanks for the stats.

Kathy Lione for her medical expertise and support and for believing in us.

Frank Lione for sharing so freely his experiences in Vietnam and the NYPD. I love you, Dad.

Shirley Kerrigan for Scripture references.

Janet, Albert, Rick, Olivia, Lisa Panzer (the Rev Doc), Connie, Dave, Marlena, Mary, Dean, Mike V., Larry, Jim, Karen, Bob, Chris, Sue, Donna, Lee, the two Linda L.s, and all our Paesanos from House on the Rock. We love you guys.

Georgie and Frankie for sharing our dream and supporting it. We love being your parents.

Our family for their love and support and for giving us so much material to work with (just kidding). We love you.

F. P. Lione is actually two people—a married couple by the name of Frank and Pam Lione. They are both Italian-American and the offspring of NYPD detectives. Frank Lione is a veteran of the NYPD, and Pam recently left her job as a medical sonographer to stay home with their two sons. They divide their time between New York City and Pennsylvania, in the Poconos. To learn more about the Midtown Blue series or to contact the authors, log on to their website at www.midtown blue.com.